MW01235285

The Stone

To Lucretha
I hope you
enjoy the story.
Let me know
what you think

Dyl H

Email: legal69280
netzero.net

The Stone

✦

A Novel

Darryl A. Hines

iUniverse, Inc.
New York Lincoln Shanghai

The Stone
A Novel

Copyright © 2007 by Darryl A. Hines

All rights reserved. No part of this book may be used or reproduced by any means, graphic, electronic, or mechanical, including photocopying, recording, taping or by any information storage retrieval system without the written permission of the publisher except in the case of brief quotations embodied in critical articles and reviews.

iUniverse books may be ordered through booksellers or by contacting:

iUniverse
2021 Pine Lake Road, Suite 100
Lincoln, NE 68512
www.iuniverse.com
1-800-Authors (1-800-288-4677)

Because of the dynamic nature of the Internet, any Web addresses or links contained in this book may have changed since publication and may no longer be valid.

This is a work of fiction. All of the characters, names, incidents, organizations, and dialogue in this novel are either the products of the author's imagination or are used fictitiously.

ISBN: 978-0-595-45679-6 (pbk)
ISBN: 978-0-595-89981-4 (ebk)

Printed in the United States of America

Prologue

I wrote: *There are days that ask questions and there are days that give answers,* my loose attempt to paraphrase Zora Neale Hurston.

My newfound awareness of the Harlem Renaissance writer signifies my own awakening that has come too late; like the toddler who touches a hot stove or someone making a wrong turn into oncoming traffic. The world closed up on me just when I had emerged from my shell. And from the inner sanctum of a Thai prison my writing is my only refuge and discovery of my true self. And what about today? There are still many unanswered questions.

Day One

Writing while lying on this cot has become increasingly uncomfortable. Unable to lay flat on my stomach, I open my diary on the pillow and enter daily reflections and thoughts with my body twisted and contorted, hips perpendicular to the bed and shoulders squared, propped by my elbows like Venus with arms. My awkward angle must have disturbed him because he kicks so hard that I inspect my body for bruises.

"I guess you can't bruise from the inside," I tell him.

I rub my stomach gently hoping to calm him and watch with some amusement as my misshapen belly gradually returns to its rotund and perfect roundness. I can still see an outline of the little foot distorted my shape. I am life giving, he is life saving, as we nurture each other in this most unlikely place for us. I'd only occasionally thought about having children, but that was more of an afterthought because there were other things in my life far more important until they told me I was pregnant.

It was a routine checkup that revealed my blessing and confirmed what I had suspected before I arrived here. At first I thought the sick feeling that crept upon me nearly every morning was my inability to digest the stuff they call food—served Bangkok prison-style. A spicy combination of rice and bean sprouts with a side of "something" that resembles meat of unknown origins is enough to make anyone sick, even a black girl raised in the South on grits and unspecified hog parts. But with my physical check up came the bittersweet news told through a translator.

"You are pregnant. Your life will be spared—for now. Doctor informed Board of Pardons. They delay execution until baby come."

The translator had the uncanny ability to sound as uncaring as the Thai doctor who made the assessment. They won't kill my baby for my misdeeds. A reprieve from the gallows, a delayed execution and an opportunity to extend my appeals was the glimmer of hope I'd prayed for, but I only have four months left.

There's an added benefit to being pregnant in a Bangkok prison—solitude. I've been removed from the general population of prostitutes and petty thieves sent here from the province of Phukit. My reward, my own cell with a cotton mattress that is more forgiving than the bamboo cot that exposed my body to an earthen floor and served as cover for roaches. It all reminds me just how far I'm away from home.

There are unseen women in the prison cells on each side of mine separated by concrete and mortar walls. I hear them shouting to each other through the small opening in the cell door that serves as our only portal in and out of this closed universe. They speak in the high chatter of Thai with different dialects and although I can't understand what they're saying my instincts tell me that it's simply the idle talk of those who have nothing else to do twenty-four hours a day.

My "roommates" don't bother to include me in their conversations because they know I don't understand Thai and they don't speak English. Yet, every morning they greet me with "Sabaai Dee Mai?"And sometimes I forget and respond in English. "I am fine."

I want to learn Thai so I often correct myself and greet them in their own language.

"Sabaai Dee." My words are hollow because I'm not doing well at all.

The girl on my left has been there for just a few days and it was only yesterday that we exchanged names. She had shouted, "Khun Cheu Arai!"

And I answered, "Dahlia. Dahlia Reynolds."

I reciprocated and asked the girl for her name as I strained to hear her reply.

"Phom Cheu … Chiang Mai," was the answer, along with a smattering of laughter.

It wasn't funny. I'd been in Thailand long enough to know that young prostitutes never give their real names and that Chiang Mai was a city north of Bangkok. I wonder now if it's even worth the trouble trying to talk to her. But I'm lonely and I need someone to talk to even if my Thai is limited.

I call out, "Hello? How are you?"

And wait for a response.

"I fine. How are you today, Dahlia Reynolds?"

It's the new girl speaking in dialectic English.

"Chiang Mai?" I ask.

"Yes."

"You speak English?"

"Yes."

I sigh. Relief is what I feel knowing that I'm not as much of an outsider as I think I am. It's not like being back home making idle conversation with my friends, but it's a start. I lift my body with its swollen torso from my cot and move to the small opening in my prison cell door. I push my face against the bars and strain to see her, but to no avail. I can hear her and she can hear me, but we cannot see one another.

"I didn't know you speak English."

She laughs. "Me educated. I study English at school before I find work to help family."

"Why are you in here?" I ask.

"Me—what you say? Call girl."

"What? You're here for prostitution?" I ask.

My question is full of presumptions. I know that the flesh business thrives in Thailand with the government turning a blind eye to its pervasiveness, so I'm surprised that she's here for something that's hardly a crime. I wait for her response.

She laughs, making me feel silly and naïve. "No, I not here for that. I here for stealing money from European. How you say? Boyfriend?"

I think. *Boyfriend? That's the term we use back in the States for "John" or "Trick".*

"They put you in lock-up just for stealing?" I ask.

"More. I steal from rich boyfriend. He mad. I go to jail."

"For how long?"

"Don't know. They say, I learn lesson, then go."

I think about the Thai justice system, no jury, an impassive judge and a more impassive attorney and here I am. I wonder if Chiang even had a trial.

"You prostitute?" she asks me.

Her straightforward question temporarily stuns me and almost stills my tongue into silence, but I guess it's only natural for her to ask me that since many of the women here in prison make their living using their bodies. Most are here, however, for other crimes. Still, I wonder if she read about me in a Thai newspaper.

I shrug it off. "No," is my answer.

"You kill three boyfriends. No?"

Chiang hits me with another straightforward statement presented as a question and my response is two-fold.

"I didn't kill anyone." I tell her.

I'm measured in my reply because I believe that most people interpret an emphatic denial of anything as an admission.

"And I'm not a prostitute."

I try to change the subject.

"How old are you?" I ask.

"Seventeen-year-old."

"How long have you been in the business?" My next question is intended to pry beneath the surface of Chiang's sex trade business in Thailand because I am curious and I have nothing better to do.

"Five year. Me twelve then. Find boyfriends."

I sigh heavily at the thought of a child losing her innocence and it pains me. I remember my own childhood and how the naiveté of a young girl was stolen away by circumstance. In that way, we are sisters.

"You, how you say? *Negro?*" She asks.

Negro? I think about the term's archaic past and its loss of relevance in America. After all, I was born in the '80s. My stomach knots up at the thought that its use here in Thailand remains the primary description when discussing people of my race. After all, they had used the term repeatedly during my trial. I decide from this point on and however much time I have left here that I'm on a one-woman crusade to rectify those outdated perceptions of my people and educate anyone who'll listen.

"I'm an African-American!"

"You American? No!?" Chiang replies, deflecting any attempt on my part to stand up for my heritage.

"Yes. I'm American. Have you ever been there?" I ask her.

"No. Been to Antigua in Caribbean once for holiday. I go to America soon, someday. Go see Michael Jackson sing. Watch Michael Jordan bounce ball."

Her words humor me. *She must be in a time warp.* Neither of the two Michaels are doing the things that made them rich and famous.

"There's a lot more to see there," I tell her.

"Why you kill three boyfriends?"

Chiang Mai has either ignored my assertions of innocence or has forgotten.

"Like I said, I didn't kill anyone!"

I'm a little more animated in my protestation. "This is useless," I mutter, so that my comment is barely audible then walk away from the hole in the door and retreat to the inner confines of my prison cell.

"Dahlia. Dahlia Reynolds." She's almost singing my name. "Please. You tell Chiang Mai what happened. Tell how you here."

I'm sitting on my bed watching a large cockroach scamper across the floor. His pace quickens in response to my half-hearted attempt to squash the life out of him. When I think, *that's no way to treat a guest* I realize that living in a state of solitude degrades not only the spirit, but the mind as well.

Like a world-class athlete recuperating from an injury, my skills at intercourse, the verbal kind, are rusty from lack of use. I think about Chiang Mai's question and realize I should tell her exactly how I wound up here. It's the kind of therapy I need.

I take a deep breath, walk back over to the hole in my door and call out, "Chiang. Are you still there?"

Even that question rings hollow since it's not likely that she's gone.

"It's a long story," I tell her.

"I listen. Have lots of time."

We both laugh at her tongue in cheek comment.

"I've been writing my memoirs since I've been in here," I tell her. "It's for my baby in case I …," I let my voice trail off.

"In case you die here," Chiang fills in the blanks.

"Anyway, I write down stuff, stuff I think about. Some of it's pretty deep, I think."

"What you mean, 'deep'?" she asks me.

I realize that the slang and nuances of urban, contemporary English are outside my neighbor's understanding. I have to explain the things I say without resorting to the usual street-honed vernacular I've picked up since leaving the sleepy Southern town where I was raised, going away to college and ultimately having moved to Washington, DC. I search for another way to tell her about my writings.

"The things I write about reflect my thoughts and when I say, deep, I mean deep thoughts."

I decide that I'll simply tell her my story, recount those events that led up to this day, this time. I'll read from my memoir and hopefully impart some wisdom and teach. After all, I'm a seasoned twenty-six-year-old and she's a young girl of seventeen who can learn a lot from me. But that can wait until tomorrow.

"Chiang, I'm feeling a little tired now. Let's talk tomorrow."

"You promise?" She asks almost begging.

"I promise."

Chiang joins the chorus of women now calling for their dinner as I retreat away and back to my cot and the inevitable cane-lashing that will be administered to the doors of those recalcitrant choir members by the bamboo wielding guards. It will effectively quell the noise made by their singing.

I've learned to blot out the banter of my neighbors so that I can focus on my diary entries because the things that I write will tell my story and how my life changed so drastically. Lying on my mattress with my baby now at peace I flip through the pages of my memoir and I replay the events of the past year.

Before that fateful day when I met the man that would change everything my diary would've read:

I got up this morning at six a.m. Got dressed. Caught the bus to the Connecticut Avenue Metro station. Got off at the Pentagon City stop. In the office at seven. Read some reports. Analyzed data. Had lunch with the girls. More reports. Sick of this shit! Go home. Talk to my mother. Wait for the phone to ring. Fall asleep with a glass of Shiraz. S.O.S. tomorrow.

But the monotony of my former life in Washington, D.C. pales in comparison to existing in a Bangkok prison and counting the days until this monotone of living day to day is interrupted by the executioner's call and I'm hurled into the abyss of whatever the after-life will bring me.

I wrote: *Death is better than languishing in this earthly purgatory the Thai fondly call, Pattaya Prison.*

That was yesterday's entry.

On the most part my writing is less philosophical than the way I described it to Chiang. It's written for my mother to read someday after I'm gone apologizing profusely for the pain I've caused her. But there's a section especially written for my unborn child with the hope that I can impart some wisdom from the grave. It isn't the wisdom I gained during my twenty-six years on earth, but what I've learned in the last two because that's when I really began to live. I think about what he told me less than a week after we met. "Learning is what you read. Wisdom comes from what you live."

I laugh even now when I think of him and his "wisdom". Corny but true, wisdom *is* what you live. And with that thought I recall his words and my mind rewinds taking me back to when we began.

Day Two

The thought of him makes me write feverishly and all of the images of him come rushing back to me. I had performed this ritual before, just last week. The thoughts and images are imbedded deep within my being. It's a place where only he had been able to touch me. Images of his face consume me, cause me to roll over on my back and stare at the ceiling with its broken plaster and an occasional fly bearing its multi-faceted eyes down on me. I call out to Chiang.

"Chiang Mai, what are you doing?"

"I waiting to talk to you," she replies.

Judging by her quick response I know that she really is waiting for me to wake up and tell her my story. So I begin to tell her.

My thoughts are now far away from the stench of Pattaya Prison and from death. I drift back a few months to last April and to my one bedroom apartment in Silver Spring, Maryland. It was a cozy and safe place like a womb made of overstuffed easy chairs, real feather pillows and a canopy bed I had inherited from my great-grandmother. I think of the large quilt that I hung with pride on my living room wall. Handmade and meticulously stitched, it told a story of my family in symbols first conjured up by my maternal great-great-great grandmother while still a slave on the Reynolds plantation.

The quilt began with the woman who was called, "Momma Set" by the slave owning Reynolds family and known as "The Beginner" by my own. There were five stick figures—four stitched in black yarn and one in white standing apart from the others. My mother had always said that the white one stood for the Reynolds' son, whom The Beginner nursed as her own. Later, it was discovered through genealogical study and research that the symbol of the white child actually represented her own son. He was my great, great grandfather. I figured that it was from him I had inherited my caramel-colored skin and loosely curled hair.

Thoughts of home overwhelm my emotions and my fanciful memories are replaced by a feeling of melancholy. I close my eyes tight to suppress the tears that are trying to force their way out and down my face. My thoughts drift away from my condo and to the times when I was "kicking it" with my girls at lunch on K Street or in Georgetown and engaging in our favorite topics—careers and men. I was always more of a listener than a contributor, which made sense considering the fact that I knew little about men and due to the secrecy that surrounded my job.

Stacy is my best friend and the unspoken leader of our Sisterhood. We grew up together in Waycross, Georgia and were roommates at Ashland University, a small liberal arts college secluded in the countryside of northern Ohio. We both moved to D.C. right after we graduated. For a year we shared a small apartment on Capitol Hill while Stacy completed her internship with *The Post* and I was just starting my job as a data analyst at the Pentagon. At first the arrangement was convenient for us. We were both saddled with student loan debt and didn't have much money, but when Stacy accepted a full-time position as a reporter and I was promoted a few months later we decided that it was time to grow up and live apart for the first time in five years.

The move wasn't a quantum leap for Stacy because within six months after we moved to Washington she was spending more time with her boyfriend than at the apartment. There were times when I didn't see her for days. She'd come and go to the point where we'd joke that we needed a revolving door. So when I got a raise we decided that I could almost afford to live on my own and Stacy moved in with Derek. As a result Stacy got the love of her life and I bought a condo. Fair exchange.

Loshamita Cunningham completed our little triumvirate. A Georgetown Law School graduate working as a lawyer at the Department of Justice, El, as she preferred, was the most outspoken, flirty and worldly of the three of us. She was from Chicago and she worked hard to put the Southside behind her, burying her background and upbringing the way some of the international criminals she prosecuted hid their pasts. In fact, I don't remember how we became friends. She just seemed to be there one day and I guess a bond developed between the three of us.

El hated her given name. "Loshamita? So ghetto," she often said. She would chide Stacy and me by telling us that our names were too gentrified and calling us both "Quita" as in JaQuita and LoQuita, made up ghetto sounding names. We all laughed whenever El called us "Quiti", her plural version of Quita. But that was El, full of catty cynicism and extremely pretentious in everything from the clothes she wore to the men she dated.

In my prison cell I often think about those times with Stacy and El and our relationship. I was closest with Stacy whom I often called, "Earth Mother" because of her natural hairdo and Afro-centric sensibility. She was Erykah Badu without the singing voice. "Baduism" could've been her religion.

And although I called El "my girl", our relationship was sometimes marked by tension. I guess it was because she was everything that I would've been if I had been less grounded and more superficial.

Glitz and glamour: that was El. But there were still things about her that I envied. El was beautiful, in a made-up sort of way. Me? I always thought of myself as plain. I didn't wear much make-up and I kept my long, curly hair pulled back into a constant bun. El, by contrast, wore Dolce and Gabbana everything and her tall equine figure with that bubble butt could stop traffic. Maybe it was my desire to be like her that drove me to a place like Bangkok and eventually to Pattaya.

I remember well the day when things began to change. Indelibly etched into my thoughts, it was a spring day in Washington and the cherry blossoms were exploding all over with their sweet and sensuous smells. Stacy had invited El and I to lunch at *J. Paul's*, an upscale eatery in the heart of Georgetown.

I was really excited about seeing my friends. It had been a couple of weeks and there was a lot of catching up to do. Stacy had written a story about teenage prostitution and the sex slave trade both here in America and overseas and the word from her editor was that she would be nominated for a Pulitzer Prize.

And El had just returned from northern Africa and was anxious to tell us about the experience. For someone who labored in obscurity and had never left the continental United States, hearing about their good fortunes would allow me to live my life vicariously through theirs, if only for a few moments.

I was the first to arrive at the restaurant that day and I reserved our usual booth near the front window where I could see the busy Georgetown traffic of cars and pedestrians. I loved this place; the restaurant, Georgetown, Washington. It was the epicenter of the known universe for many Washingtonians. Upscale restaurants, boutiques and townhouses were its legacy to the community, but Georgetown was more than Rodeo Drive on the Potomac. It's brick and cobblestone streets spoke of a history that preceded Coach, Prada and Givenchy.

The maitre d' led me to my table through the already-crowded restaurant, speaking to me in halting English with a heavy French accent. I'd been there so often that he knew me by name, which was comforting and reassuring for a woman alone.

"Meezz Ray-nalds. Eet is so good to see you. Eet has been a long time. You are looking well these days."

The "looking well" comment made me cringe. *What the hell did he mean by that? Did it mean I looked okay for someone who is so unattractive or did he mean I looked healthy?* Either way, the comment wasn't very flattering. I thought that my grandmother looks well. Why couldn't he say, *you look beautiful?*

I sat down and reached into my purse and found my compact and opened it so I could look at the mirror. I regarded the face that was looking back at me and concluded that it only looked well.

The most noticeable thing about my image was my obtrusive eyeglasses that framed my face like two headlights on a car—not a Ferrari, but a Volkswagen. I always wondered how I'd look without them, but my vision was slightly better than Stevie Wonder's with them off. My friends would tell me that I had such beautiful features—eyes, nose and lips. Too bad I hid them behind those ugly glasses. I couldn't see well enough without them to apply my makeup, scared that I'd have the clown effect when I finished. Thought about wearing contact lens, but a speck of dust in my eye felt like a tree limb so they were out of the question. And I couldn't afford laser eye surgery.

True, my eyeglasses made me look unappealing, but my wardrobe didn't help either. You see, I'm tall and slender with a curvy figure and I kept my body hidden, never wanting to attract too much attention to it or to myself. I wore clothes that seemed too large and dresses that El would laugh and call, "moo-moos".

My mother often told me that it's not how you look on the outside that's important, but what you are on the inside. Those were words that rang true, but they didn't quite explain why I chose to dress down almost all the time. Maybe it was that small-town Southern mentality that affected me and being raised in a Pentecostal Church certainly didn't help. They preached that the mind was the devil's workshop and a hint of skin on display by any woman made him work overtime.

I shook myself out of my preoccupation with the image in the mirror, closed my compact and my face disappeared along with thoughts of how I looked. I focused on where I was rather than on myself. Georgetown was one of my favorite places to hang out and to study people. Looking out the window I could see the city teeming with shoppers and it seemed that the intersection of M Street and Wisconsin Avenue was the center of the universe. It reminded me just how far away I was from Waycross, Georgia.

I looked at my watch and wondered where my girls were. *Fashionably late,* would describe El, but for Stacy, ever ready and always punctual, this was unusual. I looked around the restaurant hoping that I'd see them hanging around the door or chatting with some gorgeous guy that El always seemed to find. I was feeling a little insecure sitting all alone in this large booth. "It probably looks like I've been stood up," I mumbled.

Everyone else at J. Paul's was suitably teamed up with lunch dates, business partners and of course, lobbyists and politicians. This was D.C.

There was a strange mix of people in the restaurant that day, even for Washington. A long-legged blond was playing footsie with her date, whom I figured must have been married judging by the way he nervously glanced over his shoulder whenever she displayed any affection towards him. There was a table full of Middle Eastern-looking gentlemen whose animated conversations blended perfectly with the clatter of silverware and china. And there was a couple of young black men dressed down in the usual garb that was the signature of my twenty-something generation.

I couldn't help but size them up. *Fubu and Nautica, a strange mix of the oxymoronic urban chic.*

I quickly shifted my eyes and my thoughts away from the two men and continued to pan across the restaurant hoping that my friends would come into my view. My eyes settled on an older man eating alone. I stole a quick glance and then pretended to read my menu, but my eyes inexplicably returned for more. It was probably the way he was dressed in an impeccably sharp gray suit, ultra-white Egyptian cotton shirt with gold cufflinks barely peeking from underneath his jacket sleeves and polished Italian loafers. He had dark olive-colored skin and neatly cropped hair with a hint of white around his ears that swept down from his temples and he sported a thick evenly trimmed mustache. Even sitting down I could tell that he was fit and in great shape for a man his age, which I figured was at least forty-five or fifty.

I was careful not to stare because my mother always said it was rude and I had no intention of flirting. But I had that uncanny ability to size a man up while pretending to ignore him. In a split second my mental Polaroid camera had recorded a picture of him, which I studied until a voice broke my fixation. It was the waiter.

"Madam, are you ready to order?"

"Not quite yet, thank you. I'm waiting for my friends," I answered.

"How about something to drink? We have a special on the house, Chardonnay."

I glanced over at the distinguished looking man. He had a glass of white wine on his table, but I doubt it was some generic house wine. I toyed with the notion of telling the waiter, "*I'll have what he's drinking*" but I realized that I probably couldn't afford it, besides I had to go back to work after lunch.

"The house wine is fine," I told the waiter, believing that it wouldn't give me a buzz and I'd be able to go back to work without feeling the after effect.

I glanced over at the man once again, concluded that he was probably the handsomest older man I'd ever seen. I thought about handsome black men my grandmother and mother would talk about when I was growing up. Men who were more than just good—looking, but had something special that set them apart from all other good-looking brothers. For my grandmother it was Billy Eckstein. For Momma, Billy Dee Williams and later Denzel. Funny, I couldn't think of anyone in my generation who fit that mold.

There was something special about the man sitting in the restaurant alone that day. It was more than just good looks and expensive clothes. He had an aura about him I'd never seen in any man, like a glow that you could almost touch.

I guess I was so wrapped up in my thoughts that I hadn't noticed someone approaching. A friendly voice broke through. It was Stacy.

"Thought we weren't going to show, didn't you?" she said.

We exchanged hugs.

"Girl, I was about to leave. I've got better things to do than to waste time waiting on you heifers," I told Stacy, pretending to be mad.

"Yeah, yeah. Tell that to someone who don't know you. El is parking her car. I tried to tell her let's take a cab, but she bought that convertible Z4 and she's just showing off. Screw her anyway."

Stacy took a pause to catch her breath.

"How you doing, babygirl?" she asked me.

I was all-smiles, cheesing at my friend like I was crazy. It was so good seeing her. Derek and the demands of reporting for *The Post* allowed Stacy little time for me and it seemed we were drifting apart. But whenever we found find time to get together the love was still there and we'd talk the way we did when we were walking on some dirt road back home or in our dorm room in college.

"I'm fine, but it's you I want to hear about," I said. "What? A Pulitzer Prize winner?"

My comment made Stacy's lips drift into a wide smile. She was obviously excited about the prospect of receiving journalism's highest award.

"Well, I haven't got it yet, but my editor says rumor has it, I'm a lock. You know, it's something I always dreamed about even back in the days when I wrote for our school paper. But I don't want to say too much, might jinx my chances."

Our conversation was short-circuited when we heard El laughing. She was talking to the two young brothers I had noticed earlier. We shook our heads as if to say, "That's El."

She did that classic move as she reached into her Coach handbag and pulled out a silver cardholder. With a smile and a wink of her eye, El handed each man one of her business cards and started walking in our direction. She raised her eyebrows at Stacy and added a little extra hip action to her walk; cheeks bouncing like an Iverson crossover dribble and giving the two men a full view of her more than ample junk-in-the—trunk.

"You are such a hoe," Stacy told her in mock disapproval.

"Whatever. Do you know who that was? Jamil Forrest! Running back! He only led the entire league in total rushing yards, was the MVP and has the sexiest body in sports. Where have you Quiti been? Keep Runnin' Mississippi? Don't y'all know anything?"

This was typical El, coming through like a brown tornado and gathering up everything that got in her way. She was a woman that couldn't be missed in a club or crowded room. In fact, I always felt that if El walked into the Superdome full to capacity with eighty thousand screaming fans the place would go completely silent when she made her typical grand entrance.

"Well, not everyone gets to go to places like Morocco," Stacy shot back.

"It was Tunisia and Portugal. Had a great time. Walter used most of his playoff money to spoil me rotten."

She flashed a diamond-studded tennis bracelet so that we could see it in its full glory. Stacy leaned over as though she was whispering something to me, but intentionally spoke loud enough so that El could hear.

"I wonder how much ass she had to give up for *that* little bauble."

We both laughed hard.

"I heard that," El shot back.

She sat down on Stacy's side of the booth.

"Move them hips over Stace. Give a sister some room. You pregnant or something?"

El turned and looked directly at me for the first time. "JaQuita, how are you?" I was an afterthought.

"I'm doing great El. I was just congratulating Stacy …"

"Yeah, yeah. I know. Have you ordered? El asked, cutting me off.

"Don't worry about her Dahlia. If it ain't about El, it ain't important," Stacy said in her own defense.

I gave her a knowing smile.

"Anyway, which story was it that got you nominated?" I asked.

"The three-part story I wrote about women being forced into prostitution in Asia and sent here. Girl, if you could've seen the things I saw while I was researching my story. There's a little house in Bethesda where twenty women live and work there."

Stacy took a sip from her glass of water and looked around the restaurant as though she was about to tell us something that was highly confidential. She leaned forward and whispered.

"Did I say, women? I meant, girls. Some of them had barely reached puberty?"

The thought of a pre-teen girl servicing some fat, old bureaucrat both mesmerized and sickened me.

"Why would a grown man want to have sex with a little girl?" I asked.

El laughed and covered her mouth.

"There are a lot of sick bastards out there. It's like they're some kind of vampire trying to suck the life out of some young girl, thinking it'll restore their youth."

"There she goes, playing amateur shrink again. That's the problem with lawyers, they think they're experts on everything," Stacy interrupted.

"Damn near have to be," El said. "For example, I just got assigned to this case at the Department of Justice. International stuff. You know, James Bond intrigue kind of stuff. I'm learning about Swiss bank accounts and how money is laundered overseas and moved all over the planet. You know thieves develop elaborate schemes to hide their money and their identities. It's mind boggling."

"Well, they're adapting to a post 9/11 environment," I said.

El nudged Stacy. "Wait a minute and she'll tell us about all the high tech tracking devices, GPS, counter-intelligence crap-speak they talk about at the Pentagon."

"You know I can't talk about what happens over at my job," I said.

"I don't see why not, Dahlia. We're on the same team," El paused. "At least you and I are. Stacy works for the press. You know, government watchdog."

I played with my water, stirring my slice of lemon 'round and round with my spoon. My eyes drifted away from our table to the man I'd noticed earlier. He was still sitting there, eyes trained on the newspaper and occasionally taking a sip from his glass. I watched as he looked up to speak to the waiter and flashed a 100 watt, neon-laced smile. Stacy and El's conversation became background noise to my pre-occupation with him, but they soon noticed that I had been distracted.

"What are you looking at?" Stacy asked.

"Oh, nothing," I replied. The question reeled me back in.

"She's probably checking out Jamil. Hands off girlfriend. I saw him first," El said.

She cast another flirtatious eye towards the football player.

"Don't worry. They're not Dahlia's type," Stacy added.

Through lunch we all traded barbs and stories about everything from shopping to families to spiritual awareness and I listened intently as Stacy talked about her next big story and El about her next big criminal case. They didn't ask me anything else about what was going on at my job because it was boring and highly classified. El often referred to me as, "The Undercover Sister."

I wanted to talk about something else so I quickly turned to a subject we all were interested in—men!

It was something Stacy had said that led into it, something about Derek and how he seemed jealous that her career was moving at a faster pace than his. I translated her remarks into Stacy believing that maybe Derek would someday hold her back; his insecurities would outrun her ambition. But rather than focus on Derek, too personal, I opened the floor to a discussion about the entire male gender.

"I don't know what it is about these young brothers today," I said. "They claim that they want this so-called *Superwoman*, yet when they get her they don't know how to handle her success."

El broke in. "Yeah, they want you to look good, hold an intelligent conversation, screw their brains out with some 'head' for dessert and then get pissed when you make more money than they do."

"Well, you don't have to worry about Walter in the money and conversation department," Stacy laughingly told El. "I don't think I've heard the brother put two sentences together and there ain't no way you're gonna make more money than a pro basketball player as a government attorney."

I laugh hard. I had met Walter, El's "playmate" or "friend with benefits" on several occasions and I couldn't remember him saying anything other than, "Wuz Up?"

"Dahlia, what are you laughing at?" El asked. She was being defensive. "I don't hang with Walter for what he says. It's about what he does. I mean staying power, baby." She flashed a vixen-like smile. "Dahlia you need to come to one of his games. The brother's a power forward and I emphasize *power*, P-O-W-E-R. Besides, what does that young doughboy you mess around with do for you? The boy don't have a job and have you ever had an orgasm?"

I realized then that the things I had said about "my friend" Antoine would come back and bite me.

"First of all, he's no 'doughboy', Antoine's a music producer and the rest is none of your business."

I laughed and turned to Stacy who was already positioned with her hand in the air to slap me a "high five".

"I heard that," Stacy added. "But you know, I've been meaning to ask y'all what qualities you look for in a man. I mean tell me what would be your ideal man."

"You know what I'm looking for," El jumped in without hesitating. "Young, dumb, rich and athletic, that's why I only date pro-ball players."

I couldn't believe what she was saying. "Certainly, Walter fits that mold, but you're stereotyping," I told her. "Athletes are not dumb. But let me tell you what I look for in a man."

My thoughts flashed back to the man eating alone, the one I'd been studying. I leaned over the table close to Stacy and Dahlia and looked over in his direction.

El's eyes widened. "What? Are you talking about that old guy sitting over there?"

I nodded.

"Stacy! Stacy! You better take home-girl someplace to be analyzed. That man's old enough to be her father! I didn't have a daddy either, but trust me I don't need a father figure! That's sick, Dahlia!"

El was animated with her hands and fingers, like she was arguing a case in court.

I gave her a half-hearted smile, a look of exasperation and pierced my lips to make a shoosh sound.

"I don't mean that I'd want to get together with him," I whispered. "I'm just saying that if I had my pick of a man I'd want someone like that—classy, sophisticated."

"I got to agree with you on that. I mean look at him. He's fine. I don't care how old he is, that is a good-looking man." Stacy emphasized the words, "good-looking". "And look at what he's wearing, from head to toe, that's money and class. Bruno Magli Italian loafers, Breitling watch, Zegna suit and twenty-four carat gold cufflinks. Besides, Denzel's about that age and I bet if *he* tried to hit on you El, you'd be giving up the draws."

El broke down and laughed so hard that she doubled over at the waist and put her head on the table.

"Girl! What do you know about class? You can't even spell those designer labels with your little country ass. Besides, that's no black man. Look at his hair and skin color. He's probably Haitian or something."

She paused, pointed a finger back at Stacy and poke out her full lips, "And you're right about Denzel. If he said one word to me my panties would fly right off."

While El and Stacy engaged in their verbal battle, I took another long look at the man who'd become the center of our conversation. In many ways he looked the way I often imagined how my father would look, if I could see him now. But it was an image I had to conjure from vague descriptions given to me by my mother over the last twenty-six years. Descriptions that were amorphous and ethereal, allowing me to paint my own picture of the man, who'd seemed to have been vaporized from the dusty red Georgia clay, planted his seed almost twenty-seven years ago and disappeared.

I quickly looked away when I saw the man we were watching look up from his newspaper and in our direction and directly at me. His eyes made me feel uncomfortable like he was looking right into me and I didn't want to look back. I could see his subtle smile out of the corner of my eye. A lump gathered in my throat, I swallowed hard hoping to regain my composure. My chest heaved which made my breasts appear embarrassingly upright and erect. I guess I should've worn a bra.

I was breathing hard, almost hyperventilating the way I'd do to the point of nearly passing out whenever I was in an uncomfortable social situation.

But my therapist told me that the best way to overcome my anxieties was to confront them. So at the very least, I could steal another look at him. I expected to see his eyes, once again, looking in my direction or maybe that was wishful thinking. After all, my non-descript appearance blended into the background like I was wearing camouflage gear. Still, I was hoping that he'd still be looking at me and maybe I'd be bold enough to smile at him—but he wasn't. Instead, he stood up, placed a tip on the table and started walking in our direction. I held my breath.

I looked across the table at Stacy and El and pretended not to notice his long, confident stride that was taking him right by our table. I thought for a moment, *Oh, my God, he's coming over here.* Stacy saw the panic in my eyes and looked directly at the man. El joined in as the three of us trained our eyes on him. He gave us a slight nod, acknowledging our attention like a man accustomed to being admired by women, but we played coy and didn't speak acting as though we hadn't noticed him at all.

Stacy made a barely audible, 'uhm-uhm' sound. Our eyes followed him as he walked by, watched him as he left the restaurant and walked up to the group of young men who valet parked cars. I tried not to stare at him through the large window choosing instead to focus on the salmon patties and cheese grits made gourmet style that were sitting on the plate in front of me. El forced us all to turn when she made an unintelligible sound of her own. I looked up in time to see him slide into a sparkling, shiny black Bentley with white leather interior.

We all shook our heads as he drove away. He was royalty in a chariot. I was feeling validated for noticing him first and vindicated because I knew that El would now give me my props. Her self-absorbed materialistic view on life would force her approval and as for me, I just thought of him as someone I'd like to know.

Day Three

Sometimes you don't remember seeing someone for the first time unless there's a connection or the person stands out from the crowd. The day I saw him in the restaurant I thought it would be the only time I'd ever see him and like most strangers, he'd fade into the recesses of the city living his life in a world that might as well have been in another dimension occupying space parallel to mine. But never touching.

Songs of Desdemona—9/15/05

Somehow we overlapped and came together without touching and he without knowing, like concentric circles and it was our common center that allows me to know and to write about him.

My ride home on the Metro was filled with thoughts of home, some riddled with nostalgia, others full of dread that I would someday have to return to that sleepy little Southern town of repressed dreams. It wasn't the home at the end of a train line and a cab ride from the Connecticut Avenue stop, but *home*, the place where I grew up. My mother was still in Waycross, living the simple life on the farm with Rufus, my stepfather and with my grandmother, a kind soul we called, Stevie. But I didn't miss home. Hated the place. Never wanted to visit, let alone move back there.

Home was as distant as Mars and from an emotional standpoint just as cold. My mother had raised me alone for much of my life, with the help of Stevie then she married Rufus and he moved all of us on to his farm.

My mother was guarded about me. I was eleven and getting bumps and lumps in places that distinguished women from men and I was already five foot, nine inches tall. I believe that my mother joined the Pentecostal Church to stem the tide of my exuding sexuality. Its fundamentalist, rigid holy-roller teachings and antithetical theories of propagation was perfect for my mother to subdue the emerging woman in me.

Sex was a forbidden subject and anything that resembled sensuality was "the devil's doing." When I had my first period and cried, hysterically, my mother said nothing to calm me. She simply handed me a sanitary pad that was as big as a diaper and said, "Put this on."

My mother's fears and the obstacles they erected probably became the template for my own sexuality. In my adult life I'd become insecure and repressed in my womanhood, but I guess I rebelled against my upbringing when it came to Antoine. No, he wasn't a drug dealer like El always implied, but I wasn't sure what he did exactly. All I knew was that he would come around from time to time whenever it was convenient or when he was horny.

I hadn't seen or talked to him for several weeks and when those lapses in time occurred I would wonder whether he was in jail or shacked up with some "hoochie". Antoine was young and women said he was *pretty* and it wasn't beyond the realm of possibility that some older woman was taking care of him. So when I saw him that day outside my building looking like a puppy dog in the security monitor I was surprised.

I wasn't ready to have company and it was a Wednesday night. Unlike Antoine, I had to get up early for work the following day. My hair, still in a bun with a scarf wrapped around my head, didn't make me look very sexy. Most of all, I wasn't physically or mentally ready for an all-night sex-fest with a man who always acted like the Energizer Bunny on steroids. Besides, even with all of his humping and just as El reminded me, Antoine had never made me have an orgasm.

For a moment I stood there looking at his image on the screen without speaking, trying to make up my mind whether I should let him in or not. I eased out a heavy sigh from deep within full of resignation. *Even unfulfilling sex is better than none at all.* Reluctantly, I pressed the buzzer and when he spoke I said, "C'mon up," sounding as matter-of-fact as I could.

Antoine was a stud and I knew that was unlikely to change for many years, but I was no longer enamored with his good looks and ripped body. He had long been nothing more than a blow up doll, the male version, and he might as well have had the vacant eyes and expressionless face of a manufactured man with a big ego and a penis that inflated and deflated on command. I knew what to expect when I opened the door—the smile, framed by dimples and heightened by his green-brown eyes that always seemed to draw me in and The Look that broadcast to me and probably the entire world—*You know you want me, real bad.*

"Hey, stranger," I greeted him as he walked past me and straight to my sofa.

He smiled and planted his six-foot, two-inch frame in a sprawling position that covered more than half of its seating area. As usual he was empty handed. No flowers, no candy, nothing but himself and that "drill" he carried between his legs. For some women that was enough and for the moment, as it had been with virtually every moment I was with Antoine, I was one of those women.

He quickly removed his sweatshirt and made himself comfortable. It was clear that he was planning to stay for a while. He sat there in his sleeveless tee shirt, the kind some people call "wife-beaters" which was loosely covered up by a Wizards basketball jersey. I couldn't help but notice how cut-up his arms, shoulders and pecs were.

"Looks like you've been spending a lot of time in the gym, lately," I said.

"Yeah, trying to get ripped."

"Must be nice to have that kind of time on your hands to spend hours in the gym everyday," I said.

I was trying not to sound too sarcastic, but I was feeling a little envious because I had to work everyday yet I could barely afford to buy a workout tape and I didn't have the luxury of spending hours in an egotistical, voyeur's pit called a "fitness center."

Displaying his body had always been Antoine's version of seduction and I had to admit that seeing him like that was turning me on. For us, carnality was strictly physical without pretending that there was some kind of spiritual or emotional bond. It was sex for the sake of sex.

Antoine was sagging like many twenty-something black males who wore their pants low and their underwear pulled up high, prison code for saying, "I'm available." He reminded me of a young man I'd seen earlier that day, scampering across the street at Fourteenth and K, his pants dropping with every step. He almost tripped on his descending jeans and I laughed thinking that he might fall.

That young brother, like Antoine, was one of hip-hop's soldiers wearing his parade dress of baggy pants, basketball jersey with someone else's name on it as unpaid advertisers for the No Boys Allowed league and topped off with a baseball style cap. His cornrow braids were squeezing his brain underneath his cap. But something told me that Antoine was on the cusp of morphing into someone different, putting down the hardcore persona for a suit like a reformed Jay-Z. I guess I thought that because I'd imagined him dressed to kill the way I'd imagine men in my fantasies.

"Hey, baby," rolled from his lips like slow thunder. His voice was deep and raspy. Antoine attributed that quality to all of the weed he smoked growing up and his continuing mission to get high on a daily basis. "I was in the neighborhood. I thought I'd give you a holler."

"Yeah, I bet," I replied unable to disguise my skepticism.

"No, seriously, I been in the studio a lot lately. Working on something that's hot, real hot! Told my dude that I needed some R & R and I needed to chill. So I was rolling out this way to score some trees and I thought I'd just swing by old girl's place and see what's up."

I twisted my lips, gave him that look like I knew it was all bullshit. But it really didn't matter because my emotional investment in Antoine had been spent months ago.

"You got a car?" I asked.

"Yeah, I got wheels. Brand new Escalade with some spinning twenty-fours. Dat shit is hot!"

"Uhmm, maybe, you can finally take me out on a date," I said, again my comment was reeking with skepticism.

He'd never taken me anywhere during the entire year I'd known him. I remembered how we met that time when my friends dragged me out to *Dream*, a D.C. nightclub to celebrate Stacy's promotion to a feature reporter position and it was the first time we hung out with El. Even I could tell that Antoine and I seemed a most unlikely pair, but I thought that there was definitely a connection between us then. In fact, although a lot of beautiful women were throwing themselves at him that night Antoine ignored them all. El said she didn't get it in her typical condescending way. Pretty boy and plain Jane. He took me home and I, uncharacteristically, had sex with him. That one night defined the parameters of our relationship and it hadn't changed.

I was the clichéd "booty call" with no other labels to define what we were to each other. I couldn't call him a friend, not in good conscience because the word had a definite connotation and meaning in my vocabulary and it didn't mean someone showing up at your door, unannounced, wanting to get his rocks off.

I sat down beside him realizing that we'd have one of those awkward moments when nothing was said by people who had little in common. Antoine never asked me about what was going on in my life and if he ever tried to hold a conversation it was usually about the things he was doing. As we sat on the couch it quickly became obvious that our effort at small talk was futile and only a waste of precious time better utilized for sleeping after sex.

"I'm going to bed," I told him. "You can follow me or you can chill right here. It's up to you. Don't be offended but I have to get up early and go to work."

I guess my words were music to Antoine's ears. "I'm right behind you," he said.

I took off my robe revealing my nude body underneath. This was nothing special that I did for him. I always slept without any clothes on anyway and he no doubt, enjoyed the visual. I had a king-size bed that was perfect for two people who'd seek refuge in one of its expansive corners once they had finished coupling. I busily pulled back the comforter and fluffed the pillows that matched it as though I was oblivious to Antoine's presence there.

"Damn, girl! You got a beautiful body. I don't know why you always hide what you got. Shit, I peeped you the first time we met, all conservative and shit, but I saw right through that. I guess that's what attracted me, you know, the low-keyed, subtle thing about you."

His words rang empty against my sleepy consciousness. I was already in bed, lying on my side with my back to him. His words now totally garbled by the sleep that was trying to overtake my body and mind seemed to melt together. Still, I could feel the weight of his body as he climbed in bed and immediately pressed himself against me. He removed the scarf and loosened my hair. The few kisses he would deposit on the back of my neck would be the sum total of his efforts at foreplay.

"Are you wearing some protection?" I asked.

"Of course. I never go raw, even if it's with your fine ass," he said.

Already erect, Antoine slid between my legs and buried himself into me. He seemed to fill me up inside as he started slow and steady then quickly followed with his rapid fire thrusting.

The redundancy of his lovemaking brought no surprises. It was always the same. He would lift me up so my ass would be the mountain he'd try to conquer. Position me on my knees while he "hit it from the back", doggy-style. From this angle it was never slow and gentle, but always pounding like a jackhammer's staccato-like destruction of everything it touched, like the pounding of a man determined to get his first.

I could hear his groans and the slapping of his pelvis against my buttocks and feel the pounding inside. There was no pain and little pleasure, at least not the kind of pleasure that would send me into an orgasmic frenzy, but he did feel good.

Strange as it seems I had never had an orgasm, not from someone else's doing. Stacy said she had them all the time with Derek. El said depending on the man, she'd have one. But I wondered what it would be like to explode, to have my mind lobotomized by pleasure, leaving me stupid and drained. With Antoine I'd come to the brink and then it would fade away, obscured by his "me first" attitude towards love making. Frustration would take the place of orgasm.

I was trying to force one that night as he banged away at me. Gradually, I could feel the intensity of something building inside my body. *Maybe just maybe, this would be the time.*

We were both breathing hard and as Antoine increased his thrusting I pushed back in rhythm.

I thought, *Just a little more, I'm almost there.*

But when he screamed out in that primal cry of a man who had reached his climax of pleasure I knew that I would go unfulfilled. He quickly pulled out and rolled over on to his back as I fell onto my stomach, exasperated. Seconds later we both lay there asleep without touching, oblivious to each other's presence.

◆   ◆   ◆

Six a.m. I was already up, getting dressed for work. I'd washed off Antoine's scent in the shower and along with it the memory of our being together. I was surprised to see that he was still in my bed when I walked back into the bedroom. Usually he'd just hit and run like he couldn't wait to get out of my place.

I let him sleep a little while longer so that I could finish dressing without having to talk to him. After all, he didn't have a job to go to and he would tell me that he'd shower at the gym or when he got back home.

When it was time, I unceremoniously jarred him awake, shouting out, "Antoine! Time to get up! I've got to go to work."

He immediately popped up into a sitting position on the edge of the bed, squinty eyed and foggy brained. "All right. All right. Damn! What time is it?"

"Time for you to go and time for me to go to work. I don't want to miss my train."

He stretched and yawned like a satisfied alley cat that had devoured a fat mouse and dozed off on a patch of city landscape. He stood in front of me, condom still on but spent.

"I guess I better take care of this. You got a towel?" he said, sheepishly, as he tiptoed to my other bathroom down the hall. "Take your time," he hollered back. "I'll drop you off at your job."

That made me laugh. Antoine had never taken me anywhere and now he was volunteering to drive me to work. There was something poetic in the gesture, but I just couldn't figure out what it was.

I was sitting at the kitchen table when he sauntered in and sat down.

"Can a brother get a cup of coffee?" he asked.

"How you like yours?"

"Black."

I could feel his eyes watching me as I stood and walked to the stove to pour him a cup. I figured he was having one of those morning-after moments, the way he always did after we had sex.

I tried to ignore him when he walked up behind me and wrapped his arms around my waist, pulling me close. Antoine planted warm kisses on my exposed neck, the kind meant to ignite a fire in me, but I resisted.

"What are you doing?" I asked him.

"Ah, c'mon, baby. How 'bout a quick one for the road?"

I pulled away and headed back to the table with his coffee carefully balanced on a saucer. I was trying to maintain my composure and not get mad at him, but he had ignited a fire in me and it wasn't the kind he wanted or hoped for. I sat down, placed his cup hard on the table and allowed my feelings to fume along with the steam from the coffee. I sat there, jaws tighter than a pit bull's incensed by what I'd just heard.

"What's your problem?" Antoine asked.

He joined me at the table waiting for his coffee to cool and watching to see if I would do the same.

"What's my *problem*? I'll tell you. I haven't seen you since, what? A month or so? You don't call me. You don't take me anywhere. And have you ever given me anything? I mean like flowers, candy or bought me a birthday or Christmas present? Have you, Antoine?"

He sat there dumbstruck, convicted by his silence. I knew he had no defense, no way to comeback.

"It pisses me off that you don't respect me, that you don't make me feel special. All you want to do is screw me, get your rocks off and then vanish into thin air until you do your fucking Houdini act a month from now and I'm supposed to say, c'mon, I'm waiting for you, daddy! That's some bullshit, Antoine and now I don't believe you got the nerve to ask me if I'm down for another fifteen minutes of your mindless humping!"

I could feel the little beads of sweat that usually gathered underneath my eyes whenever I got mad and I thought it was a good thing I didn't wear makeup. I was glaring at him, not quite sure if I'd finished my rant and gearing up to start round two when he came out of his trance.

"Whoa, baby. Slow your roll," Antoine said. "Damn! Why all the drama? You act like I asked you for something important, like some money or something."

I glared at him even harder.

"So what you're telling me is that according to your value system money holds a higher place than my body. Is that what you're saying, Antoine?"

He shook his head, not disagreeing with what I'd said, but to show me that he was becoming exasperated with the conversation.

"I don't know why you trippin', but there's a ton of women who'd do anything just to have me spend a few minutes with them. Shit, consider yourself lucky girl."

"You the one trippin' if you think that's gonna impress me, telling me about other women, Antoine."

"I don't believe this shit.".

He stood up and reached for his baseball cap, twisted it backwards on his head.

"If you had a problem with me and the way we've been with each other for the past year, you should've said something last night," he said.

Antoine gave me a hard look and let out a harder breath.

"So, if you're trying to tell me that I'm using you then you should check that shit at the door because you used me, too," he added.

This was classic Antoine. He was animated, using his hands like a streetwise hustler giving a PowerPoint presentation to the board of directors of some Fortune 500 company. He reminded me of the countless number of hip-hop artists I'd watch from time to time on television and their contrived demeanor, like being in the music business forced them to walk, talk and think the same way. And I wondered how someone could be truly creative when they all were cookie-cutter images of each other.

I turned my attention back to our conversation. I guess there was some truth in Antoine's remark about me using him, but I had a different reason. Mine was no less opportunistic than his but in my own mind it was justified. I'd been with him because there was no one else around. Men weren't knocking my door down, ringing my telephone off the hook so I'd learned to settle, to check my self-esteem at the door. I decided there was no point in arguing, besides, I had to get to work.

"Look, I'm sorry. I guess I got up on the wrong side of the bed this morning. I got a lot of things I'm dealing with, O.K?"

My apology was more about myself than any concern for his feelings because his occasional forays into my life were better than none at all. D.C., after all, was a city where the women outnumbered the men twenty to one and I knew a whole lot of sisters who had their men in parcels, one piece at a time.

Antoine sipped his coffee and assumed a relaxed pose with his legs spread out and his head cocked to the side as he watched me without saying anything. He had an air of confidence that made him both attractive and despicable. And his half-hearted acceptance of my apology put it on display.

"Apology accepted," was all he said. Subject closed. "If you still need that ride I'm ready to roll."

It would take him about an hour and a half to drive from my place to Pentagon City across the Key Street Bridge and into Northern Virginia. With traffic being the way it was it was faster and easier to take the train. Besides, I'd never had a conversation with Antoine that lasted more than twenty minutes and the thought of being cooped up with him in a car for nearly two hours was causing me to break out in hives.

"If you just take me to the Metro station I'll ride the train to work. It'll save you trying to drive through rush hour traffic."

He didn't object. I didn't expect him to. So I found myself following him to his car, a pearl white Escalade with shiny chrome wheels that would continue to spin when the vehicle came to a stop.

We approached the car from the passenger side and Antoine hit the remote, unlocking the car doors and starting its engine. For a fleeting moment I thought that he might open my door, but that was just a thought. True to form, he walked to the driver's side, looked at me and uttered those famous two words every woman hates to hear, "It's open."

Well, at least El could no longer chastise me for being involved with someone who had nothing. The car wasn't exactly what I would judge as being of good taste, but its ostentatious excess symbolized that Antoine must've been doing well. I wouldn't draw any hasty conclusions about that, however. It was how a person lived that mattered, especially to El. "Let me see your P & L, your house, your financial statements. Hell, just show me your tax return and proof that you have a savings account."

Antoine saved me the trouble of standing out on Aspen Road, trying to flag a taxi cab. When he stopped right in front of the Metro's 'Stop and Kiss' drop off, I gave him a little one on the cheek.

"I'll call you," he told me.

"Yeah, I bet." *Probably in another three months.* I thought.

The Metro train was crowded like every day with what seemed like all of humanity pressed shoulder to shoulder and riding in a sardine can at seventy miles an hour. I was fortunate that the place where I got on was at the start of the line and the car was relatively empty. The closer to downtown, the more crowded the train became; a seat was cherished like having the exact change for a token.

I sat in the same seat by a window everyday except on those rare occasions when I missed my seven o'clock connection. There was nothing special about the seat, just consistency and a pattern and a way of doing things to maintain certainty in an uncertain world. Besides, I enjoyed seeing the city blurred by speed, reminding me of a collage painted by some drunken artist.

I guess in some ways seeing it this way made me think of my life and my tendency to gloss over my reality without looking at the details. Stacy would sometimes chastise me, telling me that I needed to step outside the box, to add some spice to my life, but I remained in the safe confines of my government job and the little cubicle I called, home.

Most of the people on the train had their heads buried in a newspaper or a book. Others, prodigiously devoted to their places of employment, hammered away at their laptop computers, their PDA's or Blackberry's, writing, communicating, dictating, analyzing and every other kind of "ing" associated with the desire to get ahead or just to keep up in Washington. As for my part, I just watched them impassively until I noticed that someone seemed to be watching me.

At first, I dismissed the idea that the man in the gray suit was being overly attentive and reacting to my every move because when I looked at him he'd look away. He didn't smile or nod, didn't acknowledge me in any way. I could see the remnants of a face, brown and angular, that chilled my spirit and sent shivers through my body. *Just ignore him,* I thought, but that was hard to do.

He was wearing a hat, detective-style with the brim pulled down low and wearing sunglasses that left only his nose, mouth and chin exposed. My imagination went into overdrive, sending my thoughts to spiral into some 1940's type spy movie with this guy right out of central casting. And Washington was the perfect backdrop for the story and I was the perfect heroine as the frightened damsel in distress.

The announcement over the train's intercom that Pentagon City was the next stop shook me from fantasy and slammed me back to reality. In a few minutes I'd be sitting at my desk, eyes trained on a computer screen and realizing that my life was as flat as the images it projected.

By 7:30 a.m. I was following the herd of people getting off at the Pentagon City station as they all stutter stepped to keep from walking on top of each other. The intimacy of strangers so close yet not touching beneath the surface was a byproduct of mass transportation and indicative of a hustle-bustle world that didn't foster humans connecting. I sometimes marveled at the choreography of it all while imagining the horror of a stampede if someone yelled, "Fire!" And somewhere in the crowd I was aware that the man on the train was a few steps behind me. I turned my head to see where he was and I quickened my own pace trying to put some distance between us.

I thought it was ridiculous to think that he might be following me which I guess was my paranoia. I dismissed that idea and concluded that he probably worked at the Pentagon like thousands of others, but as I approached the building's entrance I lost track of him.

Once on the safe side of the security checkpoint I turned to look back into the crowd, hoping he had re-appeared and I could get a good look at the man so that I could file his image in my memory, but he was gone. I shrugged it off, figured that he had no reason for following me and that he probably wasn't.

Whatever mystique the Pentagon held with the public before 9/11 it had tripled since that day. Security had always been tight and the civilians were subjected to detailed screening and background checks that were unrivaled in American history. Beyond the usual investigation for links to terrorist organizations and criminal history, references had to be beyond reproach and an employee had to maintain a solid credit report. El would always laugh and say, "That's why no black people work at the Pentagon because we don't have good credit."

I resented her remarks and the dearth of African-Americans working there could have been attributed to a lot of other factors, but I refused to speculate why. I had to undergo an additional layer of security screening because of my supersensitive position as an analyst. Although my department mostly crunched numbers those numbers were critical to tracking the activities of known terrorists and agents of espionage. My division was known as "COTES" or Counter Terrorism Espionage Systems.

It wasn't nearly as glamorous or sexy as it sounded, but there was a certain James Bond element to the job. Entering the building everyone was required to produce the standard government issued I.D. card with a bar code that was scanned by the guards. My department went a step farther by requiring all employees to have the palms of their hands scanned for further identification and then retinal colorization and refraction identification for further access into my section. For me the extra scrutiny was tedious and mind numbing, but it came with the job.

The pay was O.K. and the potential for promotion into the executive classification was realistic, but the job was just a job and in my mind I often dreamed of doing something else, something more creative. Still, I had privileges not enjoyed by the average U.S. citizen which included my current security clearance that was at a level eight, with ten being tops. It meant I could go anywhere in the world without restraint and without questions. A level ten flew on Air Force One or Two.

My desk was no different than it was any other day: Laptop computer with a screen saver spiraling traces of a wand being waved by an invisible fairy, notepad as blank as my enthusiasm and a picture of my mother with my stepfather's hand around her shoulder and his face torn out. That was the sum total of my desk and pretty much my life.

I clicked on my laptop and typed my password, downloaded an Excel document that had been sent by my supervisor and daydreamed over the numbers. I thought briefly of Antoine and then drifted to the beautiful older man I'd seen at the restaurant. And wondered what it would be like to be with him compared to Antoine. I could see his slow and gentle hands caressing every part of my body, soft kisses everywhere and a matured love, unselfish and making my satisfaction his priority.

It was a rude beep from my computer notifying me that I had an email that broke the spell. My section chief had sent a note advising me that he needed to see me in his office. I swallowed hard and choked back the thought that there was some kind of problem, but I still felt like someone going to the gallows as I walked from my cubicle to his office.

"You want to see me, Mr. Rhinehart?" I asked.

He responded without looking up from the papers sprawled all over his desk and with a simple gesture of his hand granted me permission to enter his office like he was a sultan or some despotic king. I quietly acceded to his command and took a seat on the other side of his desk.

I watched and waited for him to address me, curious about why he needed to see me and why he seemed so serious. A career bureaucrat, Mr. Rhinehart had always been a hands-off supervisor and not especially demanding when it came to any of the employees under his charge. Most of all he was a congenial boss whose reddish-gray hair and balding crown gave him the appearance of someone who was a refugee from the Ringling Brothers Circus. Add a red nose and a flower that squirted water and he'd be entertaining adolescent children at a five-year-olds' lawn party.

"Ah, yes, Dahlia Reynolds," he said, finally looking up from the documents. "Thanks for coming. I need to talk to you about something."

My heart sank as I listened to those words. I thought about all the reasons he could have for summoning me there and none were good.

He continued. "We've had a security breach. Someone hacked into the department's personnel files and apparently accessed personal and private information about people in this department."

I had no real reaction just, "Oh".

"Yeah, that kind of thing happens, but I'm just alerting everyone in our section that this happened so as a pre-caution, check your credit report and watch for someone trying to open up charge accounts under your name or withdrawing money from your checking and savings accounts."

I thought about what he just told me and chuckled slightly. If anyone tried to use my social security number and other personal information to secure credit or anything else they'd be in for a rude awakening. Savings? Had none. Checking account? Just enough in there to buy groceries. The rest of my paycheck was direct deposited to my creditors.

I left his office that day believing that I, like many others, could be a victim of cyber-fraud, but in my case the consequences were minimal, or so I thought.

Day Four

I don't know how he entered my mind and stayed there, but I couldn't shake him. But it's easy to drift and to dream within the limited confines of these four walls that make a prison of my body, but not of my mind. I would get to know him during the ensuing weeks, more personal and intimate than I'd ever known any man. There are things you should know.

Songs of Desdemona—9/23/05

An ill-timed kick from my baby brings me back to the present, to the now. I'm not home in Washington where my thoughts had taken me, but rather still confined and rotting in Pattaya, lost and alone. Only my memories sustain me, keeping my sanity, but memories are elusive and come and go like the tide, lapping at the shore of an island paradise. His image now faded.

I roll back over onto my side and keep writing in my diary: *Life is a series of unrequited chance. It isn't fair. It isn't just. It is what it is.*

My writing is more than thoughts it is a reflection of my state of being. I'm allowed to read a few books, mostly classics like Steinbeck and Camus which further shape my pessimism about how this scenario of life and death will play out. In Steinbeck, I confront the stark realities of life just as Camus is existential, but I find things more palatable in the whimsy of my world before I got here. And I know that Chiang Mai is waiting to hear my story.

"Why you write always?" she asks me.

"For posterity."

"Me not understand. Who is this 'pos-pos-ity'?" She fumbles through the word with her phonetic attempt at its pronunciation and I resist the urge to help her through it.

Chiang's question reflects her confusion and lets me know that although she speaks English, language remains a barrier for us.

"It's for, how you say? Not ancestors. The ones that follow me in life," I answered.

"Like your baby?"

"Exactly. Someday I hope that he'll get to know me through the things I write, whether I'm with him or not."

I wait for her response, but there's dead silence.

"Are you still there, Chiang?"

I hear her blow a sigh and sniffle away a tear.

"It is sad for your pos-ter-ity," she says.

"I guess it depends on how you look at it. I have no regrets about my baby and since we've been talking it's helped me see things a little more clearly. I guess I'm putting my life into perspective."

"I want to hear more about your life," Chiang tells me.

I eagerly acquiesce to her request and my mind scrolls back to the time I'd wandered once again into J. Paul's a few days later. I was hoping that the man who'd so intrigued me would be there sitting at the same table, eating his lunch and reading. But he wasn't.

I ate, paid the waiter and headed for the door. "Nothing ventured, nothing gained," I said, quietly.

A parting glance back into the restaurant was enough to make me feel totally ridiculous that I had gone this far. I doubled back, looking for my familiar maitre d'.

"Excuse me," I said.

"Ah, yes. Eet's the pretty Mademoiselle Ray-nolds. I did not see you. Are you here for lunch? Are you waiting for someone?"

"No, actually I'm leaving. I just wanted to ask you something. There was a man in here the other day. You know, older. Black. Nice dresser. Drives a new Bentley."

He stood still for a moment obviously listening and thinking. Then it clicked. He smiled.

"I know. Eets Mr. Powell you are talking about. He comes in here all the time. He is a regular. Generous tipper, I might add."

My heart pounded. I couldn't believe I was being so bold, asking about some stranger. The maitre d' smiled with a look as though he had uncovered some secret like children exposing a schoolgirl's crush, making the laugh lines in his face dig deep into his skin.

"I can arrange for you to meet him, Oui?"

"No, no. It's not like that," I told him. "I thought he looked familiar like someone my father knows."

He smiled even wider. It was obvious he wasn't buying what I was selling. I told myself it didn't matter what he thought. *If I was interested in an older man, then I was just interested. There was no societal taboo. Old guys and young chicks are as common a pairing as men and men, women and women, blacks and whites. If there was any stigma to it, it was only carried by those narrow-minded folks who lacked a creative thought.*

So, why did I lie? Can't explain that now. But I'd accomplished part of my goal. Now I knew the name of the man called, Mr. Powell.

Everyday for the next two weeks I found myself hurrying over to J. Paul's, a train and cab ride over to Georgetown from the Pentagon. Always at approximately the same time, 12:45 p.m., the time I first noticed him there. If it was meant to happen, meeting him, then it would happen, but I thought I shouldn't leave it entirely up to chance.

Still, it was time for self-examination. *Am I obsessing?* It was something my therapist had warned me about. Like my tendency to clean my apartment over and over and making sure that it was spotless all the time. And those insecurities I had about myself? I know, everyone has them, but mine were glaring and obvious to me even if no one really noticed. I felt like I was some kind of stalker, but I couldn't help it. I was drawn to him.

Despite my persistence my trips to Georgetown were becoming efforts in futility. I didn't see Mr. Powell and each time I walked into the restaurant the maitre d' would shake his head as if to say, "He isn't here."

I thought about D.C. as a thriving metropolis and knowing that people come and go. A chance meeting or eye contact with a stranger on a train could mean that you might not ever see him again. I railed against myself for not seizing the moment the way El would've. I should've known that that I must treat every encounter as though it was my last.

◆   ◆   ◆

After a couple of weeks of trying I decided that I would no longer pursue the stranger. I would re-assess the things that were happening in my life and move on. Antoine was coming by more often. He'd gone beyond being merely tolerated to someone I might even enjoy, occasionally. True, he was shallow and self-centered and still no orgasms, but it seemed that he was putting in the effort to make our occasional coupling into a relationship … maybe.

He dropped by two days after I'd given up my quest to meet Mr. Powell. It wasn't his typical booty call because we had a rendezvous a couple of nights earlier with the same results. Antoine had called early that Saturday and asked if he could come by. There was excitement in his voice muted by the blunt he had smoked that morning to celebrate the news he was going to share with me.

"We got a meeting with a major label," he announced. "They heard our demo. Say they love it."

"Which one? I know you've been working with different artists," I asked.

"Desire. The girl I signed. She writes, sings her ass off, pretty. Like Alicia Keys but better."

He reached inside his pants pocket, pulled out a PA. "You mind?" he asked me.

I don't know why, but I shook my head giving him the go ahead to do what he always did. Decided I'd join him with an early glass of wine. By the time I returned from the kitchen Antoine had emptied most of the tobacco out of his cigar and filled it with cannabis. He cut off the filter, sealed it and lit it up like a bonfire. A long and heavy draw and he was on the road to euphoria.

Antoine on weed wasn't exactly the picture of verbosity. Usually, he'd be in that dumb-downed state of mind as though marijuana had made him retarded. His responses would be peppered with a slowed and barely audible, "Huh?" or "Wha?" But today he was almost lucid—even after a few tokes.

"You know, I don't really know you and you don't really, really know me," he volunteered.

For me it was like stating the obvious like men are from Mars kind of shit, but his recognition was refreshing—I guess. And for him it must've been an epiphany.

"What do you want to know?" I asked. "You know I'm from Georgia. You know what I do for a living. What else is there to know about me?"

He had settled deep inside a corner of my couch, the picture of ease and contentment. His green eyes cut towards me as slits in his face and he offered them along with a smile.

"What else is there to know? Plenty, I bet. I mean, tell me about your family. Your moms and pops."

I groped for my glass of wine behind the question. Took a long gulp.

"Nothing to tell. My mom lives back home in Waycross with my stepfather and grandmother. My father died the day before I was born."

"Wow, that's deep. You miss him?"

The question confused and confounded me. I thought maybe it was the weed talking.

"How can I miss someone I never knew, Antoine?"

"I don't mean miss him, as in missing someone you knew and was close to. What I mean is miss him for what could've been. For what he might've been to you."

The comment muted me, stilled my words like I was the one who'd smoked that blunt. It revived those thoughts I had growing up, imagining what my father looked like, how he smelled and how we'd interact. I imagined him and me laughing and lots and lots of hugs. I missed that.

It was as though Antoine had reached into my thoughts, something I didn't think he was capable of doing. His comments were simple, but displayed a depth I hadn't experienced with him. But I couldn't go there with him so I retreated in my silence.

"I miss my father," he told me.

"Why did he pass on, too?"

"Nah, he's been AWOL like a lot of black men from that generation. I hate his ass for that."

"What happened?" I asked.

"You know the usual. He went on an extended vacation. Did five years at the Federal Spa and Hotel Resort. When he got out my moms was waitin' but he didn't want no part of her or me."

"I'm sorry."

"Nuthin' to be sorry about. Not your fault."

Antoine and I had something in common although it didn't exactly make us soul mates. Fatherless by design or by happenstance we'd both grown up without one and I guess that fact colored our perspective on ourselves. I thought about the conversation days later and thought about my father and what he might say about my life and my career if he was still alive.

"Do you think that part of your problem with your father is that he doesn't agree with your lifestyle?" I asked.

Antoine's smirking persona returned. "How in the hell could he ever judge me? It's his lifestyle I have a problem with. Dude's a hustler, a real life pimp."

"But isn't that what you guys in the rap game idolize? You don't talk about being doctors or lawyers. All rappers ever talk about is getting easy money, pimping 'hoes', you know that misogynistic vitriol you constantly spew out to our youth. Seems to me that your father would be the poster boy for every young brother to idolize and emulate."

I was waiting for Antoine's reaction which I assumed would be some kind of defense but he just laughed.

"Damn, girl," he said. "I know you went to college and all, but a brother from the streets can't relate to all those big words."

His words made me realize just how different we were as people. Antoine was from the streets, as he called it with a hustler for a father, their non-existent relationship, punctuated by his absence from the son's life. That apparently shaped him, formed him like clay. I also realized how our parents became some kind of pseudo-deities with the ability to create and destroy.

"What about your stepfather?" Antoine asked. "Are you close?"

"Next question." My response was flat.

"No, seriously. What kind of relationship do you have with him?"

"I don't talk about Rufus," I said.

Another hard sip of wine and I was ready to end the conversation, but I knew that Antoine would press on.

"What? Did he abuse you?" He asked.

His question evoked suppressed memories. I gave him a dispirited answer. "Yes."

"Son of a bitch! Your moms know?"

I nodded.

"And you telling me she's still with the muthafucka!"

"She's been a victim, too. It wasn't sexual abuse from my stepfather. It was physical and mental. He'd whip me for just about anything or no reason at all. Always called me things like 'harlot' and 'whore'. Told me that no man would ever want me. If I cried he'd lock me in a closet with no lights——sometimes for two or three days straight," I said.

"Damn! Did they bring you food or water? Let you go to the bathroom?"

"Most times he didn't. I'd lie on the cold, hard floor, tried to hold my body functions and when I couldn't I'd lay in my filth. When he'd let me out I used to sit in the tub for hours and scrub my skin until it was raw."

The words just slipped out of me and I sat there wishing I could take them back. I'd never confided in anyone about that experience except my therapist and there I was telling Antoine my secrets. I guess I told him because I had a need to connect with him, with anybody on a deeper level as my doctor had suggested, but why I discussed my life with Antoine is still a mystery to me. In a twisted way, I imagined it could be the foundation of a real relationship.

"What about your mother? Why didn't she stop him?"

"Partly because she was abused, too. Partly because their church said that children had to be punished. And partly because he put a roof over our heads, all three generations of Reynolds—my grandmother, mother and me."

Antoine slid back into the couch as though he was contemplating my words, my story. The thick blunt he'd been smoking was now smoldering in the ashtray. He reached for it, took it to his mouth and pulled another drag letting the cannabis fill the void left by his previous hit which was slowly dissolving away. *I must be killing his high, my words a true buzz-kill.* He let the smoke go, his green eyes peering through it made him look like a Chinese dragon with piercing jade pupils.

"I thought it was tough growing up without a father but I guess its better not to have one at all than to have someone who treats you like shit," he told me.

He took one more hit and held the smoke inside like he had taken his last grab for air before plunging deep into the murkiness of euphoric waters. I watched him as he released another plume of smoke that floated surreally over his head and into the fibers of my family's quilt that was hanging on the wall over us. I was fine with Antoine smoking until he did that.

"What are you doing?" I asked, as I feverishly fanned the smoke away from my legacy, my heirloom.

"Whoa, sorry, didn't intend no harm."

He twisted his body around to get a full view of the quilt. "Damn! That's nice. Must be real valuable."

"It's been in my family for a real long time. It tells our history beginning with our coming here as slaves."

Antoine sat there staring at the quilt without uttering a word. I assumed he was immersed in my lineage, but I also wondered if he was sizing it up and trying to guess its value. I quickly dismissed the thought. No matter what I'd ever thought about him a thief wasn't part of the description.

We spent the rest of the day hanging out at my place and when it got dark outside he left. I woke up the next morning feeling somewhat redeemed by the catharsis I'd experienced with him. There were times when I used to think that I was the only person in the world who was rudderless and abandoned by not having that strong paternal figure in my life that we all need. And my father's ghost, resurrected by a common experience haunted my thoughts for most of the day.

Day Five

Serendipity: the happening of fortunate discoveries when not in search of them. The word seemed to be the antithesis of an orderly universe where things happen for a reason, life's causes and effects and me for one, had never experienced anything close to it

Songs of Desdemona—9/25/05.

I thought about him while I sat at my desk reading reports, but my conjured up image of my father receded when I was summoned to the personnel office. A pretty young blonde-haired girl was sitting at the receptionist's desk with a stack of papers in front of her and a wad of chewing gum jammed into her mouth. Occasionally she would bite down on a bubble of air trapped inside the gum and it would pop with that aggravating sound that drives teachers to distraction and makes you want to slap the gum chewer in the mouth.

I was told that I had to fill out some paperwork and that the agency had to re-certify all of its employees who had their files corrupted and information deleted.

"What do you mean, re-certify?" I asked her.

"Your security clearance. You have to be re-certified for your clearance status."

I let her comment roll around in my head. Then thought about some of the things El once told me about the government's scrutiny over every little piss-assed blemish on its employees' records. I thought about my student loans, federal-insured, that had gone delinquent and on the verge of going into default.

I thought about how I could not only lose my clearance, but my job along with it. The government would reason, anyone who owed almost a hundred grand in student loans could be compromised by someone throwing some change in their direction to get top-secret information. I shuddered at the thought that I could lose my job because someone hacked into *their* computer and, possibly stole my identity.

"You'll have to fill out these papers."

The young woman had a bureaucratic sense of nonchalance and seemed so detached that she reeked of that "I'm just doing my job" attitude. She was the kind of person who could test my patience.

I finished filling out forms like the ones I'd filled out when they first hired me. I had to give them every little detail about my life. Answered questions about my mother, stepfather and my deceased biological seed planter, finished and handed them to the gatekeeper.

"They're running your info through the computers today. You should have something back before the day is over," she said without looking at me.

The walk and elevator ride back to my office was a long one with thoughts of my career's demise dominating my journey. I thought about the different scenarios and how they'd play out.

I remembered once when a girl was fired and how they had security with guns wearing Gestapo type, drag clothing escort her out of the building. She'd committed no crime but that's how they did things, fearful that some hundred and twenty-five pound, five foot-six female might go postal and annihilate us all.

The rest of the day was wasted by worry and I sat at my desk waiting for that fateful email or the Gestapo goose stepping their way to my cubicle. Later, I got the email from Mr. Rhinehart. It read: *Dahlia Reynolds, I need to see you right away.*

I remember the anxiety I felt as I walked down that long, narrow hall to Mr. Rhinehart's office and the familiar droplets of perspiration that always seemed to pop up on their own right around the bridge of my nose. I used my open hands to fan my face as I walked, happy that there was no one else in the hall to see me flapping my wings as though I'd take flight. I hesitated when I reached his door, but then I took a deep breath and mustered all of my courage before I knocked.

"It's open!" He said.

I turned the doorknob slowly and walked in. My supervisor was not alone. There were two other men there with Rhinehart sitting at his desk and the other two in chairs and their backs to me. Rhinehart forced a weak smile and motioned for me to take a seat in the empty chair beside his desk. It had all of the appearance of an inquisition and I knew that something was wrong.

The way the room was set up made me feel like I was about to testify in a court of law. Rhinehart sat at the judge's bench and me in the witness chair facing the two men who looked ready to prosecute me to the fullest.

"This is Mr. Robinson and that's Mr. Liles," Rhinehart said.

I nodded politely and they both responded with the grimfaced salutation, "Hello, pleased to meet you." They spoke in one voice like it was part of their routine honed to perfection from countless encounters with people as a duo.

"They're with the FBI," Rhinehart added.

Those words hit me so hard that they reverberated through my being and settled somewhere between my stomach and my heart. Both organs reacted. My stomach churned and felt queasy. My heart raced with intermittent palpitations inserted to slow its pace.

Robinson, no first name, was the first to speak after our introductions. "There's nothing to be concerned about, Ms. Reynolds. We just want to ask you a few questions."

I had learned a long time ago that whenever someone started a conversation with those fated words "nothing to worry about" it meant that trouble was on its way. I didn't respond, just waited for the questions.

He had a manila folder balanced on his lap that was in stark contrast to his large dark brown hands. I squirmed uncomfortably as he deftly opened the folder and read something to himself before he began to speak.

"It's about the background investigation the agency conducted," he told me.

I relaxed for a moment realizing I had nothing to hide. My student loan was public record and I thought that if the FBI was getting into the collection business for every delinquent student loan then the country was really in trouble.

"Do you know a Mr. Antoine Blackwell?"

I nodded. He smirked.

"You need to watch the kind of company you keep," he said.

I knew that my face displayed my confusion over his comment. I squirmed again in my chair like my thong panties were riding up on me. My body language was going to send me to the electric chair for a crime I didn't know I had committed. I cleared my throat.

"I mean, I know he smokes a little weed now and then but ..."

"Don't try and be coy with us," the second man, Mr. Liles broke through. Robinson gave him a stern look, smiled slightly and with a gesture of his hand held Liles at bay.

"I apologize, Ms. Reynolds for my associate's remark. Like I said, we just want to ask you a few questions," Robinson said.

I picked up on their act right away—good cop, bad cop—a time worn cliché, but still no less intimidating. This was the salt and pepper version. I figured that it was Robinson's role as my African-American brother to make me feel at ease while Liles would be "the man", my oppressor ready to shackle me and take me away. "I'm sorry, I guess I don't know why you're asking me about Antoine," I said.

"How well do you know him?" Robinson asked me.

"Not that well. I mean, we're friends, sort of but …"

It was Liles' turn again. "You don't know him that well and you're sort of friends but", he paused and glanced at Robinson's open folder. "He's spent the night at your place twice during the last couple of weeks and he was there just a couple of days ago."

My mouth dropped open. I looked at Mr. Rhinehart for help, but he simply shrugged his shoulders.

"I didn't know that's a crime," I said. The blood was beginning to rush to my head. They were spying on me. "Do I need to call my lawyer?"

Mr. Robinson leaned close, flashed his big brown eyes, curled his lips and displayed some of the whitest teeth I'd ever seen. He spoke in an almost whispered, "You won't need a lawyer. Like I said, we just want to ask you some questions. Do you know what Mr. Blackwell does for a living?"

"Music producer." I decided right then to keep my answers short.

He smiled even wider. "He ever talk about any of his associates in *the music business?*"

I detected the *music business* sarcasm. "No."

"Well, if he does anything in the music business it's on the side," Robinson said.

"So, what are you telling me? Is he involved in a gang? Drugs?" I asked.

Liles was chomping at the bit, waiting for his chance to jump into the interrogation.

"Yeah, Antoine's in a gang, alright," he said.

Robinson gave his partner another look as if to say, you'll get your turn, just wait.

"I guess you could call it gang activity but at a different level," he told me. "They're a lot more sophisticated than your typical red shirt-blue shirt guys. I guess you'd call them smugglers or maybe import-export entrepreneurs."

"I don't understand how any of this has to do with me," I replied.

Robinson gave Liles the nod. It was tag team time and like a television wrestler he was already climbing over the ropes to deliver his own kind of smack down.

"It's got plenty to do with you, Ms. Reynolds. Wire transfers of large sums of money from your home computer to foreign banks puts you right smack dab in the middle of all this," Liles said.

My mouth dropped open. "Are you saying that you monitored my home computer? Isn't that illegal or something?"

Liles smirked. "We got all the law we need on our side. It's called The Patriot Act. So why don't we just stop playing games, Ms. Reynolds."

"I don't know what you're talking about. I mean, Antoine's been over to my place lately and he's used my computer to surf the net or play video games, but that's all." I could feel my emotions gaining a stranglehold around my brain, but I fought back the tears that were beginning to well up in my eyes. I needed to think clearly. I shook my head. "I haven't done anything wrong," I added.

I watched as Liles reached for the folder and pulled out a sheet of paper. He unceremoniously placed it on my lap. It was a bank statement from a bank in Antigua with my name at the top. My eyes skimmed over the statement and rested at the bottom where it read: *Account Balance: $250,000.00.* For a moment I froze unable to even blink my eyelids.

"That's a lot of money for a twenty something, forty thousand dollar a year government employee. Isn't it?" he said.

I could feel six eyes all trained on me, waiting for my response. "It's not mine, I swear. I don't know anything about this." I could feel the dam break as the tears rushed down my cheeks. I took off my eyeglasses and put my hands over my face and cried.

I heard the calm voice of Robinson as the good guy coming to the rescue. "I believe you, Ms. Reynolds." He handed me a handkerchief that he had pulled from his jacket pocket and watched as I used it to dab around my eyes.

"I can give the money back," I told him as I continued to cry.

"That's not what we want from you because if we did we could've frozen the account and seized the money anytime. What we want is your assistance."

"What do you mean?"

"Your boy, Antoine is a low level player and we've been tracking him for a while. Their little posse is up to something huge and we believe they've got a part for you to play, but we need to get the main players. Right now they're insulated. We could pick him up and see if he'll turn on them, but that's a gamble because if Antoine's suddenly not around the others will disappear."

"I don't understand. You mean they want to use me to launder the two hundred, fifty thousand?"

"No, it's much bigger than that. There's a lot of activity within the group and our intelligence tells us that something's brewing and it's gonna happen soon. My theory is that they need you because of your security clearance. Either they want to bring something into the country that's real big or take something out."

"What kind of stuff do you think they're trying to smuggle in or out of here?" I asked.

"That's not important for you to know right now," Liles jumped back in. He was now sitting on the corner of Rhinehart's desk like he owned it.

Robinson spoke up. "They usually deal in fine art, antiquities, stuff like that. They've been known to smuggle ancient artifacts out of Egypt. Some of us at the department call them, tomb raiders."

He motioned for Liles to get off of Rhinehart's desk. "Sooner or later he's going to come to you with a scheme, asking you to help him move something using your credentials."

"And why would Antoine even think I'd do something illegal?"

Liles brought back that awful, sinister smirk to his face. He made a gesture like he was twisting his arm out throwing a punch, but with a twist at the end. It was sexual. I gave him a look of disgust.

"You don't have to do anything," Robinson said. "You're the bait or maybe the foil. Either way, they'll come to you, show you the easy money or make you think that what they're doing is on the up and up. As for our department, we just sit back and wait and watch until the time is right. Our goal is to expose the brains behind whatever it is they're planning and catch them all with the goods."

He stood up, straightened his tie to signal that he and his anxious partner were leaving. "Here's my card, Ms. Reynolds. Just give me a call anytime you want to talk or if you think there's something I need to know."

"Am I in danger?"

"Nah, we don't think so. I'm not going to lie. There are some dangerous elements in this group, but they need you. So you're Teflon."

"And what am I supposed to do if they tell me about all that money?"

"It's in your name—keep it, spend it if you want."

I watched as the two walked out of Rhinehart's office with Robinson leading the way. Liles gave me a parting glance and shook his head. He stopped midway. "I can't believe you didn't suspect that our boy Antoine was up to something. I mean, I've seen him while we've been on surveillance," he smiled. "Let's just say you're not his type."

◆   ◆   ◆

I left work that day confused, decided that I needed to clear my head so I ventured over to Old Town in Alexandria, Virginia, a stone's throw away from downtown Washington and the Pentagon. It was a place I'd often visit just to lose myself in this neighborhood of brownstones and earthy shops that sold antique furniture and pricey clothes. I'd often imagine myself walking into one of those stores and buying the most expensive dresses or jewelry they kept on display but under lock and key.

It didn't take long before I'd had my fill of wandering up and down Old Town's main street with my mind rapt with things I couldn't buy. It was a convenient respite from my problems but I soon grew weary of the game. There was a jazz club I'd sometimes visit whenever I was in that part of town. I wasn't really into jazz but I liked the atmosphere of the converted four-story brownstone that served as a place for folks to congregate and enjoy music that wasn't frenetic and mind numbing.

I stood in front of the Café Alexandria for a moment contemplating whether I should go inside or take a ride on the Metro back home. I could hear the sound of a live band oozing out of the front door whenever somebody more determined than I scurried past and stepped inside. I decided I would follow a smiling couple linked arm in arm as the male half of the duo opened the door for his lady and beamed as she stepped ahead of him. He stood there holding the door like a doorman at the Ritz-Carlton Hotel and waited for me. He didn't say anything, just gave me a friendly nod and dipped his head towards the entrance as though he was saying ladies first.

I walked past him, gave him a polite smile to acknowledge his gentleman-like gesture. He, in return, puckered his lips and gave me an air kiss while carefully looking past me to see if his lady was watching. I could feel his eyes examine me up and down, obviously paying close attention to my body. I glanced back to see him still holding on to his unapologetic stare as I shook my head. Here he was with a beautiful black woman already at his side and allowing himself to be distracted. *Men are dogs,* I thought.

His date was standing there waiting patiently when I walked by. She appeared either unaware or unaffected by her flirty partner but I wasn't taking any chances that she had seen him and would make me the object of her anger instead of him. I made a beeline right into the ladies room, gave myself a once over in the mirror and tried to make an assessment of my appearance and my clothes.

I had that working girl look and not the kind that sold themselves on the corners along K Street just a stone's throw away from the symbolic epicenter of Judeo-Christian morality, the Bush Whitehouse. Instead, I was in a dressed down plaid suit with the skirt clinging just below my knees, a white blouse that screamed for a fashion intervention and flat shoes from the Wal-Mart couture collection. Good judgment would have told me to leave the club immediately but I decided to stay.

Café Alexandria had always been an upscale jazz club with a mix of black and white professional people that included a smattering of civil servants blending in with doctors, lawyers and D.C. power brokers. It seemed purposely away from the beaten path that was Georgetown and perfect for a surreptitious rendezvous between some young model-type P.Y.T. and her upper middle class or wealthy and often, unattractive male benefactor.

It was the kind of place that I imagined El would someday frequent after she turned thirty-five and her prey had advanced from young pro-athletes to some middle-aged and married, rich cat who craved to have a pulchritudinous female playing arm candy to his bittersweet memories of what he once had been.

My timidity quickly gave way to a sense of exhilaration and expectation, like I was meant to be in the club that evening so I walked out of the bathroom with my head held high and made my way to the bar. It was typical D.C. club action with an older clientele. There were men lined up along the bar watching every woman who walked by like they were judges in the Miss America contest. I imagined them holding signs rating each woman and I shuddered to think how they would rate me especially considering my outfit but still I pressed on.

I found an open seat at the bar, flanked on one side by two thirty-something divas with short skirts and long legs and holding court to a pack of men playing the usual ritualistic mating game of who could be the most charming. I made a quick study of the two women.

The lady farthest from me was a plus-sized, honey-colored sister who appeared to be very comfortable inside her own ample skin. She was getting a double dose of attention from two men at the same time with them going tit for tat in each ear. I could overhear their compliments and clumsy efforts at seduction.

"Look here, baby. I got a condo on the Potomac River, a Chris Chraft, thirty-six footer docked behind it and a baby Benz." A short bald man was bragging to her in one ear.

The taller man in her other ear started laughing out loud. "Condo! Hell! Jamal's got a con-doo, as in his con-doo won't do for you, baby. And his boat, I've seen it. Just make sure you bring a life jacket and an oar cause you'll be rowing that little dingy yourself!"

They all laughed and I could tell that the competition was all in fun. I snuck a peek at her equally occupied girlfriend, a slim mocha-brown sister with clear skin, full lips and tauntingly large dark eyes. Like her comrade she was surrounded by men. It was as though they were the only two women on a planet populated by just men.

On my other side sat a man who looked like he was at least eighty-years-old drinking alone and seemed oblivious to the crowd of people jockeying to order drinks at the bar. And there I was in the middle of it all, lucky to find a place to sit.

"I'd like a glass of Shiraz," I told the bartender.

I took a sip and looked over at the old man sitting beside me with his drink as his company. He held his glass up as though he was toasting my arrival and took a sip. I smiled.

"Pretty girls should never drink alone," he said.

At first I thought it was a line, an attempt on his part to come on to me, but he quickly turned and looked straight ahead at the mirror behind the bar. I joined him in that furtive stare, beheld my own image reflected in the mirror that didn't lie. And I realized just how alone I was at that moment.

I turned away and spun my bar stool around to face the jazz combo pushing music to an adoring crowd. The atmosphere was very different from Dream, the nightclub where I'd met Antoine. The men were wearing suits like they'd gone to the Café Alexandria right after leaving their offices, calling their wives to tell them they were working late. I thought about the sign in the club's entrance that read: No jeans, No tennis shoes, No baseball caps. That meant no 23-year-old brothers standing around with straws stuck in bottles of Moet.

My eyes drifted around appreciating the club's intimate setting and its sophisticated patrons until I settled on a table across the room and the couple sitting there engrossed in conversation. It was Mr. Powell, sitting at a table with a beautiful mocha-colored woman, her hair jazzy and short the way Halle Berry once wore hers and with a prominent streak of silver peeking through her flaxen waves. But my attention was really on him.

Seeing him there so unexpectedly made my heart race. I inhaled deep, closed my eyes for a second and exhaled all the feelings that made me want to run out of the place. I looked nervously toward the old man sitting beside me to see if he had noticed my reaction, but he was still absorbed in the parameters he'd established for interacting and I wasn't in it.

I glanced over at the group of two women and four men huddled near me on the other side, but the women were too self-absorbed to notice my urchin-like presence and the men were equally caught up in them except one, that is. A big man with a shaved head was looking right at me with his eyes narrowed displaying a look of feigned concern for me.

"You all right?" he asked.

"I'm fine," I answered, unable to steady the slight tremor in my voice.

I watched him as he moved away from the group and closer to me. I braced myself for the inevitable and often clumsy introduction between strangers.

"Hi. My name is Joe," he said.

The hot air from his breath told me that he'd been drinking for a while, must've gotten off work early and came here for the happy hour discounted drinks and buffet. He extended the hand that wasn't holding a glass and waited for mine to connect.

"Dahlia," I replied.

He stared into my eyes and held my hand for too long, gave me the feeling that he wasn't going to let go. His quirky smile and clammy hand made me feel uncomfortable. I felt like he was trying to suck out a part of my soul through my appendages.

"You work at the Pentagon," he told me.

My mind reeled. I thought about the man on the train who kept staring at me the other day and followed me all the way to the security gate. I thought: *They're following me.* Of course, my thoughts were on the FBI.

"How do you know where I work?" I asked.

I eased my hand from his grip, wanted to run unable to disguise my panicked tone.

He smiled, easily. "Relax, just a guess. Most people who come here work in Pentagon City. Judging by the way you're dressed I'd say you came here from work."

"I guess that makes you a real detective," I said. I was trying my best to hide my sarcasm but it was clear and he apparently didn't care.

"Do my best. I can size up a woman from jump. Know everything about her after giving her a once over."

He leered at me like I was a t-bone steak. I was waiting for him to drool all over his cotton blend and polyester suit.

I looked at him really for the first time. "Have we met somewhere before?" I asked.

"Hey, that's my line."

"No, seriously. You look familiar."

"I guess I got one of those faces. You know, hard to forget."

I looked away from Joe and his "unforgettable face" over at Mr. Powell and the woman who was entertaining him. Judging by the way they both laughed and her touchy interaction with him they were having a good time. I thought that she was probably his girlfriend or maybe his wife and my heart sank.

Joe leaned close to whisper in my ear. The smell of martinis, beer and incongruent alcoholic beverages all mixed together nearly overwhelmed me.

"Does she know?" he asked.

I pulled back and looked at him, a puzzled expression rooted all over my face.

"Does who know what?" I asked.

"Your boyfriend over there. Does his wife know about you and him?"

He was looking directly at Mr. Powell.

"I don't know what you're talking about. That's not my boyfriend," I said. "I don't even know him."

I turned away to face the bar and my image again in the mirror while Joe stared out into the club.

"Well, know him or not, he's headed over this way," he said in a slurred whispered.

I tensed up all over and held my breath as I pretended to be totally absorbed by the images in the large mirror. The old man next to me was mumbling something unintelligible. I figured that his romance with the bottle had long-term effects so I ignored him and waited.

"Excuse me." I heard Mr. Powell say, as he squeezed in between the group huddled beside me.

He was up to the bar trying to get the attention of the bartender with his eyes, trying to connect with the man who was busily pouring drinks. I tried not to look at him, but the two women who were being entertained by the entourage of men quickly took notice. The chocolate one closest to me looked up at him and then leaned over to her friend and whispered something in her ear. They turned to look right at him, shook their heads and ogled him like he was a fresh cut of prime beef.

He seemed not to notice their admiring stares when he ordered two Grey Goose martinis then smiled at me and waited for his drinks. He was leaning on the bar with one hand to brace himself and so close that I could smell his cologne. I could see his hand with his manicured fingernails, black onyx ring and matching cufflinks coordinated to perfection. His gold Rolex watch set it all off. I wanted to say something clever, to get his attention the way El would've done or the way that guy, Joe had made his straightforward presentation to me, but I froze unable to speak a word.

I could feel electricity emanating from him or maybe it was just me and my own kinetic energy working overtime. And when the bartender returned with his drinks he pulled out a hundred dollar bill, made a gesture with his eyes towards me and said, "Get the lady what she wants and keep the change."

I smiled politely, ready to tell him that I didn't accept drinks from strangers, but before I could speak he had already retreated into the crowd and was making his way back to his table and to the beautiful woman who was waiting anxiously for him to return. I could see the two women sitting next to me follow him with their eyes as Joe and his crew seemed perturbed by the fact that they were being ignored. The plus-sized sister looked over at me.

"Honey, that's one gorgeous man. He must like you," she said.

Joe was hovering over the entire scene like a buzzard waiting for leftovers after the lions had feasted. He looked over at Mr. Powell, turned to the two women. "I don't know why ya'll so goofy and shit over that brother," he said.

There was a tone in his voice that spoke of jealousy and someone who liked being the center of attention.

The other woman spoke up.

"Nobody's acting goofy, Joe. The man is fine, that's all."

He obviously didn't like the lady's endorsement because his mouth twisted into a menacing sneer. He cut his eyes over to the couple sitting at the table on the other side of the club who were oblivious to the conversation and controversy brewing over at the bar.

"Well, the man is rude. Coming over here and pushing in front of me to get to the bar."

"Oh, calm down, Joe. I heard him say, *Excuse me.*"

The woman turned to her girlfriend. "I definitely heard him say, excuse me."

She nodded.

"Well, I didn't hear him. Besides, I think the niggah stepped on my foot."

He looked down to examine his shoes that were already scuffed up. I always check out a man's shoes, right after I look at his hands and teeth and this guy's were in need of a good polishing. But it wasn't about his shoes it was ego, fueled by alcohol and a desire to impress the ladies.

Joe took a hard swallow from his drink. Said, "Pretty ass, Geechie niggah. Dude dissed me. Think I'll just go and kick his ass."

He ambled across the room with bad intent in his eyes, making big, easy strides until he was standing right over the couple. Everyone at the bar stopped and watched as Joe stood over his prey glaring down at them. He was quiet at first, the calm before the storm then he erupted into a verbal barrage of words punctuated with, "nigger" and "motherfucker". The man that I knew only as Mr.

Powell just sat there unmoved and unshaken, ignoring the big man's torrent of insults.

My heart raced. I thought, *Oh my God! That guy is trying to fight him!* I watched as Mr. Powell smiled at the beautiful woman sitting with him, straightened his tie and slowly rose to his feet.

Both men stood over six feet tall, but the Joe guy outweighed his chosen adversary by at least fifty pounds and was probably fifteen years younger. Nose to nose, eye to eye, the two men stood there for what seemed like an eternity, sizing up each other like Tyson and Holyfield. I held my breath and waited to see who would throw the first punch.

To my surprise it was Mr. Powell who would make the first move. His face displayed no anger and none of the hostility that was evident in the eyes of the other man and most of all, there was no fear there. Before Joe could react Mr. Powell threw his arm around the other man's shoulders and neck and whispered in his ear. I could tell that he was listening intently as he offered no words of his own and his body language shifted from the combative stance he had when he first approached to that of a man who'd been conquered.

With Mr. Powell's arm still resting around Joe's shoulders, the younger man bowed to the beautiful woman, offered his hand to shake hers and bowed once again. He smiled at Mr. Powell, gave him an age-old, black power kind of handshake and made his way back over to the bar where we were all gaping at the action wide-eyed.

What happened?" I heard one of the women ask him.

I looked at the visibly shaken man, listening for his answer. He had a kind of dazed look in his eyes like he'd just gone to the mountaintop and seen the burning bush.

"I'm not sure," he answered.

His boisterous bravado had faded along with the volume and bass in his voice.

"What did he say to you?" The honey-colored woman asked. "You look like you've just seen a ghost."

Joe sipped hard from the bottle of beer he'd left on the bar unguarded.

"He said he's a lover not a fighter. Told me that we're all brothers here. We come from the same seed."

Joe was shaking his head, still looking dazed and confused like a bomb had gone off right by him, leaving him in a state of shellshock.

"That was all?" One of the women said.

Joe breathed deep, took a napkin from the bar and wiped the sweat from his forehead

"He told me he could kill me right there where I stood and I wouldn't lose a drop of blood. Said everyone would think I had a heart attack."

"And you believe that?"

Joe nodded.

I looked back over at Mr. Powell who had resumed his conversation with his date as though nothing had happened and I wondered about the power he must've had over the other man. I'd always heard that power is the ultimate aphrodisiac and whatever power he possessed it was working its magic on virtually every woman in the place, including me. I guess I was spellbound.

"Did he tell you his name?" I overheard one of the women ask Joe.

"Yeah. Mackenzie. Mackenzie Powell."

"Are you for real?" She replied. "So that's him."

Joe had turned away and was now facing the bar, gazing into the mirror behind it, reduced to a hulk of flesh. He was hunched over his drink like he was trying to make himself disappear and didn't turn around when one of his female friends said, "He's leaving".

I joined the two women watching Mackenzie Powell as he helped his lady with her chair and followed behind her. They were headed to the exit. My eyes followed him, captured his walk in slowed motion, saw a hint of metal as he closed his suit jacket and I wondered if that was his belt buckle or something sinister. Either way, I was totally intrigue by him.

Apparently the older gentleman sitting beside me had taken it all in, but without so much as an effort to turn away from the drink he'd been nursing. He sat there still mesmerized by his own image in the mirror and without looking at me when he started talking.

"I was like that young fella once upon a time," he said in a matter-of-fact way.

I thought he was talking about the man they called, Joe who was still suffering from his encounter with Mackenzie Powell. I looked over to see what the old man was referring to.

"Not him," he said. "The one who bought you the drink. I was just like him years ago."

I shrugged off the comment not intending to make it into a conversation, but he seemed intent on making a point.

"There was a time when women loved me. I could play them the way I used to play my guitar."

At that point I knew that the alcohol he'd been drinking was doing all the talking for him. I decided to see how far he would take this.

"Well, the man you're talking about isn't that young. He's old enough to be my father," I told the old man.

He took another sip from his glass and let the ice swirl around in it so that it almost sounded like a bell signaling that he was about to make some sage-like statement. I guess I was right.

"It's all relative, young lady. I'm seventy-five years old and it's not how you start, it's the journey that matters. There are babies born yesterday who won't outlive me."

He turned and faced me directly for the very first time.

"Enjoy the journey. Embrace it and live your life to its fullest. We all have just one shot so make it your best."

I watched as he slid off of the bar stool, stood semi-upright and stumbled towards the exit doors. He turned around, gave me a parting nod then disappeared. His words repeated inside my head: *Enjoy the journey. Embrace it and live your life to its fullest. We all have just one shot so make it your best.*

Day Six

The constant in life is change.

Songs of Desdemona—9/30/05/

I woke up the next day thinking about Antoine. He was being watched by FBI agents and so was I. Agent Robinson readily accepted my claims that I had nothing to do with Antoine and his gang and that made me leery. I wasn't stupid and I knew that cops often let someone believe they're not a suspect when they actually are. They did this so the person wouldn't change his routine or fly the coop.

This was weighty stuff and I didn't know what to do about it or who to talk to. El was the most logical person because she was an attorney and she worked for the Justice Department, but that was also the reason why I couldn't talk to her. And telling Stacy would be opening a can of worms. She would make my situation into a media crusade and that could put my life in jeopardy.

I decided that it all was too much to think about. I needed to get out of my apartment because I didn't feel comfortable there. I had visions of government agents sitting in some small room with headphones wrapped around their heads and tape recorders capturing every sound I made. The thought made me both angry and embarrassed.

I tried to dismiss the idea that my place had been bugged. I thought, Patriot Act or not they still needed a warrant to wiretap my telephone and bug my apartment. I decided that I couldn't worry about it and sitting around alone at home would only make things worse. It was Saturday and springtime and the perfect day for an excursion into the city.

I remember that day so clearly. It was a beautiful morning when I ventured out to D.C.'s Adams Morgan area to find a bookstore. It had always been one of my favorite neighborhoods because of its diversity. The clash of cultures was exhilarating and there was a sense of intrigue in the different languages that were spoken in the markets and cafes around Columbia Road.

I didn't have a car so I took the train to the heart of downtown and then a short cab ride to Adams Morgan. I found an interesting bookstore/coffee house that served strong Turkish espresso and baklava. Sounds of espresso machines mixed with the New Age music played in the background underscored the café's bohemian atmosphere. Couples, mostly white, sat at tables sipping and talking and looking like refugees from a Grateful Dead concert. Being there was a unique experience for me because I had never spent much time in bookstores.

I wandered amongst the various sections of books, categorized by subject matter and some by author. There was a section titled, "Rare Books" that was under lock and key and I took the opportunity to read some of the book titles. I admit that I was culturally stunted with no real appreciation for the arts and I'd never read a book purely for the enjoyment of reading.

Stacy, on the other hand, read incessantly and often told me that I was like most of my peers. We were the MTV generation of sensory overload, bombarded by video,the Internet and even TV shows on our mobile telephones.. For us, reading was like work. So when I looked at some of the books on the shelves and more importantly the prices, I couldn't believe someone would pay as much for a book as some people would for a car.

I thought of El and her constant refrain, "You so cun-try," drawing out the word to imitate her notion of how people talked in places like southern Georgia or L.A., meaning Lower Alabama. *"I guess I am country,"* I mumbled as I perused the locked book cases.

I wandered into the magazine section and picked up a copy of *Essence* to read while I drank my mocha espresso. There was a small table that was empty so I sat down. My espresso was too hot and its heat pierced my tongue leaving pain as its residue. I quickly put the cup down on the table and started reading my magazine. Flipping through the pages looking at drop-dead gorgeous, sepia-colored models, airbrushed no doubt, I fantasized about seeing myself modeling in the magazine. My world would be perfect there with my perfect teeth and vision and my hair suspended in midair for eternity captured by the camera's eye as I flipped my hair responding to the photographer's command to, *move it, baby.*

I chuckled at the idea and felt foolish for a moment and kept turning the pages. I found an article about older women and younger men; *"A Growing Trend?"* captioned.

The writer implied that there was something Freudian about a young brother and a woman more than ten years his senior, as though he wanted to do something freaky with his own mother. *Disgusting.* But I kept reading and realized that the article was really talking about May-September relationships and how they were becoming more acceptable. I thought about what I'd read and Mackenzie Powell and wondered if there was some kind of Freudian link with my infatuation as El implied that day at the restaurant. But the thought was as fleeting as the infatuation and I resigned myself with the fact that I'd never know.

I flipped through the magazine, casually reading other articles, looking at the cosmetic ads but most of all, thinking. Occasionally, I'd look up at the television monitor, listened as it spewed out the morning news, punctuated with a dose of murder and mayhem. When I heard a reporter say that a body had been found behind Café Alexandria I made a brief mental note only because I'd been there the night before.

My espresso had cooled enough to sip and savor. I loved its chocolate flavor and its smell reminded me of the cookies that Grandma Stevie made just for me. Times like these made me think of home, my mother and grandmother. In a large city like Washington surrounded by millions of people, I often felt alone and thoughts of my family even with all of the bad memories made me feel better. Add Antoine and whatever trouble he was in and me, an innocent bystander in this drive-by shooting called life I could feel myself buckling under the weight of it all.

Without warning, a sense of melancholy overtook me and I felt my emotions warm like the coffee in front of me. I tried to fight the tears but they flowed anyway. Streaming down my face, fountains of pain and regrets. I thought I was so silly for getting emotional especially over chocolate espresso. Times like this made me realize just how much I needed to keep seeing my therapist. In that moment I thought of myself as some psycho bitch, emotions unchecked, tears running like water from a leaky dike.

I feverishly searched my purse for a tissue but came up empty and the only napkin I had was now soaked with the overflow from my coffee. I looked up for a moment and quickly back down at the table. I thought I'd have to make the long journey across the café with a tear stained face and a hint of melted mascara around my eyes.

"Here, use this." I heard a man's voice speak those words as he handed me a white handkerchief. Too embarrassed to look up I reluctantly accepted the offer and used it to dab my eyes and nose. "Are you going to be alright?" he asked.

I nodded with my head down and eyes still riveted on the table. His voice was reassuring. His presence was comforting, if only for the moment. I thought he was still standing near but when I looked out the corner of my eye he was gone. I was holding onto his tear soaked handkerchief and wondering if I should look for him in the store and give it back. But I had no idea who he was or what he looked like.

I grabbed the handkerchief, made one last swipe with it around my eyes and then opened it. It was monogrammed with the initials "*MAP*".

I stood up from the table and walked around the café looking for a man I didn't know. I thought I could find him alone reading or sipping espresso but there were only a couple of men in the place and they were occupied. I went back to my table thinking the man might return. Finally, I asked the couple at the next table if they'd seen the man who gave me the hanky. They nodded. "He left," the young woman said.

I studied the monogram's fine stitching and considered its owner. It had a scent of cologne, full bodied and rich. Like a schoolgirl I folded it and put it away in my purse. It was time for me to leave, as well.

Outside the sky had that smoked-out look like the gods were about to rumble. A spring downpour was on its way. I figured that if I hurried a taxicab would find me before the rain did. There was a taxi stand further down Columbia Road at 16th Street. It would be better to look for one there than to stand outside the café, which was tucked away and hidden from traffic. I took one long look at the sky and started walking fast.

The dark, puffy clouds quickly became an ominous black overhang that was a canopy for the whole city. One raindrop turned into two, then three and then a torrent. I was running to escape the drenching and searching in vain for a taxi or even some store that could give me cover from the rain. I saw the taxi stand except it was across 16th Street and cars speeding through the busy intersection were forcing me to wait until the light changed.

The longer I stood waiting the harder it rained. A car rounding the corner in front of me hit a pothole and from underneath its indiscriminant tire spewed a tidal wave of muddy, dirty water that totally engulfed me. I was near tears and it seemed that things couldn't get any worse. *The hell with this shit!* I stepped off the curb. *Traffic will have to wait.*

A car narrowly missed me as I ran across the street. An impatient car horn barked as though by doing so I'd run back to the curb. But it was too late. My mission was irreversible. The cars were unrelenting and now I was risking real bodily harm. I stood on the yellow line that divided the street, helpless.

I looked for an opening, space to run across to the other side. I didn't see the black car behind me at first but it had stopped while other cars kept moving by. I figured it must have been some jerk trying to pick me up so I tried to ignore him. I focused on the traffic, ready to risk it all and make a mad dash across the street when the window on the driver's side slowly rolled down. "Hop in. I'll give you a ride," said the driver.

It was Mackenzie Powell!

I froze right there. Started thinking about how weird this must look to him. Here I was standing in the middle of the street, muddy and dripping wet and some man I didn't know yet wanted to meet was trying to give me a ride. I thought of El and what she'd do given the same situation and assuming it was one of the professional athletes she worshipped. Of course, she would get in the car. But I wasn't El and I always acted with caution, not willing to take any chances.

"No, that's O.K. I'm just going to catch a cab over there and then...." My voice trailed off. Just when I said that, the only cab left at the stand pulled off and sped down the other side of Columbia. "Damn!"

"C'mon. I'll take you home or at least, find you a cab."

It started raining harder and I figured only a fool would stand there and continue to get soaked. I ran around to the car's passenger side and reached for the door handle. *Oh, no. It's a Bentley,* which made me hesitate about getting inside. *The car cost more than my mama's house.* I opened the door and eased in. I was apologetic. "I'm so sorry. I'm messing up your car," I said.

The car's soft leather seat caressed my body like a warm glove. I looked around, briefly taking in its fine details. Burled wood accentuated the dashboard and ran along the sides of the doors. I started to rest my arm on the door the way I might do in a "normal car" but I quickly folded my arms underneath my breasts.

"Don't worry about it. It's just a car. The leather cleans real well," he told me. "Where can I take you?"

"If you just drop me off at the nearest train station, that'll be fine. I don't want to take you out of your way."

The sound of a car horn reminded us that we were sitting in the middle of the street. "I guess I better move," he told me. "You know, I'm no doctor but I don't think it's a good idea to stay in those wet clothes."

I was feverishly using my hands to wipe away the water dripping down my face from my rain soaked hair. "I don't exactly have a change of clothes with me," I told him.

Of course, he was right. I was cold and wet, susceptible to getting sick. I watched him lean forward and push a button on the car's dashboard then felt a surge of warmth on my cold, wet back and rear coming from the seat.

"Heated seats. It'll help you warm up. Look, my place isn't far from here. How about if I take you there? You can dry off. Maybe, drink some hot green tea—it's good for the system—and I'll make sure you get home," he said.

I was the kind of woman who'd never accept a ride from a stranger let alone go to his house but for some reason, one that I couldn't explain, I felt safe. It might have been the smoothness of his voice and his reassuring, soulful eyes or maybe it was his mature confidence. Whatever it was I felt that there was nothing malicious about him.

I guess in a way I was lucky that the rain had soaked my face, otherwise he would've seen the small beads of nervous moisture gathering underneath my eyes, again, a symptom of my being stressed out or nervous. I couldn't believe that I was riding in the car with *him*. I sat there for a moment saying nothing, afraid to move, afraid to look directly at him. I waited until his focus was on the street ahead then stole a glance in his direction.

He was dressed appropriately for a cool, rainy spring day in DC. Burberry jacket with wool gabardine slacks coordinated in muted browns and tan colors gave him an outdoor, woodsy look like he was on his way to some aristocratic fox and hound club. His jacket hung open just enough so that I could see a silhouette of his chest and stomach wrapped in a ribbed cotton shirt and I marveled at the fact that a man his age could be in such great shape.

He was cool and relaxed behind the wheel of that Bentley as though car and man was a matched pair. Together they made a bold statement of class, style and comfort. With that thought I shook myself, knowing that my thoughts were like some car commercial created on Madison Avenue but truth be told if anyone wanted to sell Bentleys then this man could be their poster boy.

"You're not some kind of serial killer, are you?" I said, smiling. "Besides, I don't even know you." The question was my own feeble attempt to break the ice or rather, the cool because his body language wasn't cold and distant just cool like he wasn't in a hurry to say or do anything.

"The name's Mackenzie, Mackenzie Powell. My friends call me, Mac. And no, I'm not a serial killer." His dimpled smile lit up the interior of the car.

"I know who you are," I said.

"You do!"

"Yeah, I was at Café Alexandria's last night. You got into a beef with that big guy."

He smiled, slightly. "Yeah, that was unfortunate. Alcohol can make a man a fool."

"What did you say to him? I mean, he came back to the bar acting all creepy and scared."

"I introduced him to my associate, Mr. Friendly."

"Mr. Friendly?" I asked.

Mackenzie opened his jacket with one hand and revealed a chrome-plated pistol. My eyes widened. Seeing it gave me a rush of adrenalin and instantly filled me with a sense of intrigue or danger.

"Don't worry. I've never used it. It's a deterrent. Some of these assholes out here see you driving a new Bentley and they think you got money. Want to separate you from the things that you worked hard to earn."

His greenish eyes softened as the thought of Joe and their confrontation passed by like it had never happened. He looked at me with the kind of concern I used to imagine my father would show me whenever I'd come in out of the rain but I wasn't seeing him as a fatherly figure.

The water was dripping everywhere.

"You know, you can use that handkerchief I left you instead of your hands to help dry off. I don't have another one with me."

I nodded and reached inside my purse, pulled out his hanky. The M.A.P. initials now made sense. Mackenzie A. Powell. I wondered what the "A" stood for but didn't ask. It wasn't important. The main thing was that I was riding in a $250,000.00 car with an older man who had somehow struck a chord in me the moment I first saw him. Like in my childhood dreams I was being rescued. It was all too surreal to imagine.

Day Seven

"Life is borne of opportunity." He once told me. This is one lesson you will learn above many. Nothing is left to chance and fate is just the manifestation of the pre-ordained.

Songs of Desdemona—10/1/06

I can write down these thoughts now in a way that has never occurred to me before I found my voice in a place that is meant to still it. Nelson Mandela's writing became more profound during his twenty-seven year stay in a South African prison. My empathy runs deep. Alone with my thoughts I peel away the layers that were once me and find something, someone deep within. But it was he who'd begun the process.

♦　　♦　　♦

I recall how he drove me to his home that day. He wasn't worried about the mud and how my clothes had soaked the car's white leather seat. The cotton dress I wore clung to my body like a cat suit and its wet chill made my bra-less breasts stand at attention. I was embarrassed but I fought against it with my arms folded across my chest, hiding the obvious.

I could tell that he was trying not to look directly at me but in a way I wanted him to do just that, to see my only perfection hidden for most of my life revealed to him through the transparency of my wet clothes. It was raining harder and he tried to keep his focus on the road ahead but I could see the pupils of his eyes drift occasionally in my direction taking in his nymphet-like passenger.

He cleared his throat of its nervous moisture, allowing the words to come out. "Did you find anything good to read at the coffee house?" he asked.

It was small talk, I suppose but it signaled that he wasn't quite as cool and comfortable as I had thought. I thought that I was the only one feeling the tension but I could tell he was feeling it, too.

"Not really," I answered. "I was there trying to find a book to introduce me to a foreign language. I'm trying to decide if I'm going to learn how to speak French, Japanese or Spanish."

I exhaled slowly, letting all of the air seep out of my lungs and then purposely slowed my breathing. The car was filled with a kind of tension, not the uncomfortable kind but the sexual tension that permeates the space two people occupy when they're thrown together for the first time.

He said something that sounded French. The air inside the car loosened.

I smiled. I was impressed. "What did you just say?"

"I said that you are pretty when wet." He laughed, dimples cutting deep into his handsome face.

I smiled again. Flattered.

"What's your favorite language?" I asked.

"French, hands-down. Speaking in French is more than communicating it's feeling with words. It's the way the lips form and pucker when you speak, sensual without being crude. I love everything about the French—the culture, the food …"

I cut him off. "And the women, I suppose."

He had a whimsical expression on his face. His eyes bounced from the road ahead then towards me and back to the road again. And every time I saw a flash of their emerald hue I became more enamored with him.

"Ah, yes, the women. There's an expression that describes the French woman but the English translation doesn't really capture its total essence. Interpreted it says, 'She walks in music' but it's so much more. It's song, dance, poetry and art and that's the total essence of the French woman."

"I'm impressed," I replied. "And black women? How do you describe them?"

"The English language doesn't have a suitable word to describe my beautiful black sisters."

"Is that meant to be a compliment or condescension?"

"What do you think?" he asked. His subtle smile told me that he wouldn't paint himself into a corner.

I mulled over the question. There is no monolith called, The Black Woman, I knew that. Diverse and complex were neutral and non-committal descriptions and applied to virtually every woman, regardless of race. Strength and perseverance, positive attributes. And victimized and compulsive and neurotic had their place in the debate but they were also universal descriptions. I concluded that French society must be too simplistic. I focused back on his question.

"I don't want to answer that," was my reply.

"That's cool. Let me ask you why were you crying back there?"

"You're getting kind of personal, aren't you?"

"I guess I can ask because you did snot up my hankie," he said. He laughed. I didn't.

I shook my head and looked downward. "I'm so silly," I said. "Crying in front of all those people, in public. You probably thought I was some kind of schitzo. I really don't know why I started crying."

"Boyfriend?"

"No. Don't have one. Not really. I guess sometimes I miss my mother and grandmother. I worry about them."

"Yeah, I know what that's like. I was away from my family when I was younger. I lost my mother during the time I was gone. I always wish I could get that time back but I can't."

He exhaled a labored breath. "Why don't you go home sometime?"

"I'd like to or fly my mother here but it's expensive from where they live and my money's kind of tight. I've got bills and my mortgage payment on my condo doesn't give me a whole lot of extra money for things like airplane tickets. Besides, there are memories there."

I stopped myself. I was getting way too personal and he was still a stranger. He turned down a side street and the Bentley rolled slowly within its narrow confines.

"My house is on this street," he said.

Day Eight

Washington is the tale of two, or maybe, three cities. Money and power supported by those who administer the mandates and the will of those who control them. And then there's the poor who exist in yet a third city. Hapless and rudderless, owing their very existence to the whim and caprice of those who don't see them, they are the underbelly of the other two.

Songs of Desdemona—10/3/05

One of the things that I loved about Georgetown was its Old World flavor. Cobblestone streets and stately carriage houses are unique to this D.C. neighborhood. There was the mystique of money here so it made sense that Mac was now motoring his Bentley smooth and effortlessly over the normally bumpy roads. He drove down a side street that was too narrow for cars to park on it and then turned into what appeared to be another street but it was actually a driveway.

At the end of the drive stood a stately home that was not quite large enough to be called a mansion but close. Still, it was unlike any home I'd ever seen before except on television or in a magazine.

"Is this your home? Mr. Mackenzie ... I mean, Mr. Powell."

He laughed. "It's Mac, all right? Yeah, I live here."

I was staring at the house, trying to keep my jaw in place, trying to hold my mouth shut. The whole scene reminded me of the Batman movie and Vickie Vale coming to the Bat Mansion. I was actually expecting some guy named Alfred with white hair to greet us in a tuxedo.

I thought about how our conversation had become more relaxed as the ride continued. It flowed and made me feel at ease. Going to his house was just as easy.

He stopped the car within a few feet of the front door. It was still raining hard but at least we were close to the house. I reached for the car's door handle on my side but Mac said, "Hold on. Sit there."

I froze like a puppy dog responding to a command and waited as he hopped out of the car, flipped open an umbrella and opened my door. I thought how Antoine had given me one of those "what are you waiting for" looks when he opened his own car door and left me outside. Now in stark contrast, a man was standing in the rain waiting with his hand extended to help me get out of the car.

I thought about young brothers of the Generation X and the low-level cool, video-vixen portrayal of women. It was hard to feel like a lady when most men I knew didn't even know what a lady was. There was a difference between them and him and even in Mac's small gesture it was obvious. I thought about young men and how they wear their manhood on their chests while older men had long ago proven theirs.

Mac opened the front door and led me inside his house. It was opulent, just as I might imagine and it looked like the homes I dreamt about as a young girl. Italian marble made the floors shiny like glass and in the middle of the foyer was a fountain with water that gently overflowed into its basin and emitted soothing babbling sounds. Around the windows were blue velvet drapes and between them were sconces that washed the entire area with soft lights. On the other side of the foyer was a spiral staircase that wound its way to the upstairs area. My reaction was "Wow", a reflex beyond my control.

I stood in one spot, afraid to move and drip muddy water on his floors.

"I'll be right back," he told me.

I watched him head towards a long hallway. He stopped in his tracks and turned.

"Excuse my manners. I didn't get *your* name. After all, you might be some kind of serial killer," he said with those smiling dimples.

"Dahlia Reynolds."

"Nice name."

I watched him disappear into the hall and return a couple of minutes later with a long cotton robe, slippers and towels.

"Here, you can put this on." He pointed to a second hallway "That leads to the pool house. There's a shower and some privacy. I'll find something for you to wear."

I watched him climb the staircase to the second floor. In that instant my heart sunk. *He must be getting me something that belongs to his wife or his girlfriend. Something probably too big and even more dowdy looking than what I'm wearing.* But then I thought about the woman he was with at the jazz club and knew that if he brought me anything that belonged to her it would be haute couture at its best.

I sauntered down the hall carrying towel and robe just as Mac had directed and right into an atrium made of glass. It captured the sun from outside and was lined with tropical plants and flowers. I could see the indoor swimming pool just ahead and a sign that read "Shower" which was pointing me in that direction. As I walked past the swimming pool I wondered what it would be like to get up in the morning and go for a swim without ever leaving the house. There was a swimming hole near Rufus' house but it was more than a stone-throw away and somehow it didn't seem quite the same.

I imagined waking up in the nude and walking downstairs to go to the pool without dressing. In my mind that was the true essence of being free.

Once inside the dressing room I quickly removed my wet clothes, walked into the shower and ran the water. I glanced over my shoulder to see if anyone was watching and for a moment thought maybe the man I'd just met had cameras installed somewhere and that this was some kind of ploy designed for him to get his jollies by watching young women bathe. I looked around the entire area trying to see if there was anything that could be disguised as a video camera.

I thought, "*Well, if he sees me, he just sees me. I've gotta get this mud crap off. I just hope no one tells me they saw me naked on the Internet.*"

I finished showering and put on the robe. It was thick and extremely soft made of 100% cotton and soothing against my bare skin. I used the towels to dry my hair and after an attempt to comb it gave up and pulled it back into the usual bun.

A knock on the dressing room door startled me and took me away from the moment. It was Mac telling me that he had found something for me to wear. "I'll leave it on the clothes rack outside the door," he said.

I waited for a moment then opened the door and peeked outside the dressing room. I couldn't see him and although I had a robe on I was shy about stepping out of the room. But I knew I couldn't stay in there forever. "*What the hell,*" I mumbled as I cautiously ventured out only to find a clothing rack full of beautiful dresses.

I'd never seen dresses like these except for the ones I longed for in fashion magazines. Like a little girl on Christmas Day I gleefully went through the rack stopping to look at the dresses and putting each one in front of me as I stared at my image in the mirror. I wore a size eight and ironically, every dress on the rack was my size.

There was a gorgeous flowered sun dress, yellow and white, and made of poplin. It had spaghetti straps with a bustier that hugged the wearer's breast and torso and it was full and wide at the bottom. I liked this one most of all. I surveyed it fully and saw that the tags were still on it. The label read, "Ferragamo" and there was a price tag dangling on the inside at the top where it fastened. The dress had never been worn.

I looked at the price and gasped. "*$2200!*" I said aloud. "*I can't wear this. His woman will have a heart attack.*" I put the dress back on the rack and started searching for another less pricey one but they all cost two to four thousand dollars.

I thought about putting my wet clothes back on but when I looked around I noticed they were gone.

"I guess I don't have a choice." I pulled the yellow and white dress off the rack. There was a pair of yellow pumps that matched and they were also my size. Finally, I saw a white wide brimmed hat with a yellow band that was perfectly coordinated with the dress and shoes. Together it was a perfect ensemble.

I strutted into the dressing room with the clothes in hand and emerged a few minutes later dressed like a sister who had arrived with a vengeance. *Stop the world. Beautiful black woman in the hizz-ouse.*

It was like I'd gone into some upscale New York boutique and chose everything myself. The hat was perfect because my hair had become a big ball of frizzy curls that topped my head like it had a mind of its own. It took me a while to push and twist my hair so that it would fit under the hat but eventually I managed to do it. I smiled when I saw myself full in the mirror.

"Damn! I look good!"

An extravagance like a designer dress was something I never could afford so for the moment I acted like I was born to wear it.

One last look in the mirror and a tilt of the hat so that it nearly covered my left eye was all I needed. It was time to find Mac. I followed the path back through the atrium and to the main house, calling out his name.

Mac was standing in the foyer patiently waiting for me. When I made my entrance he smiled broadly and shook his head in amazement.

"That dress was made for you," he said.

I twirled on cue to show it off in its entirety. I couldn't believe how relaxed and comfortable I was, displaying the outfit in front of a man I didn't know. I stopped myself.

"I'm sorry," I said. "I guess I got carried away."

"No apologies needed. You like the dress?" He asked.

"I love it. But won't your wife get upset? I mean, this is very expensive but I'll have it cleaned and sent back. I promise," I said in a rush of words.

"I'm not married. Remember?" was his response.

"How'd you know what size dress and shoes I wear?" I asked him.

"Come. I fixed you some tea," he said leading me down another hallway. "Do you like fine art?" He ignored my question but it was something that loomed large in my mind although I was too excited to consider the implications.

I thought about the woman he sat with in the club and had to stop myself from asking whether she was his girlfriend. Instead, I followed him like I was on a leash, first to the kitchen where he handed me a cup that was brimming hot with green tea.

"I don't use processed sugar, ever. So, I took the liberty of putting two teaspoons of raw sugar in your tea. Some people want honey but I tell them that honey's not that good for you."

"Ummm. It's the best tea I've ever had," I said.

I followed him through another section of the house and thought about what he said about not having a wife. *Maybe, he's gay.* That might explain it, the clothes, the refined look and the house that looked too perfect like something a woman might assemble but with a man's feel.

We entered into what he called his study room and there was nothing feminine about it. The centerpiece of the room was a rustic looking leather sofa, circa 1940's along with an overstuffed leather chair and ottoman. A large oriental rug covered most of the hardwood floor, exposing only its edges. In front of the sofa was a coffee table that had several men's magazines neatly placed on top. The walls were decorated with antique rifles and firearms that looked like something from an old war movie. And there were plants, lots of plants strategically placed by a wall full of windows. Across and opposite from the windows was a wall of books. I glanced at some of them and was reminded of the rare books I saw at the café.

"Do you like to read?" he asked.

"Oh, yes. I read a lot. I love *Cosmopolitan, Essence.* You know, stuff like that. They have great articles."

He smiled.

"Well, I meant, books. Novels. Come here, let me show you something."

He moved over to a section of his bookcase. Rubbed his fingers along a shelf of books like he was rubbing the soft skin of a woman. Smiled as though the books had some endearing quality or memories.

"Countee Cullen, Zora Neale Hurston. Richard Wright. They're all here, their writings. Ever heard of them?"

I had a blank look on my face that told him that I hadn't.

"Didn't they teach you about the Harlem Renaissance in school?"

I laughed. "They didn't even teach us about Harlem, period. Not in Way-cross."

"What about college?"

I shook my head. "Went to a small liberal arts college in Ohio. I learned a little bit about Chaucer and Shakespeare but nothing of the black experience. We, the black students, fought for classes that would be relevant to our own experience as Africans in America, but our voices were drowned out by the bleeding hearts of those who claimed they wanted to heal the racial divide, not focus on our differences."

"What a damn shame," Mac said.

"This is nice but I thought you were going to show me your art collection," I told him.

Mac nodded. "Right this way." There was a door right off the study and he used a key to unlock it, opening up a world that I couldn't have imagined in my wildest dreams. The room was huge and virtually every space on its walls was filled with a painting. I didn't know much about fine art but I could tell that the works on display were very valuable.

There was one piece I recognized because Stacy bought a printed reproduction the time we went to a Romare Bearden exhibition at the Smithsonian. Stacy's Bearden print was still rolled up after more than a year had passed and now I could see it the way it should be displayed.

"My friend has that same print. Did you buy yours at the Bearden exhibition, too?" I asked.

Mac laughed, slightly. "No, it's the original. I had it out on loan for the exhibition. It was just returned last month. One of my favorites, along with the Jacob Lawrence over there," he said, pointing.

I'm so stupid. I thought.

"Don't worry. Most people think that it's a print or at most, a serigraph. It's one of my favorites because I bought it from Romare right before he died. Actually, I pay a lot of money for original artwork and not to ego trip. They're a very good investment because they appreciate and I make money on the pieces I loan out. That Bearden has paid for itself ten times over."

With a gesture of his hand we headed to the door leading back into the study.

"I think your tea is getting cold."

I was quickly becoming mesmerized, wanting to know more about him. I sat down on the sofa, which seemed to caress and hold me as Mac found his way to his easy chair directly across from where I sat. My tea was still hot and I sipped it gingerly and watched while he drank something that appeared to be brandy.

"I hope you don't mind," he said as he lit a thin, brown cigar and lightly pulled smoke from it. He exhaled slowly and sinewy fingers of smoke lifted from his mouth forming a light cloud around him. Unlike the Black and Milds or PA's that seemed to be the thing with many of the young men I knew, Mac's cigar had a mild, sweet smell that I hardly noticed.

"That's bad for you," I told him.

"I know. There are very few vices that a man can have that'll do him some good but I think a cigarillo and an occasional sip of Courvoisier, VSOP 1948 are two worth risking."

I laughed. "I guess you should know," I said.

He laughed, too. This was the first time I had an opportunity to really look at him and to hear him laugh fully.

Actually, Mac was even better looking than when I first saw him in the restaurant. Even in the afternoon, J. Paul's lighting was dim and from the distance where I sat his facial features were obscured by the restaurant's muted lighting.

Everything about him seemed perfect from the dimple in his chin to the dimples in his cheeks all the way to his slightly curled hair. He had a thick mustache that outlined his lips without a single hair out of place and his face lacked any shadow of a beard or stubble, which made it clear and without a blemish. To top it off his eyes were hazel colored with a mix of green and gray so that when he looked at me they seemed to pierce my soul. Except for the creeping white hair that had fastened to his temples and around his ears and the salt and pepper mustache, he could be mistaken for a man at least ten years younger than he probably was.

"How old are you?"

It was another one of those stupid moments when I couldn't believe that I'd asked the question.

"I'm fifty," he answered without hesitation. "And let me guess your age. What? Twenty-five, Twenty-six, right?"

I nodded. "Twenty-six to be exact."

"Yeah, I know what you're thinking. He's old enough to be my father," Mac said.

I was smiling and nodding my head profusely. I was growing more comfortable around him by the minute, added to the déjà vu feeling I had like I'd known him somewhere before. Still I tried not to look directly into those eyes while still watching his every move as though he might vanish into thin air.

"I know it's early but could you mix a little of that brandy in my tea. I think it'll help me fight off the scratchy feeling in my throat."

"Are you old enough to drink?"

"If you are then so am I."

"*Tres bien.*"

My eyes watched as he rose and walked over to a cabinet made of glass and lit from the inside. Various liquor bottles stood in perfect order according to brand and year and all conspicuously labeled in French. These weren't the kind of liquors you'd find at some package store on North Capitol Avenue. These were imported liquors and I shuddered to think what he might've paid for them.

"This is vintage stuff and it doesn't take much. You sure you want a drink? I don't want your Mama hunting me down saying that I got her little girl wasted."

"I can take care of myself. Thank you."

It was a game of cat and mouse with an equal amount of flirting between us.

He poured a little liquor into my cup and the steam from the cognac mixing with the hot tea filled the room.

"You sure you can handle this?" Mac asked.

I didn't respond. Instead I was slowly taking all of this in, everything about Mac and his lifestyle, the ambience. In my own little world I didn't know that black people lived like this except maybe, Oprah or Jay-Z but they were celebrities and that's how they made their money—being celebrities.

"What do you do for a living?" I asked, once again surprised at my own straightforwardness.

"I'm a collector," Mac answered. He took another sip of his cognac and continued. "I collect all kinds of things, cars, houses, art, money—people."

I expected him to laugh after the "people" remark but Mac's expression didn't change. There was a kind of detached coolness about him that made me know that he was being real.

After a couple of sips I could feel the warmth of the liquor overriding the tea and causing me to sink further and deeper into the sofa. I crossed my bare legs and the dress I was wearing rose above my knees to show their smoothness and shape. The cognac made me light-headed. I was feeling seductive. I stood and tried to walk it off to get myself together. I decided I'd better focus on other things or I might attack him.

There were photographs on the wall mostly of Mac and various people all looking very important. There was a picture of him with Miles Davis and another with Bob Marley. Another picture really caught my attention. It was Mac, probably, ten or fifteen years earlier and he was posing with a familiar looking woman. Together they were a striking couple with her beauty matching his suave and debonair looks. Judging from the pose and the look on their faces they were closer than friends.

"Who is this?" I asked, pointing to the woman in the picture. "She looks familiar, like someone I've seen somewhere."

Mac stood up and walked over to where I was standing, close enough so that I could feel the heat coming from his body. That didn't help the situation and I inched away but slightly. He looked longingly at the picture.

"That's Regina Dupont," he said.

"I knew it. I knew it. She was one of my mother's favorite actresses. She starred in that movie. You know, what was it? I know—it was *Blues For Sissy* and then the other one when she was nominated for an Academy Award, *Rags to Riches*. I watched that movie over and over with my mom. Whatever happened to her?"

Mac's face turned grim. "She was killed in a car accident three weeks after this picture was taken. A tragic loss."

In that moment I regretted asking about the picture. It seemed to stir memories, made him appear melancholy. Mac stood there for a moment silently staring at the picture. He took a deep breath then turned away from the past. The air in the room thickened and I knew that it was time to bring this dream-like day to an end.

"I'd better go," I told him. "If you give me your address I'll have the clothes sent back to you."

"Keep it," he said. "Look, I'm having a little get—together next Saturday. I'd like to invite you and bring a friend, if you like."

He stood up and walked over to me and took my hand.

"I called a cab. It should be here any minute."

The doorbell rang almost on cue. The cab driver was outside, ready to take me home. Mac greeted him and handed him a hundred dollar bill.

"Take her wherever she wants to go," he told the driver. He turned to me. "Wait just one minute. I need to get your clothes."

He returned holding a leather overnight carrying bag.

"Your clothes are inside. Bring the bag when you come to the party," he said, opening the front door. I gave him a parting look, smiled demurely and did an El-type walk to the taxicab. My yellow dress flowed and the hat blocked out any hint of the girl I was when I first entered Mac's house.

I took one more look at him as the cab pulled off, wondered what had happened that day and wished I could've stayed. I thought about the dress I wore and told myself I couldn't keep it. I was so preoccupied thinking about him and the wonderful day I had that I almost didn't notice the black sedan parked at the end of Mac's driveway and on the narrow street leading up to his house. It seemed out of place there because there were no other cars parked on the street. I glanced at the car as my cab crept passed it. I couldn't really see inside through its dark, tinted windows but there was someone sitting in the car looking like a shadow. *Probably his bodyguard,* I thought.

It didn't dawn on me until I was almost home that I hadn't asked Mac for his address or telephone number and there was no way I could remember how to find his house.

It was just getting dark outside when the cab dropped me off at my home but it seemed like an entire day had passed without registering. I started taking the dress off as soon as I walked inside along with the hat and shoes. Moments later I was in my usual Saturday outfit—sweat pants and an oversized tee shirt. I neatly folded the dress and picked up Mac's overnight bag so that I could take my own wet dress out and put the new clothes inside to return them to him someday. I found a black satin dress inside the bag made to be worn after-five for a cocktail-party. There was also a note inside. It read: *Wear this to the party. Mackenzie.* The note had his telephone number and street address.

I was blown away. *Why did he do this?* He didn't know me and I certainly didn't know him but beyond that I thought about our differences. He was so much older, worldly and I presumed wiser. In fact, who was I kidding? I knew he was wiser.

We were total opposites. More opposite than anyone I'd ever known. But like positive and negative ends of a magnet I could feel there was some kind of attraction between us. In that brief encounter and with all my anticipation leading up to our actually meeing I realized that he was slowly taking control of my thoughts and I wondered whether my body would follow. I cursed myself first and then cursed him. "This is fucked up."

Day Nine

Cinderella was haunted by years of abuse at the hands of a mean stepmother and step-sisters. Til' one day a benevolent stranger bestowed something upon her that was more than external for among the gifts her fairy godmother brought her, wrapped up neatly and tied with a bow, was a box of confidence.

Songs of Desdemona—10/5/05

"I don't understand, Dahlia. You mean to tell me that he didn't even hit on you and you think that you've got a thing for him? I don't get it, homegirl. Besides, from what I'm hearing the brotha's older than dirt. C'mon, Girlfriend, he's fifty. I mean your mom's what? Forty-five or something?"

It was typical El all the way, judgmental and relentless. She was talking to me and looking at the quilt my grandmother had given me.

"Oh, lighten up, El," Stacy came to my defense. "I don't care how old he is the brother is fine and rich. I bet he knows how to treat a lady. And make love? Mmmmmm, I bet he takes it slow and easy. Shit! Viagra is the equalizer! And with it, age ain't nothing but a number."

Stacy laughed as she closed her eyes and squeezed her own body fully appreciating the moment and the thought.

"This is beautiful," El said, referring to the quilt. She then jumped right back into the debate.

"This girl can really make some choices in men. She's got pretty boy thug Antoine who don't work, has no future and will probably get his college degree in prison and then she got Ol' Mac Daddy who's loaded but probably can't get it up. You know they say that old guys' sperm turns to dust. Can't get you pregnant. Don't you want to have kids someday?"

El was shaking her head and wagging her finger, imitating what we call "ghetto-fabulous" style.

"Hell, I'd say she's got the best of both worlds," Stacy said.

She offered me a high-five but I left her hand hanging in the air. El was upsetting me.

"Ignore her, Dahlia. Are you going to his party? Can I go?" Stacy asked, practically jumping up and down.

"Me too," piped in El. "I was just kidding about that 'can't get it up' stuff."

"Well, I'm not so sure if I'm going. I mean, I can't keep the dresses and how would it look? Going to a party and I can't even buy my own dress. But I really want to see him again and I don't know why," I told them.

El was looking at the two dresses Mac had given me that were now draped over my sofa.

"Ferragamo and Jean Paul Gaultier? Girl, if you don't keep these, you're crazy," she said. "Obviously, he wants you to have them."

"Yeah, but at what price?" Stacy asked. "You know how some guys are. They'll buy a girl things and then think he owns her. They say, 'jump' and you're supposed to say, 'how high?"

"Well, I call it that old school mentality. You know, treat her like a lady. Whatever happened to chivalry?" El said.

She walked over to where Stacy and I were sitting on the sofa sipping tea mixed with raw sugar.

"When's the last time a man bought you a dress like this? Hell! When's the last time a man bought you anything?" El asked me.

She stood there with her hands on her hips waiting for my answer. Hearing no response, she held up the black dress.

"I rest my case. Now, what are you going to wear with this? I've got some black heels that would be perfect and a black and white Dolce and Gabbana handbag would be slamming. Wish I could wear this."

She turned and held it in front of her body pretending to model the dress for us. Stacy and I both smiled.

"Yeah, yeah. I know. My ass is too big," El said.

We all laughed while repeating the words almost in unison.

She turned back to face the quilt on the wall and studied it hard.

"Where'd you get this?" El asked me.

"It's been in my family for a long time. My grandmother gave it to me last year. I guess that shows how often you come and visit me," I said.

El seemed unfazed by my remark. The quilt had her mesmerized.

"What are all these symbols?"

"Don't know for sure. The ones at the top were first stitched there by my great-great-great grandmother, Momma Set. She was a slave."

"Damn, that's history."

El moved her face close to the quilt.

"What you doing, El," Stacy said. "Trying to stare a hole in it?"

"No. Just trying to read this thing."

She turned and faced me.

"Is that you at the bottom? The little stick figure with the halo?"

"Yeah. How'd you know?"

"I guess it's because it looks just like you," El laughed.

"Shut up, El." Stacy jumped in. "If they had put you on the quilt, your stick figure would have big breasts and a big ass. Probably would be floating in the air. You know, buoyancy."

El laughed. "That's a good one, Stacy."

She took her index finger and made a line in the air.

"Score one for Stacy. What about the halo, Dahlia?" she asked.

"My grandmother stitched that. I guess she's always thought of me as her little angel."

My statement conjured up images of my grandmother, Stevie. I rubbed the quilt, felt its thickness, and remembered her venous fingers stitching away, adding to our history. My thoughts flipped back to Mackenzie Powell.

"I didn't tell you, but I also saw him at Café Alexandria's a couple of nights ago. He got into some kind of beef with this real big guy."

Both Stacy and El looked surprised.

"You mean he got into a fight? Kind of childish for a man his age." Stacy said.

"It wasn't his fault. It was the other guy and there wasn't a fight. The other guy named, Joe turned and walked away like a scared puppy. Mackenzie had a gun," I told them.

"What? You're kidding." El said.

"It wasn't like that. He didn't pull it out or anything like that. He just told me when we met."

El smiled broadly.

"Girl's got an O.G. bad boy, thug," she said.

"Most good girls like a man with a rough side," Stacy said.

I reflected on her comment. I had to admit there was something dangerous about Mac and it was attractive.

◆   ◆   ◆

I spent the rest of the day deciding what I would wear with the dress. This was going to be a very chic affair and I knew that everyone there, including my friends would be dressed like they were going to Prince's 1999 party. If the world's coming to an end, you might as well dress in your best.

I often called my wardrobe, "flea market couture", reflecting my clothing budget and to some degree my tastes. For a moment I thought about buying new shoes and a purse to wear with the dress but I changed my mind. My credit cards were nearly maxed out and the last thing I needed was more debt. I resigned myself to the fact that I probably wouldn't go. For a brief moment I considered the quarter of a million dollars that the FBI agents said was stashed away in an offshore bank. My wistful thoughts took me on a shopping spree, imagining all the clothes I could buy with that money.

I was sitting on the sofa still contemplating whether I was going to Mac's party when my phone rang. My heart raced thinking that it might be him. I wanted to grab the phone on the first ring but I decided to be cool and I waited. In my mind I quickly went over what I'd say to him and I told myself to stay calm. When I couldn't stand it anymore I reached for the telephone and gave him a breathy, hello.

"Wuzzup, Baby/" It was Antoine.

My heart sank and I knew he could hear it in my voice. "Hello," was all I could say.

"Damn! It's good to hear from you, too," he told me. Antoine didn't hide his sarcasm.

I didn't apologize or explain my lack of enthusiasm. "We need to talk, Antoine," I said, flatly.

"Sure, what about?"

"Can't talk on the phone. We need to meet somewhere but not here. We need to meet someplace public," I said.

"O.K. How about at the Mall near the Monument?"

"I'll meet you there tomorrow after I get off work. Say about six o'clock," I said.

I hung up the telephone thinking that I wasn't going to worry about Antoine and the FBI. It wasn't my problem and I wasn't going to help anyone not him or the government. I just wanted to make sure that my name wasn't attached to anything—not the money, not Antoine and definitely not some big-time gang.

◆   ◆   ◆

My train ride to work the next day was filled with thoughts of Mac and the party. I pulled out the piece of paper with his telephone number and address written on it. I thought about calling him but wondered what I'd say. *Thanks for everything. I really love the dresses but I can't accept them. Will you make love to me?* I thought all would make great icebreakers.

I remembered the picture of Mac and Regina, the late movie star and my insecurities kicked in hard. There was no way I could compare myself to her but why was I even going there? Insecurity is a place for those who at least have something going on between them like the way Derek is insecure about Stacy. Mac didn't try to hit on me or seduce me. In fact, he seemed more paternalistic than romantic so I had no reason to feel insecure.

Going back to the picture I thought of how he looked fifteen years earlier. *Daaamn! That brother was fine!* And not much about him had changed over the years.

I could hardly concentrate at work and the day was just a blur. I worked on some Excel reports, took an extra long lunch break and daydreamed through much of the entire day. Several times I picked up the telephone and pushed the first three or four digits to his number but then backed down. I finally resigned myself to the fact that I didn't have the courage.

I guess thinking about Mac sped me right through the humdrum pace that usually marked my time at work. I glanced up at the clock and realized it was time to leave. Five o'clock at the Pentagon was like the starting bell being rung at the Derby. The doors flew open and a flood of humanity streamed outside like a rushing river. I never quite understood why people were always in such a big hurry to leave when they'd have to wait to get on the trains or be stuck on the parkway choking on carbon monoxide spewing from cars in front, on the sides and behind them. Personally, I always took my time because a train ride home was a train ride home but this day was different because I was to meet Antoine near the Capital and I'd almost forgot.

I decided to catch the Red Line train to downtown DC and then hop a cab over to Capitol Hill just in case I was being followed. The thought wasn't out of the question as I discovered after speaking with Agents Robinson and Liles. Add in the man I saw on the train a couple of days earlier and it wasn't only possible that they had me under some kind of surveillance it was probable.

By the time I reached the platform at Pentagon City most of the people had boarded the earlier trains that ran in succession every fifteen minutes or so. I surveyed the area looking for any familiar faces then breathed a sigh of relief hoping and believing I wasn't being followed.

I got off at the Connecticut Avenue stop and went into the same routine checking over my shoulder and scoping out my surroundings. I can't explain it but the anxiety I felt about being caught up in Antoine's mess was blending in with the suspense of playing this undercover game and it was exciting. Suddenly I was the actress Regina Dupont getting over on The Man in a circa 1970's blaxploitation movie and a long way from my job as a pencil pushing bureaucrat laboring everyday for the government.

I hailed a cab and told him to drop me off a block from the place where I was going to meet Antoine. I could walk the rest of the way.

The cool thing about meeting at the Washington Monument was that the area was wide open and there wasn't anyplace, like a tree or building to use as a shield. And there were plenty of people out there with a mixture of the hunched over, suited down Capitol Hill minions making their way home while dodging the long-haired, shirtless Frisbee throwers, who didn't seem like they had a care in the world. Add in some tourists in Bermuda shorts and straw hats it became the perfect place for a covert rendezvous.

I could see Antoine off in the distance, sitting on a bench with smoke hovering over his head in the dry, thin air like he'd been sending off signals. I had been fairly calm up until that point, but then I got scared and nervous. My heart seemed to pump louder with every stride and I told myself to just relax. I reminded myself that I'd done nothing wrong and I shouldn't be afraid to confront Antoine. If anything I should be pissed off.

He gave me one of his typical easy smiles when I walked up on him like I was simply making a social call, but his smile quickly dissipated when he saw that I wasn't responding.

"Uh, oh, you look like you about to kick my ass or somethin'," he said.

"Trust me, if I could I would." I took a seat on the bench beside him then looked around to see if anyone was within earshot. "I had FBI agents come to my office the other day. They asked me about you and about how well did I know you."

Antoine leaned back against the park bench and puffed on his cigar. He tilted his head back and playfully blew out rings of smoke. "Old black dude, young white cat?"

I nodded.

"They're just sniffing around. Ain't got nothing because if they did I wouldn't be sitting here right now talkin' to you."

"That's not the point Antoine. It's the fact that they came to see me in the first place and that I'm being spied on all because of something you're doing."

"And you couldn't tell them nothing cause you don't know nothing."

I clinched my teeth together for a moment, took a deep breath then exhaled hard. It wasn't in my nature to curse or swear very much, but his casual demeanor was forcing out the demons that resided deep within me. "What the fuck are you talking about Antoine? You don't get it. You used my computer to do something shady and you never told me anything."

"Well, if I had told you I'd have to kill you," he said with a look that was as grim and serious as any I'd ever seen. His statement rocked me for a moment until I saw his smile return followed by an outburst of laughter. "Look at your face! That's some funny shit Dahlia. I've always wanted to say that to someone like the way they do in the movies." He kept laughing.

"It ain't funny Antoine."

"Look, don't worry about nothing. We ain't doing nothing wrong," he told me.

"Well, what about your gang they say you belong to?"

"Gang? I ain't no banger. Look at me. Look at this face. You think I'd be messing around with that hardcore kind of bullshit? Hell no. It's just their paranoia. Anytime they see a group of brothers living large and ballin' they say the words, gang related. Worst thing I ever done was to catch a little misdemeanor type weed case a couple months ago."

"It doesn't add up, Antoine. I mean, why would they be following you, following me if you weren't doing something illegal?"

"Look, like I've told you, I'm in the music business trying to become a producer and I admit that some of the people I deal with are a little on the shady side but their simply investors. It costs money to produce, record and package an artist and I don't know if you've noticed but Chase ain't giving loans or investment dollars to twenty-three year old brothers trying to become the next Jay-Z."

"Well, that's all well and good but why are you using me? Why'd you use my computer to conduct your business and most of all why'd you deposit money in a bank in my name? You put me right in the middle of all this and you need to clean it all up. I don't want to be involved in any of this shit."

"The money thing was because I know I can trust you and my investors wanted to make sure that I couldn't touch the money until I had certain things in place. I mean 250 grand is a lot of cheese," he said.

Antoine gave me this real soulful look like he was about to beg for something. "Look Dahlia just chill out for a little bit—please? The money's in the account just gaining interest. Besides, I can't take your name off it because the people I work with set it up as some kind of trust and no one can touch it but you. When the time is right I'll ask you to withdraw it and you can keep ten per cent for your trouble O.K?"

His explanation about everything didn't make me feel any better about the whole thing nor did it put me at ease but I guess it made sense. I tried to do a quick analysis of everything and thought about my options but I was very confused. I knew I needed to talk to someone like El even though I didn't want to.

"I'll need to think about this for a minute. I need to figure out what I'm going to do Antoine."

"Take your time, baby. Like I said, just chill out. I'm in no hurry to do anything and I ain't doing nothing wrong but if we all panic and start looking like we're up to some dirt then the Feds will be all over us trying to make a case,"

I sat up straight, looked right into Antoine's green eyes. "What do you mean 'we'?" I told him. "Regardless of what happens and even if you tell me that everything is legit, I'm not in this. There is no we when it comes to me, Antoine."

"Yeah, yeah, I got it."

I looked around the park and down the long corridor of grass lined by trees known as The Mall. At the end of the corridor was the place where Congress met. I studied it for a moment and thought about all of the laws that were being passed there then directed my attention back to Antoine.

"Those FBI guys think you want to use me because of my security clearance. They told me that you and your people are smugglers and one implied that I'm not your type and that's the only reason you're involved with me. The white guy said that I'm not your type"

He smirked then dropped his head and shook it from side to side. "You see, that's why I know they're just fishing for something with their theories and that kind of bullshit. We don't need any kind of security clearance to transfer money from an island account to my bank account here and if my associates are some kind of smugglers they don't need you to handle their business," he laughed along with his words. "What do they think? We're gonna bring the money here in a big paper sack?"

Antoine rose to his feet, stuck his cigar in his mouth and began speaking to me through clinched teeth. "What the hell do they know about what woman's my type? I've always been interested in you because you're different. There's something there, something under the surface and waiting to break lose. But it's real, not made up. You're not flossing, you're just being you and that's what I like." He glanced at his watch. "I gotta run but like I said, don't worry."

I watched him recede into the crowd of people who had gathered near the Washington Monument realizing that Antoine was the kind of man who'd go through them rather than around. His ego would cause the crowd to part and make a path for him as he headed towards Constitution Avenue and probably to the place where he had parked his car. I guess if I were an expert in human behavior I'd conclude that he wasn't worried about anything.

◆   ◆   ◆

I soon found myself at home standing in the mirror with the black dress in front of me. I was so engrossed in my image that I almost didn't hear the doorbell ring.

"He's gotta stop doing this," I said, frustration in my voice. It was typical Antoine, coming over without calling, acting like I didn't have a life. My first thought was that he wanted me to withdraw the money when he had just told me that he was in no hurry to get it.

I was feeling a little agitated when I turned on my monitor but it wasn't Antoine standing in the lobby. It was a deliveryman.

"Yes, may I help you?" I shouted into the speaker.

"Delivery for Dahlia Reynolds."

"I'll be right there." My anticipation was high as I wondered who could've sent me something and what could it be.

I grabbed my keys and headed for the elevator. In seconds I was signing my name as the deliveryman handed me a bouquet of flowers and a large box that was gift-wrapped. I anxiously accepted the delivery. This all was totally out of character for Antoine and it made me suspicious like he was buying my silence.

I waited until I was back in my condo to read the card tucked neatly in an envelope and tied to the flowers. It read: *I hope that these will hold up better in water than you did—Mac. P.S. I realized that you might need something to wear with the Gaultier.* I opened the box to find a pair of shoes and a matching Fendi purse.

I checked the shoe size and wondered how he could've known that I wore a size nine shoe. I filed the thought away for the moment, figuring that his skills of observation were finely tuned or it was a lucky guess.

Totally blown away, I sat down on the sofa and breathed hard and deep, nearly hyperventilating. I didn't know whether to be flattered or angry. First, I wondered how he knew where I lived and then realized that the taxicab driver probably told him. Then I tried to understand why he was being so nice to me. Maybe, he really was trying to buy my affections, like Stacy said. *He's a collector. That's what he said. And what do collector's do? They buy what they want whether it's an antique or a woman.*

I picked up the telephone and dialed Mac's number. It rang a few times and then his voice mail came on asking the caller to leave a message. "Yes, Mr. Powell. This is Dahlia Reynolds. I need to talk to you. I need to tell you that I can't accept these gifts from you." I left my number although something told me he had it already.

Mac didn't return any of my telephone calls that week so I decided to go to his party. It would've been a girls' night out but Derek wanted to tag along. El said that she'd drive but we all couldn't ride in her Beamer convertible so she borrowed Walter's Hummer H2 while he was out in Los Angeles playing a game. It was appropriate for her, big and ballsy.

I nudged El, as we pulled the Hummer into Mac's driveway. Listening to Tupac and his ear shattering beats and rhymes torched with expletives, amplified by Walter's sound system was fine for the ride through the city but now we were in Georgetown and in Mac's driveway so it was time for the mute button and some "Quiet Storm".

Mac's home looked different at night. Recessed lighting bordered the driveway and soft colored lights washed over the front of the house. It had a fairy-tale, mystical quality like something you'd read about in a gothic novel just not as scary. There were young men in white jackets opening car doors for his guests and driving the vehicles away. El pushed the Hummer slowly, which looked like a bull among a group of swans with emblems for Jaguar, Mercedes and Ferrari on them.

A few minutes earlier we'd been rocking and bobbing to a heavy hip-hop beat and now everyone except me appeared to be mesmerized by what they saw. We all sat in the car not saying anything, taking everything in. Derek was the first to speak, "So, this is how the other side lives."

"Yeah, I mean, Walter's got a nice house in Potomac but he's *nouveau riche*. This is old school money. Probably a bunch of old, stuffy people in there." El paused. "Well, I asked for it."

"Well, Darlings. I think we have finally arrived. I believe it is time to meet the king. Chop, chop," said Stacy feigning a British accent as we all got out of the car.

I felt a small lump growing in my throat, a symptom of my anxiety. A deep breath relieved some of the pressure as I led them inside. At least I had my friends to back me up so I held my head high and put on a confident expression and walked into a house full of people laughing and rubbing elbows with each other.

Mac had gone all out for the party, judging by the servers dressed in tails and walking around holding trays stacked with long-stemmed glasses filled with Don Perignon. The fountain in the foyer was awash in yellow lights and pushing Crystal not water. There were servers everywhere with trays of appetizers. Most of all, the house was full of people dressed like they were in a scene from the old television show *Dynasty*.

Stacy said she had never seen so many beautiful people in one place. It was a diverse group represented by every race and nationality. Everyone was talking and laughing and apparently having a good time. Stacy pointed out all the famous people there and bragged how she had covered most of them as a newspaper reporter. There were politicians and Washington insiders along with the bottom feeders known as lobbyists. There were also a number of men from the Middle East, some dressed in robes and others in Armani.

Stacy pointed to a heavyset man who was the center of attention of a small crowd.

"You know that's the mayor, don't you?"

She grabbed a glass of champagne and made her way with Derek in tow over to the spot where His Honor was holding court.

"That's Stacy," El said. "Always looking for a story."

She looked around the room. "Where's your man?"

"He's not my man and I'm sure he's here, somewhere."

I was feeling insecure around Mac's high and mighty friends. But the way I looked belied my true feelings. The Gaultier looked magnificent on me even with my ugly eyeglasses and my hair not quite ready for the occasion. I had tried to do what I could with my "combination hair", which was part fine and part coarse. Despite my friends' urging, I'd long resisted having it straightened. I always felt that a little water and some oil would do giving me that Sheena of the Jungle look, wild and exotic.

A live jazz band was playing a sweet and soulful song that had some people dancing and others clapping to the beat. El sized up the room and noticed two men standing in a corner gawking at the bevy of young things floating around the party.

"You see those two over there?" She asked me.

"Yeah," I said trying not to be conspicuous as I turned to look in their direction.

"They own Spice. You know, the hottest club in D.C. The taller one just retired last year from pro-football and was in *Washington Style* magazine as one of the city's most eligible bachelors," El said.

She gave me that "look", the one she always had when she was zeroing in on her prey. It was El's game face. I watched as she focused, pushed out her chest and hit a walk that would've made Tyra Banks jealous. Within seconds she was talking to the two men with both smiling and competing for her attention. With El gone and Stacy and Derek being entertained by Mayor Huff, I found myself standing alone and still no Mackenzie Powell to be seen.

I asked one of the servers where I'd find the host of the party. "In the pool house. He's entertaining," he said. I made my way through the crowd, passed the atrium and walked over to the swimming pool. This was the real party. While the people in the house were standing and talking, the folks here were getting their groove on. Nothing old and stuffy here, they were jammin'.

Mac's swimming pool was covered by a temporary dance floor and with a stage that had a ten-piece band grinding out some soulful songs. I recognized Phoenix, a popular local singer leading a jazzy, bumping version of Marvin Gaye's, "What's Going On." The music made my body sway involuntarily to its beat and I started mouthing the words to the song. There was a man on stage with his back to the crowd, tuning up his trumpet. It was Mac.

He turned around and immediately hit a solo that could've rivaled Miles or Dizzy in its vibrato and Wynton in its precision. But his demeanor was low key and not showy. It was easy to see that he was having a good time and was in his element up there. And the crowd loved it. With each beat and every burst from his horn they rocked and swayed, throbbing to the music, a unified body moving like one person.

I got closer to the stage to get a better look. Mac was dressed in a black tuxedo and looked like a man ready to model in a wedding magazine. There was a small group of women standing right in front of him, cheering him on with flirtatious smiles. He responded by blowing a few notes and stopping to let the band catch up while flashing that killer smile. His eyes finally caught me standing there admiring his every move. He greeted me with a warm smile and a nod as if to say, I'll be right there.

When the song ended and the applause rained down on the band, Mac got off the stage and made his way over to where I stood. He was a little winded from playing but it didn't dampen his enthusiasm. It was clear that he was happy to see me.

He took my hand and said, "I'm glad you made it. I thought you weren't coming."

"I almost didn't. You got my message, didn't you? This is too much," I said, showing off the dress.

"It's beautiful. You're beautiful. It was made for you," he replied. "Look, buying women expensive clothes is something I don't normally do but someday if I have the chance I'll tell you why I did this for you. Besides, it's a small gesture."

"Of what?" I asked.

"My appreciation for just knowing you."

I was smiling and looking into his soulful eyes as he held my hand. There was strength in his hands. Something in them that told me no harm could come my way with him around. For that moment the world stood still. There was no band playing, no crowd of people bumping to what was now non-existent music, just Mac and I standing there talking. It couldn't have been a more perfect setting for a man and a woman who were just meeting and trying to get to know each other without being awkwardly thrown together on a first date. It was perfect until we were interrupted by a woman's sultry sounding voice.

"Hey, Mac," said the voice behind me.

She quickly moved over to his side and grabbed him by the arm like she owned it. I recognized her as the same woman that was with him that evening at Café Alexandria. Her eyes were focused on him, ignoring me as she talked about the party and how she loved his playing the trumpet. Mac listened for a moment and then stopped her.

"Felicia, let me to introduce you to Dahlia. Dahlia, Felicia."

I held out my hand but she gave me a fake smile in return and kept her death grip on Mac's arm. "Nice dress", were her only words. I read between the lines.

I found myself shrinking behind her overwhelming presence. But it wasn't just Felicia's lack of manners that made me feel uneasy, it was Felicia herself. She was downright intimidating. I sized her up. She was model-type beautiful, around forty-years old and holding it extremely well.

Her hair was perfect, short and sassy. She looked like she was pressed from a mold. High cheekbones, full lips, brown skin and a body that would rival any twenty-six year old woman's including mine. I hoped I'd look like that in fifteen, twenty years.

But it was more than Felicia's looks that intimidated me, it was an air about her like she was the Queen of Sheba and everyone else her subjects. I picked up on it right away, a diva in the classic sense buoyed by a lifetime of being spoiled by men with an attitude as clear as cellophane.

Felicia whispered something into Mac's ear and pulled him away as he gave me an apologetic smile and mouthed, "I'll be back". I was left hanging there alone and feeling slightly dejected. But it wasn't long before a young man walked over and pulled me onto the dance floor. *Screw her and Mac, too.* I jumped at the chance, grabbing something to drink as I followed. As the band kept playing I had a series of men, both young and older surrounding me on the floor and with each dance came another glass of champagne.

For that moment I felt that I was the center of the Universe. *All eyes on me.* This had never happened before. I wasn't blending into the background like someone dressed in camouflage fatigues and standing in a forest or on a sand dune. Truthfully, I loved the attention and it made me feel good not be overshadowed by El or that bitch Felicia.

As the night went on I danced to Prince, Outkast and Mary J. Mac or no Mac, I was having a good time. When I couldn't dance anymore I thought about my friends and told myself I'd better find them.

Stacy and Derek had been joined by El and they were all talking to Mayor Huff. He was in rare form and not the stoic politician I'd seen on television. When I approached the group El pulled me to the side.

"His Honor, The Mayor is talking shit," she said laughing.

I picked up on the conversation as Mayor Huff was debating the virtues of older men and younger women. *That's just great,* I thought.

"Old is better than gold, baby," he told his small audience. "The Hell with Moms Mabley. Talkin' bout ain't nothin' an old man can do for her but point her to a young one. That's bullshit. These young cats don't know how to treat a woman. Me? I'm flowers and candy and expensive gifts. You could say that I'm all that and a bag of chips."

Everyone laughed. "Bag of chips? No one says that anymore," someone said.

El had had a few glasses of something and she was ready to jump on the bandwagon.

"Yeah, you talk a good game Mr. Mayor but I know you can't handle this," she said, sticking out her ample rear and strike a sassy pose with her hands on her hips.

He leered at her ass, reached into his jacket pocket and pulled out his business card.

"Here's my personal telephone number. Call me, we'll talk about it," he told El.

Then he turned to Stacy. "If you print this I'll deny everything," he told my friend. His words were followed by a chorus of laughter.

I shook my head and turned around when I heard Mac's distinctive laugh behind me. He was a few feet away talking to one of his Saudi Arabian guests. Felicia wasn't up under him anymore but it didn't matter. The alcohol was my liquid courage and it gave me confidence. I set my eyes on Mac and stepped right to him.

"So, there you are Mackenzie Powell. I thought you deserted me," I told him.

I was ready to forgive his transgression.

"I am so sorry. Felicia wanted me to meet someone and I had to fight to break loose."

He paused and then directed his attention back to his guest. "Dahlia Reynolds, I'd like to introduce you to my good friend, Sheik Khalid Al Amin. I just call him, Al," Mac said.

I was impressed. I was thinking, *A real Saudi prince? Mac operates in rare air.*

"It's a pleasure to meet me."

My words disjointed and slurred. I was feeling no pain.

"Likewise," Al said.

He extended his hand ready to accept mine and when I gave it to him he gently kissed it. Then he gave me this long look like he was studying my face and that made me feel uneasy even with my senses dulled by the alcohol. My instincts told me not to trust him. Mac could tell that I had had too much to drink and that I was real unsteady on my feet.

"I think you could use a good strong cup of coffee," he whispered in my ear.

He took my hand and led me to the only room in the house that wasn't crowded with his guests. On the way he told one of the servers to bring me a cup of coffee.

I leaned on his shoulder as we walked and Mac put his arm around my waist keeping me upright and steady. Once in his study, I slumped down on the sofa, down so low that I almost disappeared inside its pillows.

"Was that your girlfriend?"

I forced out a drunken inquiry, still cognizant of my own insecurity. He knew that I was talking about Felicia.

"No, she's just a friend," he answered, softly. "How many glasses of champagne did you drink?"

I held up ten fingers and said, "Just two". Mac shook his head and then lifted my feet on to the sofa so that I could lie down.

"Why don't you rest here for a minute? I'll check on the party and I'll be back," he said.

My head spinning, I looked up, gave him a goofy smile.

"I will if you kiss me," I told him.

Without hesitating Mac leaned over as I closed my eyes and readied my lips. I felt his warm lips plant a kiss in the middle of my forehead.

"I'll be back," he whispered.

He turned off the lights and left.

I drifted into an alcohol-induced stupor, something between sleep and veiled consciousness. I couldn't fight it and I couldn't move so I resigned myself to the fact that I would sleep it off.

I don't know how long I was there but my sleep was interrupted by the sounds of someone breathing heavy and deep interspersed with a few moans. Even in my haze I knew that it was the sound of people engaged in some kind of carnal activity. I couldn't see much in the darkened room except the outline of two bodies, a woman leaning forward on the desk and the man behind thrusting himself against her.

It was obvious that they didn't know I was there. It didn't last long and when they finished I heard the sounds of clothes rustling to be put back in place. After that, murmurs and whispers followed by kisses. I strained to hear their words.

The man spoke: "Anybody see you come in here?"

She laughed. "Fine time to ask now."

I recognized the laugh and the voice. It was Felicia. Fear gripped me. I wondered if it was Mac with her. I brushed the thought aside hoping that he would say something else and that I could be sure.

"We can't let anyone know about this, especially Mackenzie."

The man's accent was thick, distinctly Middle Eastern. Hearing that brought me some relief. It wasn't Mac who'd been humping Felicia. I held my breath as Felicia spoke.

"What? You don't want him to know that you screwed me?"

"I don't give a fuck about that. I don't want him to know that I told you about Desdemona."

"Don't worry. I won't do anything to upset your little plan," Felicia said. "And as far as Mac is concerned I don't know her."

"That's good, trust me."

"And what about the girl?" She asked.

"Don't worry, my people are keeping an eye on her. You just follow orders and do what I tell you to do," he answered.

I could see him pull her close. Their silhouette became the two-headed monster—deception and intrigue. For a moment no words were spoken until she broke the silence.

"Just like a man. Fucks you and then wants to boss you around. Don't worry about me. I'll take care of my part. You just take care of Mac and Desdemona."

She pushed him away, pulled her dress down and smoothed it against her body. He stood motionless for a long time after she had left the room and I held my breath. I was fearful that my breathing would tell him I was there. I was hoping that he wouldn't turn on the lights to see me balled up in a corner of the couch. Instead, he walked to the door, paused and then made his exit.

I wanted to rush out of the room, find Mac and tell him about what I saw but I wasn't quite sure what was going on. I chose to curl up on the couch and wait. As I drifted off to sleep my thoughts were of some woman named Desdemona and my heart sank. I reminded myself how Felicia told the man to take care of Mac and Desdemona and the instruction had a foreboding quality to it. I thought about Mac's wealth and his riches and I feared that they might rob him or worse, kill him. I fell asleep with the words, Mac and Desdemona ringing in a head that had lost its sobriety. Mac and Desdemona sounded like a match pair like Brad and Angelina, Lucy and Ricky, Bobby and Whitney.

◆   ◆   ◆

The light from the Sunday morning sun crashed through and entered the study without mercy, unforgiving in its interruption. I was startled to the point where I sat straight up and then quickly laid back down. I grabbed my head and rubbed at my temples. I couldn't believe that I'd slept there through the night. I stumbled to my feet thinking about my friends, angered by the fact that they had left me. And where was Mac?

I walked out of the study and into one of the halls, followed it towards the foyer and the spiral staircase that led up to the eight bedrooms that Mac said were upstairs. I stopped when I heard sounds coming from the kitchen. "Mac? Mac?" I called out.

I could smell fresh coffee brewing along with the smell of something cooking. I walked into the kitchen ready to curse him out and to ask why he let my friends leave me there. But it wasn't Mac cooking it was Felicia. She was standing over the stove dressed in a silk robe and gown and with her back to me.

"How do you like your eggs?" she asked.

I was a little too shocked to answer so I asked my own questions.

"Where's Mac? Is he upstairs?"

Felicia was pretty matter-of-fact in her reply.

"Oh, I think he went to play golf with the mayor and some of his guests from Saudi Arabia."

"And he left you here?" I was looking very confused.

I know what you're thinking and the answer is no. I didn't sleep with him. Mac and I are yesterday's news. I slept in one of the guest rooms upstairs. I told your friends to let you sleep and that I'd take care of you. So, they left."

I was still foggy brained and slow to process what she just told me.

"I guess I drank too much," I said.

Felicia smiled. She seemed totally different than the way she was when we first met, even friendly.

"You really like him, don't you?" she asked. I nodded.

"I think I do but I don't know what to think. We're so different and I don't think he's really that interested in me, not like that," I said.

Felicia listened as she continued to fix breakfast.

"Mac doesn't eat red meat so there's no bacon or sausage, stuff like that. I put some croissants in the oven and there's fresh fruit if you'd like some," she said still scrambling the eggs. "The eggs are those organic, low cholesterol kind and so is the butter he uses. Personally, I like the real stuff, the kind that clogs your arteries to the point where they'd have to put a catheter in me to keep my blood flowing." She laughed at her own inside joke with its punch line that drifted over my head. "Forget it," she said.

Felicia continued. "Look, sweetie. Be careful. Mac's no different than any other man. He's got good qualities and he has bad ones. How old are you anyway?"

"Twenty-six."

"Well, you're young but old enough to know better. Ever been in love?"

"No."

"All I can say is be careful. Mac and I were an item once but that ended years ago. Like most men his age he's got some baggage and he keeps secrets. He ever tell you about Regina?"

I nodded, remembering Mac and his lost actress.

"One thing I know is that he's never gotten over her death. Did he tell you that he was driving when it happened?"

"No," I answered.

I watched Felicia intently as she busily poured, stirred and scraped. For a moment I thought that the conversation was a little too heavy, especially considering the fact that I hardly knew Mac and didn't know Felicia at all. On the other hand, she was someone to talk to and at the very least, I could pick her brain and learn everything I wanted to know about him.

"Yeah, it seems like he has a lot going on," I told Felicia. "Besides, I don't think he's really that interested in me. It's like there's something paternal in the way he treats me. Like he's my daddy or something," I said.

Felicia scraped some eggs out of the skillet onto my plate.

"I know Mac and if you ask me I think he has a special interest in you. And trust me he's not the paternal type. I've been with him. He had me asking my damn self who's my daddy?" Felicia laughed. "Here, eat this and then go up to the first guest room and change your clothes. We've got an errand to run."

Day Ten

I had refused an offer to have a mirror put in my prison cell. Comic irony, I concluded. Perceptions of self have been transformed by internal examination without regard to how the world sees me or how I once saw myself. I understand now that the beauty that emanates from within is eternal and is unaffected by my present circumstance.

Songs of Desdemona—10/6/06

My brain was still full of cobwebs as I climbed inside Felicia's car and we sped down Mac's driveway like we were on the Autobahn. I opened my eyes wide when we almost struck the same unmarked car with the tinted windows I had seen the first day I came to his house. I made another mental note.

Felicia cursed at the car like it was the other driver's fault but she didn't stop.

"I saw that car in the same spot last week," I told her.

"Oh, you've been here before?" Felicia asked unable to conceal her surprise.

"Yeah, the day I met him."

"They're probably cops or something," Felicia said.

"Why? Is Mac in some kind of trouble?" I asked.

"Nah, you know how it is. Police are always around where the rich folks live, protecting their stuff and they treat The Hood like it's a leper village. They only go in when they have to. Tell me about yourself," Felicia said. She was changing the subject as quickly as she was navigating her car.

It was the nature of small talk, prying and inquisitive to be sure but I couldn't help but gravitate to the woman I saw as my rival. I thought there was no harm in talking about my life.

"What do you want to know?" Dahlia asked.

"Well, I hear you're from Georgia. You still have family there?"

Felicia shifted gears seamlessly and the black Porsche zipped down Connecticut Avenue without stalling or lurching forward as we exceeded the posted speed limits. It was hard hearing her with the wind whipping around my ears. I was tempted to ask her to put the top up. But the combination of wind and speed, riding in a convertible sports car was intoxicating so I just leaned closer and strained to hear her every word.

"What did you say?" I shouted.

Felicia raised her voice. "I said, where's your family?"

"Oh! In Georgia. I'm from a small town named Waycross. It's near the Georgia—Florida border. My mother and grandmother still live there."

"What about your father? Where does he live?" she asked.

"My father died before I was born so I never knew him. My mother says that he was a musician. They never married."

I thought, O*ops! Too personal.*

Felicia had her eyes focused straight on the road ahead but I could tell that she was listening closely.

"I'm sorry to hear that. I lost my father a couple of years ago. He was a federal judge and a good man but real strict with my sister and me. As soon as I was old enough I left home."

"What do you do now?" I asked.

"I run my own business. A tool and die company."

Felicia's response made me jerk a little. It caught me off guard.

"I thought you were going to tell me that you did something like worked in advertising or fashion but you make tools?"

Felicia laughed. "Yeah, I make tools and other things like truck gears and machinery and airplane parts. Hey, it's a great living. I've got a factory in North Carolina and another in Michigan with my corporate offices in Chantilly, Virginia right by Dulles Airport. We employ almost two thousand people and we're growing like crazy. Thanks to several contracts we have with the federal government. Department of Defense contracts are becoming our lifeblood with the war on terrorism and all."

Hearing Felicia made me feel even more intimidated. She was beautiful, capable and obviously intelligent.

"How did you get into that kind of business?" I asked.

I tried to pretend that I was interested in the tool and die business but my interest was thinly disguised.

"I got my MBA from Wharton and I had a little money and some investors who believed in me. I thought, I don't want to work for nobody. So, I looked around and I found this company that was solid and established but the owner was getting older and was tired of the day-to-day stuff. He was ready to bag it and shut the whole thing down. I came along with a proposal and the rest is history.

We went from one hundred and fifty employees when I first took over to our present level. Our annual revenue is approaching two hundred million dollars. I figure next year we'll start turning big profits. Then I'll sell the company and find something else to do."

She down-shifted and the Porsche whined, let out a high-pitched cry and then deepened into an outright growl like it was fighting being harnessed at low speed. We whipped around a corner, hugging it tight like the car was on a rail. She pulled it out after punching the gear into third and the car lurched forward at nearly seventy miles an hour. My fingers dug into the sides of my seat, making sure that wherever the car would go I'd fly right along with it.

"Nice car," I said.

"Men aren't the only ones who are entitled to have toys," she told me.

Somehow the statement didn't surprise me nor did the aggressive way in which Felicia drove her car. I could tell that she took a back seat to no one, rich and powerful men included.

"Where are we going?" I asked.

Felicia looked over at me. "When's the last time you've been to a spa? Girl's gotta' get pampered."

She returned her eyes to the street, shifted gears and accelerated. We were crossing the Key Street Bridge into Alexandria, Virginia and over to Old Town. All the while I was wrestling with the hair that was blowing all over my head.

"We're going to have to do something about that," Felicia said, looking at my mass of curly hair.

If there was a place for a woman to get pampered it was La Femme Spa, a high-priced world of saunas, massages and some of the top hair stylists on the planet. Felicia walked in like she owned the place and she seemed to be on a first name basis with everyone from the receptionist to the manager.

"Give us the ultimate package," she told a beauty consultant. "And for my young friend here throw in a beauty consultation. I want her to have a total makeover. You know, haircut, perm and makeup."

I looked at Felicia. "Wait a minute!" I said. "Who told you I wanted my hair cut and permed? I can't afford this."

"Trust me. You need this. Besides, if you want to get Mac's attention and make him really hot for you, you'll do everything you can to enhance what you already have—he's very particular, you know."

Felicia reached into her purse and pulled out an American Express Platinum Card. "Don't worry. Mac's treat."

We were led into a dressing room and emerged later wearing robes. A steam sauna helped me get rid of the remnants of my hangover. We followed with a massage, pedicure and manicure. Felicia was taken into another room after we finished the first phase of our royal treatment and I was led away to the salon where my hair was washed and detangled.

"You have beautiful hair," said the Asian woman. I watched her study my hair like a scientist. She was running her fingers through my hair, methodically feeling its texture.

"But, you need it thinned and, maybe, a little tint to bring out color. Don't worry, when we finish, you like, very much."

"Are you the stylist?" I asked her.

"Oh no, Mr. Powell say Mr. Sinclair do hair. I prep you," she answered.

El had told me about Raymond Sinclair, the hair stylist to dignitaries, debutantes and stars from Hollywood and New York. Getting him to work on a woman's hair was like trying to get a private audience with the Queen of England. There was a waiting list for his waiting list.

"You Mackenzie daughter?"

I gave her one of those you must be kidding looks.

"The eyes. You have his eyes," she explained.

"No, I'm not his daughter. We're friends." Then my curiosity took over.

"Do you know Mackenzie Powell?" I asked.

She smiled.

"Everybody know him. He come here, say once, twice a month. You know, manicure, pedicure."

"Does he bring any other women here?" I asked.

"Oh, no. Sometime Ms. Felicia come in but not with him. Act like goddess or something. Nobody here like her. All the ladies here love Mackenzie. Men, too. He so-o-o good-looking."

She had a wishful look planted all over her face, like she had retreated into some kind of fantasy and he was the object of her desires. I watched as her dark, almond-shaped eyes took her to some unspoken, faraway place and I knew that it was time for some fantasy interruptus. I cleared my throat hoping that she'd remember that I was there.

"I sorry," she said. Back to reality, she was fluffing out my hair, using her fingers as combs.

After her assessment of my hair she summoned her team and they attacked it like it was Medusa's writhing snakes, intent to lob off my thick mane and make it more manageable. They combed through it and started cutting my hair in big wads at a time. I couldn't see exactly what they were doing but my stomach balled up into a knot each time a lock of my thick curls fell on the apron draped over me. They gave me a light perm, which tingled but didn't burn the way I'd always heard it does.

When Raymond Sinclair came in I was expecting him to be accompanied by an entourage. I also expected him to be pompous and gay, but he was neither. He was tall, handsome and dark-skinned, which made me feel uneasy about him working on my hair. It was like having a good-looking, gynecologist looking at me with my legs spread wide open and my feet up in stirrups.

He smiled politely, introduced himself, asked about Mackenzie and then asked me about myself. He wanted to know my favorite colors, hobbies and activities, as well as, what I did for a living.

"I treat every woman as a model for a masterpiece. It's not just a matter of style but a look inward so that I can sculpt a style that brings out your essence," he told me. All the while I was thinking that El would be green with envy because she bragged that she had made an appointment with him for June of 2010.

Like a surgeon, Raymond took over and used some kind of comb with blades to rake through my straightened hair. After that, he blew it dry and flat-ironed it into a style that reminded me of the hairdos I admired in beauty magazines. When he finished, the whole team stood there admiring what they'd done. Then they erupted into applause.

I felt a little embarrassed, but also anxious to see the final result. Raymond spun me around to face the mirror as I fumbled for my glasses. My mouth dropped open. The change was so dramatic to the point where I almost didn't recognize myself. What had been a wild, uncontrollable mop of hair that extended past the middle of my back was now a soft, semi-straightened Cleopatra-like hairdo that stopped at my shoulders. Someone said that I was like a moth turning into a butterfly.

"They'll do your makeup next," Raymond told me. "Tell Mac he owes me a round of golf. I want to get my money back. Tell him Lola and I will see him at the fundraiser."

Felicia was in the lobby reading a magazine when I came out and approached without saying anything. She felt my presence as I stood there beaming which caused her to look up momentarily and then at the book sitting on her lap. The double take she gave me said it all.

"Girl, just look at you!" she said.

I struck a pose, did a couple of spins so that my loosened hair would follow and snap back into place. Felicia was beaming like a proud parent watching her child take her first steps.

She said. "Wait until Mac sees you. I think he'll be impressed."

Felicia took my hand and led me out. She looked at me again, trying to fully appreciate the metamorphosis.

"Anyone ever tell you that you have the most beautiful eyes? I mean what are they—green, gray? It's hard to tell with those glasses."

"They're hazel with specks of green." I told her.

"Tomorrow, we make an appointment to see an eye doctor. You should wear contact lenses or get laser surgery."

She was talking like a woman on a mission.

I didn't respond to her directive. I was so excited about my new look that even the suggestion about wearing contact lenses didn't upset me. I was busy looking at my hair and makeup in the car's mirror to the point where I started to imagine how everything would come together if I didn't wear eyeglasses. Felicia watched, amused by my pre-occupation.

"I'll drop you off at home," she said.

I learned a lot about Felicia during the drive home. At forty-two, she had never been married and didn't have any children and never wanted to have any.

"I'm not the domestic type," she said, repeatedly.

Felicia explained that her career was important but not all consuming and she had been successful at it because, in her words, she had achieved perfect balance between her business and personal life. I was tempted to ask her about the little tryst she was involved in the night before at Mac's and to ask her about Desdemona but I chickened out. I also thought about the comment her friend made concerning some girl he was keeping tabs on but like everything else I filed it away with the rest.

"How long have you known, Mac?" I asked.

"Oh, about twenty years. I'll never forget that day I met him. I was walking down the Champs Ely sees and ..."

"The what?" I broke in, displaying my lack of worldliness.

"It's a street in Paris," she replied flatly. "He was the most beautiful man I'd ever seen and I walked right up to him and told him. I was modeling over there and we quickly got involved. I thought that he should model too, even though he was almost forty but the agencies over there said he was too exotic looking."

She laughed with the memory.

"I remember an agent telling Mac that they were looking for an All-American type and he got pissed. Told them, 'America ain't just blonde hair and blue eyes, you French pastry, muthafuckas.' That was the end of his career there." She laughed.

"What did he do then?"

"He got his hustle on. Got me off drugs. He basically saved my life."

"What do you mean, he got his hustle on?" I asked.

Felicia dumbed up on me.

"I probably said too much," she told me. "Let's just say that Mac knows how to make money."

It was almost dark when we got to my place. Felicia said she needed to use the bathroom so she hastily parked her car and followed me inside.

"Your place, it's nice and quaint," she remarked after coming out of the bathroom. "How much did you pay for it? I know. Rude question but I'm just curious."

"Too much." I left her question unanswered, figured that was really too much information. After all, I didn't ask her how much she paid for her Porsche.

Felicia flopped down on the sofa, the picture of a woman relaxed and in repose.

"Nothing takes the edge off like a day at the spa." She paused. "Nothing, except this."

She was reaching into her purse searching for something. Finally, she pulled out a joint and a cigarette lighter.

"I hope you don't mind," she said.

I said nothing but thought, what *can* I say! It wasn't like I'd never seen marijuana before. In fact Stacy and I would smoke on occasion when we were in college. And, of course there's Antoine. But most of all I didn't want to appear to be un-cool around her.

I watched and said nothing as Felicia lit up, took a heavy toke from the joint and exhaled a cloud of smoke that nearly filled my entire living room. She closed her eyes for a moment and leaned back on the couch. She looked back at me and held out the joint for me to take.

"That's O.K. I'll pass. My job drug tests, you know."

"Right," said a skeptical Felicia. "When's the last time you've been tested?"

"Well, I've never been but just in case. There have been some things going on at my job that makes me nervous about doing something like this. And I don't want to risk being random tested one day …"

Felicia cut me off. "You won't be. This is some good stuff, baby. Not that ghetto shit you folks get on the street. This is right from the source."

My resistance was short-circuited by Felicia's seemingly raw power over me, a power I didn't quite understand. I reached out and we traded the joint from her hand to mine. I took a long hit to show her I wasn't afraid and held it inside until my lungs burned. The smoke fast tracked right to my brain and I quickly felt its effect. Playfully and with a good buzz going, I blew smoke into Felicia's face.

We laughed hard and passed the joint back and forth until it nearly burned the tips of our fingers. Felicia was right about one thing—the stuff was unlike anything I'd ever tried. A couple of puffs on a thin rolled up marijuana cigarette had my head swirling and made my body numb. Time seemed to pause as I sat in a sensory stupor unable to speak and hear.

"You're high."

"You damn right, I'm high," Felicia said laughing harder. "And so are you."

"Yeah," was the only word I could utter and force through numbed lips. My mouth hung open, frozen by the effects of the cannabis. Like a character in a *Cheech and Chong* movie I'd blotted out reality and suspended my animation.

Felicia chuckled as if she had told herself a private joke.

"What's so funny, Felicia?" I asked.

She gave a heavy sigh, blew out empty air because she hadn't inhaled anymore smoke.

"You said you've never been in love, Dahlia?"

"Yeah. What about you?"

"Yeah, once and only once."

"Mac?" I asked.

She nodded. Another sigh. "Loving him put a vice grip around my heart. Squeezed out any love I might've given someone else. I had nothing left to give. Even for my poor ex-husband. Problem was, he knew it. Whenever Mac would call me I came running and the poor schmuck I married would sit there and wait for me to come back to him. I felt bad for him and sorry for myself."

"And did Mac love you?" I asked.

"Yeah, in a way. It wasn't on the same level that I loved him. I'm an adult. I knew that. Where I lost the capacity to love anyone else because I loved only him Mac lost his capacity to love me because he loved so many."

The statement confused me and I guess it was showing all over my face.

"Sweetie. Most men have only one great love their entire lives. All the other women are merely infatuations or lustful connections. Mac has truly loved a number of women but has probably never really been in love."

"Oh, so he's a player." I smiled.

Felicia turned to face me. "There's a difference between players and lovers. Players play. Lovers love. Players make love into a game. A true lover of women knows that the heart is nothing to trifle with."

"Then I guess what you're telling me is the fact that Mac didn't love you meant that he was playing you so by your own definition he's a player."

I sat back after the comment and realized I was being too philosophical. Felicia's intuitive senses must've been working overtime because she laughed hard.

"That's what weed does to some people. Makes them think they're Socrates or Plato, reincarnated, when it's just their brain's all fogged up by the drugs. You know, this is your brain and this is your brain on drugs."

I guess getting high did something else to me because I hadn't noticed that Felicia was steadily moving closer to me. Without a word she put one arm around my shoulders and used the other to massage my neck.

"You're still a little tense." She whispered.

I nodded, my eyes closed, my head was spinning.

"You know you're very pretty. I can see why Mac is attracted to you," Felicia told me.

Her voice was soft and breathy as she spoke. "Ever been curious?"

I was so into the moment that I barely heard the question or I didn't understand it.

"Curious about what?"

I felt her warm lips on my bare shoulder. Her free hand moved from massaging my neck, down along my breast and was now resting around my waist. Felicia pulled me at the waist as she moved her own body into position, ready to mount mine. I guess she probably thought that I was too high to be aware of what was happening and with my guard down she thought I was there for the taking.

She pulled my face close to hers, our lips just inches from each other's.

"You are so pretty, Dahlia. So pretty," she whispered and puckered her own sensuous lips ready to taste the sweet nectar of youth that emanated from my mouth. Slowly, Felicia moved closer and closer. My breath stilled. My heart pounded hard.

"I've been wanting to do this since the first time I saw you," she said.

She touched my lips with her own. But feeling her kiss shook me out of my drug-hazed fog. I pulled away disengaging her lips from mine.

"What are you doing?" I asked.

My tone made it clear that the advance wasn't welcomed.

But she was undeterred. "C'mon. Don't you ever wonder how it would feel to be with another woman instead of some man treating you like a piece of meat? You should know that nobody knows a woman like another woman and nobody knows how to *satisfy* a woman like another woman."

"So, you're telling me that you're a lesbian, right?"

I leaned back and put some distance between us to take some of the starch out of Felicia's advances.

"No. I'm not a lesbian. I just don't put labels on myself. I am whatever I want to be for the moment. For me, there's a time for men and there is a time for women. It's what I want when I want it," Felicia said. I could feel her conviction in her words.

She was annoyingly matter-of-fact about my reaction as though she was testing me. Maybe it was the drugs but for some strange reason I thought about one of the cats we had on my stepfather's farm, the one that teased and toyed with field mice before devouring them. The cat would trap them with his paws then let them go free momentarily and play for hours. Eventually he would tire of the game, grab hold of their tales, toss them in the air and swallow them whole. His power and self-indulgent sense of superiority over the mice made him the fattest and happiest cat on the farm. I wondered whether Felicia, like that old cat, was just doing this for sport or was she really hungry.

I amazed myself with my own sense of calm about being hit on by another woman. This had never happened to me before. I wasn't upset or flattered and ambivalence was an inadequate description. As beautiful as Felicia was I wasn't attracted to her.

"Well, I'm not there," I told her. "Call me naïve or stupid or even, country but I'll just stick to men."

I was defensive but I stayed calm.

"Oh, sweetie, you are what you are," Felicia replied.

Her voice was soothing and smooth like butter.

"That's all anyone can be in this life. I just figured that a young sister like yourself would be open—given what you have to work with. From what I hear most young brothers are either in prison, on their way to prison or gay. Face it, your choices are limited and if you think latching on to some older man like Mackenzie is the answer, then you really got a lot to learn, baby."

I was O.K. until she mentioned Mac. The comment upset me. Latching on is for leeches and I never thought I was one.

"I think you better leave," I said.

Felicia's reaction was swift. She stood up, adjusted her dress and headed directly for the door. I sat there fastened to the sofa, refusing to move. But I still watched as she stopped in the doorway with one foot inside and her pride standing in the hall.

"I'd be very careful dealing with Mac if I were you," she warned. "Oh, and please do me a favor. Don't tell him about what happened here today, alright?"

She gave my place a visual once-over like she was looking for something or trying to remember the way it looked.

"Love the old quilt you got hanging on the wall. So quaint."

Felicia slowly closed the door behind her and I heard the clicking of her high heel shoes against the hall's marble floors. Listened as the sound diminished with each step until I heard the elevator chime and realized that she would take a slow ride to the first floor and I hoped out of my life.

Day Eleven

Love is a chasm, cut deep into the soul's core and virtually impossible to cross. I built a bridge made of reeds and twigs that would bend with the wind, but not break under the burden. To traverse its span was hard, at first, but in time I learned to steady my feet, gain ground and complete the journey.

Songs of Desdemona—10/10/05

Writing prose has become the better way to express my thoughts. Hoping that whoever reads my memoir will reach beneath the surface to the depth of my spirit and explore my soul. In it you will know and understand.

There is nothing to do here inside these four walls but ponder my fate and explore my thoughts; memorializing them on the pages of this notebook gives me a measure of immortality. I realize that I digress from my story but I know it's the tenth day since I started and my pen is not guided by fingers but by heart and soul. I write, therefore, as I'm directed. Between writing and telling Chiang Mai my story I am re-vitalized with hope.

◆   ◆   ◆

I had expected to hear from Mac the Monday following my spa visit with Felicia. He had all of my telephone numbers—job, cell phone and home but he didn't call. I decided that he was probably busy, making deals or doing whatever he did as, "a collector". But not hearing from him dampened my enthusiasm about "The New Dahlia" that I was anxious to show him and it drove me crazy because I couldn't stop thinking about him.

I rushed home from work that day hoping that he had called and left a message. My anxiety level rose when I entered my building. I thought of my answering machine's familiar refrain, "There are no new messages."

I could hear my telephone ringing as I approached my apartment door. I fumbled with my keys as I clumsily unlocked it. The telephone sat on an end table right beside my sofa and I literally dove for it with an outstretched arm. "Hello," I answered.

"Hi, darling Dahlia," came an exaggerated greeting. It was Felicia. My heart sank. I know she heard it in my voice.

"Oh, Hi."

"Well, aren't we the chipper one? Hard day at work? Not a problem. Look, I'll be brief. You have an appointment for tomorrow to be fitted for your contact lenses."

I said nothing, allowing my brain to process what I was hearing. I recalled Felicia had mentioned something about contacts that day we went to the spa but I got high and I didn't take her seriously. Now things were clear and I wasn't sure it was a good idea.

I thought about everything that had happened during the last week or two. The dresses, the makeover and now contact lenses, things I couldn't afford to do for myself and now I was beginning to feel overwhelmed by it all, swept away and fearful of being lost in Mac's wake. And what about Mac?

"Are you Mac's secretary? Why doesn't he call me himself?"

Felicia laughed like she was amused by my question. "Mac's out of the country and I'm sure he'll want to see you when he gets back," she told me.

She continued un-phased by my indifference. "Everything's set up for you. Just show up for your appointment and they'll take good care of you. Bye, Sweetie." Click.

I sunk into the sofa still clutching the telephone close to my stomach. I thought about calling my therapist but the situation wasn't exactly an emergency so I turned on the television just to have as background noise and I sat there trying to process the things that were gradually changing my world.

It was six o'clock and the evening news was on the television. *Seven more soldiers are dead at the hands of insurgents. President Bush still insists that Saddam Hussein had weapons of mass destruction. Police find a burglar stuck in the heating duct at a local department store. And police have no clues about the man found shot to death behind a local nightclub. Details right after this.*

I grabbed the remote and hit the mute button. Didn't want to hear any bad news. I decided to call Stacy.

Derek answered the telephone, which didn't come as a surprise because he always seemed to be there screening Stacy's calls. It was no secret that he was possessive and a tad bit insecure but I knew that he had no reason to be that way. Stacy loved him and she wasn't the kind of woman to stray anyway. However, after a year of living together she was becoming frustrated with his attitude.

Derek and Stacy were the same age but she always thought that he was a little immature, calling him "young in the mind" because of his possessiveness.

"Hi, Derek," I greeted him in my usual friendly way.

"Wuzzup, Dahl?"

Derek had taken up Stacy's pet name, which I interpreted as a term of endearment. No matter what complaints Stacy might have had about him, I always thought he was a good man.

"Nothing much. Just trying to catch up with my girl."

"Yeah, she's here. Hey, you all right? I mean, you were pretty twisted the other night at your dude's party," Derek asked. There was genuine concern in his voice.

I sighed. "Yeah, I'm cool. Guess I got a little carried away."

"Yeah, I'll say. We didn't want to leave you there but you were so out of it and old boy told us to go on. I mean he was like your daddy or something, the way he was taking care of you. You know, overly protective. So we left. Hey, I gotta' tell you, he's real smooth. I hope I'm that way when I'm old. Anyway, I'll get Stace. Later."

I waited. Glanced up at the television. Dead soldiers' pictures on display, fresh faced and too young to die.

I could hear Derek shouting for Stacy and her impatient-laden reply.

"Damn! Derek! You don't have to yell! I'll be right there."

"Her royal-freaking-highness is coming," Derek told me.

"I got it."

I heard Stacy's words as she grabbed the telephone from Derek.

"What's up, Dahl?"

Judging from the tone of Stacy's voice it was clear she was agitated.

"You alright?" I asked.

Yeah, I'm fine. It's just Derek," Stacy answered.

I could hear the exasperation in her voice.

"Sometimes he just pisses me off. I mean, it's like he's real insecure and I have to go to New York for a dinner they're having for all the nominees and, like, he say's, 'What about me? Can I roll too?' And I tell him that it's nothing that will interest him. Besides, I'm just going for the weekend and what does he do? He pouts like a little boy."

"Well, at least *he* wants to be with you." I told her.

"Are you talking about Antoine or Mac?" Stacy's voice softened.

"Mac."

"Now that's a real man! Girl, I don't care how old he is. The brother is smooth and just plain ol' fine. I bet if y'all hook up he won't be chasing you around, checking your purse to see if you got condoms every time you leave the house or getting upset because your career is moving faster than his. Talkin' bout, 'the black man is at the bottom of the totem pole.' Give me a break!" She was ratcheting up the volume and the pitch in her voice again.

"Calm down, Stacy," I said.

I glanced up again at the TV. Saw the chaos in the desert. Blood and bombs.

I wanted to change the subject so that Derek could get off the whipping post.

"Girl, you should see me. I got a complete makeover, hair, nails, facial—the works. I went to La Femme Spa and Salon."

"You did? I thought you were broke. That must've been expensive. What? You decided to go deeper into debt?"

"Mac treated me," I said.

I was talking to Stacy and watching the screen. 'Double-U-Bush' was on now trying to look confident but not fooling anyone. He's aged at least fifteen years compared to the six he's been in office.

My thoughts shifted back to Stacy. I expected her to say something like she wished that Derek could be like Mac, but I headed her off at the pass.

"Now, don't compare him to Derek because that's not fair. O.K.? Mac's established. He's rich. I'm sure it took him a while to get where he is."

Stacy sighed heavily. "You're right. I guess I have to be patient. Maybe, I can groom Derek to be like Mac," she said.

"Well, Mac's not perfect, Stace. Guess what he wants me to do?"

"Give him a BJ?" Stacy said, laughing.

"No, girl! He wants me to get contact lenses."

"So, what's wrong with that? You know your blind ass can't see a damn thing without your glasses and speaking of glasses, do you really know how you look with them on? No offense but I've been telling you for years that those are the ugliest glasses I've ever seen. C'mon, Dahl. You can do better. You're so pretty but the glasses do nothing for you." Stacy ranted.

"I don't have a problem with the idea of wearing contact lenses. I used to but I'm thinking that with my new hairdo and all it will just complete the transformation. My problem is that he's going to pay for it," I explained.

"Girl, from where I'm standing you don't have a problem. Accept it. He can afford it. I bet he spends more money treating some of those high-powered friends of his to lunch. Dahlia, I'm not saying you gotta be like El and slut yourself around for gifts but if the brother's willing then go for it. He hasn't even tried to get inside your panties and that's a big change from anyone you've ever dealt with. All those guys want to screw you for nothing."

"You're right. You're right, Stacy but it just seems too much, especially at this early stage in our relationship, if you can call it that. I mean I get suspicious, like, what does he want from me? You know, I remember a story about this guy once who was like wining and dining young girls and then selling them into slavery and sending them to the Middle East and no one ever heard about them again."

Stacy laughed. "Girl, you're just paranoid. Like I said, accept it. The man's being nice. You should've seen the way he took care of you the other night when you got drunk. He was so-o-o-o protective. He hardly fits the mold of some white-slaving pimp."

"Yeah, like that one guy. Remember? Shortie B? The one with the hairdo like Little Richard who used to hang around the bus station in Valdosta trying to pick up runaway girls. Remember?" I added.

Stacy quickly joined in.

"Yeah, dude drove that old beat up truck with the chrome rims that were worth more than his ride."

We laughed hard as we conjured up Shortie B's image and every stereotyped caricature of the old school black man as a pimp image, gold teeth and all. But I didn't call Stacy to wax nostalgic.

"I'm confused, Stacy."

"About what?"

"It's Mac. I know I just met him but I have this strong attraction that I don't understand. It's like I've known him before and I find myself thinking about him all the time. But I don't know if the feeling's mutual."

"Relax, Dahlia. Just go with the flow. You know how you get anxious about things. Just let it happen."

I thought about what Stacy said and I knew she was right but my insecurities were taking over and the doubts controlled everything.

"He has other women in his life. There's Felicia, who I shouldn't worry about because I saw her screwing someone else that night at Mac's house. And then there's Regina."

"Who?"

"This actress who was killed years ago."

Stacy laughed. "You're worried about a dead woman."

"Silly, isn't it. But I think he still carries something for her. And then there's some woman named, Desdemona I heard Felicia talking about. It's crowded around him."

"You shouldn't worry. He's obviously interested. Just be your sweet self and everything will be fine."

I thought about what my friend told me and realized that I was getting stressed out over things I couldn't control. If I pressed the issue with Mac and tried to force myself on him I'd scare him away. I decided to relax and let things take their course. Then my thoughts shifted. I wanted to tell Stacy about the FBI and Antoine but I wasn't sure how I'd start.

"Some weird things have been happening to me lately, Stacy," I said.

"Like what?"

"Well, the other day I was on the train on my way to work and there was this man who kept staring at me but every time I'd look over at him he'd look away. But the really weird part was when he got off at the Pentagon station and I swear he was following me. And then he suddenly disappeared."

"Girl, you are being paranoid. He was just some guy who thinks you're cute. It happens to me all the time," she laughed.

"But that's not all, Stacy. Two FBI agents came to my job to talk to me."

Dead silence.

"Stacy? Are you still there?"

"Yeah, just thinking about what you said. I mean, why?"

"They say they're investigating Antoine and some kind of smuggling enterprise he's involved in."

Stacy laughed. "You told them they're crazy, right?"

"Basically, but somehow he opened up a bank account in Antigua in my name and there's two hundred and fifty thousand dollars in it and I guess they think I'm laundering money for Antoine and his boys."

"Well, we both know that's bullshit. Hell, if you'd been doing something like that you wouldn't be as broke as you are right now."

"Tell me about it. I'm not really worried about it, its just that they've been spying on me, following me, I think and they even got into my computer somehow and told me that some wire transfers had been made from it. They told me that they don't believe that I've done anything wrong but that they're watching me."

"Did you tell Antoine?"

"Yeah, he laughed about it. Said they're fishing and that he put the money in my account because it was from some investors who are supporting his music projects."

"Well, be careful, Dahlia. I always thought that there was something shady about Antoine. You talk to El about this?"

"No. I figured it would be a conflict of interest considering the fact that she works for the government. I don't want to get her into any trouble. She's a lawyer but her client is Uncle Sam."

"Let me see what I can find out. I'll snoop around and maybe I can get some answers," Stacy said.

"Be careful. The agents said that some of Antoine's associates are hardcore and violent."

Stacy laughed. "Girl, they can't be as bad as some of the international crooks I've been investigating. Besides, you haven't done anything wrong."

"But, it's still a problem. I mean this administration doesn't have a problem invading folk's privacy. They do it all in the name of national security. So what if they check my records again and next time get it right. I'll be fired for sure even if I'm not invovled," I said.

"We'll just have to cross that bridge when we get to it, Dahlia. You can't worry about it. Besides, do you really want to work for the Feds for the rest of your life? Look, I've read some of your poetry and other stuff you've written and I just think you're a wonderful and creative spirit. Right now I think you're wasting your talent tracking numbers and spitting out generic reports on terrorists and spies."

That was Stacy, always philosophical and real, the voice of sanity in a crazy setting. Her grounded Afro-centric, holistic being had always been my rock. I took a deep breath and mulled over the things she said.

"Thanks, Stacy," I said.

"For what?"

"For just being there. I love you."

"I love you, too. Now tell me about your girl, Felicia. You mean you actually saw her having sex at Mac's house? That is so scandalous. And you mean to tell me that they were talking some kind of spy type stuff? Tracking some young girl? That is so scandalous...."

I hung up thinking about our sisterhood. I hit the remote and turned up the volume on the television, let reports of death and destruction filter their way back into my world. The reporter was talking in front of Café Alexandria with file footage wrapped around his live report.

A large body draped in a white sheet, no face on display and the reporter's words: *Police have no leads or information on the man identified only as a black male, age 30 to 40. Height six-foot, four inches tall, weight 270 pounds. If anyone has any information please contact the Washington homicide unit.*

◆   ◆   ◆

Talking to Stacy lifted my spirits. I decided that I'd heed her advice and stay cool.

Later that evening my telephone rang and a man's voice on the other end identified himself by saying, "Hello, it's Mackenzie Powell," in a most formal manner.

"Hi," I said. My spirit and attitude heightened.

"Sorry, I hadn't called. I'm in Bangkok, Thailand right now on business but I was thinking about you," he told me.

I closed my eyes and listened to him on the telephone, allowed the bass laden vibration in his voice to touch me and send shivers through my body.

"It's good to hear from you," I said.

"Felicia taking good care of you, I hope."

I gave him a reticent "yes" but I wanted to tell Mac about the advances she made towards me. I thought about it but it really wasn't that deep and I suffered no harm from what she tried to do.

"Look, I'll be back in D.C. in a couple of days. I'd like to see you," Mac said. "There's a fundraiser at the Smithsonian. Will you be my date?"

I thought: *How many ways can I say, yes?*

When he hung up I had a smile not only on my face but on the inside, as well. I thought about how he had referred to himself as Mackenzie during the conversation and decided that's what I would call him. Not Mac but Mackenzie. I said his name repeatedly, allowing it to roll off my tongue and adding emphasis to the "Z". I loved the sound.

Day Eleven

*I remember gazing into the mirror like Pygmalion's pre-occupation with Galatea brought to life by love's obsession as though seeing myself, for the very first time. That was the way I felt the first time I wore contact lenses. It **was** like seeing myself for the very first time, my face unobstructed. But the contact lenses I once wore are now replaced by eyeglasses even uglier than my old ones. A "gift" of the Thai prison system.*

Songs of Desdemona—10/15/05

My first adventure with my "new eyes" would be to put on eyeliner, a hint of mascara and eye shadow the way the makeup artist at La Femme had shown me. I selected azure colored eye shadow to contrast with my hazel-colored eyes. I carefully brushed it above them one at a time, used my fingers to smooth and blend it in. Next came the eyeliner.

I used the foundation that had been specially mixed at La Femme. They said it matched my honey-brown complexion and wouldn't make me look washed out or black faced. Since it was an after-six date I chose a dark ruby red lipstick that made my full lips more sumptuous and more inviting than I'd ever seen them.

I modified the hairstyle designed by the salon with an upswept French roll with bangs in the front and long curly tresses that fell down the sides of my face starting at each temple. The bangs and tresses created a border for my face like a picture frame designed to draw the viewer right to my eyes.

My dress and jewelry would be the final brush strokes that would comprise the masterpiece that I was trying hard to be. Again, gifts from Mackenzie and delivered by messenger to my door. I accepted the gifts without protesting. But when I opened the box that contained a set of pear shaped diamond earrings weighing about three carats each, I was stunned. *Maybe they're fake,* I thought. But I already knew him to be a man of style and impeccable taste—they were real.

Other than senior prom, I had never gone to a formal affair and here I was getting ready like Cinderella for the Mayor's Ball, which was an annual fundraiser for the Associated Black College Fund. It was fitting that this would be the first time I would see Mac since the debacle of my drunken state at his party. I was determined to make amends for that night and like a latter day debutante I would make this my coming out party.

A few last minute touches. I glanced at the clock. It was show time. Mac would be here within the next five minutes. I tried to stay calm but it was almost impossible. My mind raced with thoughts about whether he would like the way I looked and whether I was kidding myself to think that I could be in that class of women he was accustomed to dating. But my greater anxiety was about how the evening would go and whether I would end up wrapped in his arms at night's end. For that part I hoped I was ready.

I told myself to relax and with the help of a glass of Merlot I was doing just that. I was giddy with excitement and I couldn't wait to see him. I hadn't been on a real date in a long time and now I was being picked up by a man who kept me from sleeping because I couldn't get him out of my thoughts. I paced around my living room then sat down on the sofa. When my leg bounced uncontrollably I got up and paced some more.

The sound of my buzzer made me jump up from my seat. I sat there trying to stay cool. I counted to ten, stood up and turned on the security monitor. I could see a tall man's image on the screen. "It's Mackenzie," he said. I decided to meet him downstairs.

"I'll be right down," I shouted into the speaker.

One last look in the mirror and the usual systems check and it was time to go. I opened my purse as I waited for the elevator. I wanted to make sure I had everything I needed for the night. A date-kit, El called it. It consisted of makeup, keys, twenty dollars in case of an emergency and cell phone along with the pack of condoms, just in case. Better to be safe than sorry, El told me.

Mac was talking and laughing with the concierge when the elevator door opened. He was dressed to the nines again, wearing a tuxedo that said Armani all over it. For a moment my heart seemed to stand still. I seemed to float right to him as my heart jumpstarted and the scent of his cologne enveloped me. I admit it. I was in awe of him.

I made a quick comparison between Mac and Antoine and the younger man's baggy pants, low-slung, hip-hop style was no match for the debonair Mackenzie Powell. I guess I must've had a smile on my face that could light up Las Vegas but I couldn't suppress it.

Mac was beaming, too. His eyes twinkled and those deep dimples cut through me. He shook his head in disbelief.

"My, my, you look magnificent," he said.

"And so do you, Mr. Powell," I replied, feigning a formal demeanor. "But you did something different, didn't you?" I gasped. "You shaved your head! Oh my, god!"

An unruffled Mac said, "A temporary change. The hair will grow back. I wanted to get rid of some of the gray so I could look younger when I'm hanging out with you."

I could tell that he was joking. Whatever reason he had for changing his appearance I was sure that it was a good one. Besides, he looked even better with a baldhead like an older version of Boris Kodjoe. I stared at his face and head.

"It's a good thing your head isn't shaped funny," I laughed.

Mac diverted the attention back to me. He seemed to be overwhelmed at the final result of his and Felicia's efforts. He gave me a once over, smiled admiringly and winked at the concierge.

"Forget about me. Just look at you!" Mac said.

The concierge was equally surprised and impressed by what he saw.

"If you don't mind me saying Ms. Reynolds, you look absolutely stunning this evening," he said. Turning to Mac he added, "You're a very lucky man, Sir."

Mac smiled politely and extended his arm to me and led me to the Bentley parked by the door. This was the Cinderella story coming to life, the way I had imagined as a child and with all the trappings—beautiful peasant girl with a handsome prince being carried away in a modern chariot. I thought, if only Stacy, El and my mother could see me now.

"I've lived in this building for over a year and that's the first time Boris over there at the security desk ever noticed me," I whispered to Mac as we left the building.

"His loss," Mac replied.

Mac hurried ahead to open the car door, letting me glide into the seat, pulling the train of my dress behind. He sat behind the steering wheel for what seemed like hours admiring the finished product.

"You are the most beautiful woman I've ever seen," he said.

I was feeling giddy about the whole experience and the only thing I could say was, "More beautiful than Felicia?"

Mac laughed. "No comparison."

His response made me feel good and added to my newfound sense of confidence. My eyes were on him as he shifted the car into gear and drove off. He wasn't wearing the Breitling watch he wore the first time I saw him, switching to a more formal Cartier dress watch. Shoes by Prada and diamond studs for cufflinks. I inhaled the air in the car and caught the sent of his cologne.

"What are you wearing? I mean, you smell good. What cologne are you wearing?" I asked.

"Acqua Di Gio."

He drove onto the Beltway and then took the Baltimore-Washington Parkway towards downtown Washington. Cruising with the sunroof open and the music of Miles Davis as a backdrop to our conversation, we talked about everything from his last trip oversees to his upbringing and his life in general. I found out that he was a Southerner, like me.

"I was born in 1955 and raised in Lafayette, Louisiana," Mac responded to my question.

1955! It seemed like a million years ago.

"My mother and father were both Creoles. All mixed up with African, French, Chinese and Cajun roots like a big pot of gumbo, which is one of my favorite foods. You like gumbo? What about crawfish etoufee?"

I shook my head. I was from Georgia. All meat and potatoes.

"You have any other family?" I asked.

"I have a son about your age."

I don't know why but I was surprised by this revelation. For some reason I had figured Mac as a man with no real family ties. I thought about a few younger men I'd dated who had small children and I swore I'd never get caught up in the cycle of child and mother with me on the outside looking in.

"What about his mother? Were you married?"

"No, hardly knew each other. I was young and dumb, touring the South with the band. There were always women for comfort between stops and I was very irresponsible not protecting myself, Now I have a son that I hardly know."

Mac sank down into the driver's seat, his body language a reflection of his regrets. There was pain there, thick and opaque yet incongruent like honey and vinegar. I thought maybe it was an act like he really didn't care because he was a man who had everything material. Some wayward bastard child would have been a speed-bump on his road to fortune. I stopped myself, shamed by the thought.

"You have any other children?" I asked.

Mac started to speak but hesitated for a moment. I thought about a musician's life—women in every town and fertilizing the countryside like Johnny Appleseed. He turned his eyes away from the road and directed them right into mine. "No. I don't have any other children," he said.

I wanted to shift gears. I was intrigued by Mac's music background. He told me how the group he played with had been the opening act for some legendary artists like, James Brown and Ray Charles, as well as, The Rolling Stones.

"Why aren't you involved in music now? You're really good, Mackenzie."

"I left when the music died," he responded.

His comment puzzled me. Music wasn't dead, as far as, I was concerned. Mac explained.

"Disco killed R & B in the 80's and Rap music buried it. I put down my horn back then and didn't look back for a long time. I gave up music and tried something else."

"I guess it's a generational thing. There's a big gap between your music and my music," I said.

He smiled. "Light years."

"What about your son? Does he share your interests in music or has he been co-opted by hip-hop like the rest of the people in my generation?" I was being purposely sarcastic but I didn't want to offend him.

Mac shifted his body in his car seat, gave the world out there an uncomfortable smile, his face turning grim. I could tell talking about his son was uncomfortable.

"I wasn't around him much as he grew up. I've tried to make up for my absence, sending him to an Ivy League college and supporting him right now even though he graduated with honors in Economics. He's a little lost, uncertain about what he wants to do with his life. I'm hoping that someday he'll go to law school."

Mac sounded like a man talking to himself and not caring who was listening or what he said. I detected a tone of melancholy in his words that broadcast his pain. I guess I pre-judged him by thinking he didn't care.

"Tell me about you, Dahlia Reynolds," Mac said. He wanted to change the subject.

I knew there wasn't much to tell but he probably knew that considering my age. I used to wax poetic, comparing my life to a novel in its first chapter. The rest was waiting to be written.

"What about your father? Felicia told me that he died before you were born but your mother must've talked about him, didn't she?"

Reminded of me of my conversation with Felicia, I regretted not going with my instincts that told me not to share much information about my personal life. I had my own kind of pain. But the door had been opened. Maybe this was the therapy I needed.

"Yeah. My mother talked about him all the time before she got married to my stepfather. He was a musician, too."

"How'd he die?" Mac asked.

"He was killed in a car accident rushing back from being on the road in Alabama to be with my mother. She had gone into labor and he was trying to get back to Georgia in time for my birth."

"I'm sorry to hear that," Mac said.

I knew that it was the usual obligatory condolence given when there's nothing better to say.

"My mother says that I look like him with my eyes and all. My father met her in what they called a "jook joint" and it was basically a one-night stand. But he called her months later and found out then that she was pregnant and that's when he told her that he wanted to be there for my birth. I really believe that if he had lived they would've been married and we would've been a family."

"You miss that, don't you?"

"More than anything. I used to dream about him when I was a little girl and sometimes, even now. And I would imagine him coming home after playing with his band and coming into my bedroom with a guitar and singing me a lullaby. And I'd fall asleep not worrying about any ghosts or demons, knowing that my father was in the next room."

Mac's comment about missing my father reminded me of the conversation I'd had with Antoine and I thought about the coincidence of the two men asking me the same question. I guess in some strange way they were echoing the same sentiment, as though somehow not having a father made me less than whole.

I laughed nervously, embarrassed by what I told Mac. Dreams of my father had always been the secrets of a little girl held close. I never shared them with anyone before.

We rode along silent after that, allowing the music from the car's CD player to carry us to our destination. The conversation had been too serious and ill timed and I was beginning to regret ever saying anything about my father. After all, we were on our way to a night of fun and magic and I knew that we were going to have a good time.

I wanted to lighten the mood again, to talk about something else during this uneasy moment.

"I like your music. Who's playing?"

"Charles Mingus. Ever heard of him?"

"No."

"Didn't think so." Mac laughed a little. "He died before you were born. You like jazz?"

"Hadn't really got into it that much."

I thought about seeing Mac at the jazz club before we actually met and how I didn't go there for the music.

"I like hip-hop. You know, 50 Cent, Tupac, stuff like that."

More laughter. "Like I said, rap ruined music. That's my opinion. But there are some I kinda dig. You know, Tupac was a poet. Had something to say. Nas and Common, I can relate. I once opened for the Last Poets in Pittsburgh."

"I don't really care about the words it's the beat that moves me," I paused. "Who are The Last Poets?" I asked.

Mac laughed again. "I guess there's really a generation gap between us. The Last Poets were just that, poets. They spoke of revolution and taking a stand against America's oppressive and segregationist policies. They were anti-King, pro-Malcolm, no bullshit, brothers. Their rap was more than inane rhetoric. Hip-hop, on the other hand has no political center. It's just chatter." He paused. "It doesn't bother you when some rap artists call women, 'bitches' and 'hoes'?"

"Like I said, it's the beat I like."

I guess I was being a little defensive because I grew up thinking that rap and hip-hop was uniquely a part of African-American culture and was just as credible as jazz or the Blues.

Mac shook his head. "I guess that's a symptom of your generation. For me, music has to speak to me. Convey a message like Gil-Scott Heron or touch me emotionally. Mingus is melancholy. Coltrane is spiritual. Miles is adventurous and Monk is frenetic. I play them according to my mood at the time. Not the other way around."

"Well, you all had Gil Scott-Heron and we have Jill Scott," I countered. I thought about what he told me how his mood dictated his music. I said, "So, are you melancholy now?"

"A little bit. But I'll get over it."

My impulses were now dictating my mood. I wanted to reach out and touch him, hold his right hand that was resting casually on the car's console, feel his smooth skin that had been re-worked into soft leather with a few fine lines that distinguished its character from the new. Most of all I wanted his hands to touch me, to feel his smooth hands that had been pampered by success unsoiled and unmarked. The thought made me warm inside, made my juices boil inside my own little cauldron. I had to shake myself before I overflowed.

Mac's voice was my salvation. "We're here," he said.

I wanted to delve into his feelings and play amateur shrink but we were approaching the Smithsonian Institute, the venue for the fundraiser and I figured the mood inside would be festive so it was time to lighten up. I was hoping that there would be plenty of time to get to know the real Mackenzie Powell.

Once again, I was in awe of my surroundings. Mac's party had its share of beautiful and sophisticated people but these were the crème de la crème. The Smithsonian's main exhibit hall had been transformed into a Las Vegas styled casino and the sounds of roulette wheels and people laughing dominated the scene. There was a receiving line at the entrance to the great room where the banquet would be held. I could see the very recognizable Mayor Huff schmoozing with people who were a part of a long line of well-wishers trying to curry his favor.

At the mayor's side was his wife who was almost as recognizable as her husband, a result of her charitable work in the D.C. area. When people said that she was "the First Lady of Washington" it wasn't simply because she was married to the mayor but because she had established her own identity and was an icon in the community. And many people referred to her as the "unofficial mayor". From everything I'd heard about Elisabeth Huff it was certain that she could be a dominating figure.

My eyes were still on her when Mac said, "C'mon, I'll introduce you to the mayor and his wife."

Mac's words caused me to recoil as apprehension gripped me. It must've been obvious because the deer-caught-in-the-headlights expression on my face grabbed His attention and he calmly placed my hand in his.

There were other dignitaries to meet and greet in the line and they all seemed to know Mac, greeting him as "Mac" or "Mackenzie" and not "Mr. Powell." There were backslaps and a few eyebrows raised when he introduced me. Most of the women were gracious and complimentary but some seemed to twist their mouths in disapproval. I could only imagine what they were thinking.

When we finally arrived at the end of the receiving line I felt like my chin would drop off from all the smiling I did just to get there. But I was learning this is what people do in high society and I had to be resolute in my own graciousness—even if my smile had to be painted on my face.

Although Mac and the mayor had just seen each other at Mac's party the two men acted like a couple of schoolboys getting together for the first time after summer vacation.

"Mackenzie, my man. Every woman wants him. Every man wants to be him." Mayor Huff's smile was so wide I thought his jaws might break.

Theirs was a genuine heartfelt embrace and animated handshakes. Both men laughed loud and without pretense, as the mayor whispered something in Mac's ear. Mac responded aloud, "Man, you're crazy." He toned it down when he approach Mrs. Huff.

"It's good to see you, Mackenzie," Elisabeth Huff told him after planting a polite kiss on both sides of his face.

"The pleasure is mine, Elisabeth," he replied. "As usual, you have outdone yourself, putting this soiree together. I think we'll meet our goals for this year's scholarship fund."

"You better believe we will. We have generous people like you to thank." Mrs. Huff turned to face me. "And who is this lovely young lady, Mackenzie? Your daughter?"

Mac smiled but the remark made me uncomfortable. I assumed that Mrs. Huff was being sarcastic. I figured she knew Mac well enough to know that he didn't have a daughter. It was clear that the dig was intended only for him but it made me want to run.

Despite her remark that bordered on being snide, Mrs. Huff gave me the warmest smile and took my hand.

"It's so nice to meet you, dear. You are so lovely. How did you wind up with an old wolf like Mackenzie Powell? Don't try to explain. I know we'll talk, some-day," she told me, whispering in my ear.

We shuffled past the receiving line and right into the banquet hall where there must've been about a thousand tables with crystal wine glasses, bottles of cham-pagne on ice for centerpieces and the finest china and silverware. A gentleman standing at the door promptly escorted us to a table near the front where the dais had been set up especially for the mayor and other dignitaries. There was a plac-ard on the table that read, "Mackenzie Powell" in big, bold letters and there were dinner settings for the ten people designated as his guests.

Gradually, the banquet room filled with people walking around looking for their tables. Mac greeted his guests and spoke to everyone at the surrounding tables. Raymond Sinclair, the man responsible for my new and improved image, winked at me and discreetly mouthed the words, *Love your hair* as he embraced Mac and helped his wife to her seat at the table. This was Washington's black high society at its best.

They were all doing what I always imagined business people and dignitaries do and I was feeling a little out of place when I overheard them talking about exotic vacations, summer homes and kids away at private schools. I realized that this was Mac's moment and I was content to quietly allow him to soak it all in. I picked up the program in front of me and started reading. There was a list of contributors on the last page divided according to the amount of money they'd given to the scholarship fund.

There was a category listed for people and corporations that had contributed between one hundred to two hundred and fifty thousand dollars and among them was the name, Mackenzie Powell. I was impressed. *This man is too good to be true.* Seeing his name reminded me of what he told me when I first marveled over his home and what he had accomplished with his life.

"With much given, much is expected." Mac said that was his credo.

The evening was full of people giving kudos to the mayor and his wife, along with recognition of a number of young students. Most had been guaranteed hundreds of thousands of dollars in scholarships and I thought about how lucky they were not to have to rely on loans to get through college.

Every once in awhile I would steal a glance in Mac's direction, watching him interact with people at his table and wondering about the possibilities a relationship with him might bring. There was an undeniable pull towards him, an attraction that was beyond physical but I wasn't certain about its source. I just knew it was there.

I guess he had sensed my stares because he reacted as though he was in sync with my private thoughts and returned my stolen glances with a look of his own, his eyes piercing, face unsmiling but lacking malice. It seemed like he was sizing me up. Those awkward moments when people are trying to get to know one another.

I concluded that I wasn't savvy enough to read him but there was this sexual tension surrounding us and I knew that I was its source. I figured that there was only one way to find out whether the feeling was mutual. If I had to I'd seduce him. The thought made me increasingly impatient and ready to leave but the night was still young. I realized that I would have to turn up the pressure.

My designer dress was a slinky silver number and stylish but not especially revealing. Although it had a plunging neckline there was a sequined shawl that covered my cleavage. It had slits on each side that shot up to my hips but were fastened together by sequined buttons all the way down to my calves. It was a beautiful dress but I wondered why Mac selected something that I thought was un-sexy. I laughed thinking that he probably didn't want his important friends to think that he was going out with some young hoochie mama or worse, a paid escort.

Well, they're going to have to think whatever they think. It was time to bring out the big guns. With an "excuse me" I made my way to the ladies' room to "powder my nose" like they say on television.

There was an older woman already in the bathroom with her face in the mirror adjusting the red lipstick that had seeped up into the thin lines above her mouth. I watched the woman probably too long. And she noticed me.

"Someday, you'll have this problem," she said, flatly.

Her comment made me retreat into one of the bathroom stalls. Whatever, she was saying was years from now and I was in the present.

I removed the shawl, wrapped it into a belt and tied it around my waist. It had the effect I was looking for, making my waist look even smaller while accentuating my hips. Next, I unbuttoned the sequined fasteners that had closed the dress's slits to expose my long legs to the middle of my thighs. With a quick adjustment of my thong panties I was ready for my own grand entrance.

The older woman had gone by the time I came out of the stall and now alone it was time to freshen my makeup. I pouted my lips to apply a new coat of lipstick. A pushup of my bra and a final look in the mirror told me I was ready.

I turned and headed for the door when I almost walked right into someone standing there, watching. It was Felicia. I didn't hear her come in so she caught me off guard. My immediate reaction was to flash a weak smile and keep walking but Felicia blocked my path.

"Well, well. It's the little farm girl turned diva," Felicia said. "I saw you come in here and I must say that I totally underestimated you."

I frowned and tried to sidestep her but she moved directly into my path.

"I don't know what you're talking about, Felicia," I said.

"I believe you know exactly what I mean. Look at you!"

She grabbed my arm and pulled me back in front of the mirror.

"That's certainly not the country bumpkin I saw that first night at Mac's place," she said, forcing me to look at my image in the mirror. "What do you want from him? I mean, I understand that young brothers out here don't offer a young woman very much with their pimped-out, wish they were thugs-mentality but I'm sure there must be someone your age you can find."

Suddenly I saw red.

"What's your problem, Felicia? I thought you and Mackenzie were *old news!* What do you mean, what do *I* want from him? What are you, his big sister or his mama? Either way it's none of your damn business what I want or what he wants from me, so butt your ass out!"

We were almost toe-to-toe, nose-to-nose, staring into each other's eyes. Felicia was the first to speak, her tone softened.

"Look, sweetie. It's not Mac I'm concerned about, it's you. Things aren't always as they appear and Mackenzie Powell may not be the man you think he is."

Her feigned concern for me was almost funny.

"You still love him, don't you?" I didn't expect an answer because we both knew she did.

I walked to the door, grabbed its handle and was ready to exit but then I turned to face her once again.

"You know, you need to be more careful about who and where you screw in the future. Somebody might be watching and listening."

My statement had its desired effect. I watched Felicia's smug expression dissolve behind her confusion over what I said. I imagined what she must've been thinking and wondering whether I saw her and Mac's friend engaged in their rapturous encounter that night in his study. But I wasn't going to spend too much time thinking about her. For her part, Felicia was speechless, held at bay by someone who wasn't even close to being her equal and for me it was a small victory.

I stormed out of the bathroom, my face still flushed, an aftermath of my rage and my taking her to task. I stopped for a moment to regain my composure being careful not to trigger a panic attack. I thought about El and how she'd react if this had happened to her and acting on cue I held my head high, pushed my shoulders back and fell into my friend's killer walk, emulating her to the max with my hips swaying and long legs flashing in and out of the slits of my dress.

All eyes were on me as I re-entered the hall without feeling intimidated by the stares. I sat beside Mac who had a stare of his own, a mostly nervous one of disbelief. Everyone else at our table had stopped talking with the men giving me that "ooh, baby look" and their wives turning a little bit green around the edges. But I ignored it all, choosing instead to direct my attention only to Mac.

Feeling like a vixen, I leaned over close to him and put my hand on his thigh so that no one else could see. I whispered in his ear using the sexiest voice I had and allowed the warmth from my breath to gently bathe its inside.

"Mackenzie Powell, I'm ready to go," I said.

I watched his Adam's apple disappear for a second and then return. He took a deep breath, held it in and blew out, giving me the impression that he was releasing the kind of pressure that would've caused a volcano to spew out its lava.

I guess my own libido was working overtime that night because my mind quickly drew an analogy to an eruption of another kind. The thought embarrassed me slightly and made me feel like I must've been a candidate for a Freudian examination, making comparisons between volcanoes and phalluses.

"So, you're ready to go home, are you?"

I shook my head. "I'm ready to go to your place," I whispered.

He cleared his throat of the nervous moisture, breaking his characteristic sense of overriding cool.

"Give a few minutes. I don't want to be rude to my guests," Mac replied, politely. Smiled.

The band had just started playing and people were heading to the dance floor to do that middle-aged soulful shuffle and dance the way my drunken uncle used to dance at every wedding and graduation.

"C'mon, let's dance."

He stood and held out his hand. I playfully grabbed it, rising to the challenge.

"You sure you can handle this?" I asked.

We headed to the dance floor with my exaggerated walk, hips swaying to the beat of the music and my legs peeking through my dress with each stride. Although he didn't think I noticed, I could tell that Mac had leaned back to look at my rear end that was cupped by the dress and prominently displayed through the fabric.

"I don't know," he laughed. "Looks like you have a distinct advantage."

Once out on the floor, Mac started a two-step with his fingers snapping to the funked up beat the band was rocking. He was stiff and inhibited, not like the men I sometimes danced with in D.C.'s nightclubs so I went into an inhibited and modified booty shake to help him get into the groove.

"Loosen up." I told him. "I know. You're just trying to be cool."

He laughed. "This is as good as it gets, baby."

I turned around and moved closer, allowing my back to press up against his chest with my ass taunting his groin. He got into the moment. His arms and hands found their place around my waist and we rocked in unison to the music. I relaxed completely and laid the back of my head against his shoulder. With my eyes closed as far as I was concerned we were the only couple on the dance floor.

But we weren't and Mac soon took control. He moved back, spun me around and kept dancing. He was smiling but with a relieved look on his face. The song ended and the band shifted gears. They were playing Frankie Beverly and Maze doing a classic slow jam. Mac pulled me close. And I fell into his arms. Wrapping my arms around his neck, dancing close and slow.

The Frankie Beverly-ish lead singer doing his best impression of the music legend sang, *I can tell by the look in your eyes that you're falling in love with me.* I knew I had that look.

Day Twelve

I held Mac's hand as we waited for the valet to bring his car and felt a touch of moisture in his palm. I squeezed it slightly as though I was reassuring him and marveled at the power I apparently had over a man who could intimidate any woman. He reacted by giving me a vague smile then focused his attention on a man and woman walking down the stairs from the building and heading in our direction. The always calm, always cool Mackenzie Powell was having an uneasy reaction as the couple came closer. He shifted his eyes away from the pair like he didn't want them to see his stare, but it was too late. The chocolate man with the familiar soulful eyes was upon us.

"Well, well, if it isn't Mackenzie Powell," the man said.

Mac forced a smile, gave him a slight nod. "Paul," he said.

"Have you met my wife, Mac?"

"I can't say that I've ever had the pleasure," Mac replied.

The woman reciprocated with a polite smile of her own then passed it along to me. I, in turn, wanted to run. I cringed underneath the man's presence and hoped that he didn't recognize me or if he did that he wouldn't call me by my name.

The air was thick with tension and Mac tried to ignore the man and his wife as he strained to see if the valet was bringing his car.

"It's been a long time," the man said.

I thought, *it was just the other day* believing he was speaking to me, but when Mac said, "Yes it has been a long time Paul" I realized that I was off the hook.

It seemed that we both breathed a little easier when the shiny black Bentley rolled up in front of us and came to a stop. The man looked at me and narrowed his eyes while I tried my best to ignore him as I hopped inside the waiting car. Mac walked to the driver's side and gave the valet some folded up dollar bills as he seemed to hesitate before he took his position behind the steering wheel.

"Nice car, Mac," the man said. He looked at his wife waiting for her to join him in his appreciation of Mac's exquisite automobile. "This is truly a great country when a man can overcome adversity and achieve whatever his heart desires." He followed the statement with a broad smile, which quickly evaporated into the stone-faced presence I'd seen in my supervisor's office just a few days earlier.

Mac was in the car and comfortable behind the steering wheel. He inserted the key, turned on its engine and waited as the seat automatically adjusted to his height and pushed back to accommodate his legs. The steering wheel retracted inward and adjusted itself to Mac's driving preference. He touched the LCD screen and quickly programmed some music and the car's interior lights then leaned over and looked at the man through the window on my side of the car.

"It truly is a great country, Agent Robinson. I hope that you and your wife enjoy the rest of your evening."

With those words, Mac shifted the car's gears and pulled off slowly as I watched Agent Robinson with his eyes watching me through narrowed eyes. The large soulful eyes were gone, replaced by an intimidating scowl that resonated in his stare. He nodded at me, letting me know that I hadn't escaped his scrutiny. The fear returned with the same kind of intensity I had felt that day when he and his pasty-faced partner came to interview me, but it soon went away. His being at the fundraiser with his wife was a mere coincidence, it had to be. But I wasn't concerned about myself at that moment it was Mac that had all of my attention.

He seemed unusually uneasy and barely spoke a word. He loosened his tie and opened the top button to his shirt. "It's getting a little warm in here," he said. "You mind?"

He adjusted the AC and seemed to breathe easy from that point on. I had a million questions about our encounter with the FBI agent, but I wasn't going to ask. I just sat back and let the nighttime air carry us. I didn't want to know why Mac seemed troubled about running into Paul Robinson and I didn't care.

We rolled through downtown Washington and drove over to Pennsylvania Avenue where Mac stopped the car near the Rotunda.

"Ever done this before?" he asked.

I looked up to take in my surroundings and noticed that there were people walking and enjoying the view. Others were parked in cars, huddled close together.

"What? Make out in a car?" I asked, feeling playful.

"No."

He got out of the car and reached for my hand. A few feet away stood a horse drawn carriage and its driver.

"C'mon. Let's go for a ride."

"You're kidding. I've always wanted to do this," I told him.

We climbed in and the driver commanded the horse to move on. I snuggled close to Mac and put his arm around me. Slow rolling in a horse drawn carriage was a way to view a side of Washington I'd never seen before and on a cool, crisp evening the Moon beckoned us.

The driver guided the carriage down Constitution Avenue and then slow trotted us towards the Potomac River and over to Haines Point. We stopped there to admire the huge sculpture of a man rising out of the Earth.

"Prometheus Rising." Mac said.

"What?" I asked.

"That's the name of the sculpture," he told me.

I had seen it before from a distance but never bothered to find out what it was called. In fact, most of the people I knew simply regarded the sculpture as a fixture in the park, one they'd cruise by on Sundays when the brothers and sisters sported fine cars in an egomaniacal game of adult show and tell.

Haines Point for us was about girls hanging out in the park showing off their legs and booties in short shorts and young men flexing their muscles in their wife beaters. The show was about the people, real ones, not a fifty-foot man made of metal and looking like he was being held down by the ground rather than climbing out of it.

"I never knew what it was called," I told Mac. "I just thought it was some giant man the artist stuck in the ground. I figured it symbolized something."

"It does," Mac replied.

I could tell that he was a little amused by my remark.

"It's from Greek mythology."

I cut him a sharp glance. "I know all about Prometheus, Mackenzie Powell," I said, giving him a playful reprimand for his condescension. "He gave humans fire after he stole it from the gods and was punished by having his liver eaten by birds, everyday. It would grow back and the birds would eat it again," I added.

I pointed to the statute. "Judging by the look on his face it must've hurt a lot."

Mac laughed. "Damn right it hurt."

Our exploration of Greek culture was ended by the carriage driver who urged the horse to move on. We settled back cozy in our seat and I snuggled even closer to Mac, allowing the warmth from his body to temper the cool night air.

"Are you cold?" he asked.

"Not right now," I answered. "Tell me about your trip to Thailand."

"Not much to tell. It was all business. I've got some special and demanding clients there," Mac said.

"Must be a real exotic place. Me? I haven't been anywhere but here and Georgia and of course to Ohio for college," I told him.

"There's a big world out there. I've lived my life to the fullest. I've been places, done so many things. Hung out with Miles at the Montreux Jazz Festival in Switzerland, listened to the great Archie Shepp play under the stars beneath the Great Pyramid in Egypt, partied at Studio 54. If I die tomorrow I'd have no regrets," he told me. He paused. "Well maybe a couple."

I thought about his worldliness, imagined all of the women that must have been in his life.

"Felicia told me you were a womanizer," I said half teasing, half in a serious vein.

I could see Mac with a smirk on his face. He shook his head. "Felicia, Felicia," he said. "Just to set the record straight, I've never been what they call, a womanizer. What you have to understand is that I'm a child of the Seventies and the Eighties. You know, pre-AIDS, women popping birth control pills like Skittles."

I smiled and decided to taunt him. "And they were all over you, weren't they Mackenzie," I said. I don't know why I said that. I didn't want to hear his answer because I knew that it would make me jealous.

"Like I said, it's a big world out there." I was grateful that he didn't answer my question. Instead, he bypassed the comment and kept talking. "We Americans are so egotistical, believing that the whole planet revolves around us."

Mac clinched his teeth, something I had noticed before whenever he was irritated or just deep in thought.

"You don't like it here, do you? Is that why you're planning to move to that place where you're having your house built?" I asked.

"Oh, you mean my house near Bahia in Brazil?"

"Uh, uh."

"It's not that I don't like it here. It's just that I'm looking for a different kind of life. I'm fifty and although I don't think that's old, I spend more time looking back than I do ahead, reminiscing about the past and agonizing about the future. I guess what I want is to wipe the slate clean and start over."

"And do you think of marriage in your new life?" I asked.

He turned directly towards me and smiled. "There's a place for it—maybe."

"And children. What about children?" I asked.

"Not sure. Hadn't given that one much thought. I mean, like I said I'm fifty and there aren't any kids on the horizon. So even if I became a father in the next two years I'd be seventy when my daughter graduates from high school."

He pushed out a breathy half-laugh. "Her friends would probably ask her if I'm her grandpa."

"And all of those friends would envy her for having such a virile, handsome and distinguished-looking father. I wouldn't be surprised if they all had crushes on you."

I let my mind race twenty years into the future. I'd be forty-six to his seventy with a grown daughter. The thought made me pause and ask him, "Why did you say, daughter?"

"I don't know. It just came out. I already have a son and you know all about that relationship but I've always thought that a father-daughter relationship is special. You know, daddy's little girl. Sons grow up and want to be your competition or your buddy, at least most do but daughters always hold that special place right here," he said, putting his hand over his chest where his heart beat underneath.

I leaned back into his chest where that heart was beating and rested my head on his shoulder while his strong left arm cradled me and I thought about Mackenzie, his little girl and me. We would be a nuclear family, living on a tropical island off the coast of Brazil if only in my dreams.

◆   ◆   ◆

When we finally got to Mac's house he quickly poured a drink and offered me one but I declined, remembering how I was the night of his party. I was feeling amorous but he seemed to be in no hurry. I followed him into his familiar study and took a seat on the sofa while he sat across from me in his easy chair.

"Why so far away?" I asked.

He smiled. "No reason," he said.

He sat there staring at me, swishing his brandy around in a large snifter but my question didn't move him.

"You're a very beautiful young woman. You remind me of someone I knew a long time ago."

No man had ever told me I was beautiful before so I wanted to savor the moment and let it soak in. I thought about the other three women I knew about who had been in Mac's life. I wondered whether he was comparing me to Felicia, Regina or Desdemona.

"Who's that?" I asked.

He sipped from his glass and wiped away remnants of brandy from the tip of his thick mustache. That wistful look I'd seen on his face earlier that evening returned.

"I'm sorry. I shouldn't talk about this," he said.

"It's O.K. I'm a big girl. Tell me."

He paused. "It was a long time ago. I met this little sweet country girl and …"

"You two fell in love?"

"Not quite, but I always wondered about the possibilities."

"I don't know if I should be flattered or insulted," I said.

"It was definitely a compliment."

Mac got up from his chair and sat beside me. I moved closer and kissed him on the cheek and then his neck. He sat almost motionless as I unfastened the top two buttons of his silk shirt and kissed him sweetly on his chest. I stopped for a moment to study the gold chain and the St. Christopher's medal he was wearing underneath his shirt.

"That's nice," I said referring to the medallion.

"It's very special. I never take it off," he replied.

I said, "Why, because of its religious meaning?"

"Partly. St. Christopher is the patron saint of travelers," Mac told me.

I touched it, held its weight in my hand, read the inscription on the back: *To, Ricky* and briefly wondered but it wasn't important. I kissed his face and waited as he turned his lips to join mine. Slowly, his arms engulfed me and pulled my body close to his. I could feel the warmth, the passion growing with every passing second. My heart welled up and my body ached with a sweet pain that anticipated fulfillment.

"Mackenzie, I want you to make love to me," I whispered. With those words I threw myself upon him, kissing his neck and chest while being beckoned by his sensual cologne to taste his entire body. I allowed my hands to touch him and to let my fingers play with the thin patch of hair that rested right above his sternum. Not satisfied my hand found its way lower and felt the fullness that was quickly growing between his legs. I breathed deep, I breathed hard and my body tingled to the point where I wanted to scream. I repeated my request but this time I was almost begging. "I want you, baby," I said.

Mac said nothing and I figured that he was as caught in the moment as I had been. But his actions were too deliberate for someone who wanted what I wanted. He shifted and moved away but not very far, clearing his throat to speak.

"This is difficult, Dahlia. But we can't do this," he said.

His words stung like arrows. I was crushed by his rejection to the point that I wanted to cry but instead, I asked him one simple question, "Why?"

"I can't tell you right now but in time you'll know and understand."

"I get it. You don't find me attractive, do you?" I asked not satisfied with his answer.

He shook his head.

"To the contrary. I find you extremely attractive but I ..." He stopped.

Mac stood up and walked towards the door leading out of the room and into the hallway.

"I've got to get some sleep. I want you to stay here tonight in one of the guest rooms and I'll take you home in the morning. Give me a few minutes to make sure the room is ready and I'll be back to get you. In the meantime, make yourself comfortable." Those words pierced my heart and I wondered how Mac could be warm and passionate one minute and so cold the next. He gave me a long look that wasn't detached like his words then turned to leave.

I watched him unable to say a word. He said I was beautiful and that he found me attractive so I didn't understand why he didn't want to make love to me. I thought of all the possibilities. Maybe he was sick or was having a problem that he was too macho to admit. Or maybe the woman Felicia talked about, Desdemona was really in his life and he was being faithful, but none of it made sense. I thought about the words Felicia said during our confrontation in the ladies' room. Maybe Mac wasn't the man I thought he was, after all.

I walked around the study trying to figure out what had happened. Deep down inside I was hoping that he'd come back and sweep me off my feet the way heroes do in some old movie and carry me off to his bedroom. No words said. No apologies made. In my thoughts, he would simply take me.

I paced the room with those thoughts as my guide, tried to lose myself in the things that made this place his. I walked over to Mac's desk and marveled at its organization. Everything was in place, put where it was for a reason. His laptop computer was in the very center and a paper shredder was on the floor to the right of the desk. His chrome-plated pistol, Mr. Friendly, claimed a spot in the middle of the desk and it made me pause. But I moved on, remembering what Mac had told me about wealthy people needing protection.

My attention went to the credenza behind the desk because it had old photographs, framed and neatly placed in rows. I picked up the first one, a picture of a baby. The year was 1957. It had to be Mac at two years old. I thought how pretty he was even as a baby.

I gently put the picture down and picked up the one next to it. It was a group of young men in their early twenties, posing in front of the camera all with wide smiles, big hair and throwing up peace signs.

Judging from their style of clothes, the picture was circa late 1970's or the early 80's. Its black and white images were somewhat faded by time, but there were two young men who stood out. They looked like brothers and they were the only ones in the group who had their arms around each other's shoulders. I pulled the picture closer and studied its detail. I could see that the young man on the right was wearing a St. Christopher's medal like the one Mac was wearing. *That's Mackenzie.* I thought.

I moved over to a picture of a little boy with large, green eyes and a big Afro that seemed to take up the entire picture frame. It was inscribed with the words, *To My Dad with Love.* I thought it must be a picture Mackenzie's son when *he* was a little boy. I put the picture back in its place when I heard the sound of Mac's footsteps.

"I'm sorry I took so long. I had to take a quick shower," he said.

I smiled inside knowing that it must've been a cold shower. I decided I wouldn't press him for anything. One thing I'd learned from my friend El was that a woman shouldn't force herself on a man or if she had to then she should do it without him knowing. "Make him think he's in control when it comes to love and sex," she once told me. "It's good for his ego and great for sex."

"I love these pictures," I told him.

I was getting ready to ask about the picture of the little boy when Mac extended his hand and said, "Come. The room's ready."

I followed, holding his hand as he led me up the stairs. At the end of the hall-way was an open door to what I assumed was his master bedroom. I took a deep breath as we walked down the long hall. My heart was pounding hard and my anticipation was growing nearly out of control.

I thought that he was playing some kind of mind game, trying to make me want him even more. But if that was the case it was a very sophisticated ploy and totally unnecessary because I could feel every part of my body screaming to be touched by him and knowing that the touch would take me places I'd never been.

I started unraveling my hair with my free hand as we walked and loosened the impromptu belt that I fashioned from my shawl. I kicked off my shoes, walked along in a dreamlike state and followed him blindly into the bedroom. He opened the door and turned on the light.

"This bed is very comfortable," he said.

Then he pulled me close and put his arms around me, engulfing my whole body. It wasn't a sensuous hug but more like a father putting his little girl to bed reassuring her that he'd be nearby and that he could exorcise any nighttime demons that lay waiting in a darkened room.

I laid my head on his chest first without speaking but trying to understand.

"I thought you wanted me," I said.

"For sex?" he replied.

The question, abrasive in the way it sounded but I knew that wasn't his intent.

"For love," I said.

He gently pushed me away so that our eyes could engage and they danced back and forth between our thoughts.

"I love on many different levels, Dahlia and it's a word I don't take lightly. For us to fall into bed now would be giving in to the physical without one soul knowing the other."

For a moment I thought, what kind of metaphysical bullshit is he running on me? But when his eyes pierced through my spirit I sensed his sincerity. But it didn't quell my longing to connect with him on that basic and most carnal level of all.

He let go of my arms, gave me a knowing smile and retreated out of the room. I decided that I wouldn't follow him. I undressed and sat on the edge of the bed, embarrassed by the fact that I'd thrown myself at him and he tossed me aside. The old, insecure Dahlia Reynolds would've accepted her fate but the new Dahlia couldn't.

Day Thirteen

Mac once told me the difference between fate, luck and coincidence is that, fate is pre-determined, luck is chance, and coincidence is just happenstance. All are related and at times intertwined but each stands on their own and the key is to understand which one is controlling at any given time. I knew that fate is beyond my control and that luck is situational, controlled by how I position myself. As far as coincidence? It was my interpretation of things that occur and of which I have some control.

What I don't understand is which of the three put me in the position I now find myself. I knew that fate brought me to Bangkok, Thailand but was it just dumb, bad luck that put me in this eight by ten prison cell?

Songs of Desdemona—10/23/05

The thing about a telephone's ring when it comes in the middle of the night is that it speaks of nothing good. My heart jumped when I heard my phone as it unceremoniously lifted me from a sound sleep in a strange bed. The room was pitch-black inside and I groped around for my purse without seeing. I cursed as I knocked it off the nightstand and its contents clumsily spilled out onto the floor. After a few swipes of my hand I found it and reluctantly answered. It was my mother.

"I'm sorry to call you this time of night, baby," she said.

I could hear her voice trembling.

"I tried to call you at home but I got no answer. Where are you?"

"What's wrong, mama?" I asked, bypassing the question.

It was rare for her to call late at night and I'd grown accustomed to knowing that calls like this were serious and often meant that something was wrong or someone was dead. It was a sign of foreboding, like the telegram that came in the middle of the night back in the day.

"It's your grandmother."

My mother started to cry.

"Somebody broke into the house while Rufus and I were at Saturday night service."

"What!"

"They hurt mama—bad. She's in critical condition, Dahlia. Doctors say she may not make it. I need you to come home right away. Tomorrow, if you can. Maybe … maybe if she knows you're here she'll get better and come out of her coma. I know if she hears your voice she'll be alright."

I listened through my mother's tears and thought about my grandmother and then about what it would take to get back to Waycross on such short notice. My credit cards were charged up to the max and I didn't have enough money in the bank to buy an airplane ticket. I also knew that my mother couldn't afford to send for me and that cheap ass Rufus wouldn't. I thought that maybe Stacy or El could loan me the money. I let my mother cry for a moment without saying anything and then tried to console her.

"Don't worry, mama. I'll be there. Trust me, I'll see you tomorrow."

I hung up the phone and rolled over on my back looking into the dark and thinking about my grandmother and the prospect that she might die before I could see her again. The thought that someone would break into the house and hurt her crushed me. That kind of thing just didn't happen in small, sleepy Southern towns. Besides, my grandmother had nothing of any real value.

I cried and rolled myself into a fetal position the way I did when I was a little girl hiding from my stepfather's wrath. I was scared and distraught. I needed to be held and reassured.

I got out of bed and walked out into the hall. Mac's door was closed now. I tapped on the door and then opened it to find him asleep on his stomach. Without saying a word I slipped into his bed and pulled my body close to his and cried.

I guess my crying woke him up. I was afraid, believing that he might tell me to leave but he didn't.

"What's wrong?" he whispered.

"It's my grandmother. My mother just called and said that someone broke into the house back home and they hurt my grandma. I've got to go home and see her."

"When do you have to be there?" Mac asked.

"I need to try and get a flight tomorrow morning. I know that the rates are sky high when you fly on short notice but I'm just going to have to do it."

I cried. And cried.

"Shooo-s-s-s-sh. Don't worry. Everything will be fine. Trust me," he said. "Go to sleep. I'll make sure you get there tomorrow."

◆   ◆   ◆

Mac wasn't in the bed when I woke up the next morning. Somehow he had slipped out undetected and I wondered whether he'd gone to play golf like he did the time I spent the night at his house nursing my hangover. Although I'd climbed into his bed with nothing on except my thong panties I was now wearing a man's robe. It was Mac's and he obviously put it on me while I slept.

It was daylight and the clock pointed to 9:00 a.m., later than I'd planned to get up. I'd fallen asleep in Mac's arms with one thing on my mind and that was doing whatever I could to make sure I'd get back home. And now the morning was well on its way and I hadn't made arrangements to get back to Waycross, Georgia. I also needed to get home and pack. I made a quick telephone call to Stacy to see if she could buy me an airline ticket but there was no answer. I started to dial El's number but decided that I could wait until I knew what my next move would be and that involved Mac.

First, was the usual morning pit stop as I made my way to the bathroom adjoining the master bedroom. Mac's bathroom was almost as large as my whole apartment with lots of windows, a Jacuzzi tub, double showers and mirrored walls.

I watched my image pee, checking out the young woman looking at me from the other side of the mirror. My hair still looked great, thanks to Paul Sinclair and his professional styling but my makeup had been mixed with my tears and lost on the pillow. I didn't see it when I got up but I was hoping that it didn't look like the tee shirts that vendors still hawk on Capitol Hill. The ones that read, "I RAN INTO TAMMY FAYE LAST NIGHT". Smudged up face-print of the former television evangelist underneath the words.

I finished and was ready to find Mac when I got curious, wondered what secrets I could find in his bathroom. Mac told me that he wasn't involved with anyone but I knew there was no better place to find evidence of another woman than in a man's bathroom.

I remembered girl talk with Stacy and El and how they said women often leave their personal belongings at a man's place. It was their way of claiming their territory the way animals use urine. Panties and makeup kits were the primary warning signs. They were like pee stains in the snow, obvious and blatant.

Stacy moved in on Derek, a pair of panties at a time until they filled a whole laundry hamper. It was only a matter of time until her draws, clothes, CD collection and all of her worldly possessions were crowded into his townhouse. Overall it was better than branding her initials on his arms.

I decided to look inside his medicine cabinet for a stray tube of lipstick or some mascara. The cabinet was clean unlike the way most single men kept theirs. No toothpaste stains running down the sides or on the shelves. No lint filled brush. Nothing that said: I'm a bachelor. I don't give a damn.

Everything was chrome and pewter, from the cup that held his toothbrush to the comb that kept every hair on his head in place before he cut it all off. Everything on this side of the cabinet was for grooming and arranged like a print ad for GQ magazine. I dismissed the idea that Mac would harbor some woman's messy eye shadow container or half-used nail polish bottle. But I couldn't resist taking a quick peek on the other side of the cabinet.

This was the side that brought meaning to the words, "medicine cabinet." Small bottles of prescription medications lined the shelves with his name written on the labels. I was hoping to find one with a Viagra label on it. But most of the labels mentioned medications I couldn't pronounce except the ones that ended in "nitrate". I knew that was for the heart.

Mac had a heart condition. It brought home our age difference and the thought that he already had a head start on me in the living department by almost twenty-five years. I started doing the numbers. Women generally have a longer life expectancy than men by at least five years. Add his twenty-five and that's thirty years I'd have to live without him assuming that he made it to seventy-five. At that point I'd only be fifty. Suddenly my fanciful thought of a future with him, the one I had conjured up during our carriage ride had lost some of its luster.

Morbid thoughts about Mac grabbed me. Still it now made sense. Bad heart, bad love. Love kills if you do it too hard. I couldn't believe my thoughts, like my mind had a mind of its own. I had to seize control. It was about my grandmother and nothing else at this point. Whatever thoughts and feelings I had involving Mac had to be put on the backburner. I had to find him and figure how to get home.

He wasn't upstairs so I tied the robe and made my way down the steps and into the lower level of the house.

"Mackenzie?"

I called out but not in a loud voice. Instead, it was meek and timid like someone who didn't want to wake the monster.

I called out again. I heard a man talking. His voice was coming from outside and echoing through the atrium from the swimming pool. I moved closer to the sound and I could tell it was Mac but he was talking loud, almost shouting. His words were infused with angry expletives peppering whoever he was talking to and leaving no doubt that he was really pissed off.

"What do you mean, I'm the one who's jeopardizing the project? That's *bullshit* Al!"

I heard Mac take a deep breath as though he was drawing energy from his surroundings, ready to return verbal fire. The voice of another man, thickly accented, broke in but with a lot more calm attached to it than Mac's.

"What about the girl, Mackenzie? Is she ready? Does she even know what you want?"

"I'm working on that, Al."

"And what of Desdemona? Have you seen her?"

"She's in a safe place, Al."

I could hear the defensive tone in Mac's voice. The other man said something that I couldn't understand and although his tone seemed calm he appeared to be persistent in making his point to Mac. I could hear Mac struggling to get his point across and frustration filled the air.

"Do you mind if I say something, Al? I said, shut the fuck up and listen! GODDAMNIT! You know as well as I do that I can deliver just as I promised, Al."

I heard them mention, New York, Miami, Paris and Bangkok several different times during the conversation. Between words in English they both squeezed in something in Arabic that I didn't understand.

I stood out of view, being patient as they argued. But I had to let my presence be known or I'd never get out of Mac's house. I stepped around the corner and walked right into the poolroom.

"Excuse, me," I mumbled. "I only wanted to find you to let you know that I need to leave. I can call a cab. It's no problem."

Mac came over to me, turned on his calm button. "I've made arrangements for your trip," he said. "You remember my friend, Al, don't you?"

Al gave me an unpleasant smile, more like a sneer. "Yes, I met you at Mac's party."

I remembered him but there was something else that was familiar and I quickly put some things together. It was Al's voice, the heavy accent and its high-pitched tonality. It was the voice of the man who was having sex with Felicia that night in Mac's study. I acknowledged him and wondered if Mac knew.

"I can't let you do that," I said in a near whisper not wanting his friend to hear me. "I can't let you pay for my airplane ticket, too."

Mac pulled me out of the poolroom, back into the atrium and out of Al's presence.

"I'm not paying for your ticket," he told me. "at least, not directly. Look I have to go to Miami today. I can drop you off."

I was amused. I knew it would take about twenty hours to drive from Washington to Miami and that there was no way he'd make it there today. "It's a really long drive Mackenzie."

"Who said anything about driving? I'll fly you there. I guess I didn't tell you that I'm a licensed pilot."

"A pilot? You're kidding, aren't you? You mean to tell me that you have your own airplane?"

"No, I lease one from time to time. I've already reserved it. I can drop you off at an airport near Waycross, I believe there's one in Valdosta, Georgia and then go on to Miami. I'll be there for about a week but I can pick you up whenever you're ready. What do you say? Is that cool with you?"

"I don't know what to say," I said. I was smiling wide. "Just, thank you, so much. You're amazing. It's like you're some kind of knight in shining armor always rescuing the damsel in distress."

"Yeah, a knight with a chink in his armor," Mac said.

I pulled close to him again, lifted my face towards his with my mouth poised to touch his but he gave me a polite kiss on my cheek. It was obvious that nothing had changed during the night or by my ordeal.

"I'll throw some things together and then take you home to change. We can be at Dulles Airport by noon."

He told me to get dressed and then retreated back to the poolroom where his friend was waiting. The shouting became muffled as I walked down the hall and back upstairs to find my clothes and all I could hear, all I could think about was the name, Desdemona. Desdemona. Desdemona.

◆   ◆   ◆

Mac dropped me off in front of my building, Said, "I've got a few errands to run. I'll meet you here in an hour."

I ran inside and hurriedly packed my clothes. I went through a few systems checks and made sure I watered my plants, took the garbage out and left a light on in my living room. Stacy would stop by just to make sure things were alright while I was gone.

I gave the place the once over stopping to take a parting glance at my family's quilt, which made feel like crying. I thought about my grandmother and how she had skillfully knitted the latest installments in the Reynolds' family history and dreaded the thought that she may never have the chance to see it again. I sighed heavily as I touched its fabric and reminded myself that someday I'd be the one recording our history. I fought back the tears, grabbed my suitcase and closed the door.

Mac hadn't returned so I stood outside soaking in some sun as I anxiously waited and thought about my trip and what I could expect when I got there. But a voice broke through my thoughts. It was a man's voice.

"Going somewhere?" It was Agent Liles this time. Somehow he had crept up on me and now he was standing uncomfortably close.

"Ah, yes. I'm going out of town. Is that a problem? I asked. I was feeling invaded and defensive. I wanted to tell him that it was none of his damn business, but I didn't. "Is there something I can help you with?"

He had the same smug expression he had when I first met him and I concluded that it must've been something he picked up at the FBI Academy in the Asshole class. I figured he was at the top of his class in that department.

"You seen your boy Antoine, lately?"

"No, it's been a couple of weeks. I figure you'd probably know where he is better than I would."

Liles moved from my side and stood directly in front of me, repeated that wicked smile that seemed a part of his nature. He looked me up and down then rested his eyes on my face. He was a short man and at five foot, nine inches, almost six feet with my heels on, I towered over him. He was looking up to me. I was looking down on him. It made an interesting metaphor that he probably wanted to reverse.

"You've done something different to yourself. Uhmm, your hair and makeup looks good on you. I guess you must've thought about what I said. You know, Antoine and the kind of women he likes."

I twisted my mouth in disapproval and tried to pretend that the FBI agent wasn't standing there. But he was and I was beginning to feel defiant.

"Look, I don't know why you're here or what you want, but like I told you before I don't know anything about anything and I'm just trying to get back home to see my family, Agent Liles!"

"Whoa, calm down Miss Reynolds. And call me Rick. I just stopped by, just in case he's around. I just wanted to make a social call on my brother Antoine. There's a lot of buzz around him and his crew."

Liles stared up at me and I glared back like we were playing a game of who'd flinch first.

"You know, you've got some real pretty eyes. I never noticed them before. I guess it was the glasses."

"I got em from my dad," I replied.

He took a deep breath like he was trying to inhale a part of me then turned an eye to the suitcase that was on the ground tucked close to my side. "You wouldn't happen to be leaving the country? Ever been to Thailand? I hear it's a very interesting place."

Everything about him reeked of sarcasm. His small talk had a purpose. Just like my encounter with his partner the night before when I was with Mac I was anxious to get away from him. I was hoping that Mac would pull up and take me away but Liles would be the one to leave.

I watched him carefully as he made his way to the familiar looking black sedan parked on the street in front of my building. He stopped halfway to the car then turned to speak. "You know we checked. That quarter of a million dollars that's tucked away in your name can't be traced to anyone except you. No rich uncle, lottery winnings, no check made out to you from some donor. We got video, compliments of the Antiguan government. It's kind of grainy and I admit the quality is poor but there's ol' Antoine and a tall, attractive black woman in shades making a cash deposit. Just thought I'd tell you. Anyway, have a safe trip."

◆   ◆   ◆

Agent Liles' visit didn't upset me although I knew that was his intent but it shed some light on the things that were swirling around me and showed me that Antoine was a key figure. Someone had hacked into my personnel files and the reason was clear. It was to steal my identity. Somehow, Antoine and a woman who looked like me went to Antigua to open up a bank account in my name with the help of information gained from my files. His excuse that the money came from an investor in his music projects didn't make sense. I thought about all the reasons why he might have told me that lie and none made sense but I knew I would have to do something rather than let things spiral totally out of control. I had talked to Stacy about it and now it was time to tell El and get some advice from an attorney. But that would have to wait until I returned.

I had no idea what to expect when Mac told me he would fly me home. I thought his plane would be like a commercial airliner only smaller with rows of seats for its well-heeled passengers. But it was more like the living room in some-one's posh South Beach home. The rows of seats been removed and the airplane was custom fitted with a sofa, loveseats, wet bar and a conference table. There was also a king-sized bed in the adjoining compartment. And I could enjoy all of this as the only passenger.

Mac told me to relax and help myself to anything in the cabin but I wanted to ride in the co-pilot's seat next to him. I guess I felt safer watching him fly the plane than just riding. He went through a series of systems checks and talked on the radio to air traffic control. When he got the go ahead we taxied down the run-way and within seconds were airborne. It would be a two-hour flight.

My mother was anxious to see me and I told her about Mac and how I wanted her to meet him. The thought made me a little nervous knowing my mother the way I do. Her parochial sense of morality would have her question Mac's inten-tions and not our age difference. But that wasn't important. I was on my way home to a place that I tried to escape and one that carried memories I'd worked so hard to put behind.

I looked over at Mac as he was leveling the plane at our approved altitude. There was the focus in his eyes that's obviously necessary when operating a com-plicated piece of equipment but now it was easing up and he removed his head-phones and smiled.

"You are free to move about the cabin," he said.

"Mackenzie Powell, you are a man of many talents. How long have you been flying?"

"It started as a hobby about twenty years ago. I took some lessons and loved it. I took more lessons, was certified and decided that I wanted to make money fly-ing. I started as a co-pilot for a charter airline, worked my way to pilot and then flew for various corporations flying the CEO's, clients and board members around. It was how I made some connections to do what I do now. Just lucky. I guess I was in the right place at the right time."

"You told me you were an antiques collector but you've never told me about your shop. I mean, where is located? I'd like to see it someday."

"I never said I was an antiques collector Dahlia. And I don't have a shop. I guess when I use the term 'collector' its more euphemistic. Actually, I buy and sell things. Kind of like a junk collector. If a client wants something, I find it, buy it and sell it to them."

The idea that Mac was some kind of sophisticated junkman made me laugh and I imagined him as a real cool Fred Sanford.

"Do you have a truck?" I asked, trying to be funny. Mac caught on right away.

He laughed. "No. I don't have a truck. Besides, the things my clients want are usually discreet and I rarely deliver them personally."

"So, what kinds of things do you buy for your clients, Mackenzie?"

"Whatever, they can afford."

He banked the airplane to the left.

"We're heading south. We should be near Valdosta in an hour."

He flipped a couple of switches and looked back at me.

"Autopilot." He said.

I had this devious thought. I remembered El telling Stacy and I about how she joined the "Mile High Club" during a flight to France. Of course, that was different. It was in the bathroom of a commercial airplane and it wasn't with the pilot. I quickly pushed the thought from my mind.

I thought about the heated conversation he was having with his friend, Al, earlier that morning and the woman named Desdemona, who seemed to keep popping up everywhere. I wondered if Mac was flying to Miami to see her. I decided to ask him right then about her.

"Who's Desdemona?"

Mac's face twisted. I could tell that the question made him uncomfortable but he fought against his surprise at my asking. I could tell that it was a subject he didn't want to talk about but he didn't ignore my question.

"Shakespeare's, Othello. He murdered her in a jealous rage," he said, flatly.

The statement spoke volumes about the subject and about Mackenzie, himself. Whoever Desdemona was he wasn't going to talk about her to me and I would learn at that time, for the first time, that men keep secrets.

◆　　　◆　　　◆

We landed a few minutes later. I'd told Mac that my mother would meet us at the airport and drive me back to Waycross and I felt him tense up when I said she wanted to meet him.

"It's a little too soon for me to be meeting your family," he said.

His response came as a heavy thud against my heart. I'd told my mother that I thought I was falling in love—for the first time in my life. In her usual way, she cautioned me about being impulsive and about sex. "No unwanted pregnancies," she said. And now he was telling me that it was too early to meet her as though he knew that the meeting wouldn't be just a casual introduction.

The airport had a terminal about the size of a small town bus station and one landing strip. Mac allowed the plane's engines to run as he opened its door and helped me out onto the runway.

"Call me when you're finished here. I'll come back to get you."

We walked towards the terminal in silence with him carrying my luggage. He stopped at the entrance, gave me a parting smile as antiseptic as a man who'd been washed clean of all emotions. I was falling in love but it was obvious there was no reciprocation. I thought about the loves in his life, the ones I knew about and I wondered if he had the capacity to care about me. I watched him as he walked back to his plane without turning around and in a moment faded to black, disappeared into the friendly skies.

I found myself standing alone in the small airport terminal remembering the reason I had made the trip. I'd expected to see my mother and stepfather there waiting but they were apparently running late. I wondered if she would recognize me with my new hairstyle and without my conspicuous eyeglasses. I was a woman and looked every bit the part. My life had changed greatly since I'd gone away to college but even more so during the last few weeks I had known Mackenzie.

I strained to see the familiar blue truck creep slowly into the parking lot and my heart was pounding. It came to a stop outside the terminal door and my mother stepped out from the driver's side. I was relieved to see that Rufus wasn't with her. She greeted me with an array of facial expressions. First a faint smile then a worried look and, finally, frustration.

"What have you done to yourself?" My mother asked as she stood there looking up at me.

"You cut your hair? Wearing makeup? And what happened to your glasses? Did you get your eyes fixed or somethin'?"

My mother's reaction put a damper on my enthusiasm. I hadn't seen her in two years and I was expecting more warmth and not condemnation. But I quickly overcame it all. She was still a Pentecostal who thought that makeup made a woman a harlot, the Devil's mistress and my grandmother was gravely ill.

"How's Stevie?" I asked.

"Your grandmother's hanging on. I think it was because I told her that you were coming home. She's got a strong will."

My mother looked around.

"Where's this young fella you were raving about? I'd like to see who he is and ask him what kind of intentions he has for my only daughter."

"Oh, he had to fly to Miami."

It was obvious that the ordeal involving my grandmother was wearing on her but I could see more on her face than that. It was the living that was displayed with more prominence than anything else. The lines on her face like crevices sown into the earth, irregular and unrelenting made her appear much older than her forty-five years. I thought of Mac by comparison. He had led the good life and although he was older than my mother he looked at least ten years younger.

"I've got to get back home. Rufus is probably worried, you know how he gets," she said.

The blood rushed quickly to my brain and with it came the memories I'd tried so hard to suppress. Rufus, the Almighty. My momma at his beck and call, trapped in an abusive relationship, trapped by circumstance, a single mother with her own mother in tow and selling her soul. A form of indentured servitude purchased by the only bidder. Rufus, the Almighty.

"Mama, this ain't about Rufus. For once, will you think about yourself first? Your mother's sick and all you can say is that man is probably worried? I don't care if he's worried, Mama. What about all the times …?"

I cut short my diatribe. It wasn't the time and it certainly wasn't the place.

"Did they take anything from the house?" I asked.

My mother shook her head as she grabbed my suitcase and started heading for the exit and her truck outside.

"It was strange," she told me. "It was like they were lookin' for somethin'. They didn't take the color T.V. or your grandmother's antique china or my great-grandmother's silver. They just tore up her bedroom, went through all the drawers in her dresser and in her closet but took nothin'. It was the strangest thing."

My thoughts told me that they were thieves with a purpose but what and why? Those were the questions that consumed and confused me. And why did they have to hurt my grandmother? Like my mother said, 'it was strange'.

Day Fourteen

I knew prisons. There is the physical like the one here in Thailand that confines the body but somehow the spirit manages to roam free. And then there's the emotional kind that traps the soul and harnesses your being without hope of escape or any kind of respite from the ties that bind and lock you up. Stunted growth is the residue that can't be wiped off or expunged from the heart. I loosed the chains of my emotional bondage when I left my momma's house and moved away.

Songs of Desdemona—10/25/05

Memories of home and my childhood rushed back like a freight train ready to jump the track. My bedroom looked the same minus the posters of Whitney Houston and Blair Underwood that once adorned its walls. My old bed seemed even smaller and I wondered how I could've ever fit comfortably in it. But it was nothing when I considered my closet and the claustrophobic times I spent huddled in a human ball, sometimes hiding from my stepfather and other times being relegated to stay there as a punishment. It was both sanctuary and prison.

It was that experience that would later sustain me when prison became my reality. I am like the caged animal, raised in captivity that has never known what it's like to roam free and, therefore, unmissed in the experience.

I slowly unpacked my clothes and placed them neatly in my dresser drawers and hung the rest in the closet. My mother said that I should unpack first before making our way to the hospital to see Stevie. The confluence that joined thoughts of my grandmother to my preoccupation with Mackenzie made it difficult to concentrate on either person, individually but it was the image of him that couldn't escape my mind. The mystery that was Mackenzie left me off balanced.

Alone in my old room, I was now trying to piece it all together. The warnings from Felicia, easy to discount but still worthy of consideration, his refusal to bed me, and my female instincts not yet fully cultivated but being tested were all telling me something. I just couldn't figure out what it was. I repeated the name

Desdemona several times, thinking about his refusal to talk about her and trying to figure out who she is.

I realized that I had to put thoughts of Mac behind me for the moment and focus on Stevie. I decided to walk down the hall to her room. It still had the look of intrusion. The only room in the house that had been ransacked it looked like Hurricane Katrina had touched down and took her wrath out on my grandmother's bedroom. The visual of the intrusion was too strong for me at that moment and I had to leave the room. I needed to see my grandmother, to hold her hand. I said a brief prayer and mustered up the courage to make the visit to the hospital.

My stepfather wasn't going with us, thank God, preferring to stay home and work the fields. It was springtime and planting season. Rufus reasoned that anytime away from the fields was time stolen from the crops the fall would bear. So we made the drive without him.

Mt. Carmel Hospital was the only hospital in Waycross, Georgia and the irony was that during most of Stevie's life black people were refused treatment there. Now my grandmother was lying there near death in stark contrast to the days when Jim Crow laws dictated the care of the sick based on their race. Living had come full circle in Waycross and so had dying.

I walked into Stevie's hospital room and froze. I could see her there lying still with tubes coming out of her body like tentacles. The steady beep of the machine monitoring her vital signs had an unsettling refrain that was both reassuring and irritating because it distracted my attention from the motionless woman. But the fact that the monitor was beeping at all, an indication that the life hadn't left her was all the reassuring I needed.

I took a deep breath and stepped to my grandmother's side. There was a nurse on the other side of the bed reading a chart with the name, Stephanie Reynolds conspicuously on display.

"She's shown some improvement," the nurse said.

"Can she hear me? Does she know I'm here?"

The nurse shrugged.

"She's in a coma and unconscious, dear. We can't say what's going on in her brain or in her spirit, for that matter but sometimes it helps to talk to them, to touch them. Sometimes they know and knowing helps their recovery."

I moved closer and kissed Stevie on the cheek. I looked at my mother who was quietly sobbing.

"Mama," I said. "You go on home and get some rest. I'll stay here. I'll talk to you in the morning."

After my mother and the nurse left the room, I held my grandmother's frail hand and then started talking to her like she was wide awake. I talked about my job and my dreams of someday traveling the world. I talked about my friends, Stacy and El and even mentioned Antoine, my Johnny-Come-Lately lover. Most of all, I talked about Mackenzie Powell, told her that I thought I loved him and that there was no other man like him.

Through the night I talked and held Stevie's hand and stroked her forehead and prayed until I was exhausted and sleep soon overtook me.

Slumped in a chair with my hand attached to my grandmother's in a life grip I almost didn't notice the slight movement of her right foot underneath the blankets. But the room was so quiet with only the monitor as background noise that I thought it was my imagination. Gradually, she moved one limb and then another until it caused her to twist and stretch her body as though she was waking up from a long nap. When she opened her eyes I knew that she had returned, if only for the moment.

I cried. I didn't just cry, I sobbed a river of tears. I cried when Rufus whipped me for spilling sugar on the floor. It was precious, he said. I cried when he back-handed me across the face for being "smart mouthed", a result of a question I asked about my 7 p.m. curfew. I cried a countless number of times on the inside at his hands but never sobbed.

"Grandma Stevie. It's Dahlia, sweetheart. I'm here for you. I'm here for you." I squeezed her hand and leaned close to her face so that she could see me.

My grandmother's eyes welled up with tears behind her vacant stare and I knew that she was on her way back. I quickly pressed the call button that rang to the nurses' station and within what seemed like seconds a team swarmed into the room, talking to Stevie, flashing a small light into her eyes and checking her vital signs.

One of the nurses turned to me and asked, "What did you do?" To which I replied. "I just prayed, that's all."

Through the remainder of the day Stevie became more and more alert and responsive and even talked in repetitious phrases and partial sentences. The most notable was her constantly repeating of the word, "father". I thought that she was referring to God and that she had been so close to him that she was trying to tell me about the experience but she made her thoughts clear when she combined it with the word, "your".

I repeated her words to myself.

"Your father. Your father. Your father."

Then it hit me. *She's talking about my father.* I thought.

"Stevie? What do you mean? Are you talking about my father?" I asked.
She nodded.

"What about my father, Grandma? Did you see him in heaven?"

Stevie mustered whatever strength she had and shook her head. She hadn't seen my father in heaven, her response to a question that was asked in an almost patronizing way. But I wondered why my grandmother mentioned him right then, more than twenty-six years after his death. My curiosity seized me.

I tried to resign myself with the thought that it was the hallucination of a gravely ill woman who'd just awakened from a two-day coma but there were other things Stevie could have talked about. After all, she had only seen my father once and that was the night I was conceived when he came by the house to pick up my mother. And in all the years that I'd known her she had only mentioned him once.

"Stevie, what did you want to tell me about my father?" I asked.

I knew that she needed her rest but I wanted to press on for an answer. Stevie opened her eyes wide and mouthed the barely audible words, "Hope chest". She repeated the words, "hope chest" only this time it was stronger and with more conviction.

I was familiar with my grandmother's hope chest fashioned many years ago from a Dutch Masters cigar box within which the old woman held her dreams both past, present and for the future. And she meticulously guarded the box, keeping it hidden—the keeper of Stevie's secrets.

There was a certain amount of intrigue in that old box, a mystique about it that somehow gripped my thoughts like the quilt I inherited. It was in a wooden trunk that was hidden under the floorboards and under her bed. I remember once watching her struggle to lift the small trunk from its hiding place and then she'd tell me to "skee-daddle" lest I find out where she kept its key.

Whenever I'd ask her what was in the box she had hidden inside the trunk, she'd simply say, "You'll learn in time, Dahlia." I could've opened it anytime I wanted because I had always known where my grandmother kept the key but I didn't.

I guess it was because I simply thought it was a place where she kept her memories, memories irrelevant to the existence of a young girl. I had never made a connection between the box and my father until now.

Stevie was resting comfortably and the nurses were now insisting that it was O.K. for me to leave. I called my mother, told her the good news. Asked her to come and get me and to take me back to her house.

My mother had straightened up my grandmother's room while I was at the hospital. I guess the news that Stevie was better lifted my mother's spirits and getting everything back in order allowed her to re-focus her thoughts.

I went to the place in Stevie's room where she hid her hope chest and I recalled the time when I was nine years old and how I spied on my grandmother, watching as she moved her bed and counted fourteen floorboards from the North wall of the room. And under the fourteenth board, loosened by a butter knife, could be found the little wooden trunk. Its key was taped underneath the bed itself. I guess she reasoned that if anyone moved the bed to get her hope chest they'd overlook the obvious place to find the key.

The one thing I could always count on was that Stevie was consistent and the fact that the place where she kept it would never change. It was like unlocking the clues to a treasure map. After removing it from its hiding place I held the little trunk in my lap and said a prayer. I took a deep breath and used the key to open it and lifted the box from inside, the one that kept the things she held near and dear.

Her hope chest was made "tamper proof" by what seemed like yards of cloth on the outside and heavy gauged plastic meticulously wrapped around its entire outer surface. I was prepared.

Armed with a pair of scissors, I used it to cut away the cloth one layer at a time until I reached the waterproof plastic. It was easier to remove and I cut through it with a single penetration of the sharp end of the scissors. I could see clearly the images of the Dutch Masters who bore a striking resemblance to the descriptions of Alexander Dumas' Three Musketeers I'd read about in college. Finally, I cut the tape that sealed the lid and carefully pried open the box.

Inside were the things that my grandmother must've treasured above anything else tangible. A tattered Bible, yarn that matched the color of the stitching in our family quilt and her handwritten last will and testament were on top.

There was also a bundle letters wrapped and held together with a rubber band at the bottom of the box. I unraveled the bands and separated the letters. Some were addressed to Stevie and others to my mother and each letter bore the same distinctive handwriting. And on each letter appeared the name—Richard Lewis, my father. My heart seemed to stop when I read the name, but then it began to race again.

Like an archeologist exploring the pyramids of Kush in search of secrets and hidden meanings, I opened the top letter, quietly read its words and instantly became connected to my past. My father had written my mother, asking about her health and the health of their baby daughter. His words were soft and reassuring. He vowed to be devoted to his daughter. *Life's complicated,* it read: *But through it all please remember that my love for her is unwavering.*

Those words hit me like a ton of bricks and not for their content, but their timing. My mother had always told me that my father died before I was born. This letter was proof that he was alive after I was born. It was obvious that my mother had lied about his passing.

I dug deeper and opened more letters and in each one he asked about me. Each letter acted like a radioactive time clock because they were dated by events that occurred in my life. Like the time I fell off my bike and knocked out my front teeth and the times I did well in school.

He wrote three or four letters every year until I was about eleven years old and around the time my mother married Rufus. That's when the letters stopped coming.

My curiosity transformed into devastation when I thought about the stories my mother had told me. He was dead to her and she made him dead to me, too. I could feel the anger rising inside.

I wrapped myself up in Stevie's bedspread, trying to process what I'd discovered and then figured that there must've been more. Digging deep to the bottom I found a large brown envelope that was stained by time. Inside there were two black and white photographs, both grainy and faded, but I could see the people in them, posing, their faces marked by what must've have been a happy time.

The first was a picture of an attractive young couple. It was the kind people would take in the drugstore picture machine a long time ago. Like a tinted memory they were two young people posing together in the small booth that captured the soul in Sepia colored strips to be memorialized for all time or at least until the picture faded. Four pictures for twenty-five cents.

I recognized the woman in the picture as my mother, many years ago. Beside her was a handsome, young man in a fancy paisley shirt. His eyes seemed to pierce through the lens of the camera and a bright smile illuminated his face. His ringlets of black hair framed his dark face, which seemed to have been sculpted out of ebony. A Michelangelo rendition of human perfection, he was art brought to life.

I stared at the man in the picture and soon realized that I was looking in a mirror. His eyes were my eyes, his nose mine. And the high cheekbones that made him both noble and refined belonged to me, as well. I had no doubt that I was seeing my father for the first time in my life.

Suddenly, I realized that the Pandora's Box had been opened and now the evils of the world had been set free. The next picture would confirm that they could never be recaptured. I knew what it was without really looking. I'd seen the picture before, recently and at a place so far removed from where I was that it might as well have been on the other side of the universe. I'd seen the very same picture of a group of young musicians at Mac's house.

The young man in the picture with my mother was the same young man in the picture of Mac's band. He was wearing a St. Christopher medal like the one that Mac had on the night before when I tried my best to seduce him. And the inescapable conclusion made me feel sick.

I remembered when I saw the picture at Mac's house and I assumed that the young man wearing the medallion and wide smile was him and I really started feeling sick. I squirmed and mumbled to myself. Nausea grabbed hold of me. I dropped the picture on my grandmother's bed, ran down the hallway to the bathroom and threw up my insides, tried to regurgitate those thoughts and flush them down the toilet.

Day Fifteen

I once read the story, Alice In Wonderland, and it frightened me. Metaphorically lyrical, it was the Queen's constant demand—Off With Her Head—that made me fearful that someday I'd be separated from my own. But it was a view of a world through the looking glass that distorted reality and my own reflection, too. It made me question what was real and to be obsessive about my search for truth.

Songs of Desdemona—10/26/05

My mother had lied and the lie had destructive consequences that couldn't have been foretold many years ago when it was first created. No one would've predicted that someday I would unknowingly find the truth about my father and fall in love with a man who was somehow connected to him. My question, did Mac know that I was the daughter of Richard Lewis, his apparently deceased friend? And what of my father? Is he alive, even still?

For a moment I had the craziest thoughts. It started with the Asian woman who'd worked on my hair at La Femme Spa and how she told me I had Mac's eyes and asked if I was his daughter—just as Mayor Huff's wife had asked Mac that question. My thoughts then degraded even further. I thought about his coolness towards me, his paternalistic presence whenever he was around me. But there were other signs he gave me that let me know he was attracted to me like the kisses.

I spent a sleepless night turning over the events of the day in my mind beginning with the first time I saw Mackenzie Powell at J. Paul's Restaurant. Was he there by some strange coincidence? That night he was in Café Alexandria's with Felicia. Was that just a coincidence? And what about that rainy day at the book store in Adams Morgan, the one that sold espresso? Was that yet another coincidence? And did he just happen to drive by that day to find me stranded and getting soaked by the rain or was he following me? I asked myself was it all just a strange coincidence or was there something else at work?

I knew I had to confront my mother to get some answers. I wasn't sure how or what to say to her but I had to say something. I decided to wait until after breakfast and after Rufus took to the fields in his noisy diesel powered tractor. It would be better to ask her during coffee when my mother was busy cleaning the kitchen.

No one said a word during breakfast, reminded me that I was definitely home again. Rufus was his usual bubbly self with his face glued to the newspaper that served as a barrier to any conversation. He wolfed down his food and left the kitchen without saying a word to anyone.

My mother believed in big Southern style breakfasts and she spent most of the morning cooking and serving, squeezing in a bite or two as she waited for the pancakes to finish cooking. And I picked over and stirred my grits with my head down rather than eat them, a thing I started many years ago whenever I was upset. It didn't take her long to realize that something was bothering me.

"O.K. Let's hear it. What is it? Rufus?"

My mother's tone was tinged with a little bit of frustration, seasoned by her years of living with that man, I guess. But I detected a new defiance in her, probably a defense built against the docility forced on her through the years.

"You lied to me!" I shot back.

"Girl, what on earth are you talking about?"

"You lied to me about my father, mama. He wasn't killed before I was born, was he?"

I felt the sweat gathering in little droplets above my high cheekbones, a precursor to crying. I tried to choke back the tears that were beginning to well up in my eyes, to choke back twenty-six years of pain but it was like trying to seal a crack in the Hoover Dam with a band-aid. Inevitably the dam will erupt.

My mother's eyes widened. It was a dead giveaway. I'd resurrected a ghost.

"I don't know what you talkin' 'bout Dahlia! You know as well as I do that your father died twenty-six years ago. I been tellin' you the story over and over...."

I cut her off in mid-sentence sobbing along with my words.

"That's just it, Mama. It was just a story all these years. He didn't die back then and you knew it. My only question is why'd you tell me that lie?"

I was fighting the tears and my tendency to hyperventilate whenever I was upset. I kept thinking, *go easy, Dahlia. Relax.*

My mother stopped what she was doing and with dishtowel in hand took a seat at the table across from me. Her gnarled fingers wiped the sweat from her brow and then formed a cover for her face. Then she cried.

"I didn't mean to deceive you Dahlia. I was trying to protect you," she said.

"Protect me from what, Mama? Were you protecting me or were you protecting yourself?"

She unveiled the pained expression that had seized her face; put her hands flat on the table. I could tell my words were arrows that found their mark deep inside my mother's heart. I didn't want to hurt her but like they say, the truth sometimes hurt.

"Baby, it was both. I loved your father the way no woman should love any man. I mean, I barely knew him and I fell so hard and so deep I thought I was goin' crazy."

She took a hard breath like she was sucking in the painful memories and holding them so they wouldn't hurt me.

"It happened the first time I laid my eyes on him. He was up on stage and every girl in the house wanted him and I felt like every song he played he was playin' just for me. It made me feel special cause' I was this little ole country gal and here he's this tall, handsome man from New Orleans or someplace and he was givin' me that look and that broad grin of his and I was helpless."

I could tell from the way she talked that the stilled waters of her emotions ran deep. Even twenty-six years of not seeing him couldn't satisfy the thirst she must've had then one that still lingered on. The floodgates were now open and letting go to talk about him I hoped was therapeutic. I thought that it could be the warm springs that would sooth her soul.

"After the show, I waited for him and he comes out with his best friend and he says to me, 'Hey, Girl. Tonight's your lucky night'. I tried to be a good girl and even though he was just passin' through I wanted him to respect me, to court me like he really cared. So I told him it was *his* lucky night and that he had to meet my momma and get her permission to take me out."

My mother's expression turned whimsical. I know that memories like honey leave their residue on everything they touch. They become the sticky fingers that can't be licked clean. I could tell that my mother thought of him often and fondly. Memories both sweet and painful but lacking the sting of the present, faded by the passing of time.

Listening to her talk softened my spirit. I listened while she kept talking, touched by the sweetness of her memories.

"He came by and met Stevie and she was so impressed because she thought he was such a beautiful man and because he was a musician. She gave him permission to take me out. I remember he was driving a shiny, black Corvette with the top down and he took me for a drive. I could feel the wind against my face. It was like running in an open field, only much faster.

We went downtown and he bought me a milkshake and we took pictures in a photo booth at the drugstore. Later, we snuck back into my room and that was the last time I saw him.

He told me he'd be back and that he'd write me. I wrote him weeks later and told him I was pregnant. I didn't think I'd hear from him again but he called and said there was no way he was leaving the road and his music career to settle in Waycross. Said I was stupid and naïve. After that he was dead, as far as I was concerned."

The truth confirmed. I asked, "So he wasn't killed trying to get back here for my birth?"

My mother's mouth turned downward. She poked out her bottom lip and shook her head.

"He wrote me and I refused to write back but your grandma wrote him and sent him pictures of you over the years and let him know what was going on in your life.

I made her promise never to tell you and that someday I would tell you myself. But I got comfortable with the lie and I really wanted Rufus to be a father to you, so I never told you. I'm so sorry, Dahlia. I'm so sorry." She cried.

I stood up and went over to where she sat and stroked her face.

"I forgive you, Mama." I said. "Do you know where he is now? My father, I mean."

My mother was still crying as she shook her head and spoke once again.

"He quit writing after Stevie told him that I had married Rufus. He just kind of vanished from the face of the Earth. He used to send you money and gifts but that stopped, too. I guess he went on with his life."

"Can I show you the pictures, Mama?"

She nodded. I opened the brown envelope and placed the two pictures on the table and watched as she picked up the dime store picture and longingly stared at the images of the happy couple. She sighed, rubbed her fingers on their images.

"He told me that his father had given him that medallion and that he never ever took it off," she said, touching the St. Christopher's medal in the photo.

My mother then moved over to the next picture, the same one that Mac had in his house. "That was the band. They called themselves, The Soul Persuasion and see, there's your father with the chain and medallion. The fella next to him was his best friend. He was some ol' fancy Creole. Nice fella. Cute like your father. Everyone thought they were brothers. They do favor, don't they?"

I nodded.

I was pointing to the image of the man I thought was a young Mackenzie Powell. "Do you remember his name?" I asked.

My mother examined the picture again. "Yeah, they called him Mac. It was on the poster, along with the names of the other band members."

She handed me back the picture of The Soul Persuasions. There was Mackenzie twenty-seven years ago posing with his arm around my father's shoulder. I studied my father's St. Christopher's medal I wondered why Mac was now wearing it. My questions had created other questions instead of answers.

I sat there trying to gather up the courage to ask her just one more question, one I was afraid to ask and even more afraid of how she might answer. Most of all, I was afraid of its implications but I had to know.

"Momma, I have to ask you something and I hope you understand but it's something I've gotta know."

Worry returned to her eyes. "What is it, Dahlia?"

I took a deep breath then clasped her hands tight with my own. I kept my head down, eyes on her hands not wanting to see her face. I started to speak but hesitated. Like I told her it was something I had to know.

"Is there any chance that the man you say was my father's friend could actually be my father?"

I kept my eyes trained on her hands but I could sense and feel a mood shift that was slowly engulfing the entire kitchen. My mother's pain was turning to horror.

"What kind of woman do you think I am, Dahlia?"

I shook my head.

"Look at me!"

Her tone had changed from apologetic to commanding. She reversed the gentle touch I had used to hold her hands and grabbed mine. She held my hands firm and tight.

"I said, look at me Dahlia! You think I'm some kinda whore? You think that I'd sleep with two men on the same night? What would make you even ask me something like that?"

I was embarrassed and ashamed, unable to look my mother in her eyes.

"It's, it's just that it looks like either one of them could be my father. I mean, the eyes. I've got his eyes," I said pointing to Mac.

My mother exhaled her exasperation. "Seems to me that a girl with a college education wouldn't make such assumptions without some proof to go on. You got your eyes from my father! He died long before you were born—and that's a fact! My word, Dahlia!"

"I'm sorry, Momma. It's just that I know him, Mackenzie. I know him. He flew me down here."

Her mouth dropped open. "He's the one you said you think you're falling in love with?"

"Yes."

She sat there motionless for what seemed like an eternity then she smiled a warm smile.

"Life is strange and full of coincidences. Mac came to visit us after you were born. He was caring and charming. If I'd a met him first he probably would be your daddy but he was a good friend to your father and he came to check on us. Didn't see or hear from him after that."

"I guess then he could tell me about my father better than anyone else and whether he's still alive," I said.

I also thought that I could find some answers to my questions about my father by talking to my grandmother who was still recovering in the hospital.

My mother let me drive the old pickup to the hospital by myself. She seemed to know and understand that I needed to talk to Stevie alone. I was talking to myself as I drove down I-75 and turned off the exit with the sign proclaiming that Waycross was the peanut capital of the world. In my monologue I would ask my grandmother questions in a way that wouldn't strain her heart or her emotions and I hoped that she would be able to answer.

Seeing her made me feel better. She still looked frail but she was alert with her eyes wide open. Her eyes smiled when she saw me although her mouth didn't move. Smiling eyes that twinkled when they captured my image hovering over her made me smile back.

"How you doing, Grandma?" I asked her, touching her hand.

She mustered a vague smile now with her mouth and said, "Hi, baby. I'm better."

I studied her face, those eyes, her vision obscured by her pain but there was clarity in her eyes that told me she could answer any question I'd ask. I knew that. I held her hand. She closed her eyes.

"Grandma, I opened the box like you told me."

She opened, closed her eyes and opened them again. Cleared her throat and the dry sound of a voice that had been stilled for several days fought to utter words.

"I knew you would," she said.

"Grandma, there are so many things I don't understand. I read his letters but he stopped writing and I have to know this. Do you know where he is?"

She shook her head from side to side. "No, baby."

"Is my father alive?"

"I don't know. He might be but I have no way of knowing," she said. "One day the letters stopped coming and I didn't hear from him no more."

"What about his family? Did he ever tell you anything about his family?" I asked.

"Just that he was from Louisiana. Lafayette, I believe but that's all."

"What about other children? Do I have any brothers or sisters?"

My grandmother shrugged her shoulders so slightly that I barely noticed. I figured that I wasn't really gaining much from this inquiry so it was best that I stopped. I wanted to ask her a few other things like did she remember much about the man who hurt her?

I took a deep breath, regarded the bruises that had painted her brown skin.

"Grandma, did you see the man who did this to you?"

"It was real quick, Dahlia. I caught a glimpse of him but I couldn't really see much of his face. He was tall, dark...."

"You mean he was a black man?" I asked.

"Not sure. I mean, I guess. His hands were brown. He grabbed my arm but he had a wool cap on that covered his face and all he said was, 'Where is it?'"

"Where's what?" I asked.

"I don't know what he was talking about. He just kept saying, 'where is it' and then when I didn't answer he hit me and that's all I remember."

I thought about the audacity of a big, strong man hitting an older woman and it made my blood boil. And then I wondered what he was looking for. It wasn't an everyday, garden-variety break-in that was obvious. But there weren't any answers, at least from my grandmother and the story of my father remained equally evasive.

"Baby. Can I have some orange juice?" Stevie asked.

She looked over at the cup sitting on the stand beside her bed and waited patiently for me to get it. She sipped from a straw and let the juice quench the dry buildup in her throat. Forced a smile.

"How's our quilt?" she asked.

Her question caught me off-guard. She'd given it to me just a year ago, said she was passing it down but I never knew why she gave it to me then but she hadn't asked me about it during that entire time not even once.

"*Our* quilt is fine, Grandma. I got it hanging in my living room back at my place in DC."

Suddenly her face tightened. Her eyes widened as though she was staring off into the past.

"That quilt is our heritage, your legacy, Dahlia. It tells a story," Stevie said.

"I know, Grandma. It tells our family's history," I replied.

"It's very old, Dahlia."

It was old, I knew that. And very valuable. I'd had it appraised once after I saw an exhibition at the Smithsonian on quilts. Its appraised value was almost fifty thousand dollars but for my family and me it was priceless. It didn't matter how much it was worth in dollars and cents, I vowed that it would never be sold.

"I know, Grandma but why you talking 'bout it now?"

She smiled, weakly. "The treasure is within."

I studied her face, knowing how right she was. The quilt was my family's treasure and its value wasn't in the patterns and symbols and its meticulous stitching. It was in the history the quilt recorded.

I decided I wouldn't press her anymore. Instead I would embark on my own journey, seeking answers to the many questions that were rolling around in my head. I kissed Stevie on her forehead and watched as she drifted back to sleep. I was comforted knowing that she would recover.

I took a commercial flight back to Washington the next day so that I could filter through the things I'd learned during my trip home. I didn't call Mac to let him know. I wanted to exorcise the demons that were beginning to pursue me in the form of questions and talking to him now wouldn't help. Questions, like did he know that I was his best friend's daughter and if he did, why didn't he tell me? And most of all, what could he tell me about the man I thought had died many years ago.

Day Sixteen

Mailbox Full. That was the message on my answering machine. It was full to capacity with telephone calls. The early ones were from Stacy making her usual "girlfriend" calls but the messages became anxious when I didn't call her back.

I called and told her that I was back in town. I was in bad need of someone else's insight, another perspective and some good old advice about those familial revelations that I'd carried back from Waycross, all the way to Washington.

Stacy was happy to hear from me. I could tell by her voice but she had the sound of a jilted lover waiting for the fulfillment of the promised, "I'll call you, later". After chastising me for what seemed like a long minute she told me how much she missed me. I said, "I missed you, too. Can you come by my place? I need to talk to you."

"I'll be right over," she said.

Even El had called while I was gone. But the overwhelming majority of telephone calls were from two men, Antoine and Mac. Their messages were filled with the urgency of men on a mission, trying to make the world standstill for some undisclosed reason.

I wasn't surprised that Mac called, after all I had flown back home with money I borrowed from my mother without calling him. But it was the calls from Antoine that worried me. I hadn't talked to him at all the week before I left for Georgia and now he was blowing up my telephone and sounding like a man bordering on obsession.

Hey, Baby, It's Antoine. Where you been? I miss you. Or, What's up, Dahl. It's Twon. I really need to talk to you. I been thinkin' bout us. Hit me up, O.K.?

Antoine had left at least ten messages with an atypical sound of begging in his voice. It was a far cry from his old pattern of not calling or his ultra-cool player persona who'd never show his cards or any emotions. I wondered whether his calls had something to do with the FBI and their investigation.

I listened to his messages and shrugged them off. I dropped my bags in the living room without a thought about unpacking. I needed a shower. So many questions loomed over my head. Most were about Mac, some about Antoine and the rest involved my father. I opened my carryon bag and pulled out the pictures I took from Stevie's hope chest. Mused over the drugstore photo of my parents and the other one of my father's band and wondered what I'd say to Mac.

I made my way to the bathroom, stripped down, dropped the clothes I'd been wearing onto the floor and ran the water until its heat steamed the glass on the shower stall and frosted my mirrors. Heat was therapeutic and soothing, healing body, mind and spirit. I allowed it to engulf me and lead me away from the things that weighed heavily on me.

I was dazed and confused by the revelations that seemed apocalyptic in nature. The world was ending, as I had known it. There had been warnings, but I didn't understand them. I changed my mind about the shower and decided to take a long bath to give myself a chance to meditate in the quiet.

I slid into the water and stretched out. Its buoyancy seemed to lighten my spirits and I closed my eyes after laying my head back. I don't know if I'd fallen asleep or just let my mind free itself, but I could've stayed in the tub for hours, oblivious to the outside world until I heard sounds coming from my living room. *Stacy wasn't playing,* I thought. She came right over just like she said and used the key I gave her to come inside.

"I'll be right out, Stace," I shouted out from the bathroom and waited for her familiar voice to tell me to take my time. But there was no reply.

"She probably didn't hear me," I mumbled, getting out of the tub. I grabbed a towel to wrap around my wet hair and another to dry my wet body, as I listened for Stacy. But it was quiet and no sounds of movement came from beyond the closed bathroom door. Knowing Stacy, I figured she was sitting on the couch, combing through the back issues of *Ebony Magazine* that sat on my coffee table. But I knew that I had to hurry because she could get impatient and would soon be ready to leave.

"Stacy?" I called her name, again.

This time I was in the living room, but she wasn't there. I looked around my small place for any signs of my friend and concluded that what I probably heard was someone in the apartment next door or that Stacy had somehow slipped past me and had gone down the hall to my extra bathroom. I walked back down the hall with a little bit of caution in my stride.

"Stacy? You in there?"

I glanced around at my bedroom door, but it was closed. I shrugged off the thought that she might be inside because the door would've been wide open and Stacy would probably be lying on my bed. I continued walking to the other bathroom, calling out her name again.

No answer.

I flinched when I thought I saw a shadow move, but I wrote it off as a symptom of my fears. I had locked the door to my apartment right after I walked inside and the door was still closed.

But my senses told me that something wasn't right. I could feel a presence in my apartment, even if I couldn't see it. Something told me to look back over my shoulder, but before I could turn I felt the weight of a strong arm grab me from behind me, gripping tight around my waist and a gloved hand suppressing the sound of terror ready to spring from my mouth, reflexive as a by-product of my fear. My primal urge to scream had been muffled, quieted by my assailant whom I felt, but couldn't see.

The gloved hand gripped my mouth in a vice made of flesh covered by leather, as his right arm held me with equal force around my waist. Fear had been my companion from the moment I felt his clutch and those tentacles engulfed me and made me more fearful by the minute.

The combination of his covering my mouth with one hand and trapping the air inside my stomach with the other, along with the way I held my breath made me a candidate for oxygen deprivation. And the consequence of a lack of air meant a lack of coherency. My mind raced without thinking and searched in earnest for the right reaction.

His grip around my stomach eased up and for a second I felt a little relieved, but it was short-lived as I felt a new reason for my terror. Cold steel was being pressed up against my throat, a flat and wide dispenser of death that had but one function and that was to kill and gut and rip through human flesh with quiet ease. But what I felt was the threatening side of the knife not the killing side and I concluded that it wasn't my life he wanted right then, but probably my body.

"Don't fucking scream! Don't cry. Or I'll cut you, bitch. I'll cut you, deep," he said. His throaty, whispered threats chilled me, made my kidneys weaken and paralyzed all thoughts and functions. If fear had a sound, that was it. The irony was that I couldn't scream even if he hadn't told me not to. My screams or any sounds, for that matter, were caught in that space between my vocal chords and my heart with both too scared to move.

"I'm going to ask you one question and for your sake you better tell me what I want to hear. All right?"

His voice and words reflected his total dominance over the situation and over me, too.

I nodded, profusely.

"Where is she?" he asked.

Where is she? I thought. *Where's who?* I didn't know who he was talking about. He removed his hand from my mouth and waited for my answer.

"Where's who?" I asked.

"Don't fucking play with me!" His tone was rife with impatience. "You know goddamn well what I'm talking about. The old lady tried to bullshit us and you see what happened to her. Like, I said. Where is it?"

His grip tightened and the dull side of his knife was slowly breaking the surface of my skin. I swallowed back my fear, concluded that whatever it was he wouldn't kill me until I told him where to find it. I thought about what he had said about the old lady, my grandmother, and how she tried to bullshit *"us"*. I realized that he or someone associated with him was the person who'd broken into my mother's house and hurt my grandmother and here he was in Washington on a cross-country quest for something or someone I didn't know. What baffled me most was how he thought that Stevie could've had what he was trying to find or that I might have it.

He was breathing hard as I was hardly breathing. His breath was full of garlic and the residue of spicy food filled my nostrils with the smell of curry powder or Creole-style gumbo. When he spoke I caught the scent of his last meal full in my face as it crept from behind and from where he stood. In what seemed like a carefully disguised voice he said, "Let's check your bedroom." It made me shudder and he sensed that, too.

"Don't worry. I ain't gonna rape your skinny ass. Just give me what I want and nobody gets hurt. Understand?"

He spun me around and pushed me down the hallway with the knife at the ready.

"Open it," he directed.

But before I could grab the doorknob he must've noticed my purse and luggage thrown loosely across the living room floor.

"Let's see what goodies you brought back."

He followed me to the living room. I tried to get a peek at him out of the corner of my eye, but his face was covered with a bandana gangsta-style and topped off with sunglasses. A Baltimore Ravens baseball cap covered his head. He was a man without a face or identity. There was no way to describe him to the police.

"Just look at the wall and you won't get hurt. Understand?"

He reached past me and grabbed my carry-on bag, dumped its contents on the floor and rifled through tubes of lipstick, makeup, panties and the precious pictures that I'd gotten from my grandmother. Disappointed, he turned and stalked his way towards me with his knife poised to kill.

"For the last time, where is it bitch," he said.

He spun me around and I felt the sting of his hand's swift contact to my face. There was anger in his blow, meant to punish me for my apparent deception. I braced myself for another one, believing that he would soon finish me with the killing side of the knife he still brandished. I squinted, cried and waited for the end. Held my breath as though I could numb myself by oxygen deprivation.

I didn't see him, either. But he came in a blur from a different part of the room. Crashing into and hitting my assailant from out of nowhere. We both were oblivious to his coming as he sent my intruder sprawling to the floor in a heap.

The knife became disengaged from the hand of my attacker and went flying across the room. There were two men on the floor in a death struggle, villain versus hero. And I could see that the hero was Antoine.

He used his six foot-two inch frame like the running back he claimed he was in high school and he drove the intruder into the wall. The heavy sounds of fighting continued as I hid in a corner of the room. There was a loud grunt, followed by stillness and a solitary figure rose from the rubble and ran for the door. It was the faceless assailant leaving in a rush with Antoine sprawled out on the floor. The worst kind of fear grabbed hold of me. It was my fear that Antoine was dead.

I jumped to my feet and locked the open door, walked gingerly over to where Antoine was lying very still on the floor and hoping for some sign of life. I thought about the knife, but it was under my sofa and the intruder had somehow subdued Antoine. I started to panic as I leaned over him. There was no blood I could see, no evidence the fluid that sustained life was seeping out of him and when he groaned and moved I felt a sense of relief.

"Antoine? Antoine. Are you O.K.?" I asked.

I struggled to roll his two hundred pound frame onto his back and watched as he fought to regain his focus and consciousness. Slowly, his eyes opened and then he squeezed them shut for a moment. He coughed and reached for his side in an effort to quell the pain of a heavy body blow left as a reminder of his struggle with the intruder.

"Is he gone?" Antoine asked.

I nodded while holding his pretty head.

"You chased him out of here," I told him.

I was barely able to speak. My voice trembled and my knees were weak and all I could think about was what might've happened had Antoine not appeared.

I guess it was his persistence in trying to reach me that brought him to my place that evening or maybe he had some kind of insight that I was in trouble.

But none of that mattered. It didn't matter to me how or why he ended up at my place. I was in dire need and all that mattered was that Antoine had fought off the boogeyman.

Day Seventeen

I write you, my son, because I want you to know that men are capable of extraordinary good and incomparable evil. More than anything, I only wanted to feel safe from them. The boogeyman that lived in my closet when I was a little girl had grown up with me. Later, he would expose himself like the pervert in the raincoat, unabashed through impulse and compulsion, bent on harm, oblivious to consequence. His objective was to torment and he could do just that because there were no hiding places in my Bangkok prison.

Songs of Desdemona—10/27/05

It took Antoine a few minutes to gather himself. He'd taken a hard blow to his ribs, had the wind knocked out of him. He was now sitting up with his back against the wall and breathing heavy.

"I'll get you some water," I told him.

He took a couple of sips, inhaled deep and let the air out of his lungs. He smiled, slightly and shook his head.

"I hadn't been hit like that since I played ball."

He looked at me, could see the concern in my eyes, mixed with the residue of the fear that had preceded his heroic arrival.

"You, a'ight?" He asked.

I nodded. I was all right thanks to Antoine, but his question brought back the reality and gravity of what had just happened. Through my attack I never once thought about actually dying, but I realized at that point, watching Antoine recover, that I could've been killed.

"I don't know what would've happened if you hadn't come along. I think he would've killed me."

"Well, the muthafucka's lucky he got that cheap shot in. My eyes were looking for that knife he had when I came in. Did you get a look at him?"

"Nah. He was all covered."

Antoine's face coursed the emotional landscape from anger to sympathetic. He could see that I had only a towel wrapped around me.

"What? He was trying to rape you?"

His anger returned.

"No, I don't think it was about that. He was looking for something, but the strange thing is that I think he was the same guy who broke into my folks' house."

Antoine looked astonished. "You mean in Georgia!" he said. "Shit don't make sense."

I agreed.

"This is the craziest thing I've ever seen Antoine and I'm scared. All of a sudden all kind of things are happening to me and I don't know and I definitely don't understand."

I looked around my apartment at the wreckage that was on display as the aftermath from the fight.

"How'd you get in?" I asked.

"Door was cracked open. Question is: How did that guy get in?"

Antoine dragged himself off the floor and walked over to examine the door and then closed it.

"No sign of any force," he said. "Must've had a key."

That was as terrifying as anything I'd heard that evening. The fact that someone had a key to my apartment and could come in whenever he wanted was frightening. After all Stacy had a spare key to my place, but she was the only one.

Antoine continued. "You need to get your lock changed."

"And call the police," I added. I walked over to the spot where all of my belongings had been spilled out onto the floor. I started searching for my cellular, buried somewhere in the rubble.

Antoine had a sickened expression on his face like the word, police, was toxic—the five-oh pandemic.

"Hold up a minute, Dahlia."

"What? Why?"

"What they gone do? Nuthin', really. Make a report? Shit like that. Keep us here all night. Or worse, take us down to the station. I mean, what you gone tell them. Dude came in here trying to rob you? You're all right. Trust me, he ain't coming back."

I didn't trust Antoine regardless of the fact that he came to my rescue. He had a ton of hidden agendas, but in some ways it made sense not to call the police. Suddenly, any mention of law enforcement made me distrustful and cautious and

I didn't need to be converted from victim to perpetrator. Besides, by the look on Antoine's face it was clear that he didn't want to talk to the police about anything. *Must be tied to the system,* I thought. On probation, parole or outstanding warrants can make a brother phobic about dealing with the law.

"What am I supposed to do in the meantime?" I asked.

He rolled a smile across his lips.

"You can stay at my place. Tomorrow you can get the lock changed and you should tell your condo management about this. File a police report once you figure out what you gone do."

I didn't know what to think when Antoine suggested that I stay at his house. I had always assumed that he lived with his momma like so many lost and aimless young brothers I knew—even if he did drive a fifty thousand dollar car. But the suggestion made sense and I was too afraid to sleep at my place that night.

I threw on some clothes and grabbed an overnight bag and met him back in my living room. He was walking around playing amateur detective, casing the place to see if the intruder had left some evidence of any kind. I told him that the knife slid under the sofa and watched as he retrieved it. It was a large folding knife with a devilish curve. Antoine closed it and gave it to me. "Evidence," he said. "Hold on to it." Satisfied that there was nothing else he moved like he was heading for the door.

"You ready?" he asked me.

I paused for a moment. I was beginning to second guess myself because in that instant I thought about this man that I'd been intimate with in a physical way with his lies and secrets. But I realized that I had to trust him regardless of what FBI Agent Liles said because if Antoine hadn't shown up I'd probably be dead.

I remembered that Stacy was on her way. "I better call Stace and let her know what happened so she can turn around and go back home where it's safe."

She was still home when I called, said something about an argument with Derek and that's the reason she was running late. I didn't tell her what happened, just that I was leaving and wouldn't be home. I hung up thinking that it might have been better to spend the night at Stacy's except for all of her drama with Derek. But my own drama was in overdrive and what I needed most was a good night's sleep.

I followed Antoine outside. He looked from side to side for any signs of danger and then helped me into his car. Forty-five minutes later we were pulling up to a row of three story townhouses in an exclusive gated neighborhood near Washington Harbor. Antoine pushed the remote control button inside his Escalade, opening the garage door.

"You live here!" I said.

"Yeah."

"With who?"

He laughed. He was obviously amused by the question.

"This is *my* place. Deed, title, taxes, insurance, all in my name."

He led me inside and into a place with hardwood floors, vaulted ceilings and modern recessed lighting. Tasteful art, the kind you might see in an art gallery, and bronze sculptures displayed on pedestals accented the environment.

"This is nice," I said. "Real nice."

I took the tour. Antoine had a shelf full of football trophies as evidence of his glory days, but this didn't surprise me as much as the plaques on his wall. These weren't tributes to his football prowess. Instead, they paid homage to his scholastic accomplishments. Dean's List, Distinguished Student and a Bachelor of Science Degree with Magna Cum Laude honors were his *fete accompli,* a testimonial to academic achievements. I was both pleased and stunned.

"I don't get it, Antoine. You always come across as some wannabee thug. You know, blunt smoking, dick holding brotha from the streets, but this is the real you."

I was holding my breath, hoping that he wouldn't take my comments and candor as an insult.

"I'm sorry," I added.

"No apology needed. It's all about the persona. You know. Street cred. Gotta have it to succeed in the rap game. So I put the academics on the shelf and act like I'm from the hood. It works for me. You know, you're the only person I let see this room," he said and paused.

"So all that talk about growing up in the hood, getting into trouble and going to prison was just that—talk."

"Yeah, if the people I work with knew that I was some geek, nerdy bookworm you think they'd deal with me? Hell, no. They want someone who can relate. Somebody who feels what they feel."

I shook my head, thought about how smart Antoine was, but also, how misguided.

"I think it's about talent, Antoine. If you can write and compose that's all that matters. Putting up a front won't help you make it, but being true to yourself will." I paused. "But you know I kinda understand your logic. The part I don't understand, especially after seeing everything you've accomplished is why you're involved with some shady business that's got the FBI looking at you.

He glared at me for a moment. "Look, I told you all that's on the up and up. They just think that a black man with money is doing dirt. I'm serious about my music."

I rolled my eyes slightly without thinking, an indication of my skepticism. "Music career! What music career? You didn't get all of this from your music, did you?"

"That's not the point and I didn't get this place slinging dope or doing something illegal. I can't tell you all my business but like I said, I'm serious about my music," he repeated the same refrain.

I could see that he was reflecting on what I'd just said. But when he said, "Let me show you my studio" I knew that he would ignore any advice I could give him.

I followed him through several rooms and to the rear section of his townhouse. Antoine opened up the double doors and we entered his world of keyboards, computers, microphones and a padded sound room.

"This is where I spend most of my time."

He walked over to the huge mixing board that dominated the area and picked up some headphones.

"I got some beats I gotta mix tonight for one of my artists. You need to get some sleep. Make yourself at home and tomorrow we'll see about getting your locks changed and making that police report."

I went to bed wondering about what Antoine was thinking and how he seemed so different. He wasn't that overactive libido-laden, self-indulgent man I'd known for the last year and although I had questions, Antoine wasn't really a thug. Instead, he was this highly educated, Renaissance man. I could tell that he was hurt by the doubts I had about him and his music, but could he blame me? The law was pressing me about him and there still remained this small matter of a quarter of a million reasons why he put that money in the bank under my name. Like J.C. once said, "If it doesn't fit, you must acquit." I guess I could turn that around and in Antoine's case say: *If the facts don't fit, you must convict.*

I knew I wouldn't rest easy that night. Ironically, it wasn't because of the break-in, that scared me, but I was no longer paralyzed by fear. What would have me tossing and turning that night would be thoughts of Mackenzie.

I found myself once again lying in the guest bedroom of a man's luxurious home and it reminded me of being at Mac's house, except the man I wanted, the man I craved wasn't in the other room. All I could think about, despite my ordeal that night, was seeing him. Add the fact that he had once known my father and that he probably didn't know that I was Richard Lewis' little girl and my anxiety level was at an all-time high.

My thoughts drifted to this growing mystery scripted as my life and I wondered how the puzzle could be solved.

◆   ◆   ◆

I woke up the next morning not to the smell of coffee brewing or Canadian bacon sizzling on Antoine's kitchen island, but to the aroma of cannabis permeating the air throughout his entire house and mixing in with the scent of fresh gardenias strategically placed in almost every room. I wandered down the stairs to the place where food should be cooking to find him sitting in a chair with the newspaper on the table in front of him, smoking twigs, internal combustion.

"Well, I see you're off to an early start," I told Antoine.

He took a puff, allowed a large plume of smoke to exit his lungs and let loose the ten thousand brain cells that were attached to the THC residue.

"It's the breakfast of champions," he said, matter-of-factly. "If it bothers you, I'll put it out. It kind of eases the pain." He was holding his ribs.

"No, it's O.K. You all right?" I asked.

Antoine lifted his shirt to display his ripped six—pack torso and a deep blackened bruise that looked like a cloud.

"I'm fine. Been hit harder playing football and kept playing." He put on his best macho man impression.

"I'll get some ice," I said.

I looked past him to the wall of windows that started from the floor, rising three stories as the rear wall of his townhouse. His place overlooked the Potomac River and the tranquil setting of water and pleasure boats. From here I could see Haynes Point and the Washington Monument in one panoramic view and wondered how a twenty-three year old black man could live like this if he wasn't doing anything wrong or illegal.

I put the ice on his bruised ribs and held it, He leaned back and sighed.

"That feels good, baby."

He had that slight smile and the look of a man whose mind was venturing into the carnal. I felt his hand touch my head with gentle strokes that begged for reciprocation. He wanted me. I could tell. But things had changed since our last mindless, sexual encounter and I wasn't feeling the way he felt.

"Not right now," I told him.

He pulled his hand away, gave me that incredulous look, like *I don't believe you rejected me.*

"C'mon, baby. Brotha went through a lot last night."

"So you feel like I owe you something?"

I was fighting my own indignation at the thought—you saved me so you have the right to screw me?

"Not like you owe me or sump'in. It's just, you know, that's our story. You never turned me down before."

I walked away from him and turned my thoughts out the window and on to the beautiful cityscape that stretched out in front of me. I didn't want to look at him right then, but I couldn't let his comment go without saying something.

"Damn, Antoine. I been through a lot lately, you know? Some asshole breaks into my place and threatens to kill me and he's probably the same man who broke into my folks' house and hurt my grandmother and all you care about is sex! I don't believe this shit!"

I still had my back to him, preferring to watch the water and the boats. I could hear the winded sound of his lungs inhaling another long toke, continuing his journey from the not so sublime to the subliminal. From his lofty perch Antoine thought I owed him. Maybe it was the madness of the reefer talking or maybe it was our history that had exalted him and made him think that the bounty of my booty was his entitlement. But times had changed and so had I.

"Look, Antoine. You know there was a time when I felt that it was enough to just be around a man like you, a man women look at and lust for and have you pay a little attention to me. To have you want me was enough. But things are different, Antoine. I'm not the same girl."

"Yeah, I can tell you had a makeover." I wasn't surprised by his sarcastic retort.

His green eyes shifted to a steely gray or maybe it was the sun reflecting through the windows.

"It's more than that, Antoine. It's a paradigm shift." I thought. *Where did that come from? Paradigm?*

"So you learned a new word? Maybe you should have said that it was an epiphany."

Antoine still wasn't trying to disguise his sarcasm.

"Whatever" was my reply..

"Is there someone else? You seeing someone else?" he asked. The question was definitely out of character because he never seemed to care what I did and whether I did it with anyone else.

I wrestled with myself and silence prevailed.

"Yeah, just what I thought. I already called a locksmith. So whenever you're ready we can go to your place and change those locks. I'll go get dressed."

I stood there fuming, but proud of the way I'd turned the tables by standing up for myself. Antoine's joint was the other thing fuming. I thought I'd better put it out so he wouldn't waste any part of his precious plant.

I glanced down at the newspaper near the ashtray, the front page. Saw a face I'd seen before. He was baldheaded with a pseudo-smile in a prison quality photo. There was an article with a headline. Read: ***MURDER VICTIM IDEN-TIFIED.***

I thought: *Oh my God! It's that guy Mackenzie almost got into a fight with that night at the jazz club!* I kept reading. They found him that same night behind Café Alexandria's in the alley with a gunshot to the back of the head. The newspaper called it "execution style". The article identified him as "Joseph Martin".

My thoughts re-wound to the night I saw Mac with Felicia at the club, the altercation, the flash of light reflecting off the gun concealed inside his jacket and the dead man. I kept reading. The article said that the police weren't sure of a motive, but they hadn't ruled out robbery. I remember the victim being obnoxious that night. Someone probably took offense.

Being drunk and obnoxious was no reason to kill a man. I quickly dismissed the thought as a strange coincidence and waited for a disgruntled Antoine to take me back to my house. But my thoughts kept taking me back to Joe, the dead man and I wondered.

Day Eighteen

Serendipity: I looked the word up in a Thai to English dictionary my captors had given me. (Note: For the first time I use the word, "captors" signifying that I am a hostage not a prisoner here. Understand the difference) Anyway, my point is it's defined as, the faculty of happening upon fortunate discoveries when not looking for them. I guess it just means, having good luck.

Songs of Desdemona—10/28/05

The ride with Antoine was a wordless journey punctuated by his occasional turning up the volume in his chariot with the twenty-two speakers. I was quiet because I was thinking about Mackenzie and the revelations my trip home had revealed. The fleeting thought that he might be my father made me feel ridiculous. I was glad I asked my mother about him, glad she erased the thought. I sat back and started getting into the music on Antoine's CD player.

It was a soulful mix of his music featuring a young female singer. I admit that I was feeling this groove, which reminded me of a pre-hip hop, Seventies jam my mother once played over and over on our cassette player.

"Who is this?" I asked Antoine.

"Some new talent I'm working with."

I was waiting for more from him, thinking that he'd tell me about the artist, but he fell back into verbal silence with the music as the foreground for our existence while we rode in his car. He was still smarting from my rebuff of his advances. A man like him had only heard the word "yes" from women most of his life and my rejection must've been a hard pill to swallow.

"She's really good."

"Yeah," that was his only word until we reached my place.

I think Antoine and I saw the dark, government issued sedan parked in front of my building at the same time and it made him jittery while it made me curious. It looked like the same car I had seen parked in front of Mac's house and I remembered Felicia's explanation about how the cops protect the wealthy. I assumed that they weren't there that day to protect some secret millionaire living in my building.

We rolled to a stop a couple of buildings down from mine as Antoine seemed to study the scene. Although our attention had been primarily on the unmarked car I quickly noticed that there was a swarm of police cars in the parking lot adjacent to my building. Antoine mumbled, "Looks like some kind of SWAT operation." My instincts told me that it was something else, something personal.

I looked at Antoine and said, "Still think they're fishing?"

He had this scared, nervous look like a kid who'd been caught by his parents with his pants down around his ankles and a Playboy magazine in one hand. He tried to speak, but his nerves were caught in his throat. He coughed, hoping that his testicles would recede back to their proper place and he would have the courage to say something. "Ah, look. I gotta go someplace. I almost forgot, I-I have an appointment."

It was my cue to get out of his car and face whatever was happening inside alone. I gave Antoine a disgusted look, twisted my lips at one corner of my mouth and shook my head. I made the long, slow walk to my building as I heard my "hero" burn rubber leaving the area.

I laughed, slightly as I opened the front door to the building. I thought: *It's probably Mrs. Sloski on the fifth floor knighting the mister with a frying pan.* But the solemn expression on the concierge's face told me otherwise.

I saw them when I came out of the elevator, police in uniforms and plainclothes and in their midst was Agent Liles standing in my doorway. I walked right up to them and said, "What's going on here? Why are you in my apartment?"

"The locals got a report of a disturbance last night. Said there was a fight and that a woman might've been abducted," he said. His nonchalant tone made me skeptical.

"Where's Mr. Robinson?" I asked him.

"If you're referring to SAIC Robinson, he's inside."

I remembered the title on Robinson's business card. SAIC meant *Special Agent In-Charge* and it made me think about the HNIC designation that black folks attached to other blacks in important positions. I walked by Liles and into chaos. There were several officers inside going through my place, turning over furniture and opening drawers with Robinson orchestrating the entire show.

"Why are they doing this?" I asked. My tone was a mixture of shock and anger.

Agent Robinson turned and gave me a matter-of-fact, "We're searching for evidence."

"Searching for what evidence?"

"Can't tell you that," he replied.

'What about a warrant? You got a warrant?" I had enough presence of mind to ask the question despite my horror at seeing my place being ransacked.

"Exigent circumstances," said Liles, who was suddenly standing at his partner's side.

I looked confused.

"It means search incident to a lawful arrest or some other extraordinary circumstance like a crime scene," Robinson explained.

"But I'm O.K. so there's no reason to search my house," I told them.

Liles had that same evil smirk painted on his face. "We didn't know that when we started so we went ahead and did our duty. You know, searching for blood and DNA just in case you really were missing."

My jaws tightened. I gave him one of my own evil stares. "And I just bet you personally searched my panty drawer, didn't you."

Liles shrugged my comment off like I had bestowed a badge of honor on him. I looked over at Robinson, my eyes pleading for help. "I haven't done anything wrong," I told him.

He said nothing as we all watched the uniformed police officers continue rifling through my belongings. One of them reached up to remove my grandmother's quilt from the wall, which in my mind was the ultimate intrusion.

"Wait! My great-great grandmother made that while she was a slave! It's a family heirloom!" I said, protesting.

Robinson signaled to the officer to leave it alone. "I think we're finished here," he said. "Miss Reynolds we need you to come down to headquarters."

"I think I asked you this once before. Do I need to call a lawyer?"

"No, I just need to show you something," Agent Robinson explained.

"And if I refuse?"

"That money in an offshore account makes you a co-conspirator so I think it's in your best interests to come along. Don't worry we'll have someone clean up this mess. Liles can stick around and supervise."

Agent Liles' smirking grin quickly evaporated.

◆   ◆   ◆

I had seen the J. Edgar Hoover Building many times and never ever wanted to go inside yet there I was sitting in a stark looking office with SAIC Robinson sitting behind an equally stark looking desk. I thought about Mac and compared his desk to Robinson's. I thought about Mac period and compared him to the FBI agent, in general and there was no comparison.

Paul Robinson was attractive and about Mac's age, but he lacked the sex appeal. He was probably a lady-killer back in the day with his soulful eyes set on chocolate skin, but I could see that the years hadn't been kind. I guess it was all of his years chasing criminals as a civil servant. El said it made you cynical. Cynicism makes you old. I concluded that Mackenzie Powell must be the ultimate optimist. I was prepared to proclaim my innocence to whatever crime Robinson thought I might have committed even if I had to subject myself to his cynical eye.

I tried not to look at him, at first, preferring to focus on my hands and the manicure that needed refreshing while I waited for him to open up the discussion. I looked around his office. Robinson had a bookcase stocked with training manuals and crime related books and on top of the case was a Baltimore Ravens autographed football. I heard him rustle through some papers and pull something from his desk drawer, but I didn't bother to look to see what it was.

"You like history Miss Reynolds?"

"I'm always interested in learning new things even if it's about something old," I replied.

He smiled, slightly. "Let me tell you a story that started back about fifty years ago. It was South Africa in the throes of apartheid. Dutch Afrikaners were running things and the black Africans were working the mines as virtual slaves. Anyway, there was one mine in particular that was so dangerous and took so many lives that the people called it 'The Hole of Death'."

Robinson leaned way back in his chair, folded his hands behind his head and continued. "When they started dismantling apartheid in 1990 one of the first things the new government demanded was to have that mine closed. However, The Hole had yielded the rarest, purest and largest yellow diamond ever found a few years earlier. The diamond weighed thirty-seven carats and it was flawless. A yellow diamond is extremely rare and this was the only mine in South Africa that produced diamonds of that hue."

He stood up from his desk as though he needed to take a break from his own history lesson. "Would you like some water?" he asked me.

I nodded and watched him open a small refrigerator that was parked under the only window in the room. He retrieved two bottles of water, handed me one and twisted off the cap of the bottle he had for himself. He took a long swig nearly downing all of the water in a single gulp then wiped his lips and returned to his seat behind the barren desk.

"Let me fast forward a little bit. This pure and extremely rare yellow diamond was stolen from South Africa and sold to the King of Thailand—a lot of people don't realize that Thailand has a monarchy. Been there?"

I shook my head and said, "No".

"The Thai love their king. I digress. As I was saying, the diamond was bought and made into a necklace for the queen with the chain made entirely of one hundred and twenty-five diamonds two carats each. This made the yellow diamond not only rare, but also probably one of the most priceless pieces ever made."

He smiled. "I know what you're thinking and you're absolutely right. Somebody up and stole the necklace. Can you believe that? Somehow it was stolen again before it ever made it to Thailand. Word was that some Columbian drug lord bought it on the black market—I hate that description——and it became the ultimate sign of his wealth and prominence in the cartel. Back in the Eighties the Columbians drug lords were notorious for their conspicuous consumption with each cartel leader trying his best to top the other."

Agent Robinson finished the last sip of his water, used his shirt sleeve to wipe off its residue from his lips. He cleared his throat.

"So this drug lord had a home in Costa Rica and that became his base of operation for exporting his products to the U.S. Well it's the year of our lord 1989 and two young African American brothers—they're not really brothers as in related by blood—strike a deal with the Columbian to bring some product into the states. To sum it all up, the deal goes bad. The Columbian stiffs them and they find a way to steal this ultra-rare, priceless piece of jewelry. Of course, the two brothers signed their own death warrant and in fact, they find one of them in New Orleans a few months after the theft and I don't need to tell you the details.

The other one is arrested by a young FBI agent for high crimes and misdemeanors and he spends five years in one of our minimum security spa and resorts," Robinson laughed. "He had been running a con game when he wasn't pimping part-time. Of course, we didn't know about his involvement in the theft of the jewelry at the time of his arrest, his partner is dead and the jewelry was never found. Basically we've been keeping tabs on this fellow ever since he was released from prison and I must say he's done all right for himself. I guess he's an example of what a man can accomplish in this country if he puts his mind to it."

I shook my head, looked confused. I was feeling a little exasperated because he was wasting my time. "What does all this have to do with me Agent Robinson?" I asked.

He leaned forward, used his hand as a brace for his chin with his elbow planted firmly on the desk. He inhaled, held it and slowly exhaled like he was using a yoga relaxation technique. "The man they found in New Orleans in a motel down in the Ninth Ward was Richard Lewis, your father."

◆   ◆   ◆

I guess I should've been stunned or at least, appeared to be shocked by the news of my father's demise, but I had never known him and I'd spent my entire life believing he was dead. The revelation in the form of his letters to my grandmother had offered some glimmer of hope that he might still be alive so Agent Robinson's 'bombshell" only confirmed what had been my truth for twenty-six years.

"My father was killed in 1990," were my first words. It was a stretch from the itinerant musician he was when my mother met him. I settled back into my chair, mulled over the agent's words and realized that there was a point to his story. "You still haven't explained why you're telling me all this."

"You're Richard Lewis' only family."

I smirked. "And I suppose you're going to tell me that he left me in his will."

"That's what we're hoping you'd tell us," he said. "Tell me where the jewels are and we can end this charade."

"I have no idea what you're talking about."

"Actually, I almost believe you. But what I believe isn't important. There are other people who think you have those rocks," Robinson said.

"What about his partner, the one who went to prison?" I asked.

"He's looking for it, too. Actually, that's why we're keeping tabs on your friend, Antoine."

It was a light bulb moment. The break-in at my family's home, my own intruder and even the stiff sitting at the desk in front of me were all looking for a piece of jewelry I didn't have. The FBI had no search warrant. It was just an excuse to search my apartment hoping they'd find the crown jewels in a D.C. suburban apartment. Robinson was law enforcement, but something about him made me uneasy. I realized my being under some kind of suspicion was a ruse.

"What does Antoine have to do with this?" I asked.

Agent Robinson smiled. "Antoine's a bit player. In fact, we're not sure what his role is. The money he deposited in that bank for you is legit except that it might be a violation of Antiguan law to falsify a deposit slip. Otherwise, we think he's some kind of front man. It's the people he works for we're really interested in."

"Who is that?" I asked.

"Your father's, partner. I put him away once and I'm going to put him away again. This time it'll be for a long, long time. You know him as Mackenzie Powell."

I sat in silence for what seemed like an eternity then the questions started accumulating in my mind. "Antoine works for Mac?" I asked the question just to confirm what the agent had told me.

Robinson nodded.

"And Mac is looking for the jewelry?"

He nodded again.

"And they think I have it?"

"Yes. It was Antoine's job to locate it. They thought that by his getting close to you you'd talk about it and tell him where they could find the diamond. I guess his boss must've figured he wasn't man enough to finish the job. You can imagine how surprised I was to see you with Mac at the fundraiser."

My heart sank. I knew then what Antoine saw in me, but the pain came in realizing what Mac wanted and the things he was willing to do to get it. I was sure that Agent Robinson could see my pain etched indelibly all over my face, but he ignored it. Unfortunately, I couldn't. I had to get out of there.

I said in a low tone, "But I don't have the jewelry."

"Like I told you, I believe you don't, but *they* don't know you don't have it," Robinson said.

I saw him look down and watched as he slowly opened the top drawer to his desk. He pulled out a beautiful brown Mahogany box that was about the size of a notebook, but thicker then gently placed it on the desk in front of me. I sat there in dumb silence.

"The Thai government wants their property bad. So bad they've offered a reward of five million dollars to the person who recovers it or tells them where it is. No questions asked. The problem is someone, a very powerful person in Thailand wants the diamond as well and he's willing to pay a lot more money for it."

Robinson slowly eased the box across his desk so that I could touch it. "Open it," he said. "Please."

I reached for it like I was under some kind of spell, my mind on overload and now de-sensitized to any shock or fear. Slowly, I lifted the box's lid with my eyes opening wider with every corresponding movement of my hand. And there it was placed on black satin, a huge beautiful yellow diamond with a chain of a hundred smaller white ones sparkling like it had been harvested from the sun itself.

"I don't understand. This is it. This is the diamond you told me about. It's not missing at all," I said.

Robinson leaned close. "This, young lady, is the miracle of science. Diamonds made by man and his friend, the computer. It's worth about twenty-five thousand dollars and made to look like the real thing," he said. "The guys in the lab call it 'Desdemona II'."

"What? Desdemona?"

"Yeah, that's the name of the original stone."

"I gotta go," I said. It was too much for me to take. My senses were on overload.

Robinson nodded. "I understand. I just want you to do one thing." He looked at the jewelry in the box. "Take it with you."

"Why?" I asked.

"Bait. Mac wants it. You give it to him. I, in return, get him and his cohorts. The Thai government can nab their countryman and maybe one day the real thing will appear."

"So, I'm supposed to just walk up to him and say, 'Here, I know you've been looking for this diamond you and my father stole many years ago,'" I said.

The agent's response was a half-hearted laugh. "I think you can be a lot more subtle than that. Just tell him you found it during your visit back home and you want to know if it's worth anything. Trust me, Mackenzie Powell will know what to do from that point on."

"And what about the Columbians? I'm sure they haven't given up looking for the real diamond. His people are probably the ones who broke into my house," I said.

"I doubt it. Most of them are dead or in prison, but I wouldn't rule anything out. We have the tape from your building's security monitor. We'll be studying it to see if we find some answers. In the meantime we'll make sure you're protected."

I had a parting thought. "I thought you said that the diamond belonged to the nation of South Africa?" I asked.

"In a way it does, but possession is nine-tenths of the law and in this case it's Thailand that has all the chips in the game. Desdemona was a symbol of South African pride, but she's lost to them. Cash is king," he answered.

"Doesn't seem right," I said.

I turned down his offer for a ride home, choosing to walk around downtown with a twenty-five thousand dollar fake necklace in my purse. For a couple of hours I walked around deep in thought and window shopped without really looking at items in the stores along Connecticut Avenue. I stopped at a small tavern on M Street and drank brandy alone and listened to a sad Billie Holliday lullaby. It only deepened my pain. A short cab ride and some courage later I was standing in front of Mac's house poised to knock on his door.

I had asked the cab driver to wait a few minutes just in case Mac wasn't home or I had lost my nerve, but his car was parked in front and that answered one of my two questions. Seeing my cab take off and disappear down the long driveway forced me to seek an answer to the second. Did I have the nerve to confront him about the things that had rocked my world since the time we first met?

I thought about what Paul Robinson told me about Mac and realized that a lot of what he said was based on suspicion and speculation. Mac having known my father was real and that was my only truth because I could prove it. Everything else I was told and I would give him the opportunity to explain.

I knocked on the door and waited. Rang the doorbell and waited. Rang the doorbell again and again like a woman possessed. The firewater I drank was my fuel. "Mackenzie! Mackenzie! I need to talk to you," I shouted. Resignation was slowly setting in and I realized that just because his car was there didn't mean that he had to be. With one last knock and kick to that obstinate door I slid down to the step, sat there exhausted and exasperated.

I had my head down sitting in a Lotus position when the door cracked open and I heard a sleepy voice that almost cracked, "Dahlia? Is that you?"

"Can we talk?" I asked followed by, "Are you alone?"

Mac had this puzzled expression, but he quickly opened the door and waited for me to come inside. "I've been worried about you. I've called and called you but all I got was your answering machine and you didn't call me back," Mac said.

He led me to his kitchen and offered me a chair. "I thought you wanted me to pick you up in Georgia. I had re-thought what I said when I left you there and I actually wanted to meet your family." He sat down.

My eyes told him that I wasn't buying what he was saying but my lips were stilled. All I could think about was that he was a shyster, a conman of the highest order if I believed Agent Robinson. I was searching for the right way to tell him the things I knew and to ask him about the things I didn't know. I decided that the best way to do it was to be direct and straight to the point.

Mac stood up and walked over to the refrigerator. He poured himself a large glass of orange juice and motioned to me.

"Can I offer you something. How about a cup of coffee? Tea?"

"No." I breathed deep, mustered some courage that I knew I didn't have before. I said, "I found out something while I was back home." Took a deep breath. "You knew my father, didn't you?"

I watched him pause and stagger just a little like he'd been shot with an arrow. Mac leaned against a counter, sipping his O.J. with his eyes studying me, piercing examination of the young woman sitting at his table, a refugee from his kindness. An ever so pregnant pause delayed an answer. He cleared his throat as I watched him squirm.

"Yes, I did. You must've found out when you went home. Who told you? Your mother?" Mac asked.

"Actually my grandmother was the one."

"But I thought she was injured and in a coma."

I nodded. "She was, but she's better now." I looked over at him, rubbed my temples. "You knew who I was all along, didn't you?"

Mac nodded this time.

"It was all part of some grand plan wasn't it Mac? The designer dresses. Taking me to high society type balls. First I thought you were just feeling sorry for this little ole country girl. Then I thought maybe, just maybe you really liked me, but it was just a game for you. High stakes like the poker you play or golf. I guess what I need to know is how far would you have gone to get what you want? Would you have screwed Ricky's little girl for this?"

I reached into my purse and pulled out the polished Mahogany box and set it hard on the table. Mac recoiled ever so slightly as though another arrow had pierced his smooth shield. But he looked me in the eyes without blinking as I spoke and his lips were sealed tight. He rubbed his chest gently through his pajama top and I reminded myself about his heart.

"What's that?" he asked, pointing to the box.

"Open it. It's what you want. It's the reason you and I are here, isn't it?" My anger was bubbling over.

I watched Mac as he opened the box much in the same way I had opened it at FBI headquarters. He was cautious and moved gingerly as he slowly lifted its lid. But his eyes smiled when he saw what was inside.

"What? How'd you know? I-I don't believe this," Mac said.

"Like I said, my grandmother told me in a way. It's yours as much as it was my father's."

I stood up and started my walk to the front door. I figured that the diamond was all Mac really wanted and that because I wasn't good at deception I would let him know that it wasn't the real thing.. I fought back the tears that were trying to besiege me, hoping that Mac would follow me to the door, but a quick glance backwards and I could see that the diamonds had him transfixed and unable to move. Desdemona was the love of his life and I was merely a pawn for this player. I reached for the door, felt the pressure of his hand on my arm pulling me.

"Wait, Dahlia, don't leave," he said.

I reluctantly retreated back to him and stood there waiting for whatever he had to say to me.

"There are a lot of things you don't know about me, about your father and about that damn necklace," he told me.

"You're wrong Mackenzie. I know everything about you, about Antoine, about that piece of rock you treasure."

He looked stunned and shaken. "You know about Antoine?" he asked.

"Yes."

"Please come back and sit down, I've got some things I need to tell you."

We sat on the floor in Mac's foyer facing each other, each in the lotus position. "That rock cost me my best friend and I hated that, but I was desperate to get it back," he said.

"So meeting me was your act of desperation," I told him.

He shook his head. "No, Dahlia, but I had to come up with a plan to get the jewels back and Antoine's way wasn't working."

I thought, *Antoine, Antoine, he was being pimped in a way, trading his body for information.* "So was it part of your plan to almost kill my grandmother and me?"

Mac gave me a heavy sigh. Another arrow into his heart. I could tell that my words carried nothing but pain. I could see a transparent coat of moisture cover the whites of his eyes and wash over his emerald pupils. "I would've never let anything happen to you or your family. That's why Antoine was coming around. His job was to protect you, to make sure that nothing happens to you. I was hoping that you'd like him, that he would like you since you two were close in age, but it wasn't my plan for him to use you. It wasn't my plan to exploit you."

Now it was my turn to shake my head, trying not to lose my thoughts of sarcasm, trying not to be lured in by his eyes. But I looked into those eyes, *damn his eyes, damn him, damn it.*

"It was all part of your plan Mac, detailed and meticulous just like you. So was it your plan to make me want you, to make every organ in my body ache for you?"

"Things like that don't happen according to some plan. I felt the same things for you, but I couldn't act on my feelings. I know it's hard for you to understand this, but that piece of rock in there is my last shot. I've been knocking around this world for fifty years, reaching for the carrot only to have it snatched away from me," Mac said.

I surveyed the area, the interior of Mac's house with all its trappings of wealth and success. "Looks like you made it," I said.

"Dahlia, things aren't always as they appear to be."

"So you figured you'd take the diamond...."

Mac cut me off. "Not just take it. That quarter of a million in the bank in Antigua is yours. Antoine said it was there for his business, but it's always been yours, a kind of a down-payment."

"Why because I'm Ricky's daughter?"

"That's part of it. You know duty and honor among thieves. Your father lost his life because of what we did. I owe him that. I owe you that much."

Mac put his hands on mine and regarded the woman sitting in front of him with his eyes. "It's crazy. Here you are, this lovely and beautiful woman and I can't think of you as a daughter. I can't think of you as Ricky's little girl. I see you now as someone I long for, someone I can't stop thinking about."

My heart welled up. His words with those eyes dispelled any thoughts that he was acting only out of duty to my father. I realized right then that I really did love him, that it was more than a crush or infatuation. I moved close to him so that I could see his soul through his hazel and green-colored eyes. Kissed him.

And like magnets we were drawn together, our lips in a lovelock as a precursor to our bodies following not far behind. We stood, pulled each other close, arms intertwined and I held on for dear love. The warmth and passion was unlike anything I'd ever experienced.

I gave him a breathy, "I want you, Mackenzie. I've wanted you since that day we first met."

Day Nineteen

I had never known love before that day, not man-woman love. I had pondered the notion of love as a young girl, fanciful and full of innocent sweetness without the grittiness of the chemical and physical longing that makes love primal. The need to be held, to touch, to experience the pleasure it can bring would come later. And when I finally tasted its juices I became a woman.

Songs of Desdemona—10/29/05

Chiang Mai is quiet and I wonder if I should continue because I'm probably boring her to tears.

"Chiang, are you there?" I ask.

"Yes. I listen. Please tell more. Tell Chiang how you love him."

Her statement causes me to pause. I remember that she's only seventeen-years-old, but I also realize that she's probably more experienced than I am in the art of lovemaking, having prostituted for the last five years. But that's from a mechanical perspective, knowing what to do versus the passion of doing. Lovemaking is to simply screwing as the factory worker is to the artisan creating a masterpiece and I assume in that sense that to Chiang it's mundane and mechanical.

I let go of my reservations because I believe that there's a lesson in my experience for her to hear. And in it she'll someday learn to appreciate the beauty of being in love and the joy and wonder it has to offer.

"O.K. I'll tell you but I must warn you this part of my story is not for children," I tell her.

She laughs, "Me woman."

I continue:

Mac held my hand and led me up the stairs to his bedroom. In that moment my own demons had ceased to exist. There were no thoughts of my grandmother or the man who'd tried to hurt us or all the intrigue surrounding Desdemona. It was just he and I and the anticipation.

We sat on the bed, kissed hard and groped at each other's pleasure spots hidden underneath our clothes. I stood up in front of him taking off my clothes, one piece at a time, slowly titillating his sense of sight and proud of what I had to offer. His eyes admiringly held my image as his breathing quickened.

His, "we shouldn't do this" was barely audible, but he didn't stop and I didn't want him to. I felt the warm air from his mouth pass over my nipples followed by the wet, stickiness of his tongue tracing slow spirals down to my valley. And he stayed there moving in slow conjugal spirals that twisted me, causing involuntary tremors that shook me to the core.

I was a virgin to this. No one had ever touched me like this. No one had ever moved me like this. I closed my eyes, made an unrepentant plea to my Creator and got lost in my feeling. When it seemed like I couldn't handle it anymore I moved away from his lips and serpentine tongue. We kissed hard again as I absorbed the aftershock that quaked by body and Mac ripped off his shirt and unfastened his pants.

I felt his readiness and then straddled his lap, allowed him to fill me slow and gentle as I sank down upon him. For a moment we just held each other without moving. Our core and centers, fully engaged, were adapting to the newness of this experience. I didn't want to move, just feel my juices surround him, labia growing accustomed to his large phallic presence.

Our stars were fully in Eros when Mac began to move his hips slow and deliberate. His motion, forward and back, side to side made me follow until we were in perfect timing and rocking in tantric-like syncopation. I closed my eyes and leaned back knowing that his strong arms would hold me safely around my waist and our motion continued. I then leaned forward into his awaiting kiss and wrapped my arms around his back and squeezed and held on for dear life.

The sounds of lovemaking dominated the room with its heavy breathing, gasps and whimpers, guttural sounds of people caught in the moment of passion without pretense, adorned with ugly faces. I could feel my transformation from the young woman who lay silent during sex, used solely as a receptacle for some man's prospective progeny to being a real woman fully engaged, enjoying giving as much as I did receiving.

"Do you want to turn out the lights?" I asked.

"No, I want to see your face. Hear you breathe in my ear. Watch your eyes, your mouth. And kiss you as I love you."

With Mac's words, I lost myself in the abyss and felt my body slipping as a torrent of waves began to build and eventually seized it. This was the orgasm my girlfriends had told me about, except words couldn't do it justice. It hit me once and then repeated itself over and over. At first, each wave was more intense than the one that preceded it. It made me want to scream, to pull out my hair, to push myself from underneath him, to savor it all.

A chorus of unintelligible sounds from two people swapping juices until we reached a crescendo and then fell apart, panting and grabbing air like it was our last. My body quivered to the point where Mac quickly composed himself, reached for me, held me, listened to me say, "Ooh, baby" over and over.

We had made love like he had invented it. Made love like it was our last. Coupling and un-coupling three or four times, I lost count, until finally we collapsed. Coition complete like I'd never known or experienced. We lay afterwards, bodies still intertwined as Mac closed his eyes and his breathing became shallow.

For a moment, fear overrode my euphoria and the pace of my heart accelerated. "Mac," I said, quietly.

No response.

I raised my voice a few decibels.

"Mackenzie!"

I sat up, shook him slightly and when he didn't move I reached for the telephone to dial "911". In my angst and hobbled anxiety I heard his deep, rich voice say, "What are you doing?" Softly.

"I thought, I thought something was wrong. Like you had a heart attack."

He smiled. "No, I'm fine," he said. "Just asleep. What? You thought you killed me, didn't you?"

I nodded.

"Death by passion," he joked.

I settled in beside him, comforted in knowing that he was all right and feeling the warmth of his body and the strength in the arms that now enveloped me. For the first time in my life I was feeling complete, satisfied, safe.

I slept through the night, awakened only by the sun washing over my face, signaling that it was morning. My eyes still closed, I reached out for Mackenzie, but felt nothing but the coolness of his satin sheets. I looked across the wide spans of his king size bed, but he was gone. I thought, *He's probably downstairs* or maybe, *he's gone to play golf.*

There was a robe at the end of the bed and I hastily wrapped it around me and went searching for him. I could hear the sound of activity coming from downstairs so I followed it.

"Mac?"

There were men in the foyer carrying furniture and boxes and working hurriedly without talking. The mansion was virtually empty. I looked around only to see a cavernous shell that now lacked any evidence of Mac's existence there.

The three men loading the truck seemed not to notice me as they busily kept their pace and systematically went about carrying out their task. I called out for Mac hoping that he was somewhere in the house, but he didn't answer. Finally, I stood in the path of one of the workers, a Hispanic looking man, and asked him where the owner of the house was. He returned a blank look without a word and I realized that he didn't understand what I was saying.

A fourth man, big and burly, chomping on a thick cigar and armed with a notepad, was coming from the kitchen. He had one of those, "*what do you want?*" expressions all over his face, which made me want to run for the door. But I stood my ground and waited.

"Where's Mr. Powell?" I asked.

He shook his head. "Don't know who you talkin' bout, young lady."

"Mackenzie Powell. The guy who owns this house," I said.

"We were called by some guy named, Richard Lewis and this is his stuff we're moving."

"Must be a mistake," I said in near reflex fashion. "Richard Lewis is my father. Richard Lewis is dead!"

The fat man blew smoke at his frustration, almost choking me in the process. I could tell that he was in no mood to debate me.

"Well then his ghost must've called me," he said.

"Then tell me, where is Mister Lewis?" I asked.

The big man shrugged his shoulders and continued to direct the other men to their tasks. What he said made me panic. There was no Mackenzie Powell, no Richard Lewis and no one else in the house. Mac was gone and so was Desdemona.

Day Twenty

A note to my unborn son: Othello made Desdemona the object of his passion, as well as his rage, unaware of Iago's betrayal. And in the end the lovers paid the price while their enemy scoffed and gloated at their undoing by his hands. Someday you will understand.

Songs of Desdemona—10/30/05

I left the house where Mac once lived and went home. Or at least to the place I called my home. I sat and waited for my telephone to ring—waited for him to call, but the silence spoke volumes and deep in my heart I felt like I'd never hear from him again. Still I waited at home. And there I found solitude, secreting myself away from the world, crestfallen.

Erykah Badu in the background on my CD player singing unintelligible lyrics, an ode to neo-soul and the forgotten classics, but it was not the words or the beat that mattered—it was a feeling.

I tried to call him, but his home number was disconnected and his mobile phone's voice mail repeated the refrain: *the subscriber you are calling does not accept calls from this number.*

Badu was still singing. Made me feel melancholy.

For the next month or more I rarely left my apartment. I called off sick from my job and barely ate. My sweat-suits and tee shirts were my uniform, the couture of the depressed and rejected. The contact lens that had opened my eyes to my new beauty were now stored in saline, floating about in lipid pools of sorrow and my hair had reverted to the curly nest that had coifed the old Dahlia Reynolds. I had become myself all over again.

My mornings meant a queasy stomach, a dash to the bathroom, a quick peek at my image in the mirror followed by my gasping in horror at my metamorphosis. Depression was making me sick and out of touch with myself and my body. Regurgitating the contents of whatever had been in my stomach the night before was the only measure of my existence.

I spent those days watching my security monitor, my only portal to the outside world. I watched the comings and goings of my neighbors, some of whom I'd never seen before others I'd thought had moved. But mostly I watched to see if Mackenzie had somehow found his way to my door.

Badu played over and over until the music became part of my culture or, rather I became part of it.

And whenever my telephone rang my hope sprang eternal, believing that it was Mac only to be dashed down to the reality that it wasn't. It was the usual calls from bill collectors along with occasional inquiries from Stacy or El checking up on me. After a few days I allowed the answering machine to speak for me, choosing to listen in discriminating silence and hoping that one of those calls would be from him—with Badu in the background.

My feelings about him ran the gamut—sorrow, rage, longing, lust—a recipe for the gumbo of funk that pervaded my little world locked away in seven hundred square feet of living space. I guess I could've dwelled there depressed and heartbroken for eternity or for a few weeks more, but that was the old me. The new one could emerge from the rubble in Phoenix-like fashion, ready to press on and search for some answers.

Answers.

They weren't there in my place. I'd never find them there. My usually pristine apartment had become a reflection of my wretched existence. Dishes piled up in the sink like mountains of neglect spoke of someone who didn't give a damn. I hadn't made up my bed for days, choosing to sleep in a bundle of sheets and clothes that I'd wash, but wouldn't fold or put away. And it didn't interfere with my sleeping.

After a month of this non-existence I knew that it was time to break the cycle. It was time to wake up. I looked at the family quilt hanging on the wall. Studied it the way El did. Its intricate detail was telling me a story I hadn't bothered to hear. It was a story of survival through horror and oppression, through slavery and Jim Crow yet it hung there proudly, resilient in its proclamation that it had survived. My family, like the quilt had survived and so would I.

I remembered my grandmother's words when we were talking about the quilt. "The treasure is within," she told me. I thought that she was talking about the fact that it was so valuable, but I realized that she meant so much more. The treasure was within me.

The one thing Mac had given me was a new sense of confidence, but I still needed help to completely restore myself. I decided to call Stacy and get my best friend's perspective, as well as, her reassurances.

"I miss you," was her reaction to hearing my voice.

She followed that with her typical scolding like she was my mother or something.

"Dahlia, I've been worried about you. I heard about your break-in. You all right?"

"I'm fine, Stacy," I said.

I hesitated behind my words. I wasn't really fine and I needed someone to talk to. I needed comfort.

I forced out, "Are you busy? I need to talk to you," fighting tears.

"Sure, Dahlia. You want me to come and get you?"

"No, don't bother. I'll catch a cab. See you in a few," I said.

I got dressed, turned off Badu and left my place for the first time in weeks.

◆   ◆   ◆

The ride to Stacy's house was quieted by my tortured soul and a grieving heart that had been broken. I cried from the moment I first heard her voice answering my telephone call and kept crying until we were sitting on her bed. And when I finally spoke I told her about everything. Stacy sighed, a gesture of sympathy and then stood up.

"I need a glass of wine," she told me. "Would you like some?"

"Maybe it'll help me relax," I said.

She returned with two large wineglasses filled with Merlot and handed me a glass. She stroked the back of my head.

"I'm sure he'll be back, honey. Maybe you're jumping to conclusions," she said.

I shook my head, assured in my own belief that I hadn't.

"Then why would he just pick up and leave without saying anything to me, Stace?"

"He'll call and explain, Dahlia. There's a reason for all this. Just give him time. Don't let your insecurities get the best of you."

Insecurities? I thought. The word rankled me, made me stop dancing at my own pity party.

"What do you mean, insecurities, Stacy?"

I shot back in a half-defiant tone.

"Calm down, Dahlia. I'm not trying to insult you."

She paused as though she was searching for the right words.

"Remember how back in high school you always thought that no one liked you? I used to tell you how pretty you were and you'd say, 'No, I'm not' and I realized that you never saw the beauty in you that everyone else could see. Something made you very insecure about yourself maybe it was momma or your stepfather. Even in this butterfly transformation you've made, it's still there."

Stacy was pointing to my chest. I knew what she meant. My doubts, my insecurities were housed deep inside of me. My insecurities had a parasitic hold on me that fed off my past, my childhood and now were attempting to devour my present. But there were reasons I had been so insecure and my best friend didn't know them all.

"Remember when we were little girls and how I missed school a lot and I'd tell the teacher and everybody I'd been sick, Stacy?"

She nodded.

"I wasn't sick, not really. It was my stepfather, Rufus. He'd beat me, lock me in my closet and scream at me, telling me I was an ugly heifer and I started believing him. He'd be full of that Pentecostal spirit and saying that no one would ever want me and that I had a harlot's soul. You know, stuff like that."

Stacy's mouth turned downward. Her eyes had that sympathetic look, like she felt sorry for me. I knew it was difficult for her to visualize what I'd gone through growing up. Her family had always treated her lovingly, her life was pristine, so sympathy towards me was natural and any empathy for me wasn't.

I continued. "All along I knew that he was saying those things to fight his own demons. The demons that made him look at me a certain way or conveniently walk into the bathroom when I was taking a bath. I knew it, but it didn't change the way I felt about myself."

Stacy took another sip from her wine glass and urged me to drink some more, but I didn't need wine I simply needed to talk, to let someone else share my pain.

"You know until Mac came along I thought I'd never fall in love with anyone. I felt that all men wanted to use me. I felt un-pretty and undesirable but somehow he was different. I thought he really cared about me, but he was simply fulfilling a promise he made to my father."

"Well, I don't think screwing you was part of the deal."

Stacy was letting her sarcasm show through. She guzzled down what was left in her glass and rose to her feet.

"A lot of this doesn't make sense, Dahlia. I mean it's all unraveling like some cheap novel. Mac knew your father. Antoine knows Mac. Somebody's either using your father's name or he's still alive. Somebody breaks into your apartment looking for jewelry your father and Mac stole a long time ago from a drug kingpin and your grandma's almost killed by a man breaking into her house miles away."

Stacy shook her head. "It doesn't make sense."

"You should've seen the way he was looking at that necklace. He couldn't wait to get his hands on it. And now I'm wondering if Mac's the man in the mask who broke into my place. I mean, the man was tall like him, had a fake accent and he smelled like Creole food or like the stuff they eat in the Middle East. You know, spicy with garlic."

Stacy jumped to her feet and grabbed her telephone. She started dialing feverishly. "Well the jokes on him. You said it's fake, right?"

"Who are you calling?" I asked.

"El. We need a lawyer's pragmatism."

I looked at my friend, smiled. "There's something else I need to tell you Stacy."

She had the telephone in her hand, but gently put in down on the bed. Her face was solemn. Stacy's heightened reporter's intuition had already broadcast the news I was about to tell her. She turned and looked right at me. "What is it?" she asked.

"I'm late Stacy."

She reached over and put her hand on top of mine, an offer of comfort. My friend, my sister—the one I called, Earth Mother embraced my situation with a hug and no words. She simply held me.

"Please don't tell anyone, not even El," I begged.

Stacy tightened her hold on me and whispered, "Don't worry. There are some things that can only be shared by sisters."

Day Twenty-One

I can write about deception. It's veiled in a cloak of sincerity. There are those who can mask it, while others can't. It's a learned skill of manipulation. The deceiver is the puppet master who pulls and jerks the strings of the deceived. And in the end the line between what is real and what is not becomes blurred by the desperate need to believe.

Songs of Desdemona—10/31/05

"This better be important."

That was the first thing El said when she walked into Stacy's townhouse. She looked around surveying the place.

"Where's your man, Stacy?" she asked. "He leave you? Gave up his manhood. Lost his balls because he couldn't compete with you and your career?"

Stacy twisted her mouth in obvious disapproval.

"This isn't about me. It's Dahlia," Stacy told El. "And if it's any of your business, he's chilling out in the Rec Room so you need to check yourself."

El sat down on the bed beside me, kissed my forehead.

"It's that old guy, huh? What happened?"

She was waiving her left hand around as she spoke and being more animated than usual. Stacy was the first to notice. "What's that?" she said, pointing to something sparkling on El's ring finger.

"Let me show you something real," she said. .

El extended out her left hand and stuck out her ample chest. My eyes followed the length of her arm all the way down to her fingers. At the end was the largest diamond I'd ever seen except for the fake ones on the Desdemona necklace.

"Walter and I are engaged," El said.

At first she was the picture of restraint, acting as though it was no big deal. Stacy and I ogled the ring, a perfect pear-shaped stone that must've been culled from somewhere in the depths of a South African mine. I could only imagine the amount of human suffering that was more than just a by-product of El's extravagance.

"It's beautiful," I told her.

"Five carats. Set him back about sixty thousand," she said, proudly.

Stacy turned sarcastic.

"I hope Walter never gets hurt playing ball. I'd hate to see his career end and him running out of money. He'll cut off your finger to pay for his knee replacement surgery."

Both El and I gave Stacy one of those, "I can't believe you said that" looks. But it didn't last long. We all stood up and gave our friend a congratulatory hug. El was getting married and I was truly happy for her. When she had absorbed all of the attention that she and her ring could stand, El turned to me and said, "Give me details."

When I finished the story all she could say was, "wow" and then she settled into a pensive expression, her lawyer's mind was turning its wheels.

"Tell me about this jewelry," El said. "Where'd your grandmother get it?"

"Apparently from my father. He sent it to her for safekeeping, I guess."

"And no one knows where the real diamond is?" she asked.

"That's what the FBI agent told me. Some guy named Robinson. He thinks I have it, but I don't. They even have a name for it called, Desdemona," I explained.

El nearly lost the color from her chocolate hued face. She shifted uneasily on Stacy's bed, put her head down and began to wring her hands.

"What is it?" Stacy asked.

"You know where I work, don't you, Stacy?" El told her.

Stacy held out both of her hands, a signal of the no-brainer expression used in our culture to mockingly become dumbstruck by the obvious.

"Duh, yeah," Stacy said.

"We all know where you work, El. Department of Justice," I said.

"Yeah, DOJ, International Crimes Division," El stood up and abruptly headed to Stacy's bedroom door. "I got to go. I have to check something out."

"What's the matter?" I asked.

"It's nothing, really. Just a hunch, I guess. I can't talk about it right now."

El turned and then stopped in mid-stride.

"What's Mac's last name?" she asked.

"Powell. Mackenzie Powell."

El seemed to file that information away in that computer mounted on top of her shoulders and housed inside her perfect bone structured face. Her expression turned grim.

"It's been a rough day. A guy I know who used to work as an investigator with the department was killed. Shot in the head behind Café Alexandria's," she told us.

My heart froze.

"His name was Joe Martin."

She hesitated for a moment giving her silent condolences, as though honoring the dead man was an afterthought, and left Stacy's house.

◆   ◆   ◆

"*Shssssh*. I could lose my job if anyone finds out that I'm showing y'all this stuff," El told us.

She was looking around the third floor reading room in the Library of Congress like a not so subtle spy as Stacy and I hovered over the neatly bound dossier that memorialized a man's life.

Stacy laughed.

"You would've been fired a long time ago if they knew about all the times your name was, 'unidentified source' or 'identity withheld' when I report for the Post," she said using imaginary quotation marks drawn with her fingers. "Don't worry, you won't get into trouble."

El's facial expression was solemn. Her words were sincere.

"This is no joke. Wait until you read what's in that file," she told us.

There was a "rap sheet" for Mackenzie Powell that listed a string of criminal convictions. Most were "theft by deception" and pandering, white collar type crimes and nothing involving any acts of violence.

"What's pandering?" I asked El.

"Pimping. It seems that Mac was engaged in the marketing and the procuring of women for hire. But it was the theft by deception conviction that sent him to prison."

"Prison?" I tried to act like I didn't know.

"Yeah, it seems that he was a conman. Ran some kind of ponzi scheme that was bilking women out of their money and valuables. He did five years in a minimum security facility outside of Lafayette, Louisiana."

"So, Mister Smooth Mackenzie Powell is some kind of pimpin' con artist. Damn! I really liked him," Stacy said.

But I was magnanimous in my own reaction to what Mac's file revealed. "People change, Stacy. Besides, when was that? What? Twenty or thirty years ago?" I said in his defense.

I looked over at El and the grim expression still lingered on her face.

"What's wrong?" I asked.

"There's more," El said. "He's a smooth career criminal who might've been the man who broke into your place and held a knife to your throat."

She took a deep breath.

The room became quiet for what seemed like an eternity as we sat there thinking about the unthinkable.

"No, no. He-he's not that kind of man." I said.

But I wasn't speaking with any sense of conviction. *What if Mac was the man who broke into my place and almost killed me and Antoine?*

"Why?" El said. "Because you think you've got a thing for him?"

And then her mouth dropped open. El looked at Stacy first and then back at me.

"You didn't sleep with him, did you?"

My response was the silence of the obvious. I'd been convicted without saying a word. I fell onto Stacy's bed and quickly assumed the fetal position reserved mostly for the protective confines of a mother's womb. *It can't be. He didn't,* I thought.

For a moment deafening silence and an air of condemnation occupied us but El, as usual would be the first to speak up.

"What kind of sick bastard would do something like that?" she asked.

"Wait a minute, El," Stacy said in a calming voice. "Let's not jump to conclusions. We don't know if Mac is the man who assaulted Dahlia."

"Yeah, well someone did and who's the likely suspect? That guy, that's who," El said.

"Damn, El! You're the lawyer here. You need to start thinking like one. I mean, c'mon. You read some twenty-year old rap sheet and you're going to condemn the man forever! Whatever happened to rehabilitation?"

"Spoken right from the textbook of the liberal left wing media. Heard the term, recidivist Stacy? C'mon you're the goddamn investigative, Pulitzer Prize winning journalist! Start thinking like one."

I suddenly felt the need to be the mediator. After all, it was my father, my life, my man, I guess. I wanted to—no, I needed to get to the bottom of this intrigue and find the truth, whatever it might be. I got up from the bed and tried to pull myself together.

"You two need to stop. This is about me and I've got to figure it all out. I'm going to find Mac." I said.

El looked surprised. "You're going to do what?"

"I'm going to find him."

El cleared her throat.

"Well before you go off on some wild desperate search for a man I think there's something else you should know."

She reached into her briefcase and pulled out another file folder, plopped it on the table in front of Stacy and me.

El turned to Stacy and said, "If I see anything remotely resembling what's in this file in your rag of a newspaper I'll disown you, Stacy."

Stacy raised her right hand like she was taking an oath of secrecy.

El continued. "Remember I told you about Joe Martin? Well, I didn't tell you everything I knew. I said he was an investigator with the Justice Department. Actually he used to work with our section. He quit and became a contractor, you know, freelancer."

El slowly opened the file folder, revealing several documents inside.

"Joe was working under contract with the government of Thailand. His mission was to find and recover the crown jewels that were stolen years ago," she said.

El flipped to a document that was stamped "Classified" in bold black letters.

"Anyway. Joe had been involved in ongoing surveillance of a gang of smugglers. He created what we call in the business, a Thread."

"What's that?" I asked.

"Like a family tree, sort of. You know, like that quilt you have except it's for a crime family."

El slid the document on the table then turned away to see if anyone was watching.

"See at the top of the tree is Phanik Kook. Minister of Thailand's Interior. Reputed mob boss who specializes in the sex trade."

El cut a hard stare in Stacy's direction.

"Don't you write any of this down, Stace."

"O.K. O.K."

"Kook has been trying to acquire the jewels on his own. Thinks he'll enhance his power in the Thai government and that will give him leverage to continue his criminal enterprise."

She pointed to the Thread.

"Underneath Kook are his non-Thai co-conspirators. There's some guy who's supposed to be a Saudi sheik named Al Amin."

"I know him. That's Mac's friend."

"Right. Well it gets deeper. Underneath Amin there's a man named, Yan Tettlebaum, a member of the Jewish mafia and right next to him is Felicia Morgan, his ex-wife."

That revelation stunned me.

I said. "But Felicia told me she owns a tool and die company."

El laughed.

"Tool and die. Yeah, right. This is the smuggling end of the organization. They bring stuff into the country like designer clothes like the dresses Mac gave you, drugs and all kinds of stuff. They also provide weapons like outlawed AK-47's, Apache helicopters. Hell, they can even get a cruise missile for anyone who can afford it. If that isn't bad enough, they're also the muscle end of the organization. So, I guess you *could* call her company a tool and *die* business as in, death."

"So where does Mac fit in all of this?" I asked.

"I'm not sure. Look here. There he is, Richard Lewis, a.k.a. Mackenzie Powell, off to the right all by himself. He's obviously a freelancer who periodically uses your father's name. But according to this report he also had an accomplice named Desdemona Lewis, probably another a.k.a."

"You got anything on her?" I asked. I was thinking how ironic it was that they had given her an alias named after the diamond.

"No, not much. Joe was tailing her. Somehow she's linked to all this. Probably knows where the jewels are."

I sat there quietly, absorbed in my own private thoughts. Thought about Mac, Joe and Mr. Friendly. Thought about Felicia, Al and Desdemona and my instincts told me that Mac wasn't the kind of man portrayed in these documents.

"So do they think that's why Joe Martin ended up dead?" I asked.

"Don't know," El said. "He was shot in the head, three times. That usually signifies more than just someone eliminating another person. That's a sign of anger, passion."

El leaned close. "What do you think, Dahlia? You were there that night, the night he was killed. You said he and Mac got into some kind of argument. Mac had what you thought might've been a gun. They find Joe the next morning with three vent holes in his brain."

"I've gotta go and find him," I said.

El shook her head.

"Girl, this is some dangerous action. You need to keep as far away as you can. You said the jewelry you gave Mac was a fake replica of the Desdemona diamond and if he or his associates find out they'll think you set them up. They'll also think you've got the real one. Either way, you're putting your life in danger, honey."

"Yeah, if he's desperate enough to break into your place and hold a knife to your throat what do you think he'll do if he finds out he's been tricked," Stacy added.

What my friends said made sense, but I was relying on my instincts about the kind of person I thought Mac was. I thought about Agent Robinson telling me that the FBI was reviewing the tapes recorded by the security monitor in my building and I knew then how to find the answer to my questions about Mackenzie Powell.

Stacy and El were still going tit for tat about Mac and how crazy I was for wanting to find him when I interrupted their lively discussion.

"Stacy, El I need your help," I told them.

It was the end of Dahlia Reynolds, victim.

◆   ◆   ◆

After a stop by El's townhouse and a quick change of clothes, we hopped into the Beamer with the top down and my bootylicious friend at the wheel, the three of us on a mission. A half an hour later we were sitting in the car in the back parking lot of my apartment building going over last minute details.

"You know what to say, don't you?" I told El.

She gave me a disdainful look. "Girl, I'm a lawyer and he's a man. And unless he's gay he'll listen to anything I say to him."

Stacy groaned. "It's four o'clock in the morning. I should be getting my rest."

We climbed out of the car. Stacy and I were dressed down in black jeans and sweatshirts and El in her come and get this dress. Together we were Charlie's Angel's only chocolate-ized. El went ahead of us walking with small baby steps to accommodate a dress that was so tight it looked like she'd been wrapped in cellophane at a day spa. Add a plunging neckline and six inch spike heels and she could stop traffic on the Capital Beltway.

Stacy and I assumed our positions behind two large bushes near the staircase that led to the building's front door while El carefully navigated the stairs. We watched as she stood in front of the glass door peering at the security guard trying to get his attention because the door was locked. I could see him from where I was hiding with his head down as he sat at the front desk probably playing video games on the building's computer. El decided that she had to be more aggressive to get the young man's attention.

"C'mon," she said as she knocked on the glass door with her long fingernails. She whispered to the two of us, "If I break a fingernail you guys will get the bill for my manicure."

He finally looked up from the computer after a couple of minutes of El's persistent tapping, got up from his station and cracked open the door. "May I help you?" he asked El.

"Oh, thank you. My car broke down about a block away and I was hoping someone could come and jump me. I mean, help me. You know what I mean, jumper cables?" El asked him in her sexiest winded voice.

"I'm sorry Ma'am, but I'm on duty. I can't leave my post," he answered. "Can you call someone?"

El took a deep breath, allowed her breasts to heave up and down with her cleavage drawing a line from her beautiful face down to her awesome body and back up, again. The capable attorney was now the helpless damsel in distress.

"I would if I could, but my cell phone is dead. I guess I forgot to charge the battery." El poked out her red painted lips into the shape of a perfect kiss and gave him an extra dose of the sad eyes.

The gatekeeper in the grey uniform was trying to maintain his professional decorum and greeted her with a stern face. I guess he was new on the job. He looked over his shoulder and then around El as if he was checking to make sure the coast was clear then beckoned her to come inside. Stacy and I watched him as he allowed El to walk ahead and we chuckled when he bumped into the door while it was slowly closing.

"She's got him," Stacy whispered.

They walked over to his station and he handed her the telephone and watched as she pretended to dial it. But he could still see the front door.

I whispered to Stacy, "She's got to make him get up from there. He can still see us when we come inside."

Of course we had accounted for every detail as part of our plan. As if acting on cue, El knocked her purse off the desk and all of its contents came spilling out on the floor. She dropped down into a squat and started picking up her things as her dress rode up and stopped just short of where her kitty was peeking out from its hiding place. The young security guard was in a trance. He stared for a long moment then hurried from around his desk to offer his assistance.

"It's time to move," I told Stacy.

We walked like a couple of cat burglars, hunched over in our black outfits as I pulled out my door key and opened the door. Stacy was about to walk inside when I said, "Stacy! Put on your ski mask." Even if the security guard was distracted the monitor would catch our images.

I can only imagine how we must have looked. El squatted down on the floor with the security guard hovering over her while Stacy and I were playing spy. We eased by our voluptuous friend as she nervously kept an eye on us and talked to the guard. The building's office was over to the right and only a few feet away from the guard's station.

El was talking loudly about anything and everything she could think of just to keep him from hearing us. "Have you played NBA Live 2005?" she asked. "I have a friend who plays for the Wizards if you need a ticket." And, "Thank you so much. Did anyone ever tell you, you have nice hands?"

I eased open the office door as Stacy and I slid through its narrow opening. She closed the door softly and waited in the dark while I searched for the lights. I had been inside the office once to talk to the manager about getting my toilet fixed, but I didn't know where they kept the security tapes. There was a television monitor inside and a VCR recording everything in the lobby. We surveyed the room and concluded that the large metal cabinet in the corner was the logical place. I grabbed the door handle and turned, but it was locked.

"Can't open it Stacy," I said.

"Let me try," she told me. I watched my friend as I listened for any sounds coming from the lobby. Stacy reached inside her purse and pulled out a letter opener that looked like a small sword and inserted it into the door's key hole.

"What are you doing with that in your purse?" I asked

She shrugged her shoulders. "I get a lot of mail?"

She turned and twisted the letter opener inside the hole until the whole lock popped out. "Sorry," she said.

We opened the door wide. There they were organized neatly according to date, the backup tapes of the lobby and the comings and goings of everyone who entered the building. I quickly found the tape marked, *April 28, 2005* and put it in my purse. It was time to leave.

We turned out the lights and cracked the door open. I could see El leaning over the security guard with her breasts practically in his face. She was laughing, pointing to something on the computer and he was smiling like St. Peter had just given him a free pass into heaven. We were ready to make our exit when I remembered something.

"We need to erase part of the tape that showed us sneaking in here," I said.

Stacy groaned, "It's going to show us leaving, too."

"I'll be right back. You keep an eye on El and her friend," I told her.

I re-wound the tape and recorded over the section that showed the three of us entering the building with El in her slut suit and Stacy and I in ski masks. I rejoined my friend who was looking through the door opening with her hand over her mouth trying to contain her urge to laugh.

"What is wrong with you?" I asked Stacy.

"El, look at her."

I took a position over the shorter Stacy's head and joined her voyeuristic gaze. El was listening to the young man's iPod with his earphones on and dancing like a video vixen. All she needed was a pole. I was waiting for the young brother to reach into his wallet and pull out some dollar bills to stuff inside her garter if she had one. The guard was totally captivated by El's sexy dance.

"Put your mask back on," I told Stacy. She looked puzzled. "The camera," I replied.

We were already scanning through the twenty-four hours of recordings by the time El made it up to my place. She walked in saying, "You owe me."

Stacy laughed. "Seems like you owe us," she said. "How much did you earn in tips downstairs?"

El gritted her teeth, gave Stacy a look of feigned disgust. "He wants to take me out," she said. "Little young dude barely out of puberty and he thinks he can handle all of this."

"He is kind of cute," Stacy chimed in. "You should take him up on his offer."

"Wake up Stacy he's a security guard, a nineteen year old security guard. I rest my case."

"She'd chew the boy up and spit him out. The boy's mama wouldn't recognize him after a night with Miss Thang," I said.

"Find anything?" El asked.

"Nah, been fast forwarding through the tape," I answered.

"What exactly are you looking for?"

"Mackenzie Powell. I wanted to see if he came through the lobby the day I was attacked."

Stacy said, "Check her out. Miss amateur detective."

I was intent on finding a clue while hoping with my heart and soul that he wouldn't show up on the tape. It was five o'clock in the morning. Stacy and El were both slouched over and asleep in each corner of my couch, but my adrenalin kept me going, my eyes focused steadfast and unyielding on the tape. With the remote control in my hand I hit fast forward and re-wind so often that my fingers were starting to get numb. Then I saw him. Saw that familiar face.

"Bingo," I shouted.

The sound of my voice woke up my two friends. A groggy Stacy looked at the freeze framed image and asked about the man in the Baltimore Ravens baseball cap. "That's not Mac," she said.

El rubbed her eyes and focused on my television screen. "I thought your attacker had on a mask."

"Yeah," I said. I was studying the image of the man now frozen in time by the pause button. "But he was also wearing a Baltimore Ravens cap like the one the man on this tape is wearing."

"You know his name?"

I smiled and quietly said, "Yeah, I call him 'Insurance'.

El closed her eyes again and mumbled, "Girl's crazy" as she drifted back to sleep.

Day Twenty-Two

I felt tired this morning, not the baby kind of tired, nothing physical but mentally exhausted. I'm tired of being confined, tired of the worry, tired of thinking about my fate. I want this tragic nightmare to end, to play itself out. My strength is waning but it is my strength and my resolve that is keeping hope alive. I hadn't lost it. Hope is the well from which I drink and my thirst is unquenchable.

Songs of Desdemona—11/01/05

I was standing at Antoine's front door wondering if I should knock or run. I thought about what I'd say, how I'd phrase the questions.

I sucked in some of the cool night air, pulling in some courage along with it. I remembered something Mac told me about courage when I was anxious about going home to see my grandmother. He quoted Winston Churchill. "Courage," he said, "is the first of human qualities because it is the quality which guarantees all the others."

I had never thought of myself as being courageous, but I guess optimism and love take courage so in that sense I was brave. I knocked on Antoine's door without timidity and hesitation.

"Chill, goddamnit!"

I could hear the bravado in Antoine's voice from the other side of the door.

"Who is it?" he shouted.

A lesser me would've shrunk away, but I recounted my courage like the lion in *The Wizard of Oz*. It only took a medal of courage to instill it in him. The courage, a placard of words placed on his chest somehow melded into the cowardly lion's spirit and gave him internal fortitude. It was a kind of reversal, strength coming from without rather than within. My medal was love and the burning desire to find Mac.

"It's Dahlia, Antoine. We need to talk."

I could almost see his eyes roll up and his head shaking through the door. I knew he was thinking. *What the hell does she want?*

Deadbolt locks, unloosed to let in the interloper standing there in my form had some kind of poetic ring to it. Throughout the year I had known Antoine it was his sometimes, intrusive forays into my world, invading my body with his manhood without revealing much of himself that had annoyed me and now I had erected an emotional barrier to him. I guess it was only natural that he'd be annoyed with my sudden appearance at his door.

"Yeah, wuzzup?" Antoine said through a cracked door.

"You got a minute? I need to ask you something."

He opened the door wide, my invitation to come in as he revealed his shirtless torso. His body glistened from the faint signs of sweat that had gathered in beads and were attached to the hair on his chest, coursing their way down the thin, hairy road that divided his stomach, cut off by his pajama bottoms.

"Sorry to bother you," I told him. "Were you working out?"

He smirked, not smiled. "Yeah, I been working out."

Antoine motioned with his eyes to the white leather sofa that made an "S" shape and took up the middle of his expansive living room. I followed his eyes to the point where two young, scantily clad women were perched on his sofa.

I hesitated. "Oh, you're busy. I can call you later," I said.

"Nah, ain't like that. We were shooting all day. That's Tanika and Sherry over there. Models. You know the deal. Part of the perks for being in the video. They get to hang out here."

Antoine ushered me through his living room, passed by the two women.

I spoke trying to be polite. The one named Tanika smiled slightly and Sherry, with her nose in a magazine didn't acknowledge my presence. It didn't matter.

Antoine motioned for me to follow him. I knew where he was heading—to his studio where we could talk in private. But I could hear music coming from that direction and I first thought he was playing one of his beats or songs he said he'd been working hard to produce. Instead, I could see someone inside the sound room, a young lady with headphones over her ears. She was mouthing words, apparently to one of the beats Antoine had produced.

"That's Desire. She's working on a new song I wrote," he said.

"She's gorgeous. Got any talent?" I asked.

Antoine gave a look like I must be kidding.

"She's tight. Can sing her lungs out and just turned eighteen. She'll be bigger than Beyonce."

We were looking at the young woman like she was in a fishbowl. I saw her lips moving, heard no sound from her just the beats Antoine had composed blaring through the speakers. Apparently she was rehearsing and not recording. Her glass-encased cage was totally insulated and soundproofed. Desire must've sensed Antoine and I standing there. She looked over at us, gave a wide and warm smile.

"Eighteen years old," I said.

"Yeah." Antoine nodded at her as though he was prompting her to continue rehearsing. "She's got a lot of living ahead."

"Yeah," I replied. "I know what its like to be eighteen with dreams."

I realized that I was sounding like someone who'd been on this planet a lot longer than twenty-six years, but I guess the last few weeks had aged me. I felt myself sinking into the doldrums of my situation and how I was feeling, wondering exactly what I was doing until Antoine broke in.

"You said you needed to talk to me, so let's talk."

I could sense some hostility in his tone and realized I didn't need to be coy with him.

"I'm trying to find Mackenzie. I mean, Mr. Powell."

Antoine shook his head and looked down at the floor. "Why?"

"It's personal."

"Ya'll must think I'm stupid or something. I know there was something going on between you two. He didn't fool anybody. I saw the changes in him."

His remark made feel exposed, like I was naked in public. Mac must've said something to him about us, but I knew he hadn't told Antoine about the night we had spent together. I couldn't worry about that and I was beyond the point of lying to cover up my feelings.

"Look, Antoine. I'm going to come at you straight. I met Mac and I've fallen in love with him, simple as that."

Antoine sneered then spoke to me through slightly open lips. "What happened? He loved you then left you?" His smirk was back. "Serve your ass right. You ain't no different than anyone else he's done that to. Just younger and more naïve, that's all."

"And what makes you an expert on Mackenzie Powell, Antoine?"

Antoine glanced over to Desire in the booth then he laughed.

"You know Mackenzie Powell is my father, don't you."

I nodded. "It was easy to figure out once they told me that you worked for him. I saw the picture in his study. Little green-eyed boy with the big fro. You haven't changed that much.

"Damn! Ain't that a bitch! Talk about a father-son activity. Doing the same chick and apparently you and I weren't in on the joke. I told that son-of-a-bitch how I felt about you, but did it stop him for a moment? Hell, no!"

Antoine's anger was turning to pain. It was something I'd never seen before, not from him. His eyes welled up with tears, as his tone quieted.

"It's the way he's always lived. Always taking. Like the way he took from my mother and gave her nothing but heartache in return. Like the way he took away my dreams of having him in my life, being there when I was young, but he left."

I looked around, considered the opulent surroundings and remembered the time Mac had told me about how he provided financial support for his rudderless son.

"Looks like he tried to make up for his absence," I said.

"Yeah, good try, but we can't get the years back and he can't undo what he did by giving me shit like this."

Antoine was now sitting down with his face buried inside his large hands. Desire could see him and she ripped away her headphones before reaching for the door inside the sound room, but hearing the sound of the door opening made Antoine look up. He motioned her to stay where she was.

I watched and studied her face, saw nothing but concern for Antoine written all over it.

"She loves you," I said.

He shrugged his shoulders.

"She's young. What does she know about love?"

"That's the point. You don't have to know anything to love someone," I said.

"Well, she doesn't know any better and I guess that's her excuse, but what's yours?" he asked.

"For what?"

"Your excuse for loving my father. I guess it's because you're young, too. Maybe if you were a little more experienced and able to read people better you'd see him for the man he really is and maybe you'd also see me for who I really am."

"And what's that, Antoine?" I asked.

"Somebody who really cares about you."

Antoine looked over his shoulder at Desire then back at me.

"I don't how to say this, but I love you, Dahlia. Always have."

That revelation rocked me, but I didn't believe him.

"Is that what you call it?" I asked him. "Or is it something else?"

"Like what?"

"Like you trying to get back at your father. Sounds like some kind of revenge thing, like Oedipus in reverse." I said.

Antoine looked up, shook his head.

"First of all, don't mention anything Shakespearean to me. I minored in English Lit in college. I can quote Oedipus Rex verbatim. I turned down a Rhodes scholarship offer to go to Oxford. So don't go there. 'Cause if you do, you're on thin ice. Secondly, you can spare me the psychological analysis. I know my feelings, Dahlia," he said.

His tone was a mix of defiance and softness, if there's such a thing, but I couldn't blame him. Antoine was a young brother with issues and probably unaccustomed to expressing his true feelings.

"I'm sorry, Antoine."

"Don't be. Feel sorry for yourself. What's that they say About the sins of the father? I don't know if you really love him or just think you do, but I know my father. He's like many black men from the Seventies. Unbridled and unashamed, 'Generation Me.' They gave in to the excesses of that time—sex, drugs, Viet Nam, music, ... forever scarred. They passed along the residue of their sins for their children to suffer and now you think you love him. I feel sorry for *you,* Dahlia."

I didn't respond because I really didn't know what to say. I thought about what Antoine said, sounding more like the Ivy League college graduate than street level, hip-hop mogul wannabe. His philosophical rant hit home. Despite my own father's reasons for dropping out of my life and then dying, there was no excuse. My father had also been laid low by the excesses of his generation, leaving me to suffer not unlike Antoine's suffering. But that was another story and in my quest to find Mac and the truth about my father's passing I had found a greater purpose. I leaned over close to Antoine.

"I really need to find him, Antoine. I think he's in some kind of trouble. Can you tell me where he is?" I asked.

He looked up at me, hurt still residing behind those green eyes, Mac's eyes.

He laughed slightly, "My father has lived his whole life on the edge. Trouble don't mean shit to him so be straight with me. Why do you want to find him? Why is it so important? He's gone. He ain't coming back, ever."

"I'm late Antoine."

"And you think you're pregnant? And you think it's his baby, Dahlia? You only met him a few weeks ago."

I breathed deep. I pulled my lips in thinking my mouth had a mind of its own and knowing that it might say something I would regret later. It did and I did.

"Sometimes a woman just knows if she's pregnant. I hope it's his baby Antoine, but I don't know for sure."

"So what you're saying is that the baby could be Mac's or it could be mine. Is that what you're saying?"

"I'm not saying either, Antoine. Just that I might be pregnant and I need to find your father."

Antoine's jaws tightened. I could see bones and muscles rippling through his face and then relax.

"I'm not sure where he is. He might be in Brazil, he might be in Thailand. Now get the fuck out of here." His voice was as low as his spirit.

I turned around and looked at Desire, still singing in the cage. She smiled at me through her concern for Antoine. I stopped in my tracks.

"You really hate him, don't you?" I said.

Antoine gave me a steely-eyed stare. "You just don't know how much I hate him," he said.

"Enough to do what you did?" I asked.

He looked puzzled.

"I saw you on the security tape. You and your friend wearing the Baltimore Ravens baseball cap. I guess you guys didn't know they always kept a duplicate," I said.

Antoine's mouth dropped open. "But you don't understand. He had me in a bind."

"I just bet he did," I replied. "You'd betray your father to save your own ass."

I smiled back at Desire and walked out of Antoine's house without looking back.

Day Twenty-Three

I flew too close to the Sun like Icarus. Rising above the clouds, my wings anchored by wax melted and I plummeted back to Earth. Some called me a fool, but most applauded my effort because I tried.

Songs of Desdemona—11/02/05

My visit with Antoine brought me no closer to locating Mac. Trying to find him in Brazil or in Thailand would be next to impossible, but as fate would have it I would overcome and do the impossible. Providence can conquer the impossible and it came to me in an unexpected visit from Felicia Morgan.

I didn't want to answer the persistent sound of someone ringing my buzzer, especially when I saw her standing impatiently at my building's entrance, but I could see that she had a sense of urgency about her and a determination that wouldn't be denied.

"Hello."

"Hey, Dahlia, it's Felicia. I need to see you, please."

She was bouncing up and down as she waited for me to buzz her in as though she had to use the bathroom. I had no idea what she wanted or why she was there so I was reluctant to let her in. But I assumed it involved Mac.

Felicia walked into my place like a tempest storm. Her demeanor was blustery and winded, at first, but she quickly settled down. She told me that Mac was in Bangkok, staying at the Oriental Hotel after spending the last few weeks on the coast of Brazil. He was in danger she told me, grave danger.

"Why are you telling me this?" I asked. I wasn't being arrogant or cynical, just real because I didn't know what I could do to help him.

"He took that diamond you gave him to Bangkok. He hopes no one will notice that it's a fake replica of the real thing."

"He knows?"

Felicia nodded. "He's a very smart man."

"I still don't know what you expect me to do. He left me," I told her.

"To save you," Felicia said. "There are people here who would do you some serious harm if they thought you had Desdemona."

"But what I gave Mac is a fake and besides, I don't have the real one."

Felicia said, "It doesn't matter. As long as they even think you have it they'll do anything to get it from you. That's why he left. He was protecting you."

I sat back and thought about what she said heartened by the fact that Mac cared so much about me.

"You still love him," I said, remembering that I had asked her that question once before and she didn't answer.

"What can I say? I've always loved him, always will."

"That's why you don't want anything to happen to him."

Felicia nodded. "Somehow, some way you've got to find Desdemona, the real one. The people over there are dangerous. The guy who wants to buy it has hired the man who originally cut the stone. He knows his own work so no matter how ingenious Agent. Robinson thinks he is Mr. Kook will know that the twenty million he intends to spend on the diamond will be for the real thing. If they think Mac's trying to pull a fast one he'll never make it out of the country alive."

I was at a loss for words, but my mind went into motion. "How'd you know about the FBI and Robinson?" I asked.

"I've got my sources."

"When is Mac meeting with Mr. Kook and his people?"

"In two days."

"I'll see what I can do."

I didn't trust Felicia, but I didn't need the people she worked for coming back to my place for a visit. I decided that as soon as she left I'd get busy and get out of the city.

◆   ◆   ◆

The first thing I did was to go to my computer. I removed the firewall and went into the cache of websites that Antoine had visited on the days he used my computer. I quickly found the website to The Bank of Antigua. I used my name to log on, but I had no idea what he used as the password to the account he set up in my name. I thought about Antoine and the way I knew him and my first attempt was to use his name "Antoine" as the password. *Password rejected.*

I then tried Desdemona, but got the same result. I knew I had just one more try and if I failed I would be denied access. "Think, think, Dahlia," I mumbled.

My mind was acting like a computer as I sat there recounting the things Antoine said that were important to him then I typed in *Desire18. Access granted.* I was in.

I read the account balance: $250,000.00. Untouched. I quickly transferred two hundred thousand dollars to an account I'd set up for my mother a few months earlier to deposit the loose change I could spare from time to time just to help. The rest was transferred to my account just in case I would be gone for a long time. Finished, I shut down my computer, took out the hard drive and put it my travel bag.

I packed my clothes and went through a checklist, made sure I have enough clothes for a long trip. I kept watching the clock and watching my security monitor. I was afraid that Felicia's visit was a precursor to trouble. Once I had everything I needed I called a taxi.

Nervously I sat waiting, looking around my little home and wondering if I'd ever see it again then my thoughts turned to my mother and grandmother and I wondered if I'd ever see them again. I looked at our quilt, studied it, told myself that I would have Stacy keep until I returned.

I had never asked anyone about its symbols and what the things meticulously woven into it meant, but I had always known it told a story. It was kind of like Egyptian hieroglyphics, a story told of kings and queens, the Reynolds dynasty. The thought amused me and made me proud.

I laughed when I thought how Stacy teased El about what her symbol would look like on the quilt, floating in air with her big boobs and round posterior. El had laughed at my stick figure. The figure that represented me was no longer me.

I looked hard at my stylized image and the little halo that hovered over my head. Grandma Stevie said I was an angel and that's why she stitched a halo on the quilt, but when I looked at it that day I saw a crown, a jeweled crown. I was thunderstruck by the thought to the point that my knees got weak.

I ran to the kitchen, got a pair of scissors and said a prayer. I begged my ancestors for their forgiveness and started cutting the quilt at the seam near the bottom where my image stood alone. Wool yarn and remnants of cotton came spilling out as I carefully reached inside its thick lining and touched something. My heart pounded when I wrapped my hand around an object that felt cold to the touch and angular and hard. I gently pulled it out while my pulse quickened. I knew what it was before I opened my eyes to see. It was Desdemona, shiny and brilliant and in all her glory.

"Thanks Grandma," I whispered.

◆   ◆   ◆

I spent the night at a cheap motel near downtown Washington, hiding my whereabouts and my movements like a criminal. I didn't call my friends, my mother, I didn't call anyone out of fear that even my mobile telephone could be traced and they'd find me. I slept in my clothes that night cautious, but not afraid. In a few hours I'd be on my way out of Washington, out of the country.

I had checked on flights to Bangkok. There was one leaving at six o'clock in the morning. I didn't book it figuring I'd just show up and buy a ticket at the airport. Everything was working according to my plan and with ticket in hand I flashed my government I.D., made it through the security checkpoint and found a seat in the waiting area near the gate.

I sat there waiting for the plane to start boarding with one eye on my magazine and the other on the clock. Occasionally, I'd look around the area where I was sitting checking for familiar or strange faces. There weren't many people traveling that early in the morning, just a couple of women with small children, some Asian-looking young people I thought might be college age and a small group of men in suits who talked loud in some Eastern language I couldn't understand. I was able to relax and breathe easy for the first time since Felicia left my place.

"Calling all first class passengers for boarding Flight 198 to Bangkok, Thailand"; Came the announcement over the loudspeaker. Next were passengers who needed assistance to board and then she began announcing the rows. I had asked for a seat in the rear of the plane and I would be one of the last people to board. When she called my row I waited so that I could be the last one to get in line. When it was time for me to go I stood up, pulled out my passport and plane ticket and got behind the other passengers to board.

I was focused on making it onto the plane so I didn't notice that there was someone standing behind me until he said, "First time going to Bangkok?"

I answered, "Yes it is" without turning around, but then the hair on the back of my neck stood up. I knew that voice. I turned to face him. "Good morning Agent Robinson," I said.

He greeted me with a subtle smile, but said nothing. I looked around for his partner Agent Liles expecting to see him standing nearby waiting like a coyote and anxious to pick over my bones. But there was no Liles, no uniformed police officers at the ready. It was just Robinson and his soulful eyes.

"Are you here to arrest me?" I asked.

He shook his head. "No. Not right now. I'm just taking a little trip. You know I work real hard. Thirty years with the department and I think I've only taken three actual vacations. I guess that's dedication. But I got a lot of vacation time built up, enough to retire this year and get a nice check."

"And you just happen to be going to Bangkok?" I asked him. I was full of skepticism and he knew it.

He gave me a half-laugh. "Yeah, I think I am. I've got to protect my interests." He pulled his jacket back and displayed the gun he was carrying so that only I could see it. "Even though I'm taking a little time off from work I'm just in the habit of always carrying my equipment. Some people take their computers, others take a Blackberry. I don't think Mackenzie would cooperate with me if I didn't have it."

"Cooperate with you by letting you take the diamond or the money he's going to get for it?" I asked.

Robinson smiled, licked his lips like it was habit and nodded to show his appreciation. "Very good, Ms. Reynolds, I think you've missed your calling. You would've been a good agent. Anyway, I could care less about the diamond. I'll just wait for Mac to give me the cash."

He stood there staring at me. I could see his soulful eyes turn deadly, but I was cool under pressure. "So this isn't about the FBI and some investigation you're conducting, is it?"

"Oh, there's an investigation. It's just that no one else knows about it," he replied.

"Agent Liles?"

"Young guy, he thinks this is about some major drug smuggling ring. You know it was easy to play on his stereotypes," Robinson laughed. "Everyone around this thing seemed to fit the profile."

"So you're freelancing. A rogue agent," I said.

"Guilty. I've worked all these years for the government and there's something about seeing a slick ex-con walk away with millions that sticks in my throat. Makes me want to spit," he said. I could sense his contempt for Mac and it was deep rooted.

"So you think you're going to go over there and just take the money, huh?" I asked.

"That's about the size of it."

I shook my head, looked down at the floor and listened as they announced the last boarding call. "I don't think so," I said.

Robinson laughed hard this time. "And who's going to stop me?"

I smiled. "You like football Agent Robinson?"

"Yeah, I'm a big fan."

"I noticed the Baltimore Ravens autographed football you keep in your office."

"So what."

"Well, it made me start thinking. For some reason it made me think about the man who broke into my apartment, put a knife up to my throat and threatened to kill me. He was wearing a Baltimore Ravens cap," I told him.

"So what, the Ravens have lots of fans," he responded.

"Like I said, it made me start thinking so I got a copy of the security tape from my building that was recorded the day of the break-in and who did I see walk through the lobby wearing a Baltimore Ravens baseball cap?" I said looking right at the agent.

Robinson swallowed hard. He cleared his throat. "I'm involved in an active investigation so what's your point?"

"Well, my point is, whether it's standard procedure to conceal your identity with a mask and threaten to kill someone with a knife?"

"You can't prove anything, baby girl. So you got a video tape of me, so fucking what?"

"I also have a knife with your fingerprints on it. You see your accomplice, Antoine, gave it to me. You do know that he's Mac's son, don't you?" I paused. "Oh, you didn't know? I'm so sorry. I guess blood is thicker than water or in this case, thicker than the drug case you had against him. The other thing I think you didn't know was that I have a friend, an attorney with the Department of Justice and there is no active investigation and she's holding onto a couple of copies of the tape just in case." I smiled politely. "You know overall, I think it's better to spend a quiet retirement with a nice government pension than to spend years in prison. My friend calls it burglary, assault, abuse of office, wiretapping just to name a few of the charges."

Robinson said nothing, just stood there dumbfounded.

I smiled, "It's time for me to catch my flight. I don't imagine you'll be making the trip will you?" I reached into my purse, pulled out a copy of the tape and handed it to him. "I thought you might show up, hope you enjoy the show."

Day Twenty-Four

I breathed deep and hard. Three hours was the longest period I'd ever spent on an airplane before this trip and the thought of the twenty-two hour flight made me feel, claustrophobic. I brought along a book, *Their Eyes Were Watching God*, by Zora Neal Hurston. Mac had suggested that it was good reading that day we first met.

I read some, slept a lot and worried more. My mind was riddled with second thoughts and questions. *This is crazy*, I thought.

The flight was long and tedious, even though the book had captivated my thoughts. I could identify with its heroine. Its combination of tragedy and ecstasy; there were lessons to be learned. Young girl's discovery of self, blooming and blossoming womanhood, defined by life and its lessons, it could have been my story. Hopefully, there would be no tragic ending.

An older woman sat beside me after a brief layover in Los Angeles. She struck up idle conversation with me, got deep and recounted her life and her experiences. An expatriated American, she'd followed a young student many years ago back to his native land while Viet Nam was raging from the twin evils of war and destruction. He died after joining the resistance but she stayed.

A farm girl from Iowa transported to an exotic and dangerous place where she didn't speak the language. She told me that the chasm between her and her lover could not have been any greater.

"Why didn't you go back home after he was killed?" I asked.

"I wanted to stay close to him. Live where he once lived. Walk where he once walked. Cry where he had cried. And when the time comes, I will die there and join him."

Fated circumstances made me realize that the woman was there, sitting beside me, telling me about her life for a reason. Lessons learned. It strengthened me and gave me courage. Going to find Mac was the right thing to do no matter what the consequences.

◆   ◆   ◆

It was nighttime when we landed in Bangkok. This was the real City of Lights. The old woman and I exchanged hugs and promised to keep in touch, then went our separate ways. I took a taxicab to The Oriental Hotel, held my courage in my chest and took the inexorable step that would forever change my life.

Moments later I was standing in front of the door with the numbers, 1245 staring back at me in polished brass. I hesitated, my hand poised to knock, but suspended by doubt. I hadn't thought about it before, but it occurred to me that Mac might not be alone. I cursed my impetuous spirit, guided by impulse and not logic and tried to think about what I would say to him.

I closed my eyes and tapped, hardly making a sound. I waited. Tried to give him time to answer, but not enough time. Weak kneed I turned to retreat back down the long hall not knowing where I'd go and what I'd do. My steps were interrupted by the sound of the door opening. Mac peeked out, our eyes met, mine fearful, his in disbelief.

"Dahlia? What are you doing here? How'd you find me?" a plethora of questions that I couldn't answer right at that moment. All I knew was that I was there.

"Come inside," he said.

I mustered a weak smile, dropped my head and followed him into his suite.

"What are you doing here?" Mac repeated.

A lump rose in my throat as I tried to force words through it. I swallowed. "I've been trying to answer that question."

He shook his head. "But how did you find me?"

"Your son, Antoine told me I could find you here." I paused. "Why didn't you tell me?"

"It's complicated."

"I know but that's not why I'm here." I tossed a small velvet bag to him. My face, unsmiling. Defiant.

"What's this?" he asked. Mac pulled the drawstring that seal the bag and poured its contents into his hand. "Oh my god, you found it!"

He raised the jewels up to the light, marveled at their beauty. "Desdemona," he said. "But how? Why?"

"My grandmother. Why? Because I love you, that's why. What I don't understand is why you left me," I said.

"I left you because I care about you."

I shook my head. "Don't believe you."

"It's for the best. You're young, beautiful, got your whole life ahead of you. I lost my judgment, lost my heart, which isn't like me."

He exhaled hard as though he was releasing some great burden.

"What can I offer you? A few years, maybe," he said. "Sometimes the hardest thing about love, the true depth of being selfless about the person you love is letting go. I have to let you go, baby. It's the only way. It's like Prometheus."

"What?" I asked.

"Remember at the park. You explained it. How he gave man fire and the gods punished him by allowing vultures to eat his liver, grow it back and then eat it again the next day. His sacrifice was for the greater good. My sacrifice is for the greater good."

I didn't know what to say. He was probably right. Good judgment on my part would've told me to run for the hills. But my judgment was obscured by my love for him and I rallied behind my own feelings. I wanted to make a case for us.

"Were you being selfless or selfish, Mackenzie? You broke my heart when you left without a word or note or anything. Was that what was best for me? Look, I know about your health, but it doesn't matter. Time is relative, we don't know how much of it we have. We can't control that, but what we can control is the quality of our living."

He closed his eyes, buried his face into his large hands for a moment and then gave me the jade-green stare." He said, "Baby, you've got to leave."

"Leave? But I …"

He stopped me. "You shouldn't be here. It's too dangerous," he said. "I've got some clients coming here any minute and you can't be here."

The knock on the door was eerie as if Mac's warning had been prompted by some sort of premonition. A man's voice called out his name through the closed door.

"Mackenzie? Are you in there?"

Mac put a finger up to his lips, telling me not to make a sound and then pointed to the bedroom.

"I'll be right there," he answered.

I watched him as he reached for the chrome-plated gun I'd seen back at his house and tucked it inside his pants pocket. He handed me the diamond necklace. "Put this away someplace safe," he instructed. Mac waited until I was inside the bedroom with the door closed and then opened the door to his suite to let his guest inside.

I could hear voices, Mac's, plus those of two other men speaking in broken English. There was laughter and the sounds of objects being brought in and placed on the floor. The mood sounded celebratory, but Mac's tone was cautious.

"Ah, at last. This is the day that we have been waiting for and for many years. Sorry about the change in plans Mr. Powell, but everything is about timing and today is the right time."

I leaned against the wall inside the bedroom and positioned my face so that I could see through the small space between the door and the jamb. There was Mac and the back of another man's baldhead and a third man in a white suit guarding two large suitcases. Laughter came from a place that was outside my line of vision and I knew that a fourth man had entered the room.

"This is a momentous occasion, Mr. Kook. All made possible by my friend, Mackenzie Powell." Someone said.

The bald man, Mr. Kook, leaned forward towards Mac who was facing him.

He said, "Then it is time. Mr. Powell, you have Desdemona with you. No?"

Mac nodded.

"Then, I would like to see her."

I held my breath and peeked through the opening and watched as Mac opened the Mahogany box that Agent Robinson gave me, the one that held Desdemona's replica and carefully placed it on the table that separated him from Mr. Kook. I thought: *What is he doing? They'll know.* I wanted to run into the room and hand them the real diamond, but I figured there was a reason Mac gave it to me and until he told me otherwise I'd hold on to it.

"She's beautiful," Mr. Kook said.

"Amazing," said the voice that was out of my view.

Mac sat back and smiled as though he was proud of what he'd just revealed to the others.

The man they called, Mr. Kook leaned over and picked up Desdemona and motioned for the other man in the white suit to come close. The man stuck a monocle in his eye. It was the kind jewelers use and he waited for Mr. Kook to hand him the object. He studied the gems closely and was taking his time. Finally he nodded at Kook who then proclaimed, "Welcome home Desdemona!"

"They think it's the real thing," I whispered.

Another voice, out of view, said, "O.K. Now let's see what you have in the cases for us."

The man in the white suit promptly dropped to his knees and opened one of the large suitcases. I could see that it was full of money, neatly stacked and wrapped. Mac picked up one of the stacks and flipped through it like a blackjack dealer. He randomly selected other stacks, flipped through them and then counted the total number. Methodically, he opened the three other cases and performed the same ritual like a man on a mission.

"It's all here. Twenty-million in bearer bonds U.S. Good as cash. In fact, it's better than cash." He spoke to the unseen voice.

"Ah, very good," said the voice. "And just think, the Thai government offers a reward of a mere five million dollars for Desdemona's return."

He laughed mocking the comparisons. He added, "This calls for celebration. Mr. Kook, I just so happen to have a couple of Havana cigars in my pocket."

I could see Kook nod his head.

"After all these years it is good to see the crown jewels returned to their homeland."

He looked directly at Mac.

"It is good that you stole them from the thieves who had taken them from my country and for that I am grateful."

"Let's just say I liberated it and I am happy to accept your gratitude. Twenty million times happier than I was yesterday," Mac replied. He added, "You should be just as thankful to my friend here. Because of him and his connections this is all possible."

I watched the man with the voice hand out cigars and then I glanced over at Mac who was sitting directly across from Mr. Kook. His face was serious, but satisfied.

The other man moved to a spot where I could now see him as he gave Mac a silver cigar case. It was Mac's Saudi Arabian friend. The one he called, Al.

"I know you won't smoke it, but at least hold it as we celebrate our good fortune," He told Mac.

Mac nodded his acquiescence.

Al then reached back into his jacket pocket and pulled out something metallic and shiny and his face wasn't smiling. At first I thought it was another cigar case, the fancy kind that connoisseurs use to store their most expensive cigars, but I quickly saw that it wasn't.

In an instant, but slowed down to a near standstill by my mind's eye, Al pointed the shiny metal tube at the man in the white suit. A silent streak of light, followed by a puff of gray smoke charted a deadly path, hitting the man square in the chest. A river of blood ran down the front of his white suit. His life's fluid left a sickening stain on his clothing. The man rocked for a moment and keeled over face first, hitting the floor with an awful thud.

I gasped, put my hand over my mouth and watched in horror. The world slowed in motion, Mac jumped, his mouth open, disbelief and fear gripped his face like a vice. He managed to say, "Al! What the hell …!", before Al turned, pointed it at Mr. Kook and fired a shot directly into his face. I saw his head rock back, blood splattering all over the room like a star exploding then it rocked forward, body stilled by the report of a deadly instrument. Next, Al pointed the gun at Mac.

I gasped again and uttered an involuntary sound. I knew Mac would be next. My sounds diverted Al's attention. His eyes were now riveted on the door that had been my shield.

"Who else is here?" he demanded.

Mac said, "No one. Al! What have you done, man?"

"Tell her to come out or you're next."

Before Mac could say anything, I emerged from the bedroom, shaken by the events. I rushed to Mac, fell on my knees and held him around his waist. I was clinging to both of our lives.

"Ah, Mackenzie, my friend. What a surprise. You brought her here without telling me. Obviously, you had a plan of your own. What a pity. I guess she'll have to die along with you. A fitting end, but what a waste."

Al looked at me and lowered his gun. "Ah, such is life."

That stunned look washed away from Mac's face, replaced by anger and rage.

"So, this was your plan all along, Al? To kill me? Do you know what I've gone through over that piece of rock? You son of a bitch! I lost my best friend, hid my past, had to go underground and now you're going to rob me?" Mac was spitting out words like fire.

He tried to stand up, but now Al quickly turned the gun on him and pointed it directly at Mac's head.

"Not so fast, Mac. Just sit tight and I'll tell you why I did this—as though you deserve an explanation," Al said.

He continued, "My name isn't Al Amin and. I'm no Saudi sheik, not even close. My real name is Yan Tettlebaum. I work for The Company."

"You're an assassin!" Mac charged.

Al's smile was sinister.

"I like to call myself a maintenance man. I clean up messes."

He inhaled his cigar hard, let the smoke billow out like a volcano displaying the kind of confidence a man accustomed to holding a .380 should have.

He motioned to the dead men.

"You see Mr. Escobar wants the jewels back even though it has been fifteen years since you stole them. And as for me, I want the money."

Mac twisted his mouth in obvious disdain for his once upon a time friend and colleague.

"So you kill us and just take it," he said.

"Dead men don't tell tales," Al replied. "But there's more to it than that."

Al was still clinging to that deadly smile. He cast an evil look in my direction, gun still pointed at Mackenzie.

"Force, violence, death. These things are the way of the world, Mackenzie. Whether you're a good guy or bad guy just depends on who's telling the tale. Right now, I'm the good guy and you're the bad one. You know, convicted criminal, former pimp who lured this sweet young woman into a life of prostitution, but you'll all be dead and it'll be up to the Thai police to figure out how it happened. My guess is that they'll call it a murder-suicide."

I started to cry. I begged, pleaded and cried. Al would kill us in cold blood and over what? Jewels? Money?

I was in the most unlikely of places, staring death in the eyes and frozen by fear. I was a long way from Waycross, Georgia and a long way from the safe existence I'd lived my entire twenty-six years. And Mac would die there, too. I held him tight and buried my face into his chest, waiting for the inevitable.

Mac's chest was swelling up. His breathing was labored and his eyes glared back at Yan with a hatred that had a power of its own. He would kill him with his stare if he could, stop his heart and suspend him in the purgatory that should have been his fate for his betrayal.

Mac looked at the carnage that surrounded us.

"I never thought that it would come to this, Al. I mean if it's about the money, take it and spare the girl."

Al took a step towards the door, the gun still trained on his two hostages.

"If this surprised you, wait until you see what else I have in store for you," he told Mac.

He opened the door and a tall, dark woman walked in. It was Felicia.

"Felicia?" Mac said. His eyes narrowed. "I should've known you had something to do with this!"

"I'm sorry, Mac," was her half-hearted apology.

Al laughed. "You see, my friend, it's not just about the money. It goes a lot deeper than that."

He looked over at Felicia.

"I think about those days and how I loved her so much, but there was always you and the hold you had over her. It was always about Mac. Whenever you called she'd go running and I was the schmuck who sat at home waiting."

"Yeah, it figures. You are a schmuck," Mac said.

He had a smirk on his face, one that displayed disdain for the man who'd pretended to be his friend and now was his worst enemy.

"So you see, Mackenzie, *it is* personal," he said.

Mac looked over at Felicia who had a pained expression on her face, but she quickly erased it, replaced it with a determined look as she started gathering the suitcases full of the bonds.

"Get the cart," Al told Felicia. "We'll put the bags on it and we can take them out to the limo. We'll be at the airport in time for our flight out of here."

"What about the rock?" Felicia asked.

"Yeah, that was good work getting her to bring to Mac the real thing. Love is strange," Al answered. "O.K. pretty girl where's the real jewelry?"

I thought quickly. There was no sense telling him that it was hidden because he was going to kill us anyway. "That is the real one," I said pointing to the replica in the Mahogany box.

Al looked at Mac. "Don't let her bullshit me Mackenzie!" He put the gun to my head. "You got ten seconds Mac! Is this the real diamond?"

Mac didn't hesitate. I guess he was feeling the way I felt. "Yeah Al, that's it," he said.

Al gave him a look of disdain. "If that's the real one then show me the copy."

"I tossed it when she brought me this one," Mac told him.

"Enough talk. It's your turn, Mackenzie. I'm sorry pretty young lady, but you are what they call collateral damage," Al said.

I looked at Felicia hoping that she would stop Al. She had a pained and anguished look on her face. She smiled nervously. "Wait baby, remember your promise. You promised you wouldn't kill them. C'mon, let's just take the money and go. So what if that is or isn't, the real diamonds, Escobar will never know the difference," she said.

The panic in Felicia's voice almost begging in her tone told me that she wasn't part of this plan.

"Felicia, you don't understand. I was paid to deliver the diamonds and to kill Mac and like any professional I always do the job I'm paid to do," Al said.

Mac stood up to face him.

"Leave the girl out of this! You got a problem then deal with me but leave her alone!" He shouted.

He eased his hand into his pants pocket as he looked his former friend in the eyes.

Al smiled and his wicked eyes narrowed. "Don't do it, Mackenzie. You know I always liked you in spite of you and Felicia. But anyway, I've got to do what I have to do. Don't worry, though, I won't shoot you in the head like I usually do. Don't want to mess up your pretty face," he said.

Al leveled his gun and fired a single shot, striking Mac in the chest. I watched his body jolt and keel over to the floor. Felicia and I cried out in unison, "Mac!" I tried to move, but my feet were anchored in fear. I screamed. Felicia bent over, checked Mac's eyes and pulse.

She said, "He's dead. He's dead!"

Those words rang in my ears and I dropped to my knees beside him without any concern for what they had in store for me. Now the conversation between Al and Felicia was muffled and unintelligible. I had no thoughts, no feelings and I was no longer afraid.

But I could sense that Al was irritated and becoming anxious. I could feel his eyes watching me as I hovered over Mac, trying to hold his head up and begging him not to die. And when Al stood over me I knew that my time had come, as well. I braced myself and waited for the inevitable. My thoughts flashed—my mother, grandmother and my unborn child were all there trying to comfort me in that last moment. I felt the sting of the force that struck my head and felt the warmth of my own blood. My world was now dark.

Day Twenty-Fiver

Mac once explained to me the differences between fate, chance, luck and circumstance. Fate was predetermined, presided over by some divine authority and had but one outcome. Chance was fortuitous and qualitative with good or bad as its only outcome. Luck came in many forms and only existed in the mind of the optimist. Circumstance never created victims or victors, but was simply all things to all people.

Songs of Desdemona—11/5/05

I rise with the remnants of sun and look out the small window that's barely large enough to allow its light to find its way into my prison cell. It is dusk, the sun is fading fast and the day has escaped. My belabored thoughts of past events and circumstances have quickened the pace of time. The day's almost gone in what seems like a blink of an eye. It's all too familiar as one day melts into the next in this, my Pattaya Hell.

It's playing itself out like a bad movie, my life that is. Far from a film noir classic, but my story is about to have an unpredictable end. I'm thinking about my trial Thai-style. No jury. Just a judge, my lawyer and a translator. They concluded that only my fingerprints were on the gun that killed three men. The irony was that I was accused and convicted of also killing the man I love.

"Me no understand," Chiang Mai said after listening in silence for hour after hour as I told my tale. Her statement jars me back to the present and my fatal reality.

"What don't you understand?" I ask her.

"You, how you say? Innocent. You not kill those men."

I smile. "You're the only one here who believes me."

Having told my story I retreat inside my thoughts and ponder what's left of my future.

♦   ♦   ♦

I think about the real perpetrators, Yan or Al and Felicia and how they got away by framing me for their crimes. They were going to kill me, too and make it look like a murder-suicide but Felicia was too smart for that. A black girl shooting herself in the head didn't make sense. I guess in an off-handed complimentary way I was too cute to mess myself up by blowing off my own head.

So, they hit me and knocked me out, made it look like the men struggled to stop me from killing them and made sure my fingerprints were the only ones on the gun. The evidence was flimsy and probably wouldn't fly in the States, but there are innocent people on death row there, too.

El told me that the key ingredient to any murder prosecution was motive and opportunity. The fact that I was the only one left alive in a hotel suite with three dead men demonstrated that I had the opportunity. Motive, on the other hand, was a stretch. They couldn't find anything solid for my reason to kill so they settled on robbery. I became the high-class call girl, purveyed upon by her American pimp for a man who had a penchant for black females, Mr. Kook. And in the end I was found with a gun in my hand and fifty thousand dollars in my purse.

Felicia had an ironclad alibi. Some State Department official vouched for her. She hadn't left the country, they said. There was no record of a Sheik Al Amin or Yan Tettlebaum ever registered in the Oriental Hotel nor did the man exist in any other sense of the word. He was a ghost in the judge's eyes, a convenient lie born from the protestations of the guilty. In the end it was I, alone, sentenced to pay the ultimate price. So I languish in a Thailand prison as four months have sped by offering me little chance of exoneration.

My appeal is running its course without a hint that the tide will be reversed. Yet, I find solace in knowing that the life growing inside me will be freed once he courses his way through my birth canal and into the waiting world. When he is old enough to be taken back to the States my mother will raise him although both Stacy and El volunteered to do the same. *He belongs with family*, I wrote my friends.

But their willingness to help brings comfort to my life of confinement and their letters set my mind at ease. Stacy writes me once a week giving me updates on what's going on back home and in Washington. She always ends her letters with the words, *Keep the faith, girlfriend.* She signs her name with a smiling face drawn beside it and a solitary tear.

El, the more pragmatic one, is my undeclared legal counsel and advocate, lending advice and encouragement. But El is also working hard with the Justice Department, trying to pull strings there to heighten awareness of my fate. Through all of her catty mannerisms and condescension there is no doubt in my mind that she's there for me.

I keep my friends' letters in a small pile beside my bed, tied with a ribbon, a remembrance of our friendship and the good times. I often pick up the stack and hold it close, smiling with the memories and then meticulously placing it back in its special place.

My routine is the same. Baby kicking with me holding my stomach and humming quietly trying to sooth his restless yearning. I know he wants to see the light outside my womb.

I wait for my supper, anxious to feed my son through me. I wait for the jailer who brings our food daily with a rude shove through the opening underneath my jail cell door and a scowl instead of garnish. But judging by the setting sun it is still early for dinner.

I used to think that the prison officials wait until dark to serve us dinner so we can't see the garbage they feed us. I guess it's their way of being merciful. But it's amazing, the adaptability of the human spirit that makes the stuff they call food not only palatable, but sometimes tastes good—sometimes. Or is that only in my mind?

As usual, dinner is forewarned by the jingle of keys strapped to the jailer's belt and like Pavlov's dogs the sound makes my mouth's saliva moisten my tongue, my anxious juices wash my gums and push themselves down my throat and back up again. Today, more than any other, I'm hungry. Still, I'm a patient animal and while I hear the cries of others believing that we all will be fed early I don't join in their chorus. I never do.

I hear Chiang Mai's door clang open, orders given in Thai and the shuffling of her feet. I rush to my door and peer in earnest through the hole, trying to get a glimpse of the young woman I know without ever seeing her face. But she's gone and I suspect that she isn't coming back.

I listen for other sounds, but I only hear the keys and something inside tells me someone is coming for me. My heart leaps, garnering hope that the keys will unlock my door and a voice tells me in English that I'm free to go home. The door flies open and my jailer, a large woman, stands there in the doorway not smiling. Her imposing, hulking figure menacingly pronounces her non-verbal communication that someone wants to see me.

"You have visitors," she finally tells me.

Those are her only words. She steps to the side, allows me to pass through the narrow space between her body and the door and then closes it hard. "Follow me," she says.

My heart races. I have no idea who's here, but it doesn't matter. I'll accept anyone just so I can see a face and talk to someone other than myself.

She leads me to the room where prisoners meet with their lawyers and tells me in broken English to sit at a small table and wait. "Sit! Dey be here."

But it's hard to sit still. I twist and move in my chair trying to contain my happy anxiety. My first thought is that it's my mother. She writes me often, telling me that she's thinking about making the long flight to see me even though she's scared to fly and has never been on an airplane. I try to think about anyone else and I remember how the jailer referred to my guest as "they" and her use of the word "visitors", as in more than one. And my excitement's dulled when I think that it's probably my lawyer and his interpreter.

The door cracks open and I see a familiar face followed closely by another set of warm eyes and a smile. I start to cry.

"Girl, look at you," El says.

She rubs my swollen belly and hugs me with strong and passionate arms.

I shake my head. "I can't believe you're here." Still crying.

Stacy greets me next and strokes my head, gives me still another hug.

"And I can't believe you would look so good being pregnant and all," she says.

For a moment it's like we're back home walking the dirt roads and talking about what we'd be when we grew up. We're little girls all over again. Our tone is light and no one would ever suspect that our reunion is being held in a prison in a faraway land. They both squeeze me until I'm nearly oxygen deprived and then we all settle down at the table.

"So, tell me. What's going on back in DC?" I ask. Stacy is almost gushing with enthusiasm.

"Derek got a promotion and they nearly doubled his salary," she says.

El's mouth twists. "Yeah, check her out, Dahlia. Everything's all peaches and cream because her man has regained his self esteem through artificial means. Like the Tin Man in the Wizard of Oz."

I'm nearly stunned by El's reflective remark. I guess she's experienced some kind of metamorphosis since I've been here.

"You still getting married?" I ask her.

"Yeah. We haven't set a date yet, but you're going to be there when I do. I want you to be one of my bridesmaids," she says.

I smile feeling flattered by her gesture, but I'm saddened by my present circumstance.

"Don't wait on me." I tell her.

El reverses her cherry smile. Her mood now somber. With earnest eyes she tells me, "I'll wait no matter how long it takes."

Those words bring us all to tears. We hold hands, crowd our emotions into that little room and cry in unison. A big collective tear washes over us and dampens our spirits. Stacy is the first to break this orgy of sadness with words of encouragement.

"You're going to be there. Trust me," she says.

I can tell that she's searching for something to say, something that will lighten our mood. But I beat her to the punch, swallow back my feelings of doom and gloom. El's perfect body with that bubble butt is my foil.

"I hope you're going to have your wedding dress custom made," I tell her, laughing.

"Why?"

"Because they're gonna have to have some extra material for all that you're dragging behind you."

We all laugh. Our chorus of tears now erupt into laughter, a joyous song like Handel's Messiah.

They're allowed an hour to visit and it's over in what seems like only minutes. It's time for them to leave. I'm overwhelmed by their gesture. They'll spend nearly two days in the air on their roundtrip flight just to spend an hour with me.

Stacy and El turn serious. "I'm writing a story about you in the newspaper. My editor let me research your case and I found out some things about the man they say you killed. Mr. Kook was a real sleaze, involved in child prostitution, smuggling and all kinds of unsavory enterprises. I'm hoping that by exposing him our government will get involved and get you out of here," Stacy says.

"Yeah, and I'm still working with my people at Justice," El joins in.

"By the way, I had someone who owed me a favor. I found you a new attorney, an American who knows the ropes here in Thailand. He's here, so don't thank me," she says, smiling.

El and Stacy give me another parting embrace and we stand there afraid to let go.

"Don't worry," Stacy says. "We're going to get you out of here." She pauses. "You never told us about the baby. Is it Mac's or Antoine's?"

I look longingly into Stacy's eyes. I'm fighting to get the words out, but there are none. Stacy waits to hear an answer, but quickly realizes that I'm not ready to tell. I know now, but I figure I will go to my grave with this secret and my son can grow up not hating the man who planted the seed that would bear him as its fruit.

Stacy shrugs it off and allows her question to fall into the void we know as silence.

"We'll see you real soon. I promise," she tells me.

The door to the room opens in front of Stacy and El and my friends start making their exit. "Wait!" I tell them. They both stop. "Big hug," I tell them.

And in our huddle I say, "Please look after him, my son and if you see that momma's having a problem raising him then take him, alright? Promise?"

"We promise."

"Last thing. Stacy, can you stop by my old place and get my family quilt and keep it, just in case," I say.

"Shoosh." Stacie tells me. "I'll get it but when you come back home I'll make sure you get it back."

I turn to El, whose red, teary eyes betray her pretty smile. "Thanks for paying my mortgage all this time, but I want you to sell it for me. It's gone up in value. Give my mama the money."

She forces a smile, sniffles.

"Don't thank me. Thank Walter. I keep telling him that he can do more for others with the twelve million he gets every year for bouncing a stupid basket-ball."

Smiles.

El takes my hand. "Don't worry. I'll look out for your mom."

I choke back my tears, didn't want them to have an image of me crying as their ever-lasting memory of me. I smile weakly and wave with just my fingers. I mouth the word, "goodbye" without making a sound and watch as they fade away. My jailer stands guard until my friends are out of view. I'm ready to return to my cell.

"Wait here!" The jailer tells me. "Your lawyer here."

I sit at the table. My back is to the door, but I can hear heavy footsteps approaching. It's the sound of a man in full stride. He walks into the room, says something in Thai to the jailer, which causes her to promptly leave us alone. Head down, I'm too afraid to look up at him.

He sits across from me and opens his briefcase, rifles through papers until he finds a legal pad and places it on the table. I don't want to see his face, didn't want him to see me. Instead, I train my eyes on the table and the yellow legal pad. Next, I watch his hands, strong and brown reach down into his case and from it he retrieves a lacquered ink pen. I catch a glimpse of his head as he reaches into his bag, see his salt and pepper colored hair pulled back into a short ponytail. There's an eerie familiarity about the man. It's Mac.

Unbelievably and unmistakably, Mackenzie, like he's returned from the dead. My first thought is that the months I've spent in this hellhole have caused me to take leave of my senses. He's dead. I watched him die. Watched and held him as he took his last breath. My stomach turns and I nearly convulse from the shock of seeing him alive. But it truly is him.

That dimpled smile is now framed by a thick mustache and thicker beard. His green eyes glow and make something inside me move. My heart flutters and my mind is trying to understand the incomprehensible.

"You died. I saw you die," I shake my head in a rapid motion as though I can shake the vision of Mackenzie from my eyes.

Mac's wide smile illuminates the room.

"I'm not an aberration although the news of my demise has been overstated on more than one occasion. But it's me, live and in living color."

I reach over and touch his hand, checking to see if he's real. I feel their smoothness, still without a hint that he'd ever done anything more with them than pick up money or swing a golf club. It's Mac, all right.

"But they said you died. They said that I murdered you along with the others and I knew it was you lying on the floor with a bullet in your chest," I tell him.

I'm truly dumbfounded by this, which causes my breathing to sharpen, a precursor to the panic attacks I'd experienced for almost my whole life. But I'm determined not to let that happen here.

"Where were you? How could you leave me here all this time thinking that you were dead?"

"It's a long story and we don't have much time. And the name is Mr. Castillion now. So don't call me Mac." He whispers.

"Long or short, I want to hear what happened. Tell me how you survived. I saw Al shoot you."

"I'll make it quick but no questions, all right?" he says.

He takes a heavy breath, unbuttons the top two buttons on his shirt and pulls out the familiar St. Christopher's medal, the one he got from my father. It's mangled. The thick gold medallion has a hole in the middle.

"It saved my life in a way," Mac says. "I suspected Al would double-cross me so I was wearing a Teflon bullet proof vest. The bullet from Al's gun was lodged in this. It didn't go through but the impact stunned me. I got up after they left and went to get help, but by the time I returned the Thai police were all over the place so I ran. I've spent all this time trying to get back here and get you out of this mess."

I paused to think about the prophetic symbolism of Mac being saved by my father's St. Christopher medal.

"But they said three men were found dead in the room."

"Yeah, the third man was Al. He'd been shot several times in the head to the point where he was unrecognizable."

"Felicia?" I ask.

"Probably. I guess she felt she owed me something. But most of all she wanted all the money. Her company wasn't doing that well. I knew that. Add the fact that she really didn't love her ex-husband. Al, Yan or whatever his name was. A few bullets to his brain, along with his sketchy history and she would be the only scavenger invited to a twenty million dollar feast."

I could tell that Mac had little remorse for the man who had posed as his friend.

"I guess the double cross was on both of us. Anyway, Felicia must've planted my passport on Al so they'd think I was the unidentifiable dead man. Remember she was the one who checked me out after I'd been shot. She knew I wasn't dead. So she killed Al, took the money and split," Mac says.

I think about what I'm hearing. It's an incredible story, but this entire saga is full of incredible stories so I'm not surprised.

Mac reaches across the table and takes my hand. "Look, we don't have much time to talk. I'm going to get you out of here," he tells me.

"Get me out? How?"

"You're going to have to trust me on this, all right? Take this."

Mac hands me something wrapped in a small piece of plastic and closes my hand over it.

"Take the orange pill when you get back to your cell. It'll make you feel sick, nauseous, you'll throw up. It won't harm your baby, I promise you. They'll think you're having a miscarriage and the infirmary here isn't able to handle that kind of medical emergency," Mac whispers.

He next hands me a rubber balloon filled with some kind of fluid.

"Put this inside of you just before the nurse comes to check on you. Make sure you untie the string at the top."

I look confused. "Inside me?" I ask.

Mac nods. "Yes, inside you and I don't mean swallow it, O.K.? There'll be an ambulance here for you. Once inside, take the blue pill. You hear me? Take the blue pill! It'll make you feel better, but you'll still be shaky. The ambulance attendants and the guards will take care of you. They'll give you a change of clothes, take me to the airport. Meet me at Gate 27, O.K?"

"Mac, I want to tell you something. It's about my baby. I want to tell you that he's...."

"Save it. We'll have plenty of time to talk, later," he says.

Mac closes his brief case and stands up. Gives me a smile. He straightens his necktie and smoothes back his long hair, Miles Davis' interpretation "Birth of the Cool" come to life.

I return Mac's smile with a weak one of my own, fighting back tears. Apprehension is the dominant expression I wear. Mac's plan is a bold one to be sure, but I have nothing to lose except my life and now, his too. He tunes into my feelings as though he's read my mind. He mouths a reassuring and silent, I love you, and then taps on the door to alert the guard that he's ready to leave, falls into lawyer mode when the large woman returns to take me back to my prison cell.

"Well, Ms. Reynolds. I will be working on your appeal and I'll let you know something of my progress in the next week or two. In the meantime, keep the faith," he says.

I almost laugh.

Minutes later, I'm back in my cold, dank jail cell, alone. I tuck away the plastic "lifesavers" that Mac has slipped me. Two pills, one orange, the other, blue. Take one first then take the other. I can hear his emphatic instruction—"once you're inside the ambulance, take the blue pill! The orange one will make you sick and you'll get a fever, the blue one will make you feel better."

I take a deep breath, exhale slowly, lick my lips and pop the orange pill into my mouth. I suppress my gag reflex, pills had always been hard to swallow, and force it down my throat. Mac didn't say how long it would be before it takes effect so I sit on my cot, wait and listen to my body.

Fifteen minutes, a half an hour and then a full hour pass and nothing happens. Then it starts with a subtle rumble in my stomach above where I'm carrying the baby, followed by dulled pain. Nauseated, I roll on my side clutching my stomach and holding him. He is still, apparently unaffected.

I call out for Chiang, at first until I realize that she's gone then I call out to the guard on duty.

"Help! Help! Something's wrong! My baby!"

The response is uncharacteristically quick. The large female guard unlocks my cell door, calls for help in Thai. I can't understand her, but I hear the word, "baby" in English. Soon, the prison nurse appears, looks confused as the guard explains. She pulls out a thermometer and checks my vital signs. She opens my legs, slaps on thin, rubber gloves ready to explore my uterus, but there is blood trickling down my legs.

"Call an ambulance!" The nurse tells the guard while she attends to me.

They quickly carry me out of the prison by stretcher and I'm put inside the awaiting ambulance driven by two men dressed in Bangkok Police Department uniforms with an ambulance attendant inside to help me. I'm still reeling from the effects of the pill I'd taken. Sweat drenches my body and face even though the night air is cold. The attendant dabs my face with a cool towel and speaks in halting English.

"You all right. Take pill now," she says.

I un-wrap my fingers from around the piece of plastic that contains the blue pill, swallow it and nod to the attendant. She's a young Thai woman about my age, complexion and height and dressed in a white hospital looking smock. She watches as the pain and nausea subsides and smiles approvingly when it's obvious that I'm feeling better.

"You change clothes now," she tells me as she helps me out of my prison clothes into a blue dress. Next she hands me a long gray trench coat that covers my body and hides my bulging stomach.

"Wear this," she adds.

She then hands me a bright red bandana to cover my hair, leaving my long ponytail hanging loose down my back.

"We take you to airport now," the girl explains.

The young woman has a familiar tone in her voice, one I've heard before.

"What's your name?" I ask.

The girl smiles, "Chiang Mai."

I'm puzzled.

"You know. Chiang Mai. Me next door."

It's all coming together now. She's the girl I've been talking to for the last few weeks. The one I told intimate details about my life. I want to ask her how and why, but I realize that this is all part of Mac's plan and only he knows how it will be played out. I say a silent prayer, put myself in the hands of God and Mackenzie Powell and sit quietly as the ambulance speeds to the airport and hopefully, to freedom.

Day Twenty-Six

I write this entry today not knowing if it will be my last or a continuation of this saga. If it is to be my last, then I will taste freedom, savor its sweetness.

Songs of Desdemona—11/06/05

The airport in Bangkok is no different than most large airports in a post-9/11 world. Like everywhere else in the world, there's an overflow of people, but here most are from the Far East rushing to make their flights to who knows where in a whirl of organized chaos and a sea of brown skin. Added to the mix are police, federal agents and various security personnel and it is business as usual.

The ambulance that carries me speeds onto the airport grounds and right up to the terminal. There are no sirens blasting to warn of my coming, just the red and white vehicle rolling to a gradual stop curbside. I sit in the back trying to let the second pill take its full effect. I can feel my baby move, which comforts me.

Chiang Mai goes into action in a manner that is unmistakably well-coordinated, planned and done in typical Mackenzie Powell fashion. She opens the back door to the vehicle and looks outside. There's a police officer directing airport traffic and standing in the middle of the road just a few feet away. There are other officers dressed in white jackets, swinging batons, walking two deep shoulder to shoulder. They're on "watch" patrol, looking for anything suspicious like a bomb or a prototype terrorist, whatever that means.

Chiang Mai stands still for a moment, watches two officers motioning drivers to keep moving. One splits off from the pair, approaches a recalcitrant driver in a late model Mercedes Benz who seems oblivious to the signs that read, "No Parking" and written in Thai and English. The cop taps on the passenger side window to get the driver's attention while his partner looks on.

Chiang Mai motions me to "come on" while the police are distracted, sensing that this would be our best opportunity to enter the terminal unnoticed. She pulls out a wheelchair. One more peek at the police officers and Chiang Mai steps out of the ambulance and grabs the wheelchair and puts it in position for me. She then motions for me to join her.

"You sick," Chiang Mai reminds me.

In other words she's saying, act like you're sick and take it easy getting out of the ambulance. I'm aware enough to know what she means. I gingerly step out of the vehicle, sit in the wheelchair as Chiang Mai takes control. She pushes me in the direction of the terminal. Although there are access ramps for wheelchairs the closest one is about a hundred feet away.

There's a sense of urgency in the air. And I can tell with Chiang Mai there will be no diversions. She struggles to pull the wheelchair with me loaded in it over the curb and into the terminal. She motions for the ambulance driver to come and help, but the vehicle is empty and we can see the driver and his sidekick retreat and melt into the crowd. Although she's tall and fit, she probably weighs twenty pounds less than I do with my baby weight.

I notice that our struggle has drawn the attention of one of the police officers and he casually saunters his way over to the spot where the pretty young woman in a nurse's outfit is trying to overcome the curb with the wheelchair and me in it. My heart races uncontrollably and with each step drawing the police officer closer comes the feeling that I should just stand up and run inside.

The officer nods at Chiang Mai as he approaches and smiles while reaching for the chair's handles. She gives him a nervous smile in return, but it quickly evaporates as she watches him take control and pull me over the curb. Once up on the sidewalk he turns me around and straightens out the chair. I can't understand what he's saying, but I conclude that he's asking Chiang Mai if she needs help getting the chair inside the terminal. Her nervous smile returns, but she shakes her head telling him, no. She then follows with a courteous nod the way they do in the East to express their gratitude.

I exhale slowly as the officer tips his hat, looks directly at me and makes a military-like about face and walks back to his partner who's still arguing with the Mercedes Benz driver. I ease out a sigh and Chiang Mai resumes control of the wheel chair and we head towards the door. But as the doors swings open I hear footsteps running and a man's voice calling out.

"Sa-wad-dee, Miss. Sa-wad-dee."

It's the same police officer approaching us once again.

I want to tell Chiang Mai to keep walking and to push faster, but he's on us too quick for any kind of reaction other than to stop and wait. I put my head down, trying to appear even more ill and hoping that he hasn't recognized me.

He stands directly in front of us, blocking the entrance with his hand resting on his holstered gun and his legs spread wide.

"Khun Cheu Arai?"

The officer directs a question to Chiang Mai.

"Dii-chan cheu, Chiang Mai." She responds.

Her voice quivers with a very rational fear of what might happen next. She nods, swallows hard and waits. I'm trembling all over.

"Sabaai Dee Mai?" he asks her.

"Sabaai Dee." Chiang Mai responds.

She laughs. It's a nervous laugh.

I sense without looking that Chiang Mai's becoming relaxed in the presence of the officer. I quickly conclude that if she is a prostitute, then talking to the police is a routine occupational hazard. I try my best to relax, wait and listen.

The officer says something else to Chiang that makes her laugh and he joins her, apparently impressed with his own wit. Now I know exactly what he's doing and the reason why he stopped us. He's hitting on her.

She plays along with him and even becomes flirty to stoke his fire and distract his attention away from me entirely. But it's clear that time is becoming our enemy and Chiang will have to extricate herself from the situation and the amorous officer. She asks him for pen and paper, writes something, hands it to him. He reads, smiles and nods as he backs away.

"Yin dee tee dai roo jak," the police officer says.

He's now walking to his waiting partner. His head held high with a stride full of confidence and bragging rights to be sure.

I look up at Chiang and force a smile of my own.

"What was that all about?" I ask.

"He ask for my phone number. I give him phone number," Chiang replies. "I hope he not know number to Pattaya Prison kitchen."

She laughs.

Chiang rolls me into the airport and tells me to get out of the wheelchair. She gives me one last look as she walks away and heads back outside and to a destination that I hope isn't back to the prison.

"Good luck," are her last words.

For a moment I stand there, my feet riveted to the floor trying to regain my composure, but it's only for a moment and I snap back realizing that I must move. I waste no time looking for Gate 27. A sign in Thai and with English written in small letters, points me to the concourse and the moving sidewalk that would take me to the place where I'm to meet Mac and to my anticipated flight to freedom.

The motorized walkway pushes me as my rapid steps quicken my pace. I wobble a little from the uncertainty of my feet and use my hand to hold the rail and keep my balance. All the while I try to keep my head down and blend into the crowd of humanity that's moving equally as fast.

A tall, African-American girl in Thailand should stick out like Oprah standing in line at a McDonald's in Compton, California and I'm aware that I'm drawing attention. I hurriedly put on the sunglasses that Chiang Mai gave me and tuck the scarf I'm wearing further down over my forehead. With my brown skin and soft ponytail I hope that I look like just another Thai girl going on a trip. But my problem is that I don't have any luggage or even a purse to carry and I wonder if that's enough to arouse suspicion.

Feeling self-conscious, I wrap the trench coat around my torso and hold it close, hoping to conceal the extra bundle that's going along for the ride. An occasional look up to check the nearest gate number lets me know I'm getting closer. I'm approaching Gate 24. I take a quick glance in that direction and then eyes straight ahead, avoiding the discerning watch of the police who are stationed at various points along the way with guard dogs poised to react to whatever threat their canine sensibilities can detect.

They make me nervous and I feel that I'd have to get there soon or have a heart attack from the tension and the pressure. My breathing is deep as though there is a shortage of oxygen. It's a pattern that seems to be the only constant I've experienced since seeing Mac at the prison. It's the only thing I can do to calm my nerves and it isn't working very well. *A shot of Vodka would help*, I'm thinking, but I don't have the money to buy one or time to stop. Besides, I'm pregnant.

I look up, check out my surroundings, staring without staring at the police. I can see the sign telling me that Gate 27 is just a few feet away. I step off the moveable sidewalk. My momentum pushes me to the point where I almost fall, but I adjust and hope that Mac is waiting. With anxious eyes I explore the seating area looking for the tall, brown-skinned brother with the ponytail and sensuous eyes. He's there, just as he said he would be. I can tell immediately that he is calm.

My spirit is lifted at the sight of him sitting in the boarding section with his head down, deep into a book. I feel like running, but instead I walk up on Mac gingerly. My heart is pounding so hard I wonder why he isn't jolted by the sound. He smiles when he notices me, but quickly returns to his book. With a slight motion of his head he directs me to take a seat. It's Mac's way of telling me not to draw attention to us. So for the moment we seem like strangers until he reaches for my hand on the armrest nearest him and clutches it. Mac's strong grip is the reassurance I need. I breathe easy for the first time in months.

"Glad you made it," he says in a near whisper without looking in my direction.

Mac keeps his eyes fixed on the pages of his book as though the whole world is inside those pages, but I realize his act is part of the diversion.

Our physical connection is brief and he relaxes his hold on my hand, pulls a smile that only reaches a corner of his mouth and continues to speak without looking directly at me.

"We'll be boarding in about twenty minutes," he tells me.

I watch as he pulls an envelope from inside the flap of his book and hands it to me.

"Your boarding pass and passport are inside," Mac says.

He looks down at the floor and at the garment bag that's strategically placed between us.

"That's yours, Dahlia." Mac says, looking at the Dolce and Gabbana bag. "We don't want anyone getting suspicious because you boarded without any luggage."

I pretend not to notice as he carefully slides the bag close to me so that I can grab its handle. I study Mac's face and embrace the moment. For four months I thought he was dead and now here he is rescuing me. We're leaving this place that had been a hell to me and we're leaving together.

Mac obviously feels my eyes watching him because he abruptly lifts his head, giving me another dose of those lady killer eyes, but he's now frozen, trance-like and unmoving. He's looking at something or someone behind me. I can hear a commotion, see uneasiness overcome his calm face as his eyes dart back and forth around me and fasten on what is unseen from where I'm sitting.

My eyes say to him, what is it? I start to turn and look, but Mac shakes his head, saying, "Don't turn around." He rises to his feet and reaches out for my hand.

"Take your bag and come with me. You see the ladies' room over there?" He says.

I nod.

"I want you to go in and go inside a stall. There are clothes inside the bag. Put your scarf and coat inside your travel bag and change clothes and take your hair out of that ponytail. Wait fifteen minutes and come out. Go directly to the gate. They should be boarding by then and get on the plane. O.K?"

"But Mac, what about you?"

"Listen, Dahlia! You gotta do exactly what I'm telling you. It's the only way, all right. Just trust me."

I turn enough to see that it's the police and security officers with dogs and they're moving at a feverish pace. Armed with assault weapons and what appear to be pictures in their hands, they're moving from one gate area to the next, looking at the picture and searching. It can only mean one thing—they're looking for me.

Mac gives me a reassuring smile, but there's urgency set in his eyes.

"Whatever you do Dahlia keep your head up, but don't look anyone directly in the eyes and go right to the gate. Get in line and get on the plane."

"And where will you be?" I ask.

He smiles, "On the plane, of course."

He kisses me gently on the lips and pulls me in the direction of the bathroom. The police are getting closer, but don't seem to notice the tall African-American couple making their way through a hoard of shorter Asian people.

My thoughts are full and anxiety high, but I do exactly as Mac tells me. I make my way into the bathroom without looking at anyone and without seeing where Mac has gone. I quickly look for an empty stall, lock the door and sit on top of the toilet, waiting and listening.

I wait a few minutes then take my trench coat and scarf off and open the bag to put them inside. There are other clothes inside for me to wear. I make the change and comb my hair so that it lies straight down, framing my face. My transformation is complete and I know it's time to leave and, hopefully, board the plane undetected.

I open the door to the toilet stall, peek out and cautiously step outside. Although I am feeling more at ease, I hold my breath, say a prayer and prepare myself for whatever might greet me in the terminal. My heart quickens when I hear the sound of someone opening the door to the stall beside mine. It's Chiang Mai. Our eyes meet, but before I can say anything Chiang puts her finger to her lips telling me to be quiet. I watch as she puts on a trench coat identical to the one I had been wearing, pulls her hair into a ponytail and then ties the same colored scarf around her head. She tops off her look with sunglasses, the ornament of espionage and disguise. Chiang Mai smiles and waves goodbye as she holds her head up high and leaves the bathroom.

I wait a few moments and make an exit of my own. Take a peek outside with the door slightly cracked open and without hesitating walk directly to the gate to get in line. Once again, my heart races and I feel a lump rising in my throat as I stutter-step my way in the line to the person taking boarding passes.

"Passport, please."

That's the voice of the woman holding my boarding pass. Reaching into the envelope Mac had given me I find my passport and pull it out without opening the little booklet and hand it to the woman. She looks at my passport and then back at me. I hold my breath and try to still my heart.

The woman's eyes narrow as though she's trying to look right through me and at that point I know something's wrong. I wait while she looks at my passport and the picture and then back at me. One more look and I wish I'd used the toilet while I was in the stall. I'm so nervous that I can feel the pressure from my bladder trying to take over and exert control over my body functions. I squeeze it back, trying to win the battle of wills over my own body.

It's taking too long. I'm thinking. Here I am. Arrest me. But just when I think the ruse is over and I'm caught, the woman takes out a rubberstamp, places a seal on my passport and motions for me to move on.

"Nice picture, Ms. Lewis," she tells me.

"Ah, what?" I ask.

My voice resonates surprise. *Ms. Lewis?* I try to adjust to my new name. Apparently, Dahlia Reynolds doesn't exist anymore, at least for now. Her demise is obvious because the Thai government holds my passport under that name.

As I walk down the ramp and to the plane I open my passport and view my photograph with curious regard. It's me, to be sure, and my new name, Desdemona Lewis, is prominently displayed. A sigh of relief is the only reaction I can muster. A couple of shaky steps and I look to see if Mac is in line, but he isn't there. Something tells me to double back, but to stay in the tunnel leading to the plane. Straining my eyes and my neck to look out into the terminal I can see him now.

There are nearly a hundred police and security personnel surrounding him. His hands held high in a submissive response to having an arsenal of guns pointed in his direction and standing right beside him is Chiang Mai in her trench coat and ponytail.

I want to run back, but I remember Mac's words, remember the consequences and hope against hope that he will find a way out of this and join me. But it's very clear that there's no way out. I've lost him again. My heart sinks low as I drag myself onto the airplane bound for a destination I hadn't bothered to know.

I hold back my tears and find my seat. Mac put me in the first class section, plenty of room for my baby and me to relax if we could. I take out a magazine as other passengers get on the plane and pretend to read still watching for him to board. The seat beside me is empty and that brings me some comfort knowing that Mac was planning to be there, too.

But I figure that as long as the plane is still at the gate there's a chance that he'll make it, as well. With each passenger I steal a glance from behind my sunglasses and as each meander their way to the back my heart sinks further. I watch as the flight attendant closes the door and feel the jolt of the plane moving away from the gate. But then the plane stops. My heart races once again.

The pilot announces that there has been a slight delay and utters an apology. I feel the sensation of moving forward as the airplane repositions itself back at the gate. Now my mind is racing. *The ruse is up. They're coming to get me.* Those are my initial thoughts then I smile with easy confidence.

Mackenzie has freed himself. He's coming to join me. I sit back in my seat feeling apprehensive and exhilarated at the same time and watch as the flight attendant maneuvers the door to open it. I ask myself what's behind the closed door; devil or angel? I take a tissue from my purse and dab at the sweat gathering underneath my eyes and feel the rush of heat that has overtaken me, a by-product of my anxiety.

I think about retreating to the restroom to hide, but I realize it would be an effort in futility. The Thai police would force the door open only to find me cowering in a corner. It's clear that I'm trapped and my only option is to sit there with my head down, listen and wait. I hear feet shuffling down the aisle, slow and methodical, pausing at every row until they stop near me.

I pretend to read my magazine burying my eyes deeper into its pages as I wait to hear someone call my name, praying that it's Mac. In the corner of my eye I can see a solitary amorphous figure, but I avoid trying to discern whether it's him or the police. Instead I flip through the pages as though I'm unaffected by whatever it is that's going on around me.

I hear the sounds of struggle. The flight attendant rushing from her position behind the cockpit is wrestling with something. I hear her words, "Let me help you" then the door to the overhead compartment slams shut above me. I know then that it's not the police. I smile, steal a look knowing that it must be him only to have my heart sink again. It's not Mac. It's the old woman I met when I first flew here to Bangkok, the one from Iowa.

She takes her seat, smiles at me with empty recognition. Apparently she doesn't remember the well coiffed black girl who had listened to her nostalgic tale of broken dreams and a love lost.

The flight attendant closes the airplane with the kind of finality that tells me that no one else will board this plane and no one will leave it until it lands at its destination. We're jerked away from the gate as the jets whine.

Once the plane taxies and makes its ascent to the skies the pilot speaks through the PA system.

He says the usual things that pilots tell their passengers. "Enjoy the flight." "Sorry about any delays." He then reminds us that our ultimate destination is Bahia, Brazil.

One last look out the window I can see Bangkok at night, the city of lights and I wonder where is Mac in all that constellation of manmade illumination. I realize that we'd reversed our lots and circumstance. Mac's freedom for my life and I question whether the trade off is fair. He is Prometheus paying the price and willingly sacrificing all for me and my baby and I understand that the depth of his love is immeasurable.

EPILOGUE

FIVE YEARS LATER. Sitting on the chaise lounge with its black and white swirling design and an umbrella that lets in just enough sun to soak my bare arms and legs I've just finished reading James Baldwin and I'm confounded by the writer's complexity of thought and his allegorical examination of black people in America. I allow my mind to absorb the words, both prophetic and profound, and place the book on my lap.

It's deep reading, probably not the kind of book one reads while sitting on the beach on an island off the coast of Bahia watching the waves play tag with the sand and my young son a willing third party to the game. But I'm not on vacation. This is my life now, uncomplicated and uncluttered. My focus is being the best mother I can be. With every wave brought in by the tide I cast a discerning eye towards the curly haired little boy.

Back in my book and thoughts I hardly notice that he's running to me and shouting in a high-pitched voice, warning me that someone's coming. I look to the ocean. I can see the yacht now anchored about four hundred yards out in the water. A rubber dingy with a motor is chopping through the waves and periodically becoming airborne. It's unusual to see anyone come ashore here after all it's a private beach, the hallowed ground where Mac had built his dream home.

I stand up, clutching my little boy's hand as we watch with interest and I'm unable to suppress the smile growing on my face. Our visitor comes into full view. He runs the little rubber raft ashore and jumps out while it's still moving. I can see his bright smile even from a distance and I eagerly wave my hand to greet him.

I see my son look up at me and then at the man who's approaching. To him it's a stranger, but he can tell that I know the man and I'm happy to see him. We're both watching intently as our visitor takes big strides right up to us and I hug him as though my life depends on him being here.

"It is so good to see you," I say.

"Same here."

"I knew you were coming, but I thought you'd be here tomorrow."

"Yeah. I got a little anxious so I told the charter captain to make a beeline here."

I look him over, smile broadly. "You look good," I tell him.

"So do you. It's been a long time."

He looks down at my son and rubs his hand through the little boy's hair. Smiles.

"He looks like me when I was that age."

I nod my agreement. "Yes. I've seen those old pictures of you."

I squeeze out a sigh full of reminiscent thoughts.

"It is so good to see you,"

I'm repeating myself, probably my nerves mixing with my excitement.

"I watched you on television a couple of months ago. Congratulations."

He shrugs. "Ain't nothing, really."

"Yeah, right. Grammy Award winner. The talk shows and gossip columns say you're going to marry that cute little young lady you're producing. Desire? Right?"

"Can't believe everything you read, can you Dahlia?"

He musters a shy smile then tells me that the gossip was right on point. He looks out onto the clear, aqua ocean.

"She's on the boat."

"Congratulations. Are you going to bring her here so we can meet her?" I ask.

He turns his head towards the boat, licks his lips and smiles.

"Yeah. I just wanted to talk to you first. You know, kinda set the stage. I didn't want to just spring her on you guys plus I wanted to meet him," he says looking at my son.

He looks around at the sprawling open-aired home that is our backdrop.

"Nice place," he says.

"What can I say, it's comfortable and isolated. A good place to raise him," I reply.

I can't take my eyes off of him. I guess my admiration is clear. He kneels down, reduces his six-foot, two-inch frame to three feet. Faces my son, eye-to-eye.

"You don't know who I am, do you?" He says to the little boy.

My son looks down at the sand, shaking his head and tells him that he doesn't.

"Well, you will. I'm your big brother, Antoine."

My son beams and tries to repeat his brother's name. It's an abbreviated version and sounds as though he's been practicing for this occasion.

"Twon. Twon." He repeats the name.

Antoine stands up and looks at the house.

"I heard your grandmother passed away. I'm sorry," he tells me.

I close my eyes slightly and nod, accepting his condolences.

"How's my girls, Stacy and El?" he asks me.

"They're both fine. You know El married Walter not long after I moved here. I couldn't come back to the States so the whole wedding party came here, everybody. It was a beautiful wedding right here on the beach."

Antoine nods his head. "I bet it was. This is like paradise here."

"Yeah," I say. "El had a baby girl last year. She's spoiling her rotten."

Antoine laughs. "And how's Stacy?"

"She's doing great. Still single. You know she's city editor now."

"Yeah. I read her byline all the time," he tells me. "And what about your mother?"

"She loves it here."

"Heard she left your stepfather."

"Yeah. I've never seen her so happy. We spoil her rotten and she loves the attention and being around her grandson. She's probably inside the house, quilting."

I add, "You've really grown up."

"So have you, Mrs. Powell. Where is he?" Antoine asks.

"Inside, he's making gumbo. He's been crazy with excitement, waiting for you to get here. Go on in. Surprise him."

Antoine takes a step towards the house and then hesitates.

"You sure?"

I nod. "I'm sure."

"He never told me how he got out of that mess in Thailand," Antoine says almost pleading for the answer to his unspoken question.

I give him a knowing smile. I say, "You know your dad, Antoine. It was a lady who saved him."

"Really?"

"Yeah. A beautiful woman named Desdemona."

"Figures. That's my pop."

I watch as Antoine disappears into the house, knowing that it will be a happy reunion between father and son. I turn my thoughts to what I just told him, about how Desdemona had saved Mac and realize the truth in my statement. She bought his freedom and Chiang Mai's, as well. It cost a million dollars, but it was worth every penny.

I always laugh when I think about Stevie acting in cahoots with my father. He told her that it was part of my inheritance and that it was for me to use as I saw fit if anything ever happened to him. That was my grandmother's little secret and no one knew—until I figured it out, that is.

The thing that surprised me was that the Thai police never found it when they searched me during my arrest and I was able to mail it hidden with my other personal belongings to Stacy for safekeeping. Once I escaped my friend gave it back to me.

Mac hired a top "real" lawyer once he was released who eventually cleared my name. Felicia was extradited back to Thailand where she's serving time in the same prison that once held me, although she's due to be released in another two years. Her confession along with a barrage of news stories in Washington and around the world about how a murdered Thai government official had been the head of a child prostitution ring helped mitigate her punishment. Throw in the fact that it was Al who killed Kook, Felicia probably should've been awarded a medal. And Stacie got another Pulitzer for breaking the story.

No one ever recovered the twenty million dollars that Felicia took from the hotel that day, but let's just say that an extra ten million mysteriously appeared in my bank account.

And Desdemona? We're inextricably tied together. One of the documents I discovered in my grandmother's box was my original birth certificate, the one I'd never seen. It read: Mother—Mahalia Reynolds, Father—Richard Lewis, Baby's Name—Desdemona Dahlia Lewis. It seems that the treasure that was Desdemona was with me all along.

I often think about how she touched so many lives. My grandmother, who was chosen as the jewel's keeper almost died because of it. And then there were those who actually lost their lives like my father and Al. And Joe lost his life trying to find her. It was Al not Mac who pulled the trigger.

According to Felicia's statement to the FBI, Al was keeping tabs on her, Mac and me, but it was a coincidence that the three of us were all at Café Alexandria's that night. Add the fact that he knew that Joe Martin had been following Mac with the hope of finding Desdemona it was a perfect opportunity for Al to eliminate Joe. When Mac and Felicia left the club that night she told him she had to meet a girlfriend there later so Mac went on home. Poor Joe playing Sherlock Holmes was on their tails, but he had had a few too many and when he went to relieve himself in the alley behind the club there was Al waiting after spying on his ex-wife. Three shots to the back of Joe's head from a muzzled pistol eliminated a threat to the gang's scheme.

We had all paid a price for something made of minerals and gold and regarded as priceless, but in the end there was a cost.

But some of us reaped the benefits of having Desdemona touch our lives and in the end we were rewarded. Chiang Mai, for example, is no longer a street prostitute. She's a film major at UCLA and almost ready to graduate, thanks to the Powell Foundation. Mac has a small Cessna seaplane that he uses to charter people around the coastal islands and to our home that doubles as a bed and breakfast. And the government of South Africa proclaimed that it was eternally grateful for Desdemona's return. No reward was ever demanded, no questions asked and no one ever identified, but both Mac and I take great pride in knowing that she's on display for the people of South Africa as a reminder that the quest for riches should never be at the expense of human suffering.

Our lives are now simple and uncomplicated, the way Mac had always wanted. And when I'm not reading I'm working on my own novel. It's a story of a woman's growth and maturity and how circumstances can dictate who we are and what we become.

I turn my attention back to the little boy and call out.

"Ricky! You be careful. Don't go out too far in the water, O.K?"

He waves. Shows that big dimpled smile.

I nestle back into my chair. Open my book and muse over James Baldwin, Zora Neale Hurston and Countee Cullen and their respective messages. I let their words play with my thoughts the way my son is playing with the water. The tide laps at my toes and touches my spirit and like the sea the words are eternal.

978-0-595-45679-6
0-595-45679-0

Printed in the United States
97762LV00004B/325-342/A

9 780595 456796